MEAT POPSCICLE DESIGNED

HUMAN
★ ★ ★ ★ ★
MADE

NO AI USED

The author, publisher, editors, and designers, feel strongly about protecting the integrity of creative works made by humans—especially the professionals who have dedicated their careers to perfecting creative arts.

No generative artificial intelligence was used in the writing, editing, or any other creative aspect of writing this novel. While the future holds possibility for ethical leveraging of this technology, this novel was created the classic way: sleepless nights, inadvisable amounts of caffeine, endless revisions and editing, and ultimately, paid work that has already supported the work of four creative professionals.

ADVANCED PRAISE FOR *HASH 207*

"*Hash 207* is a must read. It's a good story; it's a call to action. It's an anthem of hope that will put a smile on your face." – Dr. David Collins, author of *Accidental Activists*

"*Hash 207* is, above all else, a celebration of community. Like the hash, it welcomes you in like an old friend, whether you know what to expect or not—a masterfully told story that understands how weirdness and individuality make life great!" – Micah "Biff Pow" Edwards

"I couldn't put it down!" – Kim Millick, author of *Rookie Warden*

"I've never read a book more authentic about the Hash House Harriers experience. *Hash 207* is an epic and hilarious tale about the battle for the soul of a city–a riot within a love story about Portland, Maine." – Walter "I-Feel Tower" Moore

"A masterful imagination captures your attention, and doesn't let go until the last word! May the Hash go in peace!" – Heather "Crotch Thumper" Auman

"Reading *Hash 207* will inspire you to blaze your own 'True Trail' and live life to the fullest, in that dash found in 'On-On!'" – Jessi "Rimmy" Darnell-Boynton

"I laughed until I realized this is the story of my life, too. Then I finished through beautiful tears." – Randy Salisbury

Copyright © 2025 by Dave Norman. All US and international rights reserved.

This is a work of fiction. Unless otherwise indicated, all the names, characters, businesses, places, events, and incidents in this book are either the product of the author's imagination or used in a fictitious manner. Any resemblance to actual persons, living or dead, or actual events, is purely coincidental.

No part of this book may be reproduced without permission or used to train artificial intelligence.

We founded f/64 Publishing to promote crisp, clear storytelling that captures those details essential to understanding a subject. Like making a photographic exposure at f/64, this takes time and strategy…and can result in breathtaking work. The company is also named partly in honor of the association of photographers co-founded by Ansel Adams: Group f.64.

f/64 Publishing
Portland, ME, USA
www.f64publishing.com
www.hash207.com
hash207novel@gmail.com

Interior design © 2025 Dave Norman. All rights reserved.
Cover design © 2025 Jessie Darnell-Boynton. Used by permission. All rights reserved. Cover image based on original artwork by Jessie Porcaro. Used by permission. All rights reserved.

1. Fiction – Literary
2. Fiction – Coming of Age
3. Fiction – City Life

ISBN 13: 978-0-9831858-6-4

Written and published in the USA

Dave Norman

Hash 207

f/64 Publishing

The Purpose of Hashing

(1) Promote physical fitness among our members
(2) Get rid of weekend hangovers
(3) Acquire a good thirst and satisfy it with beer
(4) Persuade older members they are not as old as they feel

– Charter of the Hash House Harriers, Kuala Lumpur,
Malaysia, 1938

Chapter 1

Thursday, April 16th
White River Junction, Vermont

So it's come to this: my father standing at the conveyor belt in the mixing room, yelling about ingratitude, throwing empty mayonnaise jars at my head. And this is without a doubt the most honest moment we've ever shared.

"You ungrateful little shit!" he yells, launching another jar. It shatters on the wall behind me, chipping the brick. "This company fed you," he roars. "It clothed you!"

"So what," I bark. "I'm not putting on your old suit. Living your dream."

I wonder if he misses on purpose, or if he's just blinded with anger. His next shot clips my shoulder.

"Forget it! I'm not taking over your business."

He launches a jar into my thigh.

"You spoiled brat!"

That one really hurt.

Why did I ever come back to my hometown, to his factory? My big escape didn't work out. I got away for a while, but I didn't start over. It just didn't take, and I was still nowhere, with nothing to do, just farther away. Then my car died, and I couldn't fix or replace it without asking him for money.

"You see this?" he bellows, holding an empty jar by the mouth while he jabs at the words on the label. "This is who you are."

The label says "Schmidt & Sons Mayonnaise."

"This gave you the life you don't appreciate," he lectures. "This keeps our town employed! You will show it some leadership, and some goddamn respect."

He shows his respect by hurling the jar at me, missing, and damaging the wall.

I've backed up against the bricks to keep from falling over, my fingers rooting for purchase. This wall is older than either of us. It used to be an outside wall, where it was battered by horse drawn wagons last century; more recently by my grandfather manhandling tables in this room; and ever since by carts and hand trucks and all manner of things moved by my family and their legion of workers. I used to run my hands across this wall, imagining my finger a stylus playing the dings and scratches like the grooves on a record. What stories would they tell, of the lives of those before me? Of my father as a boy, of my grandfather as the man who turned this room into the heart of our family business?

A jar skims my ribs. It digs a little chip from the brick, recording the sound of breaking glass and my father's fury.

"You know what you are, Jamie?" he asks me. "A dreamer, an idealist. You got no sense, not a practical bone in your body."

It's amazing how hatefully he says *dreamer*, and *idealist*. It makes me hope that I am one.

The company needs me, he says; the town needs me. He won't say that he needs me, and the other things sound more flattering when he's not screaming them. But I know what he means: he has pride, and a name, to protect. Also, he is the largest employer in a very small town, whose workers need continuity and stability and someone to keep their jobs safe from being downsized by some corporation.

He took the business over from his father, and expects me to eventually take it over from him, to protect his legacy and our security and the town that's depended on our factory since before it was ours. They don't need me, personally, just someone to faithfully play the role…as he had, for his father. I get that.

I just don't want that life.

Sell it to a foreman, I'd told him. His own father had been a foreman when he bought the company on credit. That suggestion didn't go over well… Just sell it to someone with the sense, with the skill, with the desire, to carry it on, I said. I'm wise enough to realize that isn't me, but apparently not clever enough to have built a better life elsewhere. Yet.

At least I'm trying. I wonder if he ever did.

Maybe he always wanted to please his father. Maybe he dreamed of mayonnaise. I don't know, he never talked about that, only about duty, leadership, and values. Heady stuff; manly stuff. He never spoke about fears; never a word about passion, inspiration, or love. Only the kind of hard work and values, he said, that built America.

Gag me with a silver spoon.

He advances, smacking the jar against his palm. I hobble away from the wall, meeting my father halfway. I'd rather punch him than stand here silently, staring him in the eye. But I won already when he made this physical. I just wonder when he'll realize it.

"You will serve this community," he growls, "and you will live a clean, upstanding life, so long as you bear my name."

My name is James Schmidt the Third. I go by just Jamie.

He swings the jar, hitting me upside my head. I'm on the floor, surprised by how much the concrete hurts my knees. His shoes point like accusations as he looms.

The final blow doesn't come. I look up. He's staring at the label, where our family name is scuffed and stained with my blood, then throws the jar against the wall. It breaks in slow motion, the label fluttering to land atop the shards.

"A Proud Family Tradition," it reads.

"I'm sorry," I say.

But I haven't changed my mind.

* * * * *

I lick my wounds on the bridge over the White River, feeling the factory's presence behind me, staring at a statue of my grandfather.

The village council put it up on a corner of land by the town hall, when I was a boy and thought it was neat. Now it's kind of embarrassing to have a family member immortalized in copper, larger than life, gazing across the river at his factory and our little downtown as if he owned the place. He did, to an extent, as my father does now. Ownership of something you've built, though, feels different than the receipt of something you're given.

Some of the people I went to school with, years ago, are working now in his factory. Some of their parents work for the factory, and have since before I was born. No wonder I don't feel comfortable sliding into management. They've been here all along. The idea seems feudal. Perhaps they'd agree.

Many of them live in apartments my family owns. They worship in the church my grandfather endowed, pay their taxes at the town hall he refurbished, and deposit their pay at the bank he once chaired. It's a small town and there's no escaping his legacy.

He was a teenager during World War II, my father told me, working as a brewer's assistant in Munich. He survived 71 heavy bombing raids by American B-17s, a fact my father takes undeserved pride in, and then survived the Soviet occupation. They relocated the men from his village, placing him in a new life, with a new job, in a new city. He was retrained as a condiment maker, never to brew again, expected by law to lead the life assigned him by forces that seemed irresistible. The conflict had destroyed his home; the

Politburo controlled his fate.

The worker's paradise, they promised, was his inevitable reward for diligence, for duty, for shutting up and following orders. Do as you're told, they said; be grateful, they said; you have it much better than those poor saps who think they're free.

He escaped as soon as he could.

My father never told me the details, as if he feared they might be instructive.

So I don't know how he came to America, or why he chose our village, only that there were no breweries so he plied his trade for the condiment company along railroad row. He learned English. He became a foreman. Other businesses moved to bigger cities and this one faltered, good fortunes elsewhere being bad for small towns. Grandpa bought the business on credit. To keep his employees from moving away, he bought the apartments across the street and fixed them up. His loyalty was rewarded in kind as he grew the business, showing his gratitude further by refurbishing the town—remaking it in his image, sure, but not to its detriment. The people didn't need a savior, just a break, and someone to look out for them. He did, and when he passed, they spoke his name more reverently than even the name of the man of God who buried him.

That's the legacy my father had to live up to; the one I'm supposed to follow.

No pressure or anything.

This is the best spot to commune with grandpa. The trees part around his statue, the factory pulls from behind me, the view includes a number of buildings with the same brickwork—grandpa had one aesthetic, and really went for it. I'm proud of his legacy, though I've done nothing to earn it. It will always be part of my past.

It just doesn't feel like part of my future. Grandpa didn't maintain, either. He fled into the unknown, and he built something cool.

* * * * *

I can't go home, at least not tonight, so I haul myself up the stairs to Grace's apartment and knock on her door. We dated in high school, and a little since. Her door needs paint, the carpeting is worn and the hallway scuffed, because no one lives in hallways, they just pass through them. On the other side of her door is a home—a place I can lay low and get my head straight. She's my closest friend, which isn't saying much.

The door opens. I stumble through. She catches me, spinning me against the wall so I don't wind up on the floor. She doesn't kiss me, though I wish she would.

"What happened to you?" she says.

"He finally believes me."

She sighs and shakes her head. "Not this again."

"This time is different," I say, angling my head so she can see the swelling.

"I'll say." She touches it gingerly, wincing before I do, and leads me to her bathroom sink. "Who started it?"

"Does it matter?"

"Well if he started it," she says, "then yeah. I guess he believes you. What are you going to do though? I mean… you can't just leave town."

"I did once."

"Yeah," she says. "And how'd that work out?"

Grace left, too, for college. That she's back is testament to the gravity of one's hometown, especially when you don't have anywhere else to be. Except she never wanted to run away; merely to get away a little while and come back with a degree and whatever memories she made.

"He called me a dreamer," I say. "An idealist."

"I'm sure he meant them as insults."

"But they're not," I say, pulling my head from the sink. In the mirror I see myself as I am: mid-twenties, hollow cheeks, feral eyes. A far cry from who I'd like to be. The water drains down my neck, soaking my collar.

"I mean, how can you build something if you don't dream?" I ask. "How do you know what's *worth* building, what's worth fighting against, if you're not idealistic? Do you just take things as they are? That's lame."

She feels attacked—Grace, God love her, is a pragmatist. A few weeks ago she outlined her next twenty years as we lay together, our sweat cooling. She has a whole plan for making a life from her job at the Center for Cartoon Studies a block away, for buying a house up the hill in three years, for taking a full year off whenever she chooses to have kids...after she meets the right guy. To my relief it doesn't seem to be me.

"Where else did he hit you?" she asks. I take off my shirt and show her my ribs, my shoulder. Her brows knit. She touches the swelling with the back of her hand, feeling the heat.

"With what?"

"Jars."

"He beat you with mayonnaise jars?" she says. "That's just so..."

"Yeah, I know." She leads me to her bed, pulling the covers back and lying beside me with her clothes on. "You know," I say, "the street outside—"

"Main Street."

"Yeah. There's a first time you ever went down that street. Probably as a baby. There'll be a last time, too. Probably on your way to the cemetery. You ever think about that? The way it connects your past, your future, just by being there?"

"Not really," she says. "It's one way on this block. If you're looking for some kind of deeper meaning, maybe start there."

"You ever think how it connects to Route Four? To the interstate? And all the places they go, all the driveways? The house you're gonna buy someday, you can drive there now, you just don't know which one it is yet. The place you're gonna be buried—"

"I want to be cremated."

"The point is," I say, "that life is an adventure, and the trail could be anywhere. At any moment. Just right there, out the window!"

"Then why don't you go, if it's right there."

"I'd rather stay with you."

Her look says she's not buying it.

"You're afraid," she taunts. "Besides, this is where you're from. It's your future. You'd just come back again."

"Like you did," I remind her.

"And look what I have to show for it," she says. "A job. An apartment. Stability."

"Where's the excitement?"

"There's a time for that. And it was fun. But then there's being responsible, so the rest of your life isn't wrecked by the things you used to think were exciting. I've moved on. You think it's boring."

"Terribly."

"Well, no one beat me up today."

"Can I just go to sleep? Can I pretend we're a happy couple and when I wake up everything is going to be fine? Of all the nights…"

She gives me a peck on the cheek.

"I'm sorry this happened to you," she says, and I believe her. "You'll feel better in the morning."

Gentle rocking wakes me sometime later. She doesn't seem to notice me. I know that curve of her mouth. That heave of her chest. So she suspected a different kind of night when I called—that makes sense. Now she gasps, and whispers someone else's name.

What did I expect? I can't blame her.

"Call me when you feel better," she says, as I slip out her

door.

Chapter 2

Thursday, April 16ᵗʰ
White River Junction, Vermont

Where could I go? Not home. Not back to Grace. Not inside this bar I'm walking past, the new one where the students go and I know a few of the servers. I just want to be alone.

So I keep walking, past where Main Street turns into the River Road, past the last turn back into town, out where there's almost no traffic and I can walk on the yellow stripes in the moonlight.

A pickup truck slips past toward town. I wonder where it's been. This road is connected to the roads that lead all the way to Key West; to Anchorage; to Patagonia. It could have come from anywhere; I could go anywhere, on these same roads, but for the limits of my feet.

It passes again, more slowly. Making me nervous. There's an overpass for the interstate just behind me, but no ramps. The truck stops and backs up. I could run, climb the embankment where it can't go, and hitch a ride. Maybe flag down a state trooper. But I stand here, in the middle of the road, daring it to back over me. Suddenly I want to fight whoever is in there. I have no idea why.

"Hey," the driver says through his open window, pointing up the embankment. "You know how the hell we're supposed to get up there?" He has blue hair, and is around my age. He looks genuinely bewildered. I don't want to fight him
10

anymore.

"Use your phone, dude," I say. "It's kinda hard to explain."

"That dumbass," he says, nodding at his passenger, "forgot our chargers." The other man looks sheepish. He slouches in his seat.

I reach for my phone. It's gone. Probably still back at Grace's.

We are, these men and me, terrible representatives of our generation.

"Do you have any idea," he says, "how long we've been driving alongside that damn interstate? And can't get on it?"

I know that frustration, and now I don't want to be alone out here, alone with my thoughts turning mean.

"Lemme in," I say. "I'll show you the exit."

They can drop me at the gas station. Maybe I can slink back into my parents' house like a beaten dog.

The door unlocks. I sit in the back of the crew cab and direct them past the easier way to the interstate because for some reason I want to go through town. We pass the new bar, the new coffee shop, the new school, the things I don't recognize from my childhood, and all the buildings my grandfather once owned. I can see it all, but can't touch it and can't be touched by it through the truck's windows.

"We've got a keg of Harpoon," the driver says. "And some Magic Hat. We're at the end of an interstate beer quest."

"Fascinating," I say. "Turn here."

"I've had every single beer in our city," the driver says.

"Brewery," the passenger mutters. "You've been to every single brewery. That's different."

"Anyway," the driver continues, "you want to see what people like, you've gotta give 'em an option. Something they already know, and something they've never even thought about before. Give 'em a taste of both. Then see which they go back for—the familiar choice, or the new thing."

"It's market research," the passenger slurs. "We're

brewers."

"Hampshire Street Brewing," the driver boasts. "Home of the weirdos."

"Where you gettin' out?" the passenger asks.

We're on the interstate now, about to cross the state line. Apparently I've become a hitchhiker.

I turn his question around. "Where are you goin'?"

"Portland," he says.

"Me too."

Let the way forward be lit by the bridges burning behind me.

"Really..." the passenger mutters, staring daggers. "What're the odds."

"Strange place to find a guy going to Portland," the driver says.

"I met you there, didn't I?"

The passenger asks which part of the city I'm from, or who I know.

"Just passing through," I say.

They seem unconvinced.

"You heading for Preble Street?" the passenger asks coldly.

"Maybe." His gaze is slightly less brutal than my father's jars. "What's there?"

"Resource center," he says. "They're probably full for the night, though."

"What?" I blurt. "I'm not homeless!"

The passenger dismisses me with a shake of his head.

"Say, what's your name?" the driver asks.

"Jamie."

I don't want to mention my last name, and risk being linked to the world behind me. Why drag it with you when you're trying to escape?

"Just, Jamie."

They laugh and relax. *On-on*, they say together.

"Hell, you shoulda just said so!" the passenger adds. "I'm

Pabst Smirnoff!"

"And I'm Diddle Acquittal," the driver says.

"We're heading to a party at Clasp Her the Friendly Ghost's place," he says. "I can drop you somewhere on the way, or you can come if you like."

"Sounds like fun," I say.

Is this what happens when you let go and trust fate? You wind up partying with weirdoes? I should have surrendered years ago.

"I didn't know," the passenger says, staring at the night-darkened wilderness outside his window, "they had a kennel way out here."

I have no idea what he's talking about, but the truck is warm and the noise of the road is soothing. If I shut up and take a nap, I just might be okay.

"Yeah," I say, drifting off. "What're the odds?"

* * * * *

Thursday, April 16th
Portland, Maine

"Put that keg by the fridge," the driver—what did he call himself?...Diddle Acquittal?—yells over the house party noise.

Someone calls him Sherman.

"Benzo!" a girl behind me yells, wrapping her arms around the passenger. She squeezes him until he sets down the keg, then lets go so he can pour her a beer. I wonder how much more fuel this fire needs, so late on a weeknight.

"What can I pour you?" Sherman asks, handing me a plastic cup.

"Beer?"

"No shit," he says. "I mean, lager or stout? Sour? Fruity?"

I read the room.

"Something weird."

He pours something pale and pink. "That's always the right choice," he says.

I wouldn't know it's beer by the taste, but it's good. Damn good.

And popular. People crowd the kegs, pushing me away. Benzo hooked several kegs to a little panel of faucets, each topped with a hand-carved tap handle, to add a little class to the keg party. Then he and Sherman, the only people I know here, dive into conversations. I decide to be lonely by the window, to open it and clear my head in the fresh air. What the hell am I doing here? They seem to all know each other, they laugh and joke and hold court in little groups… It looks awesome. I've always wanted to belong in a scene like this. Now, I'm in the middle of it. Observing. Breathing. Enjoying the night air.

Then the window slams shut.

"Gotta keep this closed, buddy," says the guy who closed it.

"Why?"

"It keeps the noise in, so the neighbors don't call the cops."

"What about the ones downstairs?"

"Like, that guy?" he says, nodding at a tall man with a handlebar mustache like a cartoon villain. He's drinking sake from a bottle while he rants about something. "He lives downstairs. It's the rest of the neighborhood we're thinking of."

"That's considerate," I say.

"I don't know you yet," he goes on. Cheerfully. As if all the strangers like me are friends he hasn't met yet. I want to be charmed, but something's not right. Maybe it's me.

"I'm Evan."

"I'm Jamie."

"Jamie…" he says, fishing for a last name or some

connection.

"Just Jamie." His eyes open wide behind bottle-thick glasses.

"Well hot damn!" he says, balling up his fist and placing it on his head. "I'm Mr. Giggles!"

"Tricky Britches!" someone yells. The cry goes 'round the room, breaking up conversations, everyone heading now to a back room. The door is off the hinge, propped in the hallway. Evan leads me past the mustachioed man, who rants about *damn dirty hippies!*, and leads me as we elbow our way into the crowded room.

"You like bluegrass?" Evan asks me.

I've not listened to much of it before, but I'm a tourist, and I want to jump into the cage with the gorillas. Just to see what happens.

"Sure!" I say.

Then we're inside the room, with people crammed against the walls. A mandolin player leans against an upright mattress, holding it back so it won't crush the tangle of girls on a blanket on the floor. A fiddler stabs his bow in the air above them, soaring and diving around a trombone slide in a dogfight over their heads. The periphery is lined and the hallway is packed. I'm as near the middle of it as I can be without lying down in the tangle of other people's friends.

Evan says something I can't make out, then he's off, on hands and knees circling the gaggle on the blanket, looking for a way in among them.

The musicians jam—it's not a song. It's a moment. Someone hands me a glass pipe and lighter. I pass it on, unlit. From the other direction comes a different pipe, probably a different lighter. Again I pass, as the room fills with smoke. In another minute the pipes may not be necessary.

When a third one comes my way, well…why not. The woman handing it to me smiles and leans close.

"It's okay. It's safe here."

Then the first real song starts, something I recognize from the radio awhile back. Definitely not an original for this band, but clearly a crowd favorite.

"Home is wherever I'm with you," the band sings.

I'm with you! the crowd calls back.

There's nowhere I'd rather be, for as long as this lasts.

Chapter 3

Friday, April 17ᵗʰ
Hampshire Street Parking Garage

Dan Grant

"This is my city," I say to the man I'm with on the top deck of this parking garage. "I was born across town. I can see the hospital from here, and over there, that observatory is near my house on Munjoy Hill. Pretty much anywhere I go in Portland—on Casco Bay, even out to the islands—I can see that observatory and know right where I belong."

"Home is forever," the man agrees, "but the city around it? That changes every twenty years or so. Faster, if you're paying attention. You can be a steward of that change, Councilman Grant, if you play your cards right."

Those words make my skin crawl.

"Imagine all that trash," he goes on, standing near the edge of the parking deck, "Just gone—poof!" His clenched fist opens like a magician's, but the trash on the street below is still there. "And in its place," he continues, pointing at a brand new bank over on Fore Street, "more of that!"

"More banks?" I ask.

He is a slick real estate developer, and particularly aggressive. There have been many like him before, all rotten. I bring each of them up here and one look is all it takes, one look at my city, and they tear off into fantasies of how their investors want to make my home better—for me.

I like it the way it is, for the most part. So I smile, as I'm smiling now, and imagine nudging them over the barrier wall. Adding a little more trash to the street below.

"I mean, more of the finest buildings," the man continues, "attracting the finest businesses, the finest *people*, to renew... um...places like *that*."

He points with a crooked finger at the Hampshire Street neighborhood anchored by Gispert's a rundown bar that's been there since the dawn of time.

When I'm up here on the parking garage, I can smell the bay. On a clear day, I can see Mt. Washington, or the horizon way out in the Atlantic. I can see my district and half of Portland and I can point out where things are and were and trace the march of progress right up to the edge of Hampshire Street, where it stopped.

I could tip this creep and a dozen more over the edge, pile the bodies good and deep, and they'd just keep coming. From Boston, from New York, from DC. Everyone wants a piece of the action when the market's hot. But there is something different about this guy. If I could put my finger on it, I could figure out his angle.

"We'll clear away those firetraps," he says, dismissing the tenements along Hampshire Street. "We'll add some street level shopping, with luxury townhomes above. We'll fix the sidewalks, we'll even repave the streets—if that expedites the permits—and from this squalor, Councilman, we will build the future of your great city."

"By destroying that part of it that's in my district."

"Change can be delayed, but never stopped. You're either in control of it, or it fucks you."

"Listen, buddy," I say.

"Maxwell," he corrects. "Maxwell A. Naylor, of—"

"Right. You have no idea how many times I've stood right here, heard this same shit, from...my God, I could swear it's been you. Every time."

"But has anyone else," he crows, "been this ambitious?"

"Yeah, and more."

"Have they been backed by a firm like Merritt Capital?"

"And better."

"Have they offered you a silent partnership?"

"Yup," I lie.

"Then what will it take?"

I've got him now.

"What you propose," I say, "may be in my district. But you need the whole council behind you. You need the *mayor* behind you."

"All we need at first," he says, "are a few promises, some expedited permits maybe, and the right friends. The rest comes later, as our friends' fortunes improve. What's good for a few, after all, can be good for many."

Over the edge he goes, in my mind, all the way to the pavement. *Splat.* The gutters drain to Casco Bay. Feed his gore to the lobsters.

Men like him will keep coming, though eventually they'll come to other people. Then they'll roll into my neighborhood with their plans and their machines and make things into what they want, around me. I'll watch from the observatory, cursing them, powerless. That's one vision of the future.

"Mayors can be made," Max says. "They need a cause, and they need campaign funds. I'm offering you both."

"They also need votes," I remind him.

"The cause brings the people," he says, "and what better cause than making the streets safe? Than bringing the neighborhood up? Imagine the next generation, coming of age in gleaming townhomes with street level shopping, in a neighborhood with a quality of people better than…that."

From the street below I hear the familiar sound of a retired fire truck with benches where the water tank was, benches covered in tourists. Shirtless guides gyrate around them to a song played through hidden speakers—*It's Raining*

Men. I peer over the barrier wall as a homeless man toasts the spectacle with a tall can of beer, hollering.

"Hallelujah!"

Max shudders.

"Think of the children, councilman."

* * * * *

I didn't shake his hand for the children. I shook it for myself—for my dignity, for my future, and yeah, because I'm scared. He has a point. My district is changing—the *city* is changing—and there's only so much I can do as a councilman to make sure it's done right, and to keep unneeded change out of *my* neighborhood. There's a lot more I could do as mayor, and a campaign this fall will be expensive. Power feels way better than fear.

Besides, there's plenty of work to be done here on Hampshire Street, and if he's willing to fund it, well... change isn't all bad. Especially when it's inevitable. Take these buildings, along this sidewalk on Hampshire Street. You can't sit on the stoops before the sun dries all the piss. The sidewalks are so jagged you have to shovel them one slab at a time, so the tenants usually don't bother. In the summer, you've gotta pick your feet up to keep from tripping, like you're marching, and make sure they don't come down in dog shit. These things can be improved.

And that building over there is wrapped in tarpaper, for Chrissakes, like it's the Great Depression. One side is covered in some hippie dippy mural of wheat fields and hops vines and dancing bottles. Right in the middle of it, some asshole spray painted "Irish IRA." What the hell were any of these people thinking?

Then over there, across the street, there's a deck for each floor of that building, and they're all about to fall off. Or maybe the building is going to fall away from the decks. Hard telling. Who knows what horrors lurk behind the deadbolted doors... And the fire escapes! Half of them lead into thin air! The rest hang on sideways. If a fire doesn't kill the poor bastards crammed inside, the fire escapes will! This is a land forsaken by Code Enforcement.

Here comes another embarrassment, a big guy in unlaced boots wearing some kind of tunic, made of...my God, he's wearing animal pelts. Pelts! Just walking up the sidewalk like he owns the place, talking to some dweeb in Coke-bottle glasses who needs a change of clothes and...a job. It's a weekday! They're young enough, able enough. It's like they've sprung from the cracks in the sidewalk.

And here comes our Street Preacher! That crotchety old bastard, holding my favorite of his different signs, the one that says "Drunks, Rebellious Women, Sex Addicts, Liberals, Party Animals...God will judge you!" He's got his eyes on the man in the pelts now, and by the way he holds his sign he'd rather swing it.

"You there!" he yells. "Have you heard the good news?"

"What's that?" Pelt Man says.

"That the Kingdom of Heaven is open for even the likes of *you!*"

"Hey," the guy in the Coke-bottle glasses says with a leer, pointing to the sign. "I know her!"

"Who?" the preacher demands.

"The woman who all those things on your sign describes! She's lovely, a real nice gal."

The preacher looks like he's about to burst into flames. He lowers his voice.

"The wages of sin, young men, are *death!*"

"Everyone dies," Pelt Man says. "Even you. Get over yourself."

"I have nothing to fear," the Preacher says. "I am not enslaved to a life of vice and sin!"

"Well you should try it sometime," I can here Coke-bottle glasses say. "It's *really* fun. On-on!"

"Fornicators!" the preacher yells as they walk past him and into Gispert's. "Drunkards! Womanizers!" His words echo off the brick walls, like he's condemning this whole street. "Your end is near!"

Chapter 4

Friday, April 17ᵗʰ
Houlton Street

Jamie Schmidt

I wake up on the ground with this dark brown taste in my mouth, and everything hurts. I'm beneath a canoe, on some blanket. A sliver of light shows it's daytime out there. A little breeze slips in with the light, but otherwise it's stifling in here.

Out there—I just know it—is the headache I deserve. I rock the canoe to get fresh air, and here it comes: bam. The headache rolls me out into the light, coughing and gagging.

What a new beginning!

There's a bottle of water with a note.

"On-on!"

It's signed, PorME H3, like I'm supposed to know what that is.

So this is the first day of the rest of my life. Every morning is. But damn…

I roll to my knees, then stand and look around. I'm at the far end of a dead end street, with little houses hemmed in by the backsides of bigger houses here in…the parked cars have Maine plates, with pinecones and a bird and the motto "Vacationland." One car has a bumper sticker saying "The way life should be!"

The building beside this canoe is three stories tall with

23

windows shut tight against a lovely morning. Last night there was a party up there. I remember it vaguely. The building has two front doors, unmarked, windowless, locked. I knock, but no one answers, so I spread the blanket over the canoe to air out and take my water down the street. I pass through a warren of parked cars and tiny fenced yards and emerge on a wider avenue lined with brick homes and trees growing through empty spots in the sidewalk.

A man walks an enormous dog on a gleaming chain past American flags, rainbow flags, and ironwork painted rustproof black. The paint is chipped around some doors but not others, and some of the metalwork is rusty. It's hit and miss—a picture perfect street at first glance whose blemishes show when you look closer. They make the beauty feel real, though. Real and accessible.

My God I'm hungry. I reach for my phone to search for... Whoops. That's right. I left it behind. There's gotta be somewhere to eat, but how to find it when I'm not sure what I'm looking for?

At a playground on the next block, a boy stares at me from the top of the jungle gym. He can't climb any higher, and doesn't seem to know what to do next. I have no idea either, kid, but good for you. You've made it. Now climb something taller. I nod at him as I pass, and find a little café farther on.

It's called the Ohno. I slip inside. Coffee urns guard the counter. Wine bottles line the walls. Flyers for yoga classes and gallery openings paper the entryway. The cashier wears a mauve t-shirt—this is the kind of place where I'm certain they use words like *mauve*. I order a pair of their heartiest sandwiches.

"This is going to sound strange," I tell the cashier, "but where exactly am I?"

"The Ohno Café," she says.

"Of course. But, where?"

"Brackett Street."

She swipes my credit card.

"I mean, what *city*?"

The machine beeps angrily.

"Portland," she says, coldly. "And your card's declined."

Her register is covered in bumper stickers with cheerful lobsters and cartoon moose that mock me.

"Sorry," I say. "Try my debit card." I feel the judgement of the line behind me, half a dozen people who haven't had their coffee yet, further delayed by my apparent poverty. "There's plenty of cash in that account," I add, regrettably. I can feel their eyes rolling.

The machine beeps angrily.

"Sir—"

"I've got cash!" I want to pull a wad of bills from my wallet and flash it around, show everyone that I'm not *broke*, it's just a problem with the technology. And I didn't just sleep under a canoe because I *had* to, but because I *wanted* to! I don't know where I am, per se, not because I flipped out and ran away from home, but because…because I'm on an adventure!

"Here!" I say too loudly, handing her a ten dollar bill.

"It's twelve fifty," she says.

Which leaves me about three bucks, and a mystery.

I slide the change into my pocket like treasure, and ask to use their phone.

Her look says a lot about her plummeting opinion.

Someone puts his hand on my back.

"You can use mine, buddy." I turn around to find a stern-looking man in a department store blazer staring at me.

"Let's just step outside," he says.

* * * * *

"Jamie! You're alive!"

My mother sounds more surprised than relieved.

"Yeah," I say. "Why?"

Her words have those rounded edges from the zinfandel-Xanax cocktails that keep her docile in captivity. My mother could have been someone; instead she married my father, who already was someone, saving herself the hassle. In such a small town, I don't blame her. I don't envy her, either.

"When you didn't come home last night—"

"I'm an adult, mom," I remind her.

"Grace said you stormed out! And no one's heard from you, not even the police!"

"The what?"

"I called the hospital, too, Jamie. There's no sign of you!"

"Because I'm fine!" I say. "I'm just in…did you really call the police?"

"Of course!"

"I just lost my phone, I'm not dead."

"And thank God for that! Hang on."

The line goes quiet. I stare at the man in the cheap blazer, who hasn't taken his eyes off his phone.

"She's impossible," I say to him. "But, she's my mom…"

"How can you be fine?" she says, back on the line. "*Fine* people don't just vanish."

"Did you take another call?"

"Phone's been ringing all morning, dear. That was Karen, she read that you're missing in the paper, and—"

"The newspaper!"

"—she wants to bring me a pie. To help with my *grief*, dear."

"But I'm not dead! Look, mom, I've got three bucks left, and my cards stopped working… Do you know anything about that?"

"Your father cancelled them this morning."

"I've been gone one night!"

"Well do you want your identity stolen?"

"You're impossible! How am I supposed to get home?"

"Ask your father, he just came in."

"Jamie!" my father barks. "You're alive!?"

"Yeah..."

"Well you're still dead to me! Here's your mother."

"Jamie," Mom says sweetly, "maybe you should stay dead awhile."

"So you can get sympathy food?"

"Yes, and while your father writes you out of his will."

"You're joking."

"I don't know, dear. But just lie low, okay? Ring if you need me."

"But mom, I'm broke and—"

She hangs up.

"You didn't tell her where you are," the man says as I hand his phone back.

"She has caller ID, she'll figure it out."

"Then she'll think you're in Rhode Island," he explains. "That's where I'm from."

Good. I don't want to be found for awhile.

＊ ＊ ＊ ＊ ＊

But I still need money to live on, so with my remaining sandwich I'm off to find my bank's nearest branch. I round a bend and the neighborhood changes dramatically. The brick homes are behind me, while ahead are newer buildings of concrete and glass with street level shops and restaurants and bars, places I might go on vacation or take a long lunch. Places I can't afford on the cash in my wallet, and suddenly I feel shut out. I'm an imposter—I look like I belong, like the kind of guy these places are designed for, but at the moment can't afford a bowl of soup.

At the moment, I remind myself. I want to get away from my father, my hometown, all that, but not from the comfort of *all* my security. I dreamed of leaving my old life behind, and I guess I have…but not of waking beneath a canoe, broke and homeless for real. Fortunes change quickly, and I'm sure I can change mine back.

Congress Street is a canyon of glass and concrete and granite cornerstones. My bank is apparently just a few blocks away, through the Arts District, so I'm left to walk and wonder about what's behind those windows up high. Are those apartments? Are they offices? What goes on in the city above the street, and how might I even get up there to find out? I don't see any buzzers, don't see any signs. Maybe if I was supposed to know, I'd notice the unmarked entrances; if I had any business here, I'd know where the stairs are. If I wasn't an imposter, I wouldn't be relegated to the sidewalk.

I see it across a plaza: my bank.

I choose the teller with the brightest hair. She's about my age, and judging by the pinks and blues and the piercing in her brow, hasn't let a bank job dim her shine.

"How may I help you?" she says.

"I just need to clear up a little confusion," I say, explaining how my cards have suddenly stopped working. She runs them through a little machine, and smiles that smile people get when they're relieved a particular problem is not theirs.

"Your cards have been cancelled," she explains, "due to a fraud alert."

"Please un-cancel them, everything's fine."

"I can't do that."

"Then let's issue new ones." Tugging at my hem, I continue, "I'd like to buy a clean shirt, you know?"

"They'll have to be mailed to the address on file."

"What! Why?"

"Corporate policy, sir—you don't want your identity stolen, do you?"

"I can't steal my own identity!"

She smiles blithely. Who would even want to be me right

now?

"Can we get a manag—"

"Excuse me," the manager says, materializing like the Ghost of Bad News Present, "but there's nothing we can do for an account of your type."

"Then," I say as politely as fear and anger allow, "I'd like to make a withdrawal."

She clacks at her keyboard and informs me that my checking account is frozen.

"The account co-signer," she explains, "attempted to close it this morning."

"No!"

She smiles, this time hopefully. "But there's a limit to single-day transactions on accounts like this, so a balance remains." She tells me how little, and my heart drops through the floor.

"That asshole," I say. The manager makes a disapproving noise, his brow reaching implausible levels of furrow. "When can I get what's left?"

"Tomorrow," she says. "But I'd be here early. Whoever gets to it first, can take it all."

I thank her for the tip, and force a smile. I tug again at my hem. "Still need a clean shirt, you know. Let's make a withdrawal from my savings account."

"It was closed this morning."

"No! Fuck no! He can't—"

"Sir!" the manager barks, "I'm going to have to ask you to calm down, or leave."

"How could he even do that?"

"Well," she says, "that balance was much lower, so…"

"Are you saying," I look at her nametag, "Carrie, that I have…three dollars to live on today? That's what's in my wallet. Three. Dollars."

"You can help yourself to a coffee in the lobby."

"No," the manager says, "he can't."

"Is there anything else I can help you with, sir?"

"You haven't helped me with anything."

I can feel the manager's breath on my neck. My grandfather chaired a branch of this bank. My father once owned its building! I don't have much money of my own— well I didn't, anyway—but what I had I earned. Now my flimsy plastic keys to that security are useless and I'm getting turned out like a vagrant.

Because now I *am* a vagrant.

This is not what I wanted.

But I guess it's what I asked for.

Chapter 5

Friday, April 17ᵗʰ
Monument Square, Portland

Jamie Schmidt

No one ever improved things by shitting on the world around them, so I take a walk to clear my mind. There's nowhere to go, nowhere to be, but back here in the morning, so I pick a direction and follow it, crossing by a library and down a street as mean and ugly as my mood. There's a bus station here, and I catch myself walking toward it, stopping because three bucks won't even get me outta town. Maybe I could beg.

But no. I'd rather get caught stowing away with the baggage—honest theft is more dignified than begging.

Maybe I could hitchhike—it worked once, when I didn't mean it to. Could the same mistake get me out? Somehow, I doubt it…but this road feels like it leads somewhere, maybe to an interstate. I might as well find out.

* * * * *

There are worse things than wandering the streets on a weekday, and they might include loitering on that corner over there. Across the way a group of disheveled people huddle over paper cups and cigarettes. They argue and shove and sit and stare and prop their feet on suitcases tied shut with rope.

31

Maybe they don't have anywhere else to be, either.

The sign behind them says "Preble Street Resource Center." I remember it being mentioned last night.

So I found it after all. Or maybe it drew me here, in some way I don't want to understand.

"Spare some change?" a woman asks robotically. I say no, politely, and have the urge to apologize as well. Her stare is blank, though, and what flicker of attention she paid me is gone. To avoid the hard-eyed crowd, I turn left down Portland Street. The name seems auspicious, given that I'm in Portland, but the broken glass on the sidewalk and the heavy locks on the windowless doors are just depressing.

Near the end of the block, at the point of a triangular building, some cops make three men sit on their hands. They're on my side of the street, so I keep walking, away from the homeless shelter, towards the men—curious.

"Back off!" a cop barks. I'm caught off guard.

"Whoa," I say. "I'm just walking here."

"Walk over there!" he snaps, flicking his baton open and pointing with it toward a crumbling sidewalk.

"Okay," I say, holding my hands in front of me, "I'll just move alo—"

"Now!" he screams.

"Are you being assaulted?" another cop asks in this weirdly chipper voice as he flicks his baton open, too.

"No," I say, "just moving along…"

Then I realize he's talking to his buddy. They laugh at me, this menacing, brutal kind of laugh I've never—not ever—heard before.

I don't even look both ways as I run across the street to get away from them.

* * * * *

So I walk as fast as I can to get out of this neighborhood,

32

right past a row of dumpy taverns guarded by rough looking men smoking cigarettes. The smoke in the air and beer on their breaths reek of decay. I keep my eyes down and try to look mean.

Across the street, I'm surprised to find a park with a duck pond. Men sit on benches, smoking, drinking from paper bags and feeding the birds. They've found places to be for today.

I keep walking.

A side street leads me past the yawning mouths of garages, through the hot grease smell of fast food places I can't afford right now. There's a strip mall anchored by a pawnshop and a payday loan place. A train rolls behind them on tracks that separate the strip mall from a jail.

How in the hell did I wind up here? If I was in a better mood, where would that take me?

"Your attitude," an old guidance counselor said, "determines your destiny."

If he could see me now!

Beyond the strip mall, a large stone building looks surprisingly familiar. My father makes mayonnaise in a building like it, only smaller. The rails behind this one connect all the way to his building, more intimately than highways. And though it's the last place I want to be right now, I want to touch that rail and feel that it can take me back home.

I shake the thought from my head, and wonder: where's the rest of the railroad station that should be here? This is a secondary building, not a terminal. Its granite corner stones and magnificent stonework were laid to stand for centuries, as if the glory days of the railroad would never end. But where's the rest of it? I look over where the grand terminal should be, and there's the pawn shop.

The sidewalks keep going, and so do I, climbing a bluff to get a view of the harbor from a little park. Piers reach into the nearby water, with lobster boats tied along low-slung sheet metal buildings. Along other piers, sailboats bob beside newer brick offices. It's a waterfront in transition.

Across the street, a bright yellow excavator stalks toward an older wooden home with its bucket raised high. A sign on the fence around the site says "Merritt Capital Improvements." The bucket tears at the building's roof. A window shatters, glass sparkling as it falls. Beauty in the brutality. The clapboard siding creaks and snaps and a section of wall falls away, landing at the foot of the excavator.

Another swipe reveals a bedroom, the walls now open to the air on both sides. A closet stands open, stuffed with clothes. The excavator shakes the house's frame and the front door swings open on an entryway full of potted plants and children's toys, just heaped there. Someone left in a hurry.

Why?

Did they die, with no one left to clear out their stuff?

Was there intrigue? Misfortune? Choices, or bad luck?

The excavator peels more walls from the house and suddenly I need to know if this is the result of specific misfortune, or because of something larger that could happen to me, too. I look around for somebody with comically awful timing, running toward the excavator waving a fistful of documents. But no one's coming to stop this thing that is clearly not right and so it keeps happening. Cars roll past. Cyclists glide by. And now I know that no one is coming to save the toys, or the house, or the lives left behind, and that you can't always go home again.

Chapter 6

Friday April 17ᵗʰ
Hampshire Street, Portland

Dan Grant

"You're slumming it tonight, Councilman Grant," Jude said to me from behind her bar. Gispert's isn't my first choice, but I'm getting prematurely nostalgic for the things I know won't last.

"I have kinder words for it," I replied.

The walls are wood paneled and covered in beer signs and posters for the Portland Sea Dogs. The trim is nicotine-stained from before we banned indoor smoking, as are the frames around the photo collages. They're labelled with all different years, huge spans of time between, and none of them recent. A lot of the people in those pictures are dead now. I knew some of 'em, but they were old when I was young and their town is mine now. This is my bar too, I guess, the consequence of spending a life in one place—you inherit things you don't necessarily want.

"I'd say," I told her, "that I'm 'getting some local color.'"

"You're part of that local color," she said, "and it's gonna cost ya three fifty."

She slid me a pint brewed around the corner, and set my change—two quarters—beside it. I left it on the bar as a tip. She left it on the bar, presumably, to mock me, until I slide a dollar bill alongside.

35

"Does anyone ever order the eggrolls?" I ask, nodding at a handwritten sign on a microwave.

"Not twice."

"I can't remember," I fib, rubbing the sweat from my pint glass, "what was here before this bar."

"Another bar."

"And what do you suppose will be here after?"

"*Definitely* another bar."

"I remember when the city wanted to tear this whole neighborhood down, for the arterial road project. Put in a lane right where I'm sitting."

"Well," she scoffs, "they didn't."

"It was such a near miss, though. Things could have been so different…but this is better, right? The Hampshire Street neighborhood?"

"Suits me just fine," she smiles. "The rest of town is getting too expensive for me. You know you've gotta drive out to the mall to buy underwear? A city ain't livable if you can't buy underwear without leaving."

"I have never thought about that."

"But we're holding out. Besides, they put that road in anyway, right over there, so who cares? What was even there before, buncha grass?"

"About a hundred twenty buildings. Taverns, grocers, God knows how many people living upstairs… It was a neighborhood, Jude."

"Uh huh…"

"They had to get the trucks from the interstate, to the waterfront, and the narrow little streets weren't working. So they erased an entire neighborhood, *for the greater good.*"

"Watcha care about all that for?"

"I'll tell you this, Jude. There's lots of people looking at Hampshire Street, India Street, thinking it's about time to… 'renew' is the word I hear a lot. Whispered, of course."

Jude laughs, jangling the sequins on her shirt. "Lemme

guess—them people puttin' up condos ain't nobody from here can afford?"

"Yup."

"They wanna 'renew' something, they can start with Grant Street."

"They have. Three of those firetraps are coming down. They're evicting two hundred people! And that's just a little project."

"Well you keep 'em the hell away from here. I like things just the way they are."

"Yeah," I say, thinking about my own neighborhood—too close to evade the eye of progress for long. "Me, too."

I didn't come here to start feeling sorry for the place, but to pay some kind of homage. Now as I stand in the doorway, I imagine Naylor rolling down the street in a bulldozer. He's wearing a bright yellow hardhat, aiming the machine for Gispert's, and directly at me.

* * * * *

I wouldn't normally walk Hampshire Street after dark, but the pre-nostalgia is strong. I want to know this place as it is, so that later I may judge how far it's come, and myself, accordingly. It's a nice enough night. The bone-white steeple of the Cathedral of the Immaculate Conception glows up the street, lighted like a beacon pointing toward heaven. It draws me past the unmarked doorways, wary of a group of young people loitering on a stoop, drinking beer. One of them has blue hair. Another—a girl, I think—has hair of all different colors like she couldn't make up her mind.

Loudly she says, "Wait, he's coming back!"

"Which one," Blue Hair asks. "Knife-guy?"

"No," she says, "the other guy. And he's got a—"

"Shovel!" says another. "Dude's got a shovel!"

A man rounds the corner waving a shovel and hollering,

entering the Hampshire Street intersection like an arena. Then I see who he's after—a man rushes along the sidewalk, straight toward the guy. They're yelling angry nonsense.

"Come on knife guy," Blue Hair cheers.

"Get him, shovel dude," the girl yells.

"Five bucks on knife guy!"

"No man, shovel dude all the way!"

It's a hobo gladiator battle by streetlight, silhouetted against the church's glowing spire. I don't know who wins—I don't stick around to watch, unlike the degenerates placing bets. I duck down Newbury Street, leaving Hampshire and my nostalgia for it far behind.

Chapter 7

Saturday, April 18th
Monument Square

Jamie Schmidt

I've been awake and hungry since dawn. Sitting here with my back against the bank's glass doors, I watch a guy in a purple felt hat, felt robes and bright boa, stroll through the plaza with a shopping cart full of cans. Another dude rocks down the sidewalk whistling the one note he can whistle, really giving it everything, scaring the seagulls off their trashcans. I'd do bad things for a good meal right now, but the smell of sun-warming dumpsters and bus exhaust keeps the worst of my appetite in check.

Otherwise, it looks like a fine day, and I dream of what all it might bring. Certainly not another night beneath the canoe. I'm done with that.

Keys jangle in the lock behind me. I look up at the disapproving face of the branch manager. He stiffens, jerks the keys from the lock and steps back to make me open the door for myself.

The teller from yesterday is still setting up her drawer.

"I'm not quite ready yet," she says, "so if you could—"

"Sorry," I interrupt, "for being a jerk yesterday."

It's been gnawing at me. She looks surprised, like people don't usually apologize for being assholes.

"Would you like to try again?"

"What, like with flowers?"

"To make your withdrawal," she laughs.

"For whatever's left, please."

She logs into the account, then frowns. "Someone else is trying to withdraw from this account too," she says. "But you're in the cue first."

"How much does he want?"

"It doesn't say. But, if you want to leave any funds available…"

"As much as he left me yesterday."

She counts a pitiful little pile of bills and closes the account. So this is it—what's left of my life savings, in my pocket. A hundred ninety bucks. Security, shelter, food, in paper form, no longer safe in a vault or behind a computer.

Outside, the skateboarders now look mean. They could whip me with the chains on their wallets and take everything I have. The men smoking cigarettes are watching me, too, waiting for their chance. The scene, so recently charming, takes on this awful edge now that I have so much—*everything*—to lose. I can't trust anyone, and have to stay on my guard.

But what if…

It's crazy, but I imagine tossing those bills in the air, throwing my head back and laughing as I walk right through the little shower and out toward whatever comes next. With nothing left, I'd have nothing to lose—I'd be free.

Then I'd need strangers instead of fearing them. I'd be free to trust them! Such a bizarre thought, to put myself at the mercy of others, even of luck itself, when I've tried so long to stand on my own. But where's my stubbornness gotten me?

Unemployed, nearly broke, and homeless.

What did I get by trusting strangers, and whatever brought us together? A ride, a party, a place to sleep…a bottle of water, with a friendly note.

I'm close enough to zero, I tell myself; I don't have to

throw my little money away. Besides, I earned it, didn't I? Even though it came from his business, how deep does that stain run? So I'll keep it, and just trust that whatever dumb luck got me here won't leave me now.

It's a beautiful day.

In a beautiful plaza.

And a beautiful chance to start over.

* * * * *

Saturday, April 18th
Bell Buoy Park

Kate Dorsett

"Kate!" my friend Devon whispers to me. We're standing behind our portable tables, trying to sell our art.

He nods at the bovine couple nosing through the prints on his table. There are a lot of people in Bell Buoy Park, but no one's looking at my jewelry right now. His glance says it all: keep an eye on these people, your jewelry table is next.

"And this one?" the tourist asks. He's holding one of Devon's prints up to the sky like it's a slide or something, like light is supposed to come through from the backside.

"That's the Super Moon," Devon says, "with the Immaculate Conception Cathedral's spire. I shot it just up thataway, up Hampshire Street."

"I like the moon you added," the tourists says, now scratching at the plastic sleeve like he expects the moon is a sticker. "It's huge!"

"That's just the way it was."

The man stares at the image while his wife mouth-breathes beside him. I've been selling art in this park long enough, I know what's coming, and it's not a sale.

"No," the tourist says with this kind of dad-voice, "you

41

did *something* to it. The moon never looks like that."

"I waited eight months to get that shot."

Devon digs in and here we go: artist vs civilian. I bet this doesn't happen in galleries, where a piece's worth is presumed and its price isn't questioned.

"I scouted locations. I planned the composition so the spire gives a sense of scale—that's how it works. No cheap manipulation. Just craft, and the science of the Moon Illusion."

"Ah ha!" the tourist snaps, dropping the picture like a forgery. "So that's your trick!"

Devon tries to explain the moon illusion, but the man backs into the stream of people flowing from the ferry terminal into the Old Port and disappears.

"How many are on the boat today?" I ask. The city publishes a list of cruise ships due in port, and how many souls are aboard. Many of them disembark to see the Old Port, wandering past this park on their way. We can set up our tables anywhere that we're not blocking a doorway or fire escape, or getting too much in the way. No one makes a living from just this, but I wouldn't be able to afford my apartment without the extra income. I hope it's a good boat this morning, for my friends.

Then there's the hope of catching the right eye—someone who falls in love with your work and wants to show it in their gallery, or sell your jewelry in their store somewhere exciting...because the stores around here don't sell our stuff. Not often. And the coffee shops with my friends' paintings on the wall, they're great, but you can't launch a career or pay your rent with those sales, or by listening to all the managers who say *no, no, no.*

There's a hundred ways our luck could break, but only if we're here, taking our chances—being seen. And ideally, appreciated. That means bearing our souls through our art, haggling with cheapskates, and falling in love with life again each time someone seems to *get it*.

And then there's Brigitte. I see her through a break in the crowd, standing outside her souvenir shop across the street. She has a clipboard. She's watching us, taking some kind of note. I stare at her until her eyes meet mine and her mouth twists in this horrible way. Sometimes she crosses the street, into our territory.

"Time to go," I tell Devon.

"Aren't you taking the later ferry?"

I nod toward Brigitte.

"Oh..." he says.

"You should come out with us," I say, but I know he won't. He has a wife and a kid and when he's not working—for the paper, or for his art—he's busy with them.

"Someday," he says. "But today, I'll hold our ground against *her*."

I watch Brigitte follow a customer into her store, then collapse my table and leave it with Devon. My friends smile as I walk past their tables. A few pack up to join me at the gate for the next Peak's Island ferry. We'll leave the market behind, and for the rest of the day, we'll *create*.

* * * * *

Saturday, April 18th
Tommy's Park

Jamie Schmidt

I'm glad I didn't throw my cash in the air. It would have looked awesome, and really made a statement, but I just bought a hotdog from a guy in a park and that's hard to do without money. I asked him how long he'd been selling hotdogs from his cart right there, and he said thirty years.

"Thirty years?" I said.

"Thirty years…" he said.

"Why?"

"Why not? I like it."

I couldn't figure it out. Thirty years selling hotdogs outside?

"This is my office," he explained. His voice was gruff, but he was getting a kick out of the moment. "It's never boring. This place, Tommy's Park? It's changing all the time, the people too. I meet folks from all over, and I don't gotta go nowhere. Even the same people, they get the same thing for years, that don't get boring, just comfortable."

"You from around here?" I asked him.

"I am now."

"How's that?"

"You stick around long enough, do something useful, before you know it, you're part of something. The way everything was when you started, that changes, and once it's all changed and you're still there, guess what—now you're part of the way things are."

"I just got here," I said, "and I'm looking for the soul of the city. Where do you think I should go?"

"Down Exchange Street. That's what everyone comes here for," he said. "The Old Port…"

Did he mean the bars, the cobblestone street, the waterfront…

Following my heart, like the hot dog guy told me, brought me along the waterfront to a little park with a bright red buoy. A guy my age with a fiddle busked beside it in a plaza ringed by elaborately staged card tables. People stood behind them, like there's some kind of art festival today.

The vendors were packed tightly, except for some table-size spaces at odd intervals. A photographer sold prints next to one of those spaces. I wondered who might have been there earlier, and what I might have learned from their art… or from them.

I carried on through the park, following foot traffic along a pier. Yellow-and-white ferries nudged the pier, waiting, while a larger ferry spin its stern toward a vehicle ramp. Its rails are lined with people, waving at the crowd around me. The crowd waves back. The ferry isn't ready to disembark, so we stare at each other through a short, uncross-able distance, and wave at each other again.

"Just Jamie!" someone says. I turn, and it's Evan, the guy in the glasses who closed the window on me at that party. "It's you again! How are ya?"

"Fine, thanks," I say automatically. "And you?"

"Better once I get to the island! Is this your first Sacred and Profane?"

I have no idea what he's talking about.

"Well...I'm not sure where I'm going, honestly," I mumble.

"Then come check it out! There's this big old fort underground," he says, "with all these spooky rooms. Artists go out there just after the Super Moon, and make installations inside. Candles everywhere, performers… Last year a dancer nearly set a dude on fire. But he was alright."

"So it's some kind of art fair? Like that one," I nod toward the park.

"No, no," he says. "That's where my friends sell art for tourists. The Sacred and Profane is more expressive. There's a donation to get in, but otherwise, nothing is for sale. It's about the moment, the meaning...it's about connecting! Through *art*. It's my favorite thing about Portland. I had to see it again, so I'm here—for the early ferry so I can help set up, and get in free."

"I like free."

I look across the harbor at what I think is the right island, out at the edge of the open ocean. I've come this far, but it feels like I have farther to go.

"Need a little more help?" I ask.

"All I can get!"

* * * * *

Saturday, April 18th
City Hall

Dan Grant

The mayor's office will need a few updates if—when—I win this fall. I'll keep that painting of the Rum Riots, of course, but not the contemporary art. It's just too—

"Dan?" the mayor interrupts my daydream.

"Yeah?"

"Since it happened in your district, I thought you might have some insight. Maybe an idea how to keep it from happening again?" We don't usually meet on Saturdays, but news travelled fast about last night's skirmish. People get stabbed in cities, sure, but bring a shovel to a knife fight, and people talk.

"It's a crying shame," I say. "But I understand it. The Old Port is full of police at night, on account of the nightclubs. We've run the bad element out of my neighborhood—it's quiet as the grave, finally. So the real trouble makers, they're stuck in between, in these concentrated little pockets...like Hampshire Street."

"It's also an opportunity," she says. "Don't you think?"

"Obviously." When bad things happen, just groom the public's fear and give it a direction that you control, then ride that energy as far as you like—even all the way into office. It's slimy, but...proven.

"There's interest in redeveloping Hampshire Street," she continues. "That could be the solution to violence like this in your district."

"Violence like this?" I'm the only one who gets to talk bad about my district... "That's the first blood spilled on

Hampshire this year!"

"You've seen the transients there. The beer cans and graffiti? It's so…unsavory. And that bar, what, Sangria's?"

"Gispert's."

"Whatever. It attracts the wrong element."

"It attracted me last night…"

"Look, Dan—your district has the second-lowest tax base on the peninsula. I bet you can turn that around with some clever handling of this opportunity. And the right friend."

"Lemme guess…"

"His plan sounds lovely, don't you think? The rest of the city is coming up so nicely. A few places still stick out."

My eyes rest on a boutique hotel through the window. The newspaper used to own the whole building. They kept it humming with the presses in the basement and the stringers dashing in and out, back when newspapers needed that kind of space down town. Now the hotel uses typewriter keys for elevator buttons, and on hot days in the right corridor you can still smell the editors' cigarettes.

"We've got a helluva lot of hotels for a city our size. But you know what I like about that one? They didn't destroy the place. It's kitschy, sure, but the trick to renovating *well* is keeping the old character while you add new layers. It's harder to bring a place up than tear it down and start over, which is why I still don't like Naylor's plan."

"I think the people are ready for change," she says. "Especially after last night."

"Change, yeah. But not to get forced out for more luxury condos."

"I know how you feel," she says, and I can see in her eyes she means it. "We overshot the mark a few times, always with the best intentions. It happens. I want to keep Max busy somewhere he can do more good than harm. We can't hold the developers off forever, and it would be a disservice to our city anyway…so why not use them to clean things up?

Hampshire Street could use it, and you know that."

"Maxwell Naylor," I say, "is a greedy, pandering dirtbag."

"I don't want to dance with the devil either, Dan, but things like last night? They could be different. It's time."

"People want to know if it's an isolated incident," I say, accepting my role.

"Violence indicates a neighborhood in peril," she says. "Say that at your press conference this afternoon."

"Okay, okay..." I make a mock military salute. Ever faithful guard-dog!

"Make them feel like something needs to be done," she adds. "Make the whole city feel that way, Dan."

"Naturally."

"Blame it on that bar. It's everything wrong with the neighborhood, and its space can be much better used."

"For condos..."

"We're thinking of calling it the 'Cathedral District.' You've got the Cathedral of the Immaculate Conception at the very end of the street, then St. Peter's a block away, and some nice places for a Sunday brunch at the far end of Hampshire. A rather remarkable turn from what it is now, right?"

"I suppose you'll shut down the bar, condemn a few buildings, then have Naylor swoop in and rebuild my district for me?"

"No Dan. That's what you're going to do. Because," she says, turning towards the window, "it's what's good for Portland. Think of the children."

Chapter 8

Saturday, April 18th
Peak's Island

Jamie Schmidt

"This is an odd place for an art fest," I say to Evan.

The old fort is completely overgrown, and tucked on the ocean-facing side of the island away from the summer homes with their manicured lawns. Trails lead through tangled foliage over a long, hollow mound with enormous passages cut through each end. Fancifully dressed artists carry sculptures and boxes into the yawning darkness, and emerge empty-handed.

We slip inside among them, the air suddenly cold, the way outlined by flickering tea candles that shrink in the distance. I put my hand on Evan's shoulder so I don't lose him. A ways on, we reach what must be a low point in a sloping floor—the day-lit chamber at the far end reveals itself by degrees, silhouetting demonic shapes with horns, with wings, contorted limbs, curves studded with bristles... They drag things that scrape and shush.

"Stay away from the walls," Evan says.

"Yeah, the candles..."

"No, the rebar. This isn't exactly a safe space."

"Then how'd they get a permit?"

His laughter echoes through the corridor.

Flashlights play across the walls, revealing swaths of

graffiti, some of which seems quite good. On the day-lit wall at the end of this tunnel looms the Monopoly Man. The moneybag over his shoulder shows the imprints of hands and feet trapped within.

"This used to be a naval gun battery," Evan says. "The big rooms at the end, those had canons aimed out to sea. The rooms we're passing, those were powder magazines, storage, offices. They drove ammunition back and forth through this corridor. That's why it's so wide. It was built for war, and here we are—using it for peaceful creation."

"So you're one of them?" I ask. "An artist?"

"No, I just... Lemme introduce you to someone. She always sets up in the radio room."

He finds the right passageway, between glow sticks on a doorframe. A woman works by headlamp inside. Her voice seems to come from the light itself.

"Surprise, surprise," she says, dryly.

"We're here to help!" Evan chirps.

"And get in free, right?"

"Well..." he says.

She laughs.

"No, that's perfect. I lost an actor." Her light blinds me. "And I could use a third, honestly."

"This is just Jamie," Evan says.

Her eyes widen.

"Seventh Heaven," she introduces herself.

She must have seen the look on my face.

"Or, you know," she continues, "Kate is fine—we're surrounded by civilians. Can you help me break the legs off this mannequin?"

The plastic breaks with a snap and she asks Evan to carry them outside to give to whoever needs legs. Alone together, she explains the installation as I help her pile jewelry onto the legless mannequin.

"This is for my play," she says, "a little something that's

come over me. These are my failed pieces, the ones that didn't sell." She lifts a pendant made of square-shaft nails and copper. "They weigh this poor dummy down, crushing her. All these ideas that came to nothing. All this rejection. Still, she tries to stand."

"That's not going to work out too well," I say. "We broke her legs off."

Her headlamp shines on me like a prison spotlight.

"She doesn't need 'em for the first act, and that's all we've got."

"What would happen in the second?"

She turns back toward the mannequin.

"I don't know yet. She's up against a lot."

"Well I'm happy to help," I say. "If I get to keep my legs."

We arrange boxes marked "ART" in big block letters. They're empty—just props. Evan returns, to my astonishment, with the teller from the bank.

"Sorry I'm late," she says. "Day job, you know..."

I hang back, outside the light from Kate's headlamp. She walks us through our opening places: Evan, near the door, so he appears behind whatever audience we can fit in this little room. The bank teller—Carrie, I recall—in a corner. Kate near the mannequin. She hands me a flashlight and stages me in a far corner.

"When I clap," she says, "shine this on the mannequin. I'll say a few words, then when I clap again, shine it on me. After that...shine it on whoever's talking. Or whoever you want, I don't care. Make it confusing—it *is* confusing. Then when Evan calls for you—"

"Whom am I playing?" I ask.

"You're playing the part of the broom."

"The broom?"

"Here." Carrie hands me a foxtail brush. "It's all I could find."

"I want you to knock those boxes over with it," she

51

continues, "then slowly come after us—like you're sweeping us out of the room."

"Alright…"

"It's all improv," Kate says, "but here's the idea. We're on a sidewalk. Carrie, you're playing Brigi…you're playing whatever name I come up with. You're a powerful landlord, let's say, and you don't like that artists on the sidewalk are competing with the tourist shops that rent from you. You've got the ego of a crime boss. And you *don't* think they're real artists. I'm playing a street artist—just your average, everyday person selling jewelry from a card table."

"Wow," Carrie says. "Big stretch right there."

"So you're going to accost me, and insult me, and call me everything you can think of. You want me *gone*. You want me *dead*, but you don't have henchmen. We'll argue about what makes something into art, who gets to sell it on the street… you've got a racket to protect, so you're really going to tear into me."

"After I vanquish Carrie," Kate continues, looking at Evan, "the light's on you. You're a developer. You're gonna walk through here and talk about tearing the buildings down, putting up condos. Say something about putting in a wine bar, I don't care. You want to drive me away, but not personally—*you* have henchmen. His cue," she says, pointing to me, "is at the end of your spiel when you say 'It's time to clean up these streets!' "

"What's my character's name?" Evan asks.

"The Man," she says. "You're perfect for it."

"Because I'm a dude? That's so—"

"Because you're the banality of evil! The face of privilege, tut-tutting around like you own the place, slumming it for the aesthetic, going home up the hill when you've got what you need."

"Damn, Kate…" he says. I shrink into the darkness.

"What? I'm just psyching you up! You'll do fine—we'll

all be fine."

* * * * *

Saturday, April 18th
In front of Gispert's

Dan Grant

"And now," Mayor Tennerly announces, "please welcome Councilman Dan Grant."

It's a small crowd for my press conference, but a friendly one dressed in the uniform of our people: khakis, windbreakers, hats with golf logos…all good people, and largely, from higher up Munjoy Hill. I don't think there are many here from this neighborhood. That's just as well.

"Our strength," I say from my little podium, "is in our diversity!" I love it when they clap politely. "But there is one type who is *not* welcome in *my* Portland: violent criminals!"

"And queers!" Someone yells. Thankfully the applause mostly drowns him out.

"What happened here last night," I continue, "when two armed men took to the street, could have swept up and injured any one of us!"

The crowd sucks wind—what a horrible thought!

"Now, I'm not the type to hang around outside of *bars*," never mind that I'm standing in front of Gispert's, "but the point remains: violence and the circumstances that cause it have no place in our community!"

They applaud on cue again, and for the moment it feels like I could ride that affirmation all the way to the mayor's office.

"So I have called upon Chief Boyer of the Portland Police Department to step up enforcement in this neighborhood, and crack down on the social ills plaguing the good people of Hampshire Street!"

I smile at Boyer, whom I pulled away from the station at the last minute to be here. He scowls at me. I hope the crowd thinks he's just treating the moment with all due tough-guy sincerity.

"Public intoxication!" I continue, pointing to a window air conditioner piled high with empty beer cans. "Vandalism!" My finger pokes toward a newspaper dispenser balanced upside down on its coin box. "Graffiti! And even, just last night...attempted murder!"

I pause for dramatic effect.

"This will not be tolerated in my district!"

Here, here! they cheer! Sweet music!

"Not in my Portland!"

Grant! Grant! Grant! Their chant warms me like sunshine. At last I turn sideways and beckon the chief to the podium.

He's all dolled up in dress blues, with shiny black gun belt and mirror-polished shoes—a true professional, with a true professional's disdain for being away from the job.

"We have reviewed the challenges facing this neighborhood," he says, "and will take a closer look at Gispert's liquor license. As they are believed to be a contributing factor to the continued unrest. Like last night." He looks at me for validation. I urge him on.

"So I've ordered my men to increase their patrols. To step up enforcement of nuisance complaints. And keep a lid on civil unrest."

His eyes are in constant motion, searching the crowd for troublemakers. Unlike his disciplined men, the public at large is liable to do or say crazy things—to push back at his authority. Will his ego be able take it? The crowd eats this up, though. Waiting for a chance to cheer, and go home.

I nod at him to wrap it up.

"Let's clean up these streets."

The crowd erupts!

"Thank you, Chief Boyer!" I say, making a big show of my applause. "Let this serve as a warning to the hooligans, the drunks, and the rabble—you are not welcome here!"

Grant! Grant! Grant!

"Thank you councilman!" the homophobe yells above the applause. I wish he'd shut up. "We're counting on you!"

*****

Saturday, April 18th
Peak's Island

James Schmidt

The spectators are due in a few minutes, and we're ready to go. Evan and Carrie scurried off to set up her installation, so I walk with Kate down the long corridor between the rows of tea lights, taking it all in. Glow sticks float past, wrapped around costumed performers and artists clad head to toe in black—wraiths, watching, ready to read the crowd's reactions from the darker corners of the labyrinth. No one knows me down here, but anonymous in the dark, no one knows I don't belong, either.

"So how do you know Mr. Giggles?" Kate asks me.

"Who?"

"Evan…"

"I don't, really. Why do you call him Mr. Giggles?"

"Same reason he calls you Just Jamie," she mocks. We're interrupted by blood-curdling moans and rush to the next room to find a large body made of oversized stuffed clothing, pierced with homemade arrows. Where the head should be is a laptop playing a video of a mouth, the lips twisting and smacking as from hidden speakers the moans become shrieks of agony. Or is it ecstasy? I can't say.

"So you're not a hasher?" She sounded relieved.

55

"I have no idea what that even means."

"It's just this weird little thing I do with my friends."

The arrow-pierced dummy moans in ecstasy.

"Yeah, this is pretty weird…"

Her laugh is the brightest thing in these catacombs.

"No, this is a different kind of weird. They're both responses to our environments. Both are ways of dealing with stress and dancing with parts of ourselves we keep buttoned up. But I won't tell anyone that you're an imposter."

It's been a long time since I've wanted in on a secret so badly.

"Then I won't tell anyone about yours, either," I say.

"And what would that be," she asks.

"That's obvious. It's the story in your play."

"Yeah, it's…more cathartic than interpretive," she admits. "But here's the actual secret: it's a spiritual warmup for taking real action. Against real, existential threats to my community."

"I'm sure it'll all work out."

She pins me with the beam of her headlamp, searching my wincing eyes for some suggestion that I know what I'm talking about.

"You're an optimist," she says dryly.

"Maybe? I'm just trying to get out from under my own stuff too."

"How's that going?"

"I'm lost in a cave on an island and I don't know where I'm sleeping tonight."

"Sounds romantic."

"Do *you* have a place to sleep tonight?"

"Yeah."

"That's probably why."

Someone enters the room behind us. I shine my light on the mannequin as Kate takes her place in a dark corner, ready to begin once Evan and Carrie arrive.

"Excuse me," the person says. "Are you the artist?"

"No."

"Well, do you have any idea what this is all about?"

"None."

* * * * *

We run the play six times, each time a little different as Kate finds the right words and the right ways to scream them. Between performances Carrie and I check on her installation: a room full of pillows made from old t-shirts and fabric she printed with words of love on one side, and hate on the other.

"People keep turning them over," she said, "so the nice words are on top. We have to go flip them back."

Evan struts through our productions waving his finger, tearing off into fantasies of how to make our implied city better—at Kate's expense. Then he gives my cue and I knock over the boxes labeled "ART" and sweep Kate away with my foxtail brush. The audience follows us out of the radio room each time. Often they boo, but they don't boo the show—they boo the message.

So I ask Kate about the second act, which will not take place on stage. How might she turn the boos into cheers?

"I don't know," she says. "But I'm closer to figuring it out."

The spectators dwindle and Kate calls it a wrap. We drag the mannequin into the doorway and stack the "ART" boxes behind it, blocking off the room. In the corridor, in the swirling sounds of clanking props and recorded moaning, she says we're done. We can go now. Then she sets off toward the failing light at one end of the corridor, where it appears to be dusk above ground.

"Aren't you afraid," I say, following her, "that someone's gonna steal your jewelry?"

"Let 'em," she says. "I'm ready to move on." Then she adds, "But I'll pack up whatever's left before I leave the island. Littering sucks."

We emerge into a pastel evening, the fort behind us and the ocean beyond. The sky is pink and blue, pale yellow around the tips of easy-going clouds. I see Kate clearly for the first time. Her face looks softer aboveground—tranquil, as if a storm has passed. The four of us weathered it together.

Kate leads us along a narrow path through wild grass and brush, toward a towering pile of driftwood, scrap wood, and boxes. Someone dressed as Pan in a half-goat costume with hooves splashes liquid on the woodpile while chanting. Those around the pile are dressed as fairies or demons, or things I can't understand, or just wearing flannel and jeans.

"No!" Evan yells, taking off running. "No, no, no! Goddammit Speedwanker!"

Pan darts out of the way as a man throws a Molotov cocktail onto the pile. It ignites Pan's fuel with a *whoomph* I feel in my bones. An orange fireball rides a plume of choking smoke into the pastel sky. The demons and fairies and Pan all cheer.

"I guess the show moved out here," I say.

"Show?" Kate says. "No, this is real."

* * * * *

They wandered into the crowd to find food, leaving me at the edge of the fire for a moment to remember how hungry I am. And that I don't have a place to sleep. And that for all the comradery around me, I don't actually know anyone—not in a way that's useful for food or shelter. Dusk has a special kind of urgency when you don't have a place to sleep.

But I have one option: a fancy little inn near the island's ferry terminal. I walked past it earlier. The porch was full of guys like my father, reading newspapers in Adirondack chairs in the middle of the day. It looks like a nice place, with a little restaurant. My parents took me to these places as a kid, so I can just imagine the rooms, with the clean white sheets and the pillow cases that someone irons. A clean shower. I could wash my clothes in the sink, and probably should. Yeah…it's expensive, but haven't I been through enough?

I wonder where these people will sleep tonight. They don't look like the vacation inn kind of crowd. Does the ferry run all night? The bonfire is big enough to last. I'd rather be here than alone again, but how could I stay? Now, a clean bed…that's appealing. I can start over again tomorrow, a little closer to absolute zero, but with a nice breakfast. And a newspaper, on the porch, in an Adirondack chair, watching the parade of whoever slept out here, coming down to the ferry.

Isn't that porch where I belong?

When I was a kid, my father warned me about exactly this kind of scene. I thought he was making it up. I can hear him now:

"Normal people don't screw around doing pagan stuff in the woods. Burning effigies! What kind of life is that? 'Artists.' Ha! Who would employ those people? Not a bank! Not a corporation! Not *me!* You take life seriously, or you'll wind up with the likes of them, going nowhere!"

By the light of the moon, someone sings by the fire. *By the bright shining light, by the light of the moon…* More voices join—Kate. Carrie. Evan. *Have you ever met a hasher, who didn't like to kiss? By the bright shining light of the moon?*

They sing together by firelight and there's nowhere I'd rather be.

And now they're throwing art on the pyre: papier-mâché, wooden dummies, the cardboard boxes marked "ART." I hear Evan yelling *Nooo!* and see one of Carrie's t-shirt pillows sail over the fire. It must be soaked in fuel, because it bursts into flames and burns like a comet.

"Dammit!" Evan yells. People cheer.

Kate startles me and laughs when I jump.

"Thought you might need this," she says, handing me a paper plate with a salad. "It's all that's left. Sorry to scare you."

"It's cool," I say. "I was just deciding if I should…"

"Jump into the fire?"

"It'd be warmer in there at least."

Carrie walks over holding a red t-shirt. She shows me the design she printed: a macaw with its beak open, either singing or yelling, above the words "Free Speaker."

"Thanks for your help," she says. "This is my last one, I thought you'd like it. Down in the tunnel, you were pretty much just a voice, you know? So I thought 'Free Speaker,' that'd fit."

I thank her.

"Just Carrie!" someone yells from the undergrowth. "Last ferry! Let's go!"

"Just Carrie?" I ask.

"Well," she says, "I have to make one more trail before I can get named. How many have you got left?"

"I don't know…" I say. "What's a trail?"

"Come on!" the voice yells.

"Maybe I'll see you tomorrow?" Carrie says and slips away.

Evan rocks out of the bonfire shadows.

"That idiot's gonna kill someone."

"Who?" Kate asks.

"Speedwanker. My eyebrows might never grow back."

"Well, at least they got the plaster sculpture to finally burn, right?" I say.

"Just so long as he doesn't burn *everything* straightaway," Evan says. "It's gonna get cold tonight."

"You're staying out here?" Kate asks him.

"Yeah!" Evan is suddenly chipper. He turns his shoulder

to me, butting me out. "I brought an extra sleeping bag, just in case, you know…someone needs it."

"I have to work tomorrow," Kate says. "Two cruise boats are coming in. I have to pay some rent."

She turns to me and asks where I'm sleeping.

"I haven't figured that out yet."

"You could sleep with me. My roommate's gone."

Evan's jaw clenches and what's left of his eyebrows rise.

"Take her bed," Kate continues as if she never meant to imply anything else. "Just leave it as you found it, she'll never know."

"Or," Evan says, "you could stay here—I mean, we've got food, I can find some beer, you can use my other sleeping bag…"

I could buy a night of lonesome comfort. I could steal one in someone else's bed. Or I could ride out this adventure, dodging their drama as I figure out where to flee in the morning.

"I'd like to stay here."

She smiles like I've passed some kind of test.

"Goodnight," she says, melting into the night. "And don't get Jamie into trouble. He's a virgin."

Evan chortles, then laughs right in my face. "You're not a hasher?"

"I have no idea," I say "what you're talking about."

"Someone who hasn't hashed isn't Just- whatever the fuck their name is. They're Virgin- whatever the fuck their name is. You can't go around claiming to be something you're not."

"I haven't."

"Stick with me," he says, suddenly sly. "I'll show you a thing or two about this town."

Maybe I'll sneak off to the inn.

"Kate," I say, "She's a…"

"Hasher," Evan says, "I brought her into the group. Then she brought me into this one."

"This isn't hashing?"

"No," he explains "This is a gathering of the arts community. Hashing is a drinking club with a running problem—it's short for Hash House Harriers. Our members overlap. People can belong to more than one group, dude."

"I see."

He sighs.

"I've loved her since college."

"That's tough, man."

"Yeah."

The awkwardness threatens to last forever. I'm relieved when it's broken by a primal scream from beyond the firelight.

"What the hell is that?"

"Christ...!"

"Doubtful..."

"I mean, that's Seasquatch."

A bear of a man dressed in pelts and a Viking helmet stomps into the firelight.

"Goddamn pitiful fire!" he yells, stabbing the roaring bonfire with the end of a wooden staff. "Grow, ya bastard! Unnnhhh!"

"Seasquatch!" someone yells. "No!"

"It needs a sacrifice!" he bellows. "Where's a virgin?"

"He flipped out at a house party once," Evan says. "I watched him destroy a car with a hammer."

"A hammer?"

Now he's twirling the staff, the flaming end searching for a target. People scatter, regrouping on the very edges of the clearing. The flames cut the air with a *whoomph*.

"So, he's not an actor?"

"Nope..."

He draws bright crescents in the sky with the fire, spinning his staff faster. Sparks fly into the brush. It's beautiful, the way a volcano is beautiful.

"Seasquatch, no!" they yell. "You're gonna set the woods

on fire!"

"Where's my virgin?" he bellows.

The flaming staff slows. He thrusts the cold end into the fire until it catches, then he sets it spinning, blue flames trailing yellow, cutting arcs that *hiss* and *whoomph*.

A lone figure stands up to him—the mustachioed man from the house party.

"Squelch your damn big stick!" he orders Seasquatch.

Seasquatch moves around him, his enormous body remarkably graceful. He whirls like a dervish, tails rising from the pelts, flinging a halo of sparks.

Unnnnnhhhhh!

Then he disappears into the catacombs, their walls glowing as if the bowels of the Earth are on fire. Inside, someone shrieks. His laughter echoes. Then hear him pounding the walls, shaking the island, thumping a rhythm that grows deeper, fainter, until all is still.

"Well," Evan says, shrugging. "Find me when you're ready to sleep."

Chapter 9

Sunday, April 19ᵗʰ
Summit Coffee House

Dan Grant

"I'd think, Mayor, you'd be glad to renovate that neighborhood—get rid of the riffraff. They're bad for business." I could tell by the way her knuckles shook that Lillian wanted to throw her coffee in Max Naylor's face. I sat back, a party to their meeting because it involves my district, glad for the moment I wasn't crossing swords with either of them.

"That's appalling," she replied. "My constituents are *not* riffraff."

"Your 'constituents' seem to be running the asylum on Hampshire Street," he replied in measured tones. It's loud in here, and busy, too. He's careful to speak only so we may here, without broadcasting to the Sunday morning crowd every detail of our business. "I heard about some kind of altercation, what—a man with a crowbar? Another with a rake? And no arrests!"

"It was a shovel," I clarified, "and a knife." Lillian shot me the *just shut up* look.

"I don't think redevelopment can come soon enough," he sighed. "Which is why we're here."

"And the City Council will keep blocking your applications," Mayor Tennerly explained, "until you first
64

secure the permits—and then break ground—on an American Housing Act offset site."

"We've been over this," he said. "The first tenement owners are ready to sell *right now*. Each development includes as many budget-priced units as will be removed from the housing stock."

"A three hundred thousand dollar, one-bedroom condo," she said, "is not 'affordably priced.'"

"Well, amortized over thirty years through our partners—"

"You're not displacing condo-buyers! You're running out blue collar workers, some disabled folks and young bohemians…"

"And they've made their neighborhood so lovely, haven't they?"

"You're not even close to the letter of the law, Max, much less the spirit of it."

"So what you're saying, is that we have to replace your current slum with a shiny new slum, is that it?"

"With truly affordable housing offered first to those displaced," she said. "That's the law."

"And I suppose you want it somewhere out of the way," he went on, "like out in the bog by the runway, with all the jet fumes?"

"No," she said, "we're putting hotels out there."

"Quaint spot…"

She rolled her eyes.

"How about replacing the derelict railroad buildings at the far end of the waterfront?"

"We're putting hotels there, too."

"Then, in Back Cove, by the middle school, where those ugly trees are?"

"No! That's a park!"

"You're right, Lillian," he said. "Bums already live there. I'd have to create an offset for their tent sites."

"The new units must be on the peninsula," she explained.

I admire Lillian's professionalism. I'm ready to throw my own coffee at him. "That's the point of offsetting housing losses *on the peninsula*."

"Of course," Max said. I watch as he deftly slips a folder from his briefcase and opens it on our table. The moment I recognize the zoning map and assessors' tables, I know we've been played. "So that leaves the lowlands just past your Million Dollar Bridge."

"That would be an ideal spot."

If she's surprised, Lillian doesn't show it. I know she's wanted to do something with that eyesore for years; all the better to keep him busy far from my neighborhood. Max drops his finger on the map, right on Yard 8, an overgrown tangle of industrial debris along the mouth of the Fore River.

"It was in your district as councilwoman. Right, Mayor?"

"Indeed."

"And the prior owners returned it to bare ground as a condition of foreclosure?"

"Mostly," she said. "The utilities are still in place. It's ready for development."

"So if we were to buy it from the city, say…tomorrow— for just the remaining balance owed—then we could have permits for both sites, there and Hampshire Street, within a week?"

"Tomorrow?" she scoffs. "It'd be more reasonable—"

"Tomorrow," he interrupts. "And permits within the week."

"I'll have to get the city accountant to figure the selling price—"

He tells her exactly how much is owed the city, adds ten percent, and still comes in well under market value. I wouldn't be swayed, and I hope Lillian won't be either.

"And fourteen thousand dollars for the elementary school in that district," he says. "Which is more than their share of the tax on a sale at market price—we don't want the children shorted. I love children, don't you?"

She glares at him, though the deal is, finally, sweet enough. I'd take it, anyway.

"Tell me, Lillian—what's on that land right now?"

"Just some trees," she says, "and a bum camp I'd *love* to get rid of."

He smiles, raising the dregs of his latte for a toast. "That shouldn't be hard at all."

* * * * *

Sunday, April 19th
Bell Buoy Park

Kate Dorsett

"I nearly had a fight on my hands, Kate," Devon tells me as he moves a crate full of matted prints out of my way. The largest photos are of lighthouses, of course—give the audience what they want. "But I saved your spot."

I thank him and cram my card table between his display and a woman selling little framed fish made of glued-up seashells. If we were organized, my jewelry wouldn't belong as the transitional display between them...but we're not organized. At all. I like that.

"So how was Sacred and Profane?"

"Transcendent," I say. "Cathartic. Empowering. Here..."

Last night I typed up a final version of my play and printed a few copies for anyone who gives a damn. I hand him one.

"This thing has teeth!" he says, glancing through it.

"C'mon, you haven't even read it."

"No, but some of the language jumps off the page."

"Well, I was inspired..."

I cover my table with a sheet of black velvet and hide

the other copies underneath, weighed down by the jewelry I display on top. This is the tourist stuff, the kind of sea glass pendants and polished stones on silver wire that sell here—art with a commercial focus. My other pieces, the more inspired ones, don't do as well. So I protect them, like the copies of my play hidden beneath the velvet.

But I'm feeling brash today, so I brought my new favorite piece for the center: a small wreath of square-shanked, blackened nails. It's too large to be a pendant, but just right to be a centerpiece. There's no price tag on it.

I wove the nails together and soldered the seams with shimmering silver. They're from a meatpacking building that burned down a few blocks from here. There's a hotel there now, but I snuck in ahead of the bulldozers and found them in the ashes. They're so fine, so delicate, but they've survived the fire that freed them from wherever they were stuck. Now it's not about the things they held together, but about their resilience.

"That belongs in a gallery," Devon says, nodding at the wreath.

"It'd give someone tetanus," I say.

"I'd like to give *her* tetanus," he says, cocking his chin toward a woman crossing the street.

"Brigitte…"

Here she comes, through the early morning crowd of power walkers and joggers. The first cruise ship hasn't even disembarked yet… She squares up against this nice old man selling his oil paintings of birds, and raises her phone to record him.

"You!" she barks. "Where's your business license?"

He yawns in her face like she's the most harmless thing in the world.

"You again?" he says. "Come over here to harass us because you're bored?"

"Pardon me for caring about the law! Where's your

license? Where's your tax ID? You have to charge sales tax for all—"

He shuts her up by casually sliding his paperwork from beneath a flyer. We don't need permits to be here, but most of us at least have our paperwork in order for sales tax. Even the mafia is afraid of the taxman.

"Hunh!" she grunts, and stomps toward the seashell artist beside me.

I don't know that artist well, but we chat sometimes. She survived some kind of cancer, and now, she donates most of her proceeds to that cancer's big charity. She has an office job. She doesn't need to be here…and certainly doesn't need to put up with this.

"You know, Brigitte," I say, drawing her attention away from the seashell artist, "*you're* the problem."

"What did you say!" she squawks, aiming her phone at me.

"Let me closed-caption it for your video," I say. "You. Are. The. Problem. Brigitte. If you'd display our work, put it on your walls and have little shows for *us* instead of out-of-towners, we'd send plenty of people in to see it. We'd send customers straight to you! It's called community—we help each other, and we all benefit. But you don't want to do that."

"This town has plenty for the *real* artists! We don't need this—craft fair—clogging the sidewalk and hurting *real* businesses."

"You wouldn't know art if it smacked you across your tits."

"Then what do you have to say for…this!" She waggles her finger at my wreath of nails. "It's gonna give someone tetanus!"

"I say that we sell more of our work from card tables, than you ever could from a store."

"I wouldn't even show it!" she snaps, storming back across the street.

"I heard someone smashed a muffin on her windshield this morning," Devon whispers.

"Was it you?"

"I thought it was you!" he says. "I wonder what that means—smashing a muffin on a windshield."

"Maybe resistance for its own sake," I say. "Maybe when that's all you can do—a muffin!—that's good enough."

"Still, though," I add. "I wish it had been you."

* * * * *

Sunday, April 19th
Peak's Island

Jamie Schmidt

I woke up to Seasquatch sniffing the back of my head, saying, "I don't know you..." I tried playing dead, as if Evan's sleeping bag would keep me safe. Then he picked me up, adding "...and that's perfect." He threw me over his shoulder and carried me away from the smoldering fire, through the undergrowth covering the naval fort. Branches scraped my sleeping bag and when the trail got steep he pulled us along with his free hand, never shifting my weight. I figured I should just go with it.

He set me down on this concrete bib over an old gun emplacement with a spectacular view of the ocean. I give up my charade of playing opossum.

"And you don't know me, either," Seasquatch says. "Not any more than they do." From up here we can see them sleeping in twos and threes in the weeds around the ashes, Evan sleeping by himself near a trailhead. "Except, they *think* they know me."

He wears his pelts from last night, and his Viking helmet. I see the helmet is plastic. The pelts are real.

"I've been awake for a couple days straight," he continues, "and I've finally got it figured out!"

"What's that?" I ask.

"Freedom!"

"Well, God bless America!"

He stares at me.

"No, like...*freedom*, freedom. Revolutionary self-determination! I was in the tank the other night—"

"The tank?" I ask.

"Drunk tank. I wasn't even drunk, just, they didn't know how to handle me. I was at Gispert's with Yeastmaster and Captain Skankaroo, talking about the Last Freedom of Man, and wound up in the tank again, and that's when it hit me: they hadn't taken my belt! I could hang myself with it."

"But you didn't."

"The point is, I could have."

He's pacing, working himself into a fine state. Over his shoulder the ocean is calm and inviting.

"You got a job?" he asks.

"Not anymore."

"Good for you! I don't either, but you gotta have money to live, right? So you take a job when you need one, you steal, you figure it out to survive. We don't have a choice—we have to interact with power, with society. We have to participate somehow, or we starve. Even if you tell the world to go fuck itself, resistance is interaction. That just validates the whole thing."

"What whole thing?" I ask.

I don't want to know what's on his mind, just the tenor of his thoughts and whether the man who is crazy enough to abduct me like a fairytale princess is also crazy enough to harm me in some spectacular way.

"True autonomy is a myth," he says. "A nice one, but what I'm talking about is the *last* freedom of man."

"Which is?"

"The freedom to live on your own terms because you have the means and courage to choose an alternative. It's the ability to live, through the freedom to die."

"Come again?" I wish a crew of burly paramedics would swarm from the bushes and haul him back to the tank.

"I didn't ask to be born. And I'll eventually die, if I wait around for something to kill me. I can do a lot in the meantime, which is the meaning of life or whatever, but the one thing I can truly control—the last freedom of man—is the freedom to choose life in the presence of a real alternative."

From beneath the pelts he draws a derringer, the kind with two barrels—one on top of the other. If he's on some suicide kick, I wonder whom the second barrel is for.

"I choose to live!" he bellows, thrusting the gun toward heaven. "Because I have a choice! I am enlightened!"

The moment passes and he shows me the gun.

"I could bring down a bear with just one of these barrels," he says, "and still have the other one for me."

"So if you choose life," I say, "what's with the gun?"

"It's practical," he says, stowing it beneath the pelts. "I could use my belt, or jump off a bridge, or… The point is, each moment I have the means and will to die but don't use them, I'm making the decision to *live*. It's the most empowering feeling in the world."

"That's batshit crazy," I say, suspecting he's more of a threat to himself than to me.

"I've been called worse." Then he continues, "What's the one thing that's against every religion? It's not killing—religion is *full* of homicide. The one thing so repugnant, that it's almost never even mentioned despite being very common?"

"All kinds of things," I say. "The world is full of tragedy."

"Suicide. The paper always says, 'passed away unexpectedly.' The cops write, 'accidental firearm discharge.' Yeah—pops was cleaning his rifle in the bathroom. Bullshit."

"I'm sorry to hear that…"

"Think about this," he says. "Every power structure, from government to religion to your own family, has a stake in your continued interaction with them. And every single one of them is against you killing yourself. Why?"

"Because they care about me?"

"Sometimes. But it's not *you* who matters to the government, your boss, the economy—only what you do: vote, produce, and consume…*participate.* We are their sources of power, and if we take ourselves out, we weaken them. So they don't let us. They make it illegal, they call it a sin. They criminalize being homeless, because you're not working for them or paying anyone to sleep outside! You're not free until you can say 'enough already!' and really mean it."

His bloodshot eyes are pleading, but I'm not sure for what. A good night's sleep? A drink? A hug?

"But why take it all the way to death?" I ask. "Why not just run away? Something less final."

"I've done that," he says, with a hint of sadness. "I've cut ties, cast off, run away—the more people need you, the more things you have to do, and be, for them. You don't get to choose who *you* are, what *you* do, so you end up trapped in a life you never asked for. Give me *radical* freedom."

"But work, and people, and being part of society, that gives people purpose. And that's healthy."

"Only on your own terms," he says. "And you're not free until you're ready—and able—to give everything up."

"That kind of freedom," I say, "sounds awfully lonely."

"It is." His voice is stoic, his breathing labored. "But it's also a thrill to be alive and free. Life is an adventure! One I choose—on my terms—between real options."

I stare at his pelts and plastic Viking helmet.

"Maybe you should start over," I say, "with a completely clean slate."

"I'd love to," he says, "but I can't get away from this city."

"We're on the uninhabited backside of a small island in the bay."

He laughs at me.

"It's all the same if you can't *stay* away," he says. "So I've been spending time out here, when I'm not on my boat."

"You have a boat?"

"It broke free during the king tide after the super moon," he says. "It's marooned by Hash Henge. I'm just squatting—I live wherever the spirit puts me. You can't get too pinned down, or…things start happening."

"Like what?"

"You get sucked into all kinds of relationships. Causes need you. You end up losing the self, getting wrapped up with others and pretending you still have a choice. You'd better love where you are—it has a profound effect on *who* you are, like it or not."

"I don't live anywhere at the moment," I admit. "I guess that means I'm free."

"Right on!"

"I left because didn't like what my future looked like back there, or who I would have become by staying."

"Where was that?"

"Away." I figure it's hard to run away from the past if you keep bringing the details up. "It just asked too much of me."

"You know," he says wistfully, "there's something that never asked anything of me."

"Your gun?"

"My bo staff. I'd just give it energy—just put it in motion—and see where it wanted to take me; what it wanted to show me. It was a kind of release. It burned up, though, so I have to make another one."

"I saw that," I say, wriggling from the sleeping bag. "It was beautiful."

He stares at me, his eyes suddenly vulnerable.

"Your fire dance was pure art. I know it wasn't a show—it

was way more real. It was transcendent."

"Yeah, well…"

"I felt bad," I say, standing, "when they yelled at you to put out the flames, and knock it off. It's like they didn't really *get* it."

"I could really have gone for a virgin," he says.

I shake my head. So he creates the caricature as much as anyone, and hides behind it…

"That's not it," I say. "You were in your element—it was *pure*. I wanted to watch longer, but there's no way I was following you underground."

"For the best," he says. "I had to work through some shit."

"That's why I'm way out here, too."

"I didn't think you were just a tourist," he says. "Tourists sleep in beds."

"Tourists come to see things," I say. "I'd like to be part of something."

"Yeah?" he scoffs. "What?"

"I have no idea. Just, something stronger than the draw of what I left."

"Which is where?"

"White River Junction."

"That's not so bad."

"It is if you're a Schmidt."

"Like," he says, "the mayonnaise? I love that stuff!"

"The same…"

"Wait, that's your family?"

"I've been groomed to be the third generation in our 'Tradition of Excellence.' I mean, my name's James Schmidt the Third, for fuck's sake."

"Whoa! So you're loaded, right?"

"My father is," I admit. "Not me."

Seasquatch busts out laughing, deep and loud and sneering.

"All that I said about freedom? I'm broke, dude. My

philosophies, that's all I've got. Rebellion is pure when you're poor. When you're rich, shit, what are you rebelling against? Having it made? That's just ingratitude! What the hell are *you* doing sleeping on the ground?"

"I'd rather be an honest failure," I say, "than a dishonest success as someone else's idea of who I should be."

"You're a stubborn son of a bitch," he says. "Pride like that kills people."

"Sometimes it saves 'em. My grandfather fled the Soviets," I explain, "and whatever future they had planned for him. He was an entrepreneur, a creator, not a maintainer. Not a yes-man. He left that whole world behind and built something for himself. That's what I'm proud of him for. That's what makes sense."

"Yeah, there's more glory in creation," Seasquatch agrees, "than in maintenance."

"Damn straight. So that's why I'm sleeping on the ground. You want to build something you know is yours, you gotta start from scratch."

"My man! How's that feel?"

"My back hurts," I say. "And I'm filthy."

Chapter 10

Sunday, April 19th
Hampshire Street

Jamie Schmidt

Seasquatch laughed when I told him about the mix-up with my name, and how people were introducing me around as a hasher until Kate burst their bubble.

"She's like that," he said. "I should know, I've loved her since college."

"You too?"

"It's a great big small town," he said.

He insisted I show up to a hash, but wouldn't tell me anymore than a place and a time: somewhere called Gispert's, about ten minutes from now. I follow his sketchy directions from the ferry terminal through the shiny tourist district toward a hill rising at one end of the city. I come to a corner where the buildings are clean, tall, and new on one side of the street, and on the other, rather seedy. The brick walls slouch. It's an abrupt change, with a vagrant about my age on the corner holding a sign.

"Ask any local about Gispert's," Seasquatch said. "They'll tell you where to go."

The vagrant is busy getting yelled at by a guy in khaki shorts and a pink golf shirt. He's carrying on like, *Get a job!* and *Do something with your life!* When he's done, the guy hands the bum some money and walks off with a smile. I

77

can see the sign now: "Yell until you feel better. $1." The bum looks familiar. This town is getting to me.

"Excuse me," I say. "I'm looking for Gispert's…"

"Yell it!" he yells.

"I'm looking for Gispert's!"

"Why!"

"I have no idea!"

"Why!"

"Because I've never been here before and I don't know anyone and everything is weird and I just want to sleep in a real bed and is that too much to ask?"

"Feel better?"

"Kinda." I try to give him a dollar, but the bank only gave me large bills. I ask if he has change for a fifty.

"That's Gispert's over there," he says, pointing to the shortest, seediest building in sight. There aren't even windows, just places they should be that are bricked over. "You can buy me a drink at the hash."

"You know about that?"

He laughs,

"I'll see you there."

* * * * *

Sunday, April 19th
Gispert's

The bar is full of people my age dressed in bright running clothes, drinking cheap beer and laughing at stories. A man wearing a pith helmet and running shoes chats in a corner with a woman dressed head to toe in costume—mouse ears, fabric tail, black whiskers painted across her cheeks.

I'm alone in their crowd, trying to figure what thread unites them, as the vagrant shows up with his sign. He high-fives his way to me and orders a beer, setting his sign against the bar. I see he's updated the prices.

"...and $5 to hit me."

"It's a public service," he explains. "People carry around all this stress, all this frustration. We have rigid ideas about how our lives should be, and when they don't work out, we get angry. Some people explode. There's got to be a better way."

"Like taking it out on you?" I ask.

"It's honest work."

"Then what do you do," I say, "so *you* don't explode?"

"This," he says, indicating the crowd of hashers. "Puerile silliness and drunken tomfoolery. It keeps modern life in balance."

I pay for his beer as a woman with blonde hair and a beaded necklace runs up to him. The beads spell "Cummybear."

"Speedwanker!" she says, leading him away from the bar. "How was the Sacred and Profane?"

Evan catches my eye from across the room. He's holding a small pie in one hand and a toy rat in the other. There are more pies on the tables, and more toy rats, some of them cute, some of them scary. Evan is about to walk toward me when Carrie steps through the front door, silencing the room. Her hair is up in a bandana, her eye covered in a patch. She holds a plastic cutlass.

The hashers reach for their pies. They reach for their rats. A man with long dreadlocks saunters up, blueberry filling smeared across his face, and puts an arm around her shoulders.

"What the hell are you doing?" he asks with theatrical disappointment. "I said on the phone, this is the pie-rat hash!"

"Aw, you guys!" she gushes, all smiles.

"On, out!" the man in dreadlocks says.

The bar quickly empties into the parking lot, leaving behind cans and bottles and bewildered locals. Following

Evan out the door, I hear an old man mutter.

"This town's gettin' too weird for me."

They gather in a circle with a tall man in the middle wearing knee-high socks that say "BEER" in proud letters. He blows a vuvuzela to quiet the circle.

"Welcome to the two hundredth running of the original Portland's Hash House Harriers," he yells. "Come over here if you wanna make something of it! Can I get an on-on?"

On-on! the circle yells.

"What we're doing today," he says, looking each person in the eye and settling on me, "isn't a pub run. It isn't a 5k. It isn't necessarily fun! We're looking—"

"—for beer!" the circle yells.

Evan slips in beside me.

"I'm glad you made it," he says.

"Seasquatch invited me."

"I'm you're RA…" the man in the circle announces.

"That's Thor the Wanker," Evan explains. "He's one of our religious advisors."

From my right, Carrie whispers, "It also means 'resident asshole.'"

"…and these are the marks we're following!"

He stands amidst a panoply of marks drawn in chalk on the asphalt. There are arrows, circles with letters in them, the letters BC69. They look like the hobo sign language carved on telephone poles and underpasses, each mysterious shape holding special meaning to those initiated in their rites.

"When you come to one of these," Thor says, pointing with his foot at an S in a circle, "that's a 'song check.' We wait here for the slowest to catch up, and sing a dirty drinking song. Then we run and look for more arrows…because arrows lead to beer!"

"We have to run?" I ask Evan. "But everyone's been drinking already!"

"Well you can walk," he says. "Just don't take too long."

"Where's it end? I'll just meet you there."

"We have no idea," he says. "And before you ask, we have no idea how many miles we'll cover, or how long it'll take, or where we'll go along the way. Trust the trail, and the people around you. The joy is in the journey."

"…and we have a virgin!" Thor looks me in the eye again. "Get your ass in my circle!"

"Test him!" Evan yells.

"What is your name?" Thor asks.

"Just, uh, Jamie?"

"No!"

I've never been booed in public before, and they're giving it their all—really going for the humiliation.

Carrie stage whispers, "Virgin Jamie."

"Virgin Jamie!" I yell.

The circle cheers.

"Where are you from?"

"New Hampshire!" I lie.

The circle tuts and clucks.

"Who made you come?"

"Seasquatch!"

They suck wind and mutter.

"Most importantly," Thor says, lowering his voice and placing a hand on my shoulder. "Why are you here?"

Carrie whispers, and I repeat, "To drink!"

Hooray! they cheer.

"Now that we know who you are," Thor says, letting me go, "you need to know who we are!"

"Mr. Giggles!" Evan says as they sound off around the circle.

"Sea Ration!" says a woman with a jazz singer's smoky bedroom voice.

"Pabst Smirnoff!"

"Enema of the State!"

"Thunderguts!"

"Diddle Aquittal!"

…until Carrie introduces herself as "Just Carrie!"

"Who we're gonna name tonight!" Thor announces ecstatically. "But first…let's find the beer!"

The circle disperses in every direction, feet stamping up and down the street and across parking lots, hashers carrying their plush rats and half-eaten pies. The guy in the pith helmet takes an appraising glance down an alley and saunters off, leaving Carrie and me alone.

"Well that was different," I say.

"Come on," she teases, "let's go find trail!"

I follow her along the border between the old neighborhood and the yuppie one, past outdoor seating for an oyster bar. Weekenders cram around small tables on the sidewalk, attacking oysters nestled on heaps of ice chips. Their conversations stop as we run past, Carrie waving her plastic sword, and me, running as best I can in sneakers and pants.

"Are you?" Carrie yells the length of the street.

"On, two!" someone shouts back.

"I've only found one arrow," she says. "It's probably back that way."

Frantic whistles and the droning plastic horn call us back.

Carrie and I pass the oyster bar again. I can feel their eyes upon me. We're not just a harmless spectacle anymore. We're the kind of people who *yell* in the streets—who *cause a scene*. How dreadful for the vacationers, sipping their wine and cocktails, spending God-knows-how much to eat oysters at the sidewalk tables.

That's the kind of place my father goes on vacation. Those are the regional sales directors, the project managers, the people I'm supposed to be like, spending the kind of income I'm supposed to make, sitting safely on the far side of a decorative rope that separates the café from the street where I run to catch up with the hooligans.

Where I run to catch up with my people.

* * * * *

Sunday, April 19ᵗʰ
Franklin Street

Dan Grant

"Afternoon, Councilman."

"Afternoon, Admiral."

We share a moment in the median, watching our dogs do their business. For all the important things I still have to do today, the important places to be and people to meet, for these moments I'm captive to the toiletry needs of my dog. So is the retired Admiral, and others the world over.

"How did it come to this?" I ask.

He knows what I mean.

"I gave the Russians hell," he says. "For thirty years, I—come on, boy, hurry it up—chased 'em across the oceans. And now?"

He shrugs.

"Times change," I say.

He nods.

"Usually for the better," I say.

He looks at me like I'm crazy and leads his dog away. I pick mine up and head for home, up Munjoy Hill along Congress Street.

"He's just grouchy," I comfort my dog. She wags her tail into my back, *thump, thump, thump.* "Everything is alright."

Then I hear it: whistles blaring, voices shouting, the sounds coming from way down Hampshire Street. A man my age in a pith helmet trots out from an alley, his gaze on the ground as he takes his one man safari past the drug store and cathedral. Over his shoulder he yells *on-on!* and the whistles start up again, drawing nearer. Around the Hampshire Street corner comes a woman dressed like a rat!

Running!

"On, on!" she yells, leading a parade of her generation's unwashed, unemployable dregs. Covered in tattoos. Long hair. Garish clothes. They're carrying pies! And toy rats! One of them lopes past, eating a slice, making a fool of himself and a mess of my sidewalk as the others hoot and holler and carry on. This is some kind of Friday night, bar district shenanigans, in broad daylight. In front of the church!

My dog barks, and I don't blame her.

"It's okay, baby girl," I say. "It'll be over soon."

She licks my hand.

"Daddy's gonna clean this place up," I whisper, scratching her behind the ear as the caravan of rejects thunder past.

I just hope it's not too late.

* * * * *

Sunday, April 19ᵗʰ
White River Junction, Vermont

Carol Schmidt

"Any word yet?"

"About what, darling?" I ask my husband as if I'm not enjoying myself.

"About peace in Tibet, Carol, what the hell do you think?"

"Jamie's not *in* Tibet." He's in Rhode Island, or somewhere, and I don't think he's coming back. Not before work tomorrow. Maybe not ever. *I* wouldn't.

"Wherever he is," James says, "the police will find him."

I claw my way up the arm of the couch and give my eyes a moment to focus. He's dressed for golf, but I haven't the faintest idea if he's just come back, or about to leave.

"You haven't given that up?" I ask. "What if he doesn't want to be found?"

"They can't close a missing person's case until they find the missing person. Even if I call it off, which I won't. What if he's snapped? We can't take any chances."

"Of course, dear," I say, pleased to see there's still gin in my decanter. The pills are awfully dry without it. "Do you honestly think he's coming back?"

"From Providence? That's what the caller ID said, right?"

"It did."

"Well yeah, who the hell stays in Providence?"

"I mean," I say, sinking back into the couch's embrace, "to all this?" The living room window faces east, overlooking our town and the distant Green Mountains. I know every building here, every family, and all of their secrets. Surely they know mine. I used to dream of a reason to leave; of a chance to see the world. I was never sure about the details, so I never saw a chance. And what's wrong with marrying well? It was a different time, and I've not gone without comfort since.

This valley is my home, but I've known since he was little that it would never suit Jamie. He has too much of his grandfather in him.

I remind my husband, "His brother ran away to the military."

"Three and a half more years," James says, "until we get Peter back."

I scoff.

"Now Jamie's run away, too," I say. "And why do you think that is?"

"Because he's ungrateful."

"There may be other reasons, dear."

"Like what!"

I wash down my afternoon pills and smile out the window. Soon I'll be home again in my mind, touring the

French estate my dream lover left me. I'll tour my vineyards. I'll sample the ice wine. There are many reasons to run away, and many ways, too.

Chapter 11

Sunday, April 19th
Yard 8

Dan Grant

Max Naylor's black town car is probably the fanciest vehicle to ever pull into this forsaken wasteland along the river. My dog drools on my lap as we roll to a stop near a stand of birch trees that grow from a mound of trash and sodden clothing. They mark a well-worn footpath into the undergrowth. There's a hobo camp back there, nearer the water—one of four I know about. Max has a job because people will pay just about anything to live on the peninsula. We're here, because at the other end of the spectrum, people will endure a lot to live in the city for free.

An enormous pickup pulls alongside. Max rolls down his window and stares up at the driver. I can barely hear his voice over the idling diesel engine.

"You've surveyed it?" Max asks.

"About eighteen trucks worth of pylons and rubble. There's some trash, maybe a truck's worth. Shouldn't take but a day, and we'll have those trees down too."

"Anything else?" Max asks.

"There's a sailboat marooned along the seawall. You want us to push it into the tide?"

"Don't bother," Max says. "And the bums?"

"About twenty, maybe twenty five. Mostly gone during

the day, which is convenient."

"It is."

"We papered 'em twice, just like you said—notices a month ago, a final warning last Thursday."

"Excellent."

"I've got an in with the cops, so we're backstopped with law enforcement. They've got a kind of protocol."

"Good! Business as usual, then."

"Business as usual, sir."

The truck pulls away with a diesel rumble. I notice the out of state plates match the ones on this towncar.

"I hope that satisfies you, Councilman," Max says, "that we're serious about our timetable."

* * * * *

Sunday, April 19th
Commercial Street

Jamie Schmidt

"Camera!" Carrie says as we follow the trail-marking arrows along a running path near the water. I'm tired and several drinks into the evening from a stop we made on a hillside, overlooking the bay. The arrows led us into a stand of trees in a hillside park, then into a clearing with a spectacular view—a little place hidden from sight that I would never have guessed was there. The person setting trail left a cache of beer, and we drank our fill.

I feel it sloshing in my stomach, and wonder how they all seem to be running so effortlessly. As exercise, hashing seems useless…but so far it's been really fun.

"Why do you keep saying 'camera'?" I ask between breaths.

"That guy back there," she says, pointing her plastic cutlass at a group of tourists behind us, "was taking our picture."

"Yeah, we're kind of a spectacle."

"Which I love," she says, "but some of us have public images to protect."

She explains that the hash, for all its carefree folks, welcomes a number of buttoned-down, professional members too.

"I don't believe you," I say.

"Come on!" she says, "I'm a bank teller!"

"You're right," I gasp, trying to keep pace.

"That old guy," she says, "in the pith helmet? He's a librarian!"

"You're lying."

"He's not even from here, he's just visiting. He hashes all over!"

I shake my head.

"Iron Pansy, in the rat suit?"

Far ahead I see the fabric tail swishing methodically as she sniffs out trail.

"She's a teacher," Carrie says. "We have a *lot* of teachers. Something about working with kids, I think, drives them to drink."

I can imagine which of my old teachers would have loved this. And if any parents knew… The costumes, the aversion to cameras, it all makes sense.

"And that's why we use hash names," she says. "To further separate the real world, from…this."

The guy with the dreadlocks sprints past me, slapping me on the ass, daring me to catch up. I can't.

We pass the ferry terminal, slowing to a walk so we don't jostle the tourists. They stare. Carrie yells *Camera!* a few more times. We gather around a large S in a circle, drawn on the concrete in Bell Buoy Park—right in front of Kate and her table full of jewelry.

"Can I get a note?" Thor the Wanker yells, smiling at

Kate, "for the illustrious Seventh Heaven?"

Kate leads a spirited parody of an old cartoon theme song.

> *Hashers,*
> *Meet the Hashers,*
> *They're the biggest drunks in history,*
> *From the,*
> *Town of Portland!*
> *They're the leaders of debauchery*
> *Half-minds, trailing shiggy through the years,*
> *Watch them, as they down a lot of beers,*
> *Down down,*
> *Drink it down down,*
> *Down, down down down down down down down,*
> *Down down down down down,*
> *Down down down down, down, down!*
> *On, on!*[1]

The pack disperses, leaving me at Kate's table.

"So this is what you were talking about?" I ask her. "Hashing?"

"Isn't it great?"

"It's sure something."

The jewelry on her table is remarkably different from the pieces on her mannequin yesterday—except for a wreath of nails in the middle, and a pendant necklace made with a matching nail. The rest are things my mother would buy on vacation, which makes sense here. A few of the other artists at their tables look familiar from the Sacred and Profane, too, but not their art. I guess this is what sells.

"So this is your day job?" I ask.

"Hardly," she says. "But it funds my art. What's *your* day job?"

"I don't have one right now."

---

1 The editors acknowledge this common parody is based on the original lyrics from *The Flintstones* by Hoyt Curtin and William Hanna and Joseph Barbera

"So…" Evan says. He snuck up behind me! "…you really are homeless."

Why is he suddenly standing here? His words come back to me.

I've loved her since college…

Get in line, buddy—behind Seasquatch.

"I'm temporarily displaced," I say. Then, smiling at Kate, "But I'm finding more reasons to stick around."

"Hash four more times," she says, "and we'll give you a name."

"Unless you do something really stupid," Evan adds. "Then we'll name you on the spot."

"Or brave," Carrie says, jogging back by us.

"So where are you staying tonight?" Kate's words are a shot across Evan's bow. I know I'm being used against him, but the way she speaks, the look in her eye—there's something more than a cold war. She's earnest, and I wonder why she cares.

"I hope I don't have to sleep on the ground again." Looking at Evan, I add, "No offense."

"I think it's exciting," Carrie says. "You just show up—no plans. Trusting strangers. It's so…reckless. And free."

"And stupid," I say. "But I'm glad it's working."

"My roommate—" Kate says. Evan cuts her off.

"I have a guest bedroom."

"Evan has a *really good job*," Carrie explains, as if rationalizing his good fortune.

"It'll be great," he says. "After the hash, I'll even show you around town. But we should really go find trail…"

Up the street, someone yells *on, on!*

"I can just get a hotel…" I protest, glad to see a faint smile on Kate's lips.

"No," Evan says, firmly. "I'll put you up tonight—it's hashpitality."

I look to Carrie for an answer, a better idea, *anything*, but she's silent.

"Well...okay," I say reluctantly.

It's a matter of budget, comfort, and a way out of this moment.

Kate's eyes flash. Deep within are the shapes of things she wants to say. Not knowing what, drives me mad. I want to see her after the hash. I have so many questions—about yesterday, about today, about this place. There's a challenge in her voice, and comfort in her smile, and I wonder what I might learn from getting to know her more. No wonder Evan still carries his torch.

"I want you to have this," she says, lifting the pendant necklace from beside her wreath of nails. "It'll keep the bad energy away."

It rests lightly on the collar of the t-shirt Carrie gave me.

"On, out!" Evan says, leading Carrie and me away. I jog a few steps before looking over my shoulder at Kate.

She's smiling.

* * * * *

Sunday, April 19th
Franklin Arterial

Officer Buffone

My partner was sitting beside me in our cruiser, droning on about something—God knows what—when this rusted-out beater rolled a red on the Arterial.

"Let's roll," he said, and hit the lights.

I pulled it over and ran the plates, all pretty standard, then went and checked her license.

"Jude," I said, 'cause as soon as I got to her window I knew her from Gispert's, "just what the hell are you doing running a red in front of me?" I pointed back to my car, a fully marked unit, big ass light bar, high-vis decals…

"Sorry officer Buffone," she said. "Been a long day."

I told her it's about two hundred fifty bucks to run a light. That's a lot of money for some people, and with a car like that? I asked if she had a damn good reason, something I might understand, but right then, my phone rang. It was the chief, so I stepped aside and took the call.

Dispatch told him who I pulled over, and he was breathing hard from running somewhere to call me in private. I like Jude, but I like my job more, so I said "Yes, sir," and "I read you, chief," and I went back to that window and told Jude to get the hell out of her car right then so we could search it. My partner didn't know what was up, but he followed along. We're tight, this side of the thin blue line.

"I said," I told her, "step out of your vehicle, *now!*"

She did not comply.

In fact, she rolled up her window and turned the car back on and I thought for a moment that I'd have to break the glass and haul her out, but, she's not exactly going through that window easily.

"Quit resisting!" I yelled. We had our Tazers out, so I aimed at the back window and shot. It wouldn't do anything but make the report look better, which was what the chief was going for. My partner fired too, just 'cause I did and he didn't want to be left out. The barbs dug into the safety glass as she pulled away, ripping the cartridges from the Tazers, and dragging them behind like cans on a newlywed's car.

Then we chased her, glad we didn't get cut up on broken window glass.

"What's that all about?" my partner asked as we drove.

"Boss's orders," I said. "Give her a hard time. Make a good report. Find anything, anything at all so we can haul her in."

"Jude?" He didn't believe it, or, didn't want to.

"Yeah," I said. "Whatever…"

Other cars pulled aside for us, and it's a straight shot up

93

Franklin. I let her pull away a little—she was doing exactly the speed limit, so I had to slow way down. Nothing ever goes the way you expect it.

"Check our speed," I said.

"Eighteen miles an hour."

"Yeah, well, keep watching." I floored it, and closed the distance in a heartbeat. I had to slam on the brakes to keep from hitting her.

"Fifty one," he said.

"That's going in the report," I said. "That's a high-speed pursuit."

He shook his head and cursed. Jude signaled her turn and we followed her to a parking space on Hampshire Street, where her door flew open. I was on the sidewalk in a flash.

"Just whaddaya think you're doing?" she said as I caught her, spun her against her car and cuffed her.

I told her she was under arrest, and on what charges. Nothing too bad—just following orders. She was fuming, but shut right up, like she's been in the back of a squad car before.

"Your tie clip's busted," my partner said.

I looked down, and sure enough, the clasp was broken from the effort.

"And," I said over my shoulder, through the air holes in the Plexiglas divider, "assaulting a police officer."

She harrumphed all the way to the station.

* * * * *

Sunday, April 19th
Portland Police Department

Chief Boyer

Of the men in my department I can absolutely count on,

Buffone stands alone. He's served under me since I was a captain, years before I made Chief. In that kind of time, I've come to appreciate his...enthusiasm.

"I brought her in," Buffone said to me in the hallway outside our interrogation rooms, "just like you said, Chief Boyer."

I clapped my hand on his shoulder and looked him dead in his dull, bovine eyes.

"You're a credit to the force, Buffone."

Inside the gray little room, where the furniture is bolted to the floor, I ask Jude why she ran the red light. She looks at me across the table like it's her filthy little bar, and she wants to kick me right out.

"He's got some nerve!" she says. "Who's gonna pay for my window!"

I remind her of the charges against her: fleeing and evading an officer, disobeying a lawful command, resisting arrest, disobeying an electronic signal...even, as Buffone stretched it, assault on a police officer.

"Oh, come on," she says, trying to cross her arms and then remembering that one is cuffed to the table.

Buffone looks at me meekly and pulls his clip-on tie away from his uniform to show where the clasp is broken. I pinch the bridge of my nose.

"No doubt you've suffered some property damage," I say, "in the course of racking up an impressive list of charges."

"Harrumph!"

"But now, we're just gonna have a little chat."

Buffone looks at me suspiciously. Her glare could cut bulletproof glass. I don't want to be here either, but my door has been darkened lately by too many men in suits. So here we are, late on a Sunday, each of us wanting to be anywhere else.

"I'm wondering if you have any insight," I say, "into the recent uptick of violence on Hampshire Street."

"He hauled me in," she reminds me, "because I ran a red light."

"I'm prepared to forget that," I explain. "Right Buffone?"

He nods.

I continue, "Because I'm more interested in how you might help us bring the neighborhood up."

She pulls angrily at the handcuff.

"The fight the other night," I say, "with what—a garden trowel and a post hole digger?"

"It was a knife," she says, "and a shovel."

"Regardless, did you know those men? Where they customers?"

"Who were they?" she asks.

"See, we don't know—they got away. Poof. But it's my profound hope that we can keep these sorts of things from happening again."

"Uh huh," she says.

"Maybe you've wanted to renovate Gispert's. Serve a more...upmarket clientele. One that's better for the community."

"Chief, I run a tavern, not a neighborhood association."

"And you've been at it for *years*. Maybe you're ready to retire?"

"I want a lawyer," she says.

I remind her that windows are cheap, these charges are serious, and there are more important things to worry about than paperwork and lawyers. There's no need, even, to press charges if she doesn't press the issue.

"Maybe you'll help us bring up your neighborhood," I say, as Buffone uncuffs her from the table. "It's good to have partners in the community."

"Yeah," she says, "and it's good to know where you stand."

Chapter 12

Sunday, April 19th
Hash Henge

Jamie Schmidt

We follow the bone-white trail marks across a gravel lot in the failing light. They lead us to the tree line, past a mound of moldering clothes, and into a scraggly little forest. The path is strewn with trash, and winds past squalid campsites. Running single-file, I trust that if the guy in front of me doesn't stumble, neither will I.

We emerge along a seawall in a burst of moonlight, running over broken glass that twinkles underfoot. The trail wends back into the trees, past great ragged mounds of trash, piles of broken asphalt, and more campsites. I feel many eyes upon me, but it's probably my imagination—the campsites appear deserted, and their fire pits are cold. I follow the guy with the dreadlocks, the trail, and the distant call of *on, in!*

Trail ends near the water in a clearing lined with slag piles and mounds of broken granite.

"Beer grenade!" Thor yells. I catch the silvery glint of a can arcing toward me and bat it out of the sky. It splits on the ground, hissing. Evan swipes it and slurps the foamy spray.

I catch the next one as he finishes.

"Welcome to Hash Henge!" he says, panting and wiping his mouth. "Land of mystery!"

"It looks like a bum camp," I say.

"The bums call it Sherwood Forest," he explains. "Pan Am Railways calls it Yard 8. But it's Hash Henge to us…and my God, just look at it."

A hopeful fire burns in the clearing, tended by the faster hashers. Others climb on slag piles and stacks of creosote-soaked railroad ties. Rotten pylons reach from murky waves along the seawall, surrounding a weather-beaten sailboat. Farther along, the pylons support the remains of a pier. I can just make out the silhouette of someone scampering along its edge.

"I can't deny its charm," I say.

A cardboard box ignites, raising a tongue of flame that casts long shadows on the trees.

"Circle up!" Thor yells.

"Coming!" yells a tiny voice from the edge of the pier, followed by a splash, then from above the water, "Whoops!"

"Sea Ration, no!" yells dreadlock guy as he climbs out toward her. A small section of pier collapses with a splash and she laughs, deep and hearty.

"This is fun!" she yells.

"And the hairs…" Thor sings. The hashers sing the line back, roaring into the opening song of their closing circle as the rescue operation unfolds behind him.

"Welcome to the exciting conclusion," he yells, undaunted, "of our two hundredth running! Can I get an on-on?"

"On-on," Sea Ration yells from the pier.

Thor calls the hare into the circle. He's been ahead of us this whole time, marking trail, so this is the first good look I get at the guy: whip-thin, with a magnificent handlebar mustache. I remember him from the bonfire last night, and from the house party too, ranting about *damn dirty hippies*. Here he is, cavorting by firelight at the edge of the sea.

"What do you have to say for yourself?" Thor yells at him.

"At least I had fun!" he says, accepting a beer.

"And I thought it was a shitty trail!" Thor bellows, leading into a song disparaging the trail, the hare, and concluding *I would rather drink some beer than run a shitty trail!*

"We sing the same songs," Carrie says, startling me, "every week. It's kinda boring, but kinda comforting too."

"Still," Evan says, "we could use some new material."

"Now get out of my circle!" Thor yells, calling others in to atone for sins both real and imagined.

"You're up soon," Evan says slyly.

They toast, roast, and serenade more hashers with filthy drinking songs.

"Virgin!" Thor yells, pulling me into the circle. "Remind us again…just who the hell are you?"

"Virgin Jamie?" I say.

"With confidence!" he yells.

Virgin Jamie!

Their cheer warms my soul.

"And why are you here?"

"To drink!" I yell, hoisting my beer to thunderous applause.

"Mr. Giggles!" Thor yells, "Take this virgin by the hand, and…"

Roll her over oh so softly, they sing to me as he spins me slowly in place.

Gently in the grass,
This is what we live and die for,
A piece of virgin ass!

Evan bends me over and the group spanks me, sloshing their beer, pulling me upright again and plying me with more drinks.

"You are no longer 'Virgin Whatever The Hell Your Name Is,' " Thor yells, "but 'Just Whatever The Hell Your Name Is,' until further notice. Now get out of my circle…we need to name Just Carrie!"

They close their ceremony with "Swing Low, Sweet Chariot," accompanied by a well-rehearsed dance that Evan explains, afterward, is an old rugby tradition that hashers embrace the world over.

"Teams in the UK," he says, "figured out all the little gestures, the motions, and after matches, the players sing it. The first guy to screw up has to buy a round for, like, thirty people. So of course it made it into hashing..."

"So there's more than just this hash group?"

"All around the world," Evan says with pride. "Anywhere serious people need a little break from reality."

The hashers mingle and fill plastic cups from skinny kegs with handmade labels. A search party raids the woods, returning with armloads of cardboard and sticks and construction debris for the fire. Hashers take positions around a mound of granite rubble, where Carrie claims her place of honor above the flames.

"It's a helluva thing, ain't it?" Evan says.

"It's been a very strange weekend," I admit.

"It keeps me going. You know, I have an office job."

"I heard."

"Those guys," he says, pointing across the circle, "work for a moving company. We've got some artists, like Kate. Diddle Acquittal, he was a lawyer! Now he makes beer in his basement. You know what we all have in common?"

"This?"

"But you know why? Because the other six days a week, we take things so damn seriously. Whether scraping by, or trying to get ahead, man, *everyone* has a struggle. Las Vegas exists for a reason. So does hashing."

"What's that?"

"Escape, man! The harder you've gotta button yourself up, the harder it's gotta come out somewhere."

"That's very punk rock," I say. Though I want to say *Right on!* something about Evan makes me play Devil's Advocate. "But punk isn't for everyone. Some people settle down, have kids..."

"Some of us do," Evan says. "Then we see 'em once or twice a year. But it hasn't happened to me."

"So this works for you?"

"Better," he says, "than a lot of things. And it sure beats going crazy."

Iron Pansy, still in her rat costume, wanders over to harangue Evan.

"What lies are you telling the new guy?" she mocks.

"He's convincing me," I say, "that all this makes sense."

Her sweat-smeared whiskers twitch.

"You've gotta suspend your disbelief," she says. "In any other light, this would be *absurd*. Just go with it. If you're not having fun, you're doing it wrong."

"I think I will."

I would like to someday not need a group of friends who meet by firelight, on islands or seawalls near bum camps. I'd like to not need spectacle as diversion, because I've found where I belong, set down roots, and built something worth celebrating by the light of day. There's a time for that.

But until then, I want nothing more than what they have right now, in this strange little city by the sea.

* * * * *

Sea Ration returns from the pier, stumbling on the uneven ground.

"Did I miss it?" she asks.

"No," Thor says. "She's about to go on."

The light paints Carrie's face a vivid orange, fire dancing in her eyes.

"Come at me," she says with provocative confidence. "I'm wide open!"

"Wide Open!" someone yells. Iron Pansy writes it in chalk on the side of a granite block.

"What's your strangest sexual fantasy?" Sea Ration asks.

Carrie straightens her back and cocks her head, deep in thought. Thor takes the moment to explain the basic rules: everyone gets a turn to ask whatever question they like. Carrie may answer with the truth, or a lie, or whatever she chooses, so long as she's having fun…and entertaining the rest of us. It's clearly hazing, and as she delivers her first answer, then her second and third, it's clear as well that she's enjoying herself.

"Are namings the same for guys?" I ask Iron Pansy.

"Of course!" she says, offended. "We're not sexist against dudes!"

So everyone with a name has been through this, unless as Evan said, they earned one on trail. Those who were there, know the stories—behind *Thor the Wanker*, behind *Seventh Heaven*. I want to know them, too, but it's impossibly rude to ask.

They are largely my age, it seems, and largely single, largely struggling with the things I thought I would have figured out by now. But who isn't? Things don't work out for everyone at the same pace. So here we are, breaking taboos in the firelight because it beats being serious and alone somewhere else.

"If you could adopt the form of any animal," the mustachioed man says, "for the purposes of mating…what animal would you be?"

"A least weasel," she says. "They're the cutest things *ever*."

"Least Weasel!" Thor yells. "Put it on the rock!"

Iron Pansy writes it in chalk.

Now it's my turn to ask a question. I'm embarrassed, but give it a go.

"How did you lose your virginity?" I ask.

The hashers cheer.

Carrie's story ends with her finding five dollars that fell out of the guy's pocket.

"How old were ya?" Evan yells.

"It was on my eighteenth birthday," she says.

"You were barely legal," he says, "and you made five bucks?"

"Yup."

"Legal Tender!" he shouts. The name goes on the rock.

The fire burns brightly, giving Thor ample light to read out the names. They elicit boos and cheers and thundering silence. He crosses off the names that don't fare well. It comes down to Legal Tender, and Least Weasel.

"We'll settle this," Thor says, "the old fashioned way. I need a volunteer!"

Carrie points to me.

"You'll represent 'Least Weasel,' " Thor says. Then, dragging Evan into the circle as well, "And you'll represent 'Legal Tender.' "

The hashers chant, *Pants off! Dance off!*

The fire in Carrie's eyes says, *don't let me down.*

Evan pulls his shirt off and hits me across the face with it, throwing it at my feet. I remove the t-shirt Carrie gave me, the one that says *Free Speaker*, and smack him right back. He dances an awkward striptease as they chant *Pants off! Dance off!*

The spirit overcomes me as well, and soon the whole circle is dancing, ripping off their shirts, their pants, flinging beer on each other and on us. The daytime world is hours away. We're safe together here in Hash Henge. Iron Pansy was right—this is absurd.

And it's wicked fun. I must be doing it right.

* * * * *

Sunday, April 19th
Munjoy Hill

Jamie Schmidt

"You really should have won," I say, charitably, as we seek shelter on his porch from the beginnings of a storm.

"I am the better dancer," Evan says, "but Least Weasel—gotta admit, that's a fun name."

He opens the door on a stairwell leading to the second floor.

"After you," he says. The carpet is tattered and crusty where it meets the wall, and the handrail wobbles like it's only screwed into the drywall. I don't trust it. I'm woozy, I'm boozy, I'm exhausted, but I'm glad to be in from the rain.

A lamp glows in his living room, just bright enough to reveal the martial order imposed on the place: perfect stacks of books, sorted by size; a fantail of gaming magazines spread on a coffee table; plants that don't need watering and may actually be plastic… He flips on a brighter light. I wince. A cat darts behind his couch. When I can see again, I notice a trail worn through standing dust between the couch and television, the living room and kitchen, the bathroom farther on and a bedroom down the hall. I'm afraid to touch anything, or step outside the path.

"Relax," he says. "We're home."

My nose twitches from the dust and dander as he shows me the guest bedroom, where the chaos missing from the common area has taken refuge. A bare mattress slouches off a bedframe, linens twisted and sulking in the corners. I can't explain the shredded paper, or the tangle of cords, or the pile of books with their paper covers ruined, or the grease stripe along the wall—terrible things must have happened on that mattress, leaving the wall an oily mess.

"I don't use that room much," he says. "Sorry it's not ready."

There is no way I can stay here.

"No problem," I say. "I'll settle right in."

Evan walks to the window. The neighborhood falls away,

down from the crest of this hill and out where the heavy sky meets the bay. There are no stars tonight, but the raindrops on the window glimmer.

"I never get tired of this view," he says. "Even on nights like this."

"It must be spectacular."

"I can't imagine living anywhere else."

"That must be nice."

"I've gotta be at work tomorrow," Evan continues, walking toward the bathroom, "but I'll get you up early enough we can do breakfast."

I might not even be sober by then. I certainly won't be *here*.

"Sounds good."

"Sleep well," he says. "And don't mind Lumpy, she's alright for a cat."

I tiptoe into my bedroom, disturbing as little dust and dander as I can. I stifle a sneeze, and then a second one. The sheets are filthy and I regret touching the mattress as I shove it back onto the frame and make the bed as best I can—for appearances. The cat comes in and hacks a hairball onto a pile of sheets. She looks at me disdainfully.

On the blank backside of a ripped-off paperback cover I write him a note.

I woke up early, it says. *I didn't want to wake you or trouble you for breakfast—you've done so much already. Thank you.*

In a fit of mirth, I add, *I hope to see you around!*

I wait by the window for the sound of his bedroom door closing. The windowpane feels cold, and the rain has picked up. From the high I felt on the hash I now regret everything and feel desperately sorry for myself here, in a squalid room with a cat named Lumpy.

What the hell am I doing with my life? This isn't fun anymore.

Maybe I'm doing it wrong.

I leave my note in the hallways and escape. Evan's front door closes behind me like a vault door. There's no going back—not inside, not home, not to some place in my mind that doesn't exist.

The only way is forward. There's nothing holding me here, or anywhere. I could find a cab, have it take me to a bus station, and disappear to a new city—another fresh start. There is nowhere I need to be, and no one to notice I'm gone—not in any big way. I'm nearly as free as Seasquatch claims to want...

...and it's crushingly lonesome.

* * * * *

Monday, April 20th
Old Port

I hailed a cab outside a place called "Mama's Crowbar."

"Where to?" the driver asked. The bus station had its appeal, but sitting out of the rain, in the cab, I felt better about staying in Portland. I want to see Kate again. I want to thank Carrie for looking after me. There are groups like theirs in every city, I'm sure, whether they're hashers or united by some other interest, but I have an in here—with this group. With these people. So I might as well see where it leads.

My grandmother had a saying: Bloom where you're planted.

"A hotel," I say. "Any one of 'em."

"You ain't got a reservation?" The dashboard clock says it's after one in the morning.

"Nope."

"Whatever, man," he says.

The lights of the Old Port shimmer. The rain washes away the chalk arrows and flour dots from our trail, surely soaking the embers at Hash Henge. By morning there'll be no trace, and the hashers will be at work using real names once again.

"The bar's still open at this one," the driver says, stopping in front of a new-looking place. "They call it, 'The Longshoreman's Rest.' 'Cause they knocked down the Longshoreman's Association Hall to build the hotel."

"Quaint," I say.

"They ain't gonna tell you that at the front desk!"

The receptionist hardly looks me in the eye. I'm a mess, and no one, apparently, pays cash at hotels like this one. It takes a bribe to get a key, hitting my dwindling funds hard, but then I'm inside my room, barring the door, hanging my filthy clothes to dry and telling myself it's worth the cost to stay.

I glance at the deserted street below, like a stage awaiting a production. I wonder what it'll look like tomorrow. I wonder who I'll meet down there.

And not if, but how, I'll see Kate again.

*****

Monday, April 20th
Quebec Street

Evan

It's dead silent in my apartment. There's no way to sneak out without the stairs creaking, so I knew he was leaving. I waited for the front door to close, and walked down the hall anyway. My cat was there, lying at the top of the stairs, staring at the closed front door.

"I get it," I said to Lumpy. "It's always the same."

They don't usually leave notes like his, though. I read it by lamplight—some bullshit about getting up early, not wanting to trouble me for breakfast... It sounded so polite.

But it wasn't even two in the morning yet. It's the boldface lying that does it, and the old wound it opens. Asshole...

Every now and again I try to be nice to the new guy. I hope my friends like him, and that he likes me, and that he remembers me as he gets popular. Someday, that could be my way back into the middle of this group I practically started.

I was one of our early members. Hashing has been around in other cities since before my grandpa was born, but it only came here a few years ago. I got my name before any of us really knew what we were doing. Now the people who named me, none of them hash anymore. They've moved on—gotten married, had kids, been driven out of town by rising rents... But I'm still at it, because why not? It's fun, it's social, and a lot of couples meet at the hash. I'm waiting for that to work for me.

People last about two years, except for a few who make it a lifestyle. About once a year someone comes along—they've got the right something about 'em, and everyone loves them right away. Suddenly they're everywhere, making things happen...stepping on toes. They don't know the history. Or relationships. They shake up the order of things and move on, not giving a shit what they leave behind.

Just Jamie seems like that type. He appears out of thin air, and suddenly, he's everywhere—the hash, the house party, in Kate's play... I see the way she looks at him. She's met him twice! And Carrie, she rolls out the red carpet for the guy. What's he done, but show up?

I brought Carrie into hashing. I got some of her housemates into it, too, just so she'd try it, and now so many of them live together that we call it our own Hash House—like the original Hash House in Malaysia, back in the 1930s. That one got its name because their house cook was lousy and only cooked skillets full of random things thrown together—hash. They played the children's game "Hare and Hounds." So they became the harriers of the Hash House, or, later, the

Hash House Harriers. We call ours the Titanic, because it's big, lists to one side, and for all it feels like an institution, there's yet an air of doom about it. But it's all ours, and it's pretty damn special to have so many hashers living together. They owe that largely to me, but... Here I am.

I don't like having roommates anyway.

Maybe if I'm his friend, Kate will see me differently. Or Carrie. Or, hell, any of them. A guy gets popular, he can bring anyone up with him, before he knows the history that's held the guy back.

He hid behind this little page of lies. I'll hide behind my smile. Maybe it'll work out for both of us.

Because something's gotta give, eventually. My twenties didn't work out the way I'd planned, or now, my thirties either, but maybe it'll finally work if I just try hard enough. If I keep the right friends close.

Or the right enemies, closer.

Chapter 13

Monday, April 20th
Fore Street

Jamie Schmidt

No matter how bad it is, free coffee always tastes great. Last night was the best money I've ever spent, even the twenty bucks I slipped the maid to wash and dry my clothes. I have no earthly idea where I'll sleep tonight, so leaving this hotel is a one-way trip away from running water and comfort, but I don't care. The rain washed this city clean, and maybe part of me, too. I have all day to figure things out.

I like what Seasquatch said about his flaming stick— that he just had to set it in motion, give it some energy so it could show him the way. That's how walking feels today, like all I have to do is stay on my feet, keep moving, and everything will work out. Maybe that's a wayward traveler's last desperate hope, but at least it's comforting.

Then I see her: Kate, riding past on a bicycle. My heart leaps into my throat. I can't call out, can't say a thing. She looks over her shoulder for cars, and sees me—in clean clothes, clutching my paper cup of complimentary coffee, standing beneath the hotel's sign.

She flashes a victor's grin as she rides away.

* * * * *

Monday, April 20th
City Hall

Mayor Lillian Tennerly

"So what I'm saying, mayor…"

Brigitte Kennedy arrived at my office unannounced. I wish she'd made an appointment, so I knew what I was getting myself into this morning.

"…is that we have three good reasons to pass this legislation."

I glance at the sheet of paper she handed me. It's a hopeful stab at writing an ordinance that will prohibit anyone from selling anything on the sidewalk, whether or not they have a tax ID—a measure she aims squarely at the artists near her shop in the Old Port, but which will affect the entire city.

"Legitimate businesses," she says, squaring her shoulders indignantly, "pay sales taxes. Those so-called artists? There's no real way to know, is there? The city is being robbed, the state is being robbed, and they're competing at an unfair advantage."

"I didn't think," I say, "your store sold anything like the art on their tables."

"A few of my tenants sell similar things, and that's my second point. These people operate as unlicensed businesses. They don't pay rent, they don't maintain our buildings, they don't employ staff…they don't contribute to the economy! We're competing for the same tourist money, but they take that money away from businesses and go spend it on drugs, or whatever."

It frustrates me the way she makes a good point, then just…ruins it.

"And third, they clutter up the parks and sidewalks so you can't hardly get through. What if there's a fire, and they're blocking an exit? Or a fire lane?"

"The police watch for that," I explain, "and I haven't heard of any problems. They seem to self-govern, like they don't want to get in trouble. Imagine that."

"Have you seen the performers though? Don't want to get in trouble, my ass—pardon me, mayor. They've turned Bell Buoy Park into some kind of circus. Isn't the city liable if someone gets hurt because you *didn't* shut that down?"

"You make excellent points," I say politely. Her feud isn't news to me. I smile and hear her out, though I don't share her anger. I'm worried about the scene down there, too, but from a…diverging viewpoint. "Have you brought your concerns to the artists?"

"To who though? They have no leadership! They have no structure! It's a free for all down there, and it's costing me business! Other cities don't put up with this!"

"New Orleans does," I argue. "Among others. Some see street artists as a draw to their businesses."

"We're not hurting for tourists. But we've gotta get 'em through our doors, and we can't if they're clogged up on the sidewalks staring at crap!"

"I understand your frustration," I say. "So your ordinance…"

"Would fix all that. Feel free to make it all, *legal*-sounding, but that's what would make my tenants and me happy."

There's not quite a dozen signatures on the bottom of the page. The intent is clear: prohibit all sales of anything on the sidewalk, prohibit the display of any art on public property without a permit, and investigate a few of the artists, by name, for tax evasion. One name seems familiar: Kate Dorsett.

"Would you like me," I ask, "to also have Chief Boyer frog-march them into the sea?"

"That would be delightful."

I promise my full attention on the matter, and shoo her out the door. When I reread her little missive, it's with sadness—I like the carnival atmosphere, the energy of the place, the people it attracts... More than three hundred cruise ships a year visit my city, and disembark right by the vendors. Those ships could sail on past, but they stop here for the Old Port and the ad hoc art fair. It's like that in most ports of call. I want to thank every performer, every street musician, every artist at their tables, for being part of that attraction, and for representing our city with smile...even though I have to balance the needs of our actual businesses, too. That's the crux of my job: striking balance between what keeps us running, and what makes it worthwhile to live here.

The art scene, the music scene, the food scene, the things that make Portland so much fun, are evolutions during my lifetime. Change is inevitable, but it really seems like now, in the final year of my term limit, we're *actually* teetering on some kind of brink. We've worked hard to market ourselves as a destination. Now, more people want to *stay*, at least seasonally, and we can't build hotels and condos fast enough. It might be a great problem to have, but it's easy to become a victim of your own success. They come for the restaurants, the galleries, the music...but not to work *in* those places.

I'm worried about those who've made us such an attractive place to live, and those who keep us running, because they increasingly struggle to afford to stay here. They're replaced by those who can buy in, but don't usually contribute beyond their patronage. We're loving our city to death, while my job is to keep it healthy.

My heart goes out to the artists Brigitte fights. They contribute to that bohemian vibe, that attraction that's so marketable for people like Max—who solves some of our problems, like turning blight into high end condos, but creates altogether new ones. Even Brigitte is an important part of keeping this city employed and attractive to tourists, but so is Kate and the other artists she wants driven into the sea.

This will be someone else's problem next year, but it's my

problem now—and my opportunity. Max wants his permits. Brigitte needs an answer. There's no need to move hastily, though the longer I wait, the more likely others may be to take matters into their own hands.

*****

Monday, April 20th
Fore Street

Jamie Schmidt

Maybe it's the caffeine, but every door seems open to me now, and every shopfront, inviting. This narrow little street is some kind of road to the future, I can feel it, with Kate somewhere up ahead. I lost sight of her around a corner, and she showed no signs of slowing, but still I follow, her spirit guiding me. I like how the more I trust my journey, the more things seem to work out.

There's a man sitting on the sidewalk with a sign that says, "Anything helps, God bless." People walk past just wide enough they don't brush against his knees. He looks at me, and for once, I don't look away. I wonder if the money in his cup might be more than I have right now. I'm on my last five bucks, a single bill in my wallet.

"Spare some change?" he says mechanically. There's something in this moment that makes it different—something about me, and the way I see my very near future in the dirty spot on the sidewalk beside him. It doesn't feel real. The difference between us must be something more than money.

"What do you need it for?" I ask.

"Food, you dipshit."

"How do I know you won't just spend it on liquor?"

My father's condescending words, pouring from my

mouth, as if from the bill in my wallet—our last real connection.

"If I spend it on liquor," he says, "that says something about me, don't it? But if you can help a guy out, and don't, that says something about you."

I'm so close to that romantic notion of being completely broke, and the difference is a measly five bucks of my father's money.

"You're right," I say, handing him the bill. "Thank you."

I step more lightly than I've ever stepped before. Maybe I'm an idiot. But I'm a free one.

Farther on, an old wooden lobster trap in a window catches my eye. It's cut away to reveal a diorama. There are oddly shaped light houses, a blue plastic dolphin, and a picnic set with red rubber lobsters and a large ear of corn. Then I notice the little twist-type bases on everything—they're vibrators.

I walk quickly on, past a head shop and tattoo parlor, loving how this town just puts it all out there, all right in the open between a fancy hotel and a gelato shop, as if it knows that keeping itself buttoned up is a sure way to explode.

"Whoa!"

I nearly collide with a man carrying an enormous box.

"Sorry!" I say.

He disappears into some hippie shop with crystals in the window. The far end of the box floats past, carried by a man with a familiar beard.

"Pabst Smirnoff?" The passenger from my ride to Portland, and one of the hashers at the naming? It must be!

"Hey dude," he says, disappearing inside with the box. I wait for him to come back out, impressed that already I've seen two people I know. What is it about this place?

"Just call me Benzo," he says, returning to the sidewalk. "We're not at the…you know."

"Right…"

115

"You're still around?"

"Yeah, just...doing my thing."

I read the logo on his shirt: Portland Muscle Movers. It matches a stencil painted on the side of a box truck double parked across the street.

"Which is what, exactly?" he asks.

"I haven't figured that out."

"Cool. You wanna make some money?"

He explains they're short staffed this morning, and that boxes of salt lamps are really heavy.

"It's twelve an hour. You dig?"

"Fifteen," I counter.

"Nice try," he says, leading me to their truck.

Chapter 14

Monday, April 20th
Rosemont Group, Inc.

Evan

Even by Monday-standards, it's been a lousy morning. First Jamie bails out of my place with his lying little note, and now here I am, hiding a hangover behind sunglasses—inside. Nobody bothers me here in the cafeteria at work. The programming manual I pretend to read scares them off, leaving me free to nurse myself with coffee in corporate Purgatory.

Above the salad bar hang the portraits of our leadership. Managers hang down low, hidden by bins of lettuce and croutons. Their ascending ranks climb the wall in this pyramid that's supposed to be motivational. Our CEO grins from the pinnacle. I used to want to be him. I used to think I could.

Now I imagine him sitting at this table, chatting me up with his fucking Ivy League smile.

"So how's work coming?" he'd say. "We love that program you wrote, what'd you call it?"

"Crystal Ball," I'd say.

"Right, right, we should have kept that name. But you know…"

His name is not Kevin. I call him Kevin in my daydream anyway because I'm better than guys named Kevin.

"So Kevin," I'd ask, "do you believe in the meritocracy?"

"Of course!"

"Then why hadn't you worked a day for this company before they hired you as CEO? Whatever happened to paying your dues?"

"You should know that," he'd say. "People are naturally suited for different roles! You can groom them to be their best selves, but there's an optimal place for everyone. Crystal Ball figures that out! You wrote the program. Do you believe it's right?"

"It's the best goddamn program I've ever written."

"And that's why we love ya, champ!"

Even in my daydream I can't bring myself to throw my coffee in his face.

Crystal Ball was supposed to put my face on that wall. Probably behind the salad bar, sure, but it was supposed to lift me from my cubicle to an actual office, with better pay and less drudgery. I put my soul into it, and the result is nothing short of magic.

I'm a programmer attached, for the moment, to the human resources division of a large corporation. Our HR drones have all these assessment tools. Every time one of them comes back from a conference, they inflict a new personality survey on us. I stitched our databases together, linking performance evaluations, personality surveys, the actuarial tables from our in-house insurance, adding a dash of magic and a sprinkle of borrowed code, and voila: a virtual crystal ball to peer into every single employee's future.

Now Kevin can forecast anyone's greatest utility. It's supposed to keep producers from being promoted into management before they're done optimally producing, identify those who've peaked, and elevate into management those talentless hacks who are better at ordering people around than actually working. Imagine if you knew, to the dollar, an employee's peak return on investment, and could keep them there, milking their productivity until the perfect moment to move them around or get rid of them. It would make men like Kevin into gods.

And it has. He loves me for it. So why am I slumming it in this cafeteria instead of napping in a corner office?

"You haven't run that program on yourself," I imagine Kevin asking, "have you?"

"Absolutely not," I'd say. "That's a fire-able offense."

"Right you are!"

Of course I ran Crystal Ball on myself!

It clearly states where I'm most useful, and how long to keep me there. It says when, and how, I'm likely to die, and how much I'll cost the company insurance plan as I circle the drain. It recommends a specific date to terminate me to avoid having to pay me a pension, as my long-term utility isn't worth the expense. I stared at those dates—at my mortality, in black and white, and the path backward from there to here.

I'm barely into my thirties. It says I've peaked already, and it's in the company's best interests to keep me right where I am until I quit or reach my termination date. I taught it to create glass ceilings, and it told them where to put mine.

How's that for gratitude to your creator.

"Because you know," Kevin would tell me with a straight face, "that program—she's a real beauty—already figured out the best career path for you, and the best ways we can reward your loyalty! You won't get that anywhere else, bub."

Maybe that kind of glass ceiling *is* everywhere else. I feel like I've peaked in more places than here; it's hard not to generalize. Take the hash—I've been with 'em since near the beginning, but I've never been asked to lead. I see new people, they get popular, they throw parties I'm invited to at the last minute, they lead the hash awhile and then pair off and go make families and are replaced by guys like Jamie who just repeat the cycle.

I am everyone's acquaintance, but no one's lover or hero, forever in the background—a non-playable character in everyone's little video game life.

Where's the room for growth? I've peaked in this job, in this town, and if I go somewhere else, I'll just start off on a worn trajectory to this same place because you can change your location but not yourself. That's what makes Crystal Ball so useful—that people don't fundamentally change.

I taught it that.

Still, I'm tormented by hope—that things can be different. The more I hope I'll get a promotion, a partner, that Jamie might be an ally instead of a liar, all these things I want, the greater the cruelty when nothing changes. Hope needs mystery. Crystal Ball runs on certainty. I've increasingly replaced the warmth of hope, with cold faith in certainty.

My daydream of Kevin disappears, replaced by this thought that dogs me about, of all things, the Titanic. People prayed and begged and sang until the end. Even as the doomed ship slid beneath the waves, there were those who hoped for impossible salvation.

I identify more with those who jumped.

* * * * *

Monday, April 20th
Outer Washington Ave.

Jamie Schmidt

Riding in this moving van is a blast! High above the other cars, strapped into the middle seat, this ride feels unstoppable. The company owner sits beside me. As he drives, he fills us in on the move ahead.

"We're on a tight deadline for this one," he says. The man's name is Karl. I recognize his mustache from the party, from the Sacred and Profane, and seemingly, everywhere. "Forty five minutes. Exactly."

Benzo sits on my right, sandwiching me in the middle.

"Jobs like this one aren't much good for business," he tells me. "But that's not why we do 'em."

"Don't listen to him," Karl says. "Of course that's why we do 'em. There just happens to be a little more to this one."

"He just doesn't want us thinking he's a big softy, or we might ask for a raise."

"It's just business," Karl says. "Nothing personal."

"What are you taking about," I ask.

"This client…" Benzo says, looking sideways at his boss. Karl nods to keep going. "…said her boyfriend is an abusive jackass, and she's had enough. So we're moving her while he's meeting his parole officer. We're supposed to clear her stuff out and whisk her off to this new place before he gets back. Bossman won't even tell *us* where that is, we just ride along."

"Sounds intense," I say.

"Nah," Karl says. "Just another job."

"The hell it is," Benzo argues, "or you wouldn't have called in Seasquatch."

Karl pulls into an empty parking spot in front of a row of dumpy apartments. As soon as his door opens, so do the doors on several nearby cars. Immediately there's a swarm of guys on the sidewalk in matching brown t-shirts. Seasquatch ripped the sleeves off of his.

He stands guard at the door while we pack her life into cardboard boxes. The smoke detector chirps. The television's on. The sense of dread has me looking to Seasquatch for reassurance. When we're finished, he nods for me to follow him into the bathroom.

"This isn't happening," he says, pulling his derringer from his waistband. "So watch real close and shut up."

I watch him unload the barrels, open the medicine cabinet, and hide the loaded cartridges inside a crumpled box of bandages. He swings the barrels closed and hides the derringer again beneath his shirt. On our way out the door, he pulls the client aside. I can just barely hear his whispers.

"They got him on a felony, right?"

"Yeah," she says.

"If he comes after you, you call his parole officer and tell him there're bullets in the medicine cabinet—'cause there are now—in a box of bandages. A felon in possession of ammunition? That's seven years of breathing room for you. Got it?"

Her horror turns into laughter, and then a look of steel-eyed confidence.

"Everybody out!" Karl yells.

* * * * *

Monday, April 20th
Interstate 95

Unloading the truck went smoothly, though it was just the three of us. Something about the aftermath of danger and the client's fresh start made the boxes feel lighter. By the end I felt truly part of their rhythm, the wordless way we moved through space without colliding. It's surprising, the quick camaraderie that comes from sharing labor.

We're in the moving van again, heading back to Portland as the sun sinks low behind us. I have no idea where I'll sleep tonight, but for the moment I'm safe, and comfortable, and the wide open sense of freedom high above the middle lane is the greatest feeling in the world.

"Do you have any more jobs like this?" I ask.

"You fishing for work?" Karl says.

"Maybe."

The road is smooth and feels limitless—nothing behind me, the whole world ahead. I could ride forever in this moment, especially if it means having to make no more decisions.

"We have plenty of work," Benzo says, relaxing beside me. "But not quite like this, just more of the usual stories."

"Like what?"

"Sometimes a family's gonna have a kid, so they move to a place with a yard. Or they're coming to Portland for a job. These shipping containers come in from all over, a whole household packed inside. They pay us to unpack 'em, and put the furniture together. We've moved a lot of out-of-staters onto Munjoy Hill…"

"And a lot of people off Munjoy Hill," Karl says, "and out of town. It's just economics."

"How so?"

"Pretty straightforward," Karl explains. "Your hard luck cases, they move downhill, like to Grant Street or off the peninsula. People coming up, they move to Munjoy Hill, or if they're really doing well, the West End. We've got condos popping up everywhere, and there, it's always people moving in."

"They're usually from away," Benzo adds.

"Well yeah. No one from here is going to pay those kinds of prices for a glorified apartment! But you compare them to Boston, they're cheap."

Benzo mutters something I can't make out.

"Embrace it, Benzo," Karl says. "The only constant is change, and it's literally your job to make that happen."

"So why'd you move here?" Benzo asks.

"I haven't. I'm just passing through."

"You've been 'just passing through' a while now," he says. He relates to Karl, not unkindly, the story of picking me up from the side of a mountain road two states away.

I continue the story, skipping the part about sneaking out of Evan's apartment, and play up being kidnapped by Seasquatch.

"Well," Karl says, chewing on his words, "he's known to do that."

"It's been a weird weekend," I say.

"And now?"

"I have no idea."

"You need a job?" Karl asks.

"I can give him the drug test," Benzo says. "Today's four-twenty, after all, I've got a little on me…"

"Quiet, you," Karl says. "Don't scare off the new hire."

They fall into comfortable silence, as if a great decision has been made.

"I'd stick around for a job," I say. "This one, anyway."

"Just show up when I need you," Karl says. "No strings attached."

"I don't have a phone," I explain.

"Really?" Benzo asks.

"Or a place to stay," I add.

"You know, a housemate of mine just moved down to Boston," Benzo says. "Their room's up for rent."

"Yeah?"

"Gotta warn ya, though," Benzo says. "It's not for everyone. I live in something of an….antonymous collective."

"Damn dirty hippies!" Karl taunts.

"Where?"

"On Hampshire Street," he says proudly. "We call it the Titanic. It's Portland's hash house."

* * * * *

Monday, April 20th
Hampshire Street

Dan Grant

Max hangs a left onto Hampshire Street, the Cathedral

of the Immaculate Conception receding slowly behind us as we pass the edge of a seedy strip mall. The tenements slouch on either side of the street, their facades sagging around good bones that somehow manage to hold their roofs up. There's a metaphor in there, but also an urgent need for code enforcement.

He *tsk, tsk, tsks,* as we pull nearer a building wrapped in roofing shingles.

"Just look at that, Councilman Grant," he says, nodding subtly at a mural splashed across the shingles. This is the mural I saw before, with a golden sun framed by brewer's paddles and hops vines, rising over a field of wheat. There are dancing bottles, and new this time, some sort of hobo signs—arrows and circles with letters in them, in a similar artistic style. Someone tried to cover over the graffiti in the middle of it—Irish IRA in spray paint—but the dark black letters show faintly through the cover-up. Nothing is sacred on this street; not unobtrusive plainness, not even attempts at art.

"What an eyesore," Max says. "And on a street with such potential!"

"What would you put there?" I ask.

"Well it's next to that ratty little bar—part of Phase Two. One building, Councilman, situated across both lots. We'll have street level shopping, put in one of those trendy microbreweries, with twelve residential units above."

"Where will they park?" I ask.

"It's a walkable city," he replies. "Let's focus on that selling point."

I nod.

"Directly across the street," he continues, "that's Phase One. Clearing that building shouldn't be a problem when we get the permits this week from Lillian. It'll be bare ground soon. Then it's a matter of clearing out the rest of the undergrowth, as it were, while the police clean up the streets."

"How many of these properties do you already own?" I ask bluntly.

"Enough to get started," he says. "Then it'll be a simple matter of convincing the holdouts to sell...expediently. These things fall like dominos, especially when the police do their part."

"All for the greater good," I say.

"Just imagine it," he continues. "Ranks of gleaming new townhomes! Their bricks all in a line, their windows evenly spaced, their corners proud. A damn sight better than...this."

He waxes poetically about his plans, painting a vision so extraordinary I can nearly see the colors, nearly feel the warmth radiating from brick facades. Max has a bit of the showman in him, and showmen are artists of a sort. I look at the mural, which he proposes to destroy and replace with a new creation, and wonder about the artists displaced by his artistic vision.

"Seems ironic," I say.

"What the hell are you talking about?" he snaps.

"Nothing," I reply. "Sorry I brought it up."

I roll my window down to get some air and am inundated by the sweet, wet smell of steeping grain.

"Where's that awful smell coming from?" he asks. "The nearest brewery is a block away."

A door stands open in the mural. Thick, white steam billows out.

"It's coming from closer than that," I say, pointing.

Max rolls the window down, sniffing the air like a bloodhound.

"What's that address?"

"Three sixty nine Hampshire Street."

He smiles this Cheshire grin and dials his phone.

"Boyer," he says firmly, "I'd like to report a nuisance—a *suspicious* nuisance. On Hampshire Street..."

126

Chapter 15

Monday, April 20ᵗʰ
Hampshire Street

Officer Buffone

I parked my cruiser in front of a fire hydrant 'cause it's the only spot open on Hampshire Street, and surveyed the surroundings. You don't want to rush into a call that looks quiet from the outside, even if it's just some bullshit nuisance complaint. If you see people hollering in the street, maybe a fight with guys taking their shirts off, you know what you're in for. But who knows what you're gonna find on the other side of one of *these* doors. It's the quiet calls that get weird.

I walk to a door propped open in this hippy dippy mural, on the side of the building I'm told to investigate. I stand behind it, listening to people talking inside and bang things around. It sounds like a kitchen and smells like a brewery. Steam pours out the door.

"Portland PD!" I announce, rounding the door. "Keep your hands where I can see 'em!"

There's a guy in there with blue hair, holding a wooden paddle, and a woman about to throw a lever on a boiling cauldron to drain it through a rubber hose. They have a fan rigged up to blow the steam out the door, right at me.

"Did you come to help?" the man asks.

Flippant little shit...

"Yeah, I'm here to sample it," I say. "Whaddaya think?

Someone complained about the smell."

"Of beer?" the woman asks. "In this neighborhood?"

"They call, I answer," I say, stepping down a few wooden steps into their basement. The space is filled with big glass jugs, coils of copper tubing and rubber hoses, cases of bottles, ranks of skinny kegs... Someone's hobby has gotten away from them. There's nothing illegal about brewing your own beer, and these days, I can't even cite 'em for the marijuana I smell. But the chief was adamant about the nuisance complaint.

"You happen to own this place?" I move my hand from my holstered pistol to the citation pad clipped to my gun belt.

"Yeah," the man says. "Are we being detained?"

"No, no, carry on. What're you brewing, anyway?"

The woman starts saying something. The guy cuts her off.

"What's your probable cause to enter my property?"

"A reported nuisance, caused by an operation I could clearly observe through an open door. That's my probable cause, bucko."

"If we're not being detained," he says, "then we're going to keep working." He calls her something like Cummy Bear and she throws the lever. The liquid drains, making a little whirlpool in the cauldron.

"If it stays hot too long," he says, "it changes the carbohydrate structure and we screw the batch."

"Is that so?"

"I've got ninety seconds until I need to cut the flow. Is there something I can help you with?"

I fill out the citation for a bullshit little fine, and hand it to him to sign.

"You can accept this fine the easy way," I say, "or the hard way. Your choice."

"A fine for what?"

"Creating a nuisance," I explain. "But carry on, by all

129

means. Smells good."

He stares at me with these cold, hard eyes, like a lawyer or something, trying to figure me out. The chief told me not to interfere with whatever's going on—just cite it, and report back directly.

And give whoever owns the place a friendly warning.

Mr. Blue Hair signs the citation without saying a word.

"You should bear in mind the city's Disorderly House regulation," I dutifully inform him. "This is strike one for ya."

"Czech Yourself," the woman says.

"Excuse me, miss?"

"It's a pilsner. You asked what we're brewing."

* * * * *

Monday, April 20th
Hampshire Street

Jamie Schmidt

Karl's money feels good folded up in my front pocket while I sit on my wallet—thin and empty, not a dollar remaining of my family's money. Sixty bucks isn't much, but today it means dinner, pride, dignity…and with Benzo's help, a place to stay tonight. The promise of more tomorrow or the next day, maybe even a regular gig to work my way up from, makes the idea of spending it a little easier.

We pull up on Hampshire Street in front of a sad, three story house that seems held together with duct tape and hope. A guy with scraggly blue hair bounds out the front door and down the stoop, straight at our truck—it's Diddle Acquittal!

"You remember Sherman, from the night we picked you up?" Benzo says.

"So that's his real name…"

Benzo flings his door open and hops out.

"You just missed the fucking cops!" Sherman says.

I wave goodbye to Karl as Benzo hears the news.

"They just fined me for brewing!"

"What the hell, man?" Benzo asks. "That's not illegal!"

"He said someone called in a nuisance complaint. About *the smell!*"

"That's bullshit!" Benzo looks up at the windows along the street, maybe looking for the rustle of a curtain or something to give away the complainer. He yells it again, loudly enough to be heard through the window fans across the street.

"Easy, tiger."

"Who does that? Who calls the cops instead of working it out, neighbor to neighbor?"

"Maybe it's one of the new people," Sherman says. "Maybe they're from somewhere neighbors only talk to each other through lawyers."

Benzo shakes his head.

"Damndest thing, though," Sherman continues. "Cop says 'Carry on.' Doesn't make me shut it down or anything, just hands me the fine and leaves. Cummy Bear and I are about to start cleaning up, you wanna help?"

"This guy can," Benzo says, clapping a hand to my shoulder.

"You're still around?" Sherman asks.

"I guess I am."

"Just Jamie lives in our attic now," Benzo says. "He's got a job and everything—we're making an honest citizen out of this hitchhiker."

"Does he now?" Sherman says. "Well, can you muck out a mashtun?"

"I have no idea," I confide. "But show me how, and I'll do it."

They lead me around the side of the house and in through a door in a spectacular mural. The basement is humid and smells like wet grains and mildew.

"Welcome to the boiler room," Sherman says theatrically, "of the Titanic—Portland's original hash house. Everyone who lives here is a hasher, and we all pitch in to brew."

"Why do you call it the Titanic?" I ask.

"Because the basement floods, she lists a bit to port, and we're struggling here in the midst of an inhospitable landscape."

"He means, we can't afford anywhere nicer," Benzo says.

"The peril adds to the camaraderie," he jokes. "And if everyone pulls their weight, we just might make it."

"But still, you call it the Titanic. That implies a certain… trajectory."

His eyes are set and humorless.

"I'm well aware of that."

* * * * *

Monday, April 20th
The Titanic

My room is an orderly hollow in their attic, an otherwise cluttered mess with piles of clothing and garish costumes. I pick my way through dusty brewing equipment smaller and cheaper looking than what they use now, past a jumble of bicycle parts and boxes of swing-top bottles, to get my hands on a man-sized costume of a slice of blueberry pie. Stenciled across the front it says National Pie Day 2011. Beside it, in a pile on the floor, is Iron Pansy's rat costume.

Dormered windows face in cardinal directions: to the south with a view of the city; to the north, looking up the slope of Munjoy Hill; to the west, where the sun just now sets behind some cathedral; and to the east, where the last pinks and golds fade over the water. The bare rafters are like the ribs of an enormous fish that's swallowed me whole, my fate belonging for the moment to something greater than myself.

There's not a scrap of insulation anywhere. This might only be a two season space—freezing in the winter, sweltering in the summer. Just right for now, though. I wonder how long I'll need it.

The hatch into my attic home swings open. Sherman climbs up.

"Settling in well?" he asks.

I pick my way back to my bed and throw my wallet on the bare mattress.

"There," I say. "All moved in."

"Thanks for sticking around to clean up after dinner," he says.

We ate in the living room on the second floor. Carrie lives here, too—she cooked spaghetti she cheerfully described as "freegan." Apparently that meant she'd scavenged the ingredients from dumpsters behind grocery stores.

"They're not even spoiled at all," she told me. "It just hits the expiration date, so they've gotta throw it out. You could live pretty well, just on the waste in this city."

I washed the dishes and thanked her for cooking. Apparently everyone takes a turn.

"Least I could do," I say to Sherman, "for a Least Weasel."

He chuckles.

"You're in luck," he says. "Skull 'n Bone Her just moved out on Saturday. You snapped this place up without even knowing it."

"Where'd he move?"

"*She*," Sherman corrects, "moved to Boston for a better job. She was a cook at this restaurant, the Back Room, but she got priced out of Portland. Staying here, she lasted as long as she could."

He's charging me seventy five dollars a week. I ask how that's so unaffordable.

"It's the rest of life," he says. "She had student loans, credit card debt, still needed to eat. Getting ahead wasn't even in her plans, she'd told me—just hanging on. You know that story though, right? It's the story of our generation."

"For some of our generation," I say.

"When her roommate bailed on her, she lost her apartment and wound up here."

"So you're like a halfway house, for hashers?"

"I guess. We're their last stop on their way outta town, or—" he nods at me "—the first stop on their way in. There used to be other houses like mine, for the crust punks and the scene kids and a couple art collectives, but...this is a dying breed. Here, anyway."

I point to the pie costume.

"National Pie Day?" I ask.

Sherman laughs.

"That was the first thing I went to in this town. It was what made me decide to buy a house here."

"What does one...do...for a Pie Day?"

"Oh, the usual," he says. "This guy, who introduced me to the hash as well, rented a Grange Hall. We wrote poetry about pies, little plays about pies. Made a shitload of pies and had a feast. Kate was doing this little play—Dance of the Sugar Pie Fairy, I think she called it—that ended with her absolutely, completely covered in pie. It took an hour to clean up. My God it was beautiful."

"Lemme guess. You've loved her since college."

He stares at me like I'm missing something obvious.

"She's...not my type. But as I stood there at the edge of the stage, throwing pie at her like she'd asked me to, I looked out at these people having just the silliest time, really just *going for it* unselfconsciously, and I thought: damn. This town is just weird enough for me. Maybe I can find, or make, someplace to belong. So I started looking for somewhere I could afford, and this was it."

"Are you talking about Pie Day?" Carrie says, climbing into the attic. "We should do that again."

"Was that a hash?" I ask.

"No, just, one of those random Portland things that used to happen more back in the day," she says.

"So you stayed," I say to Sherman.

"I did. And you people, my lodgers, make it possible to afford this place and hold out against the pressure to sell."

"Where'd you come from?" I ask.

Over dinner, he'd mentioned he was from away. The housemates spent the meal peppering me with questions, though, so it was hard to learn much more about them than how I now share a house with Sherman, Cummy Bear, Carrie, and Speedwanker—who lives on a high-walled, velvet-lined couch they call the Initiative Sapping Apparatus.

"Sherman was a lawyer," Carrie explains, "until he grew a soul."

"Hey, I resemble that remark," he laughs. "I was in family law—mainly, ripping families apart in divorces. It was the only paying work I could get out of law school. Turns out there's a high turnover rate. Who knew that helping clients fuck over people they used to love would suck so much?"

"I'd think a lawyer could afford a better place than the Titanic," I say. "No offense."

"You'd be right," he says. "But I'm not a lawyer anymore. You know what I learned from it? Besides how to destroy someone's life? I learned how power pretends to be truth. That the whole legal system is this juggernaut fueled by money and ambition. It takes people who want to fight for what's right, and lets them suffer for their idealism until they burn out, or give in to how easy it is to make money off misfortune. They treated righteousness as a prize instead of a motive—whoever wins is right, all else be damned. I paid off my loans and got the hell out of San Diego."

"That's a far way away," I say.

"That's the point. This is as far as I could run without falling into the ocean."

"Well to be honest," Carrie says, "he passed the Maine Bar exam, so technically…"

"I'd be stupid not to," Sherman says. "But I don't practice anymore. I'm *done* with all that. It's nothing but bright skies, and beer brewing, from here on out. It's an absolute luxury to be able to chase your dreams. And if you do, you gotta show that chance respect—you've gotta take it seriously, and run with it 'til you either succeed or fail spectacularly."

I point to a poster tacked to the rafters behind him. It's a hand-painted likeness of this house, with the title "Hampshire Street Brewing."

"Is that the dream?"

"The current one," he says. "There have been others. It's suicidal to think you can't change."

"What's your dream?" Carrie asks me.

"I'm trying to figure that out," I say. "People tried to sell me one, but I never bought it. I'm a little more worried at the moment about paying for food and making rent, which is actually kind of a load off."

"I came here just to get away," she says. "That was the entirety of the dream—get away from Madawaska, to a place where I can actually get a job with a living wage, in a place people aren't desperate to leave. I found that here, so, I'm happy."

"What's next?"

"I could get away farther," she says. "But what's the point? I like it here, and I'll stay as long as I can."

I'd like to think I'm here for reasons at least as noble as Sherman running away from the misuse of his talents, or as romantic as Carrie leaving the countryside for the big, exciting city. But suddenly I feel self-conscious, like I'm here on a lark.

I guess the antidote to that, is to make something of

136

myself. Not just a job—a calling. Maybe it's a misplaced sense of optimism, but it feels like it's just around the corner.

"You know what?" I say. Some previous tenant painted a true trail arrow on the floor, pointing toward the fire escape leading down to Hampshire Street. "I think I'll just keep following those things, and see where they lead."

Chapter 16

Saturday, April 25th
Shady Leprechaun Irish Pub

Jamie Schmidt

"Welcome to hash number two oh three…" Thor the Wanker shouts, calling us to the opening circle.

We're in the back of a vaguely Irish pub, finishing the details on our white pancake makeup and thick, dark eyebrows. I look past him at the bar, and here comes Kate, wearing a black and white striped shirt, black leggings, a picture of Marcel Marceau swinging from her necklace. She's all decked out.

"…the Mime Hash!"

I take my place in the circle as Thor carries on, Kate sidling up beside me.

"Let me fix your eyebrow," she whispers.

I hand her a grease pencil I borrowed from Cummy Bear.

"Hold still," she says.

"Still as a statue."

"And be quiet!" she laughs, then mouths, *Quiet as a mime.*

"Hey!" Thor yells at us. "We're mimes today, so shut up! Whistles only on this trail!"

I glance around the circle, afraid to move my head as Kate finishes. My eyes meet Evan's. He's inscrutable behind his makeup, but through his glasses, his eyes seem cold and distant.

Kate finishes my makeup with a wink.

"On, out!"

* * * * *

Saturday, April 25th
Sherwood Forest

Seasquatch

The thing I love about living on a sailboat, is the way it lulls me to sleep. It rocks like a cradle, and sleeping below the waterline, the hull turns into this kind of…echo chamber. I love the thrumming of the lobster boat diesels. The churning of the cruise ships' screws. All those deep, organ-sounds, like a womb and I'm a baby again and everything is gonna be okay.

Beep!

Then this damn beeping cuts through. It doesn't care that I've got the gangplank up, it comes right aboard and burrows into my head and I just—

Beep!

I've gotta find where it's coming from. And kill it!

Beep!

It sounds like the backup alarm on heavy machinery. The machine can't get me out here, but the sound covers the little gap between my railing and the seawall with ease. I pull the covers off and climb above deck to see what the hell's going on.

Far across Hash Henge and Sherwood Forest around it, there's this stand of birch trees. They stick up, bone-white, over the others. They're all trying to break out in leaves. Doing their best. It's that time of year for new life. But the birch trees, their limbs, they're swaying. Then there's the damn *beep!* and I hear another engine sound, one from through the trees, and now—

Holy shit!

—the birches fall into the woods. Their trunks snap like gunfire.

I check my sight lines through the trees, these lanes where I can catch glimpses of people moving around. I don't see anybody.

Beep!

The engines rev and bring more snapping sounds, scraping sounds, clunking sounds. Those must be smaller trees and all the other junk in their way. Where is everyone? Where's the defense of Sherwood Forest?

I shake my fist uselessly. This aggression will not stand.

* * * * *

Saturday, April 25th
Yard 8

Officer Buffone

"How many does that make, Buffone?"

"Twelve, sir!" I report. "Nine for Preble Street, and three for the clink."

"Only three?"

"We got one on a failure to appear, one had oxies in his pocket, one just won't give his name. The rest are clean. That's an even dozen, sir!"

Behind the chief a bulldozer plows into some birch trees at the edge of Yard 8. That sad little hobo jungle's time has come.

"Well Buffone, it'd damn well better not be a baker's dozen."

"Sir?"

I know there's no one else in there. We papered that

camp a couple days ago with notices to get the hell out. They were printed on orange pieces of paper. We papered 'em again yesterday with bright yellow paper. Most of the notices were gone this morning and the fire circles were cold when we marched through in a line, beating the underbrush with our nightsticks. Those twelve were too stoned or hungover to get away.

We had to get 'em out before the crew could start clearing the trees and debris. They've got dump trucks lined up, and excavators to load 'em, and bulldozers to scrape that place clear off the earth. It's a helluva sight.

"We gave 'em hell, sir," I report. "We beat those bushes like a deer drive."

"What do you know about deer drives?" the chief snaps, then tells me he's assigning my partner to run the paperwork on the three guys we're detaining. "I want you to stay here until those trees are down."

"But sir, then I won't—"

"That's an order, Buffone. I need a man here in case anything happens. And if it does…" He clasps a hand on my shoulder. His face blocks my view of the yellow machines behind him. "…I want it to happen to you."

* * * * *

Saturday, April 25th
Outer Commercial Street

Jamie Schmidt

I thought we made a spectacle before with the pies and the rats and all, but this weekend…wow. We ran through the Old Port as a pack of twenty wannabe mimes, keeping silent except for the whistles. We performed the old gags on street corners, like being trapped inside invisible boxes; carrying a pane of glass across the street; playing tug of war with an invisible rope. The tourists loved it. One of them tried to tip Kate, but she folded their dollar bill into some kind of flower and handed it back, blowing them a kiss.

I heard a tourist on the sidewalk talking loudly to her friend.

"This is the creepiest thing I've ever seen. There's, like, so many clowns."

Some people just don't get it.

Ahead was a brick building painted with a logo for the Star Match Company. There's a check where the trail disappears. Most of the kennel ran ahead, toward Hash Henge farther along this road, figuring they'll find trail again in that direction. Mr. Giggles veered to the right, through some undergrowth toward an old railroad tunnel, to scout for trail there.

I was near the back of the pack, so I followed Giggles. If he found the way, I'd be second to the cache of beer. If he didn't, I'd be able to blow my whistle to let him know to quit looking in case he's too far away to hear everyone else—like playing cutoff man in baseball. He hadn't said a word to me all day, but it's more than just playing the role of mime really well. There's an edge to his stare. He knows I bailed on him. I'm sorry.

So if I can help, even subtly, I will.

The whistles sound far behind me. I blow mine for Evan. He turns around, heading back, and catches a toe on a rock. Down he goes, face first into the gravel.

Ouch…

I offer him a hand; he bats it away. He's bleeding from the mouth and his palms are skinned, but he hasn't broken character. It's just the two of us, and I don't care if he talks, but he's dead-silent. Just looks at the blood dripping onto his palm.

Marcel Marceau would be proud of his dedication.

142

To make him feel better I pantomime his run, exaggerate his fall, and throw myself on the ground. I mix a little humor with the pathos. He smiles through blood-streaked face paint, showing off a chipped tooth, but doesn't help me up.

I stand and give him my best *it's all gonna be alright* look. He pulls away. Turning back toward the road, I see Kate watching us. When I jog past she runs beside me, putting her hand on the small of my back, speaking with the crinkle in her eyes.

It's alright. You tried.

We pick up trail behind the Star Match building and disappear into a scraggly urban forest across the street from Hash Henge. They've got a lot of heavy equipment milling around over there. I don't know why.

Kate takes a moment at the edge of the forest to stare at the machines. There's no surprise in her glare. It's like she expected them somehow and now, there they are, and there's nothing she can do about it. I wonder why for a moment, but mostly, I just want a beer, and for Kate to reach out to me again.

* * * * *

Saturday, April 25th
Sherwood Forest

Seasquatch

I want to rip the backup alarms off those machines and silence their damned beeping forever. First things first though—the camp seems deserted, but you never know. With the machines bearing down I want to be sure. I catch glimpses of their yellow blades and buckets as I pick my way through the trees, glancing in tents and pulling aside tarps. There's always someone passed out in their camp, always someone asleep in the weeds. Did anybody check for them?

There are these little scraps of paper on the ground, orange squares and yellow ones—warnings that the camp will be busted up on the 25th.

That must be today.

I don't find anyone in the tents, but their stuff is still there, like they were chased out by wolves. There's no one sacked out in the weeds, or the lee of the great railroad tie pile. Or anywhere in Hash Henge, either. So I draw closer to the frontline, where the air is full of this new earth smell like tea leaves and coffee grounds and chocolate—the way spring is supposed to smell. But they're ripping the trees out by their roots. And through it all, that infernal *beep!*

A bulldozer pushes its way through the trees to my left, then backs up to widen its path. Straight ahead an excavator uses its trench digging claw to attack the boulders and railroad ties of Hash Henge. The fire pit disappears as the claw drags rocks and dirt through it. The old railroad timbers chatter as they're dragged to a debris pile. The claw swings back toward the granite block we write on during naming ceremonies. It's too heavy to haul away, so the claw pushes it over the seawall. Then the excavator loads the debris into a dump truck that hauls Hash Henge away.

The driver sits there in the cab, its doors open to the breeze. He's listening to music through headphones, placid as a cow being milked.

Then he drops the bucket on a little camp, right on a ragged tent I checked a moment ago. No one's in there. Could he have known it was empty? He didn't seem to care, and just brought that bucket down. It's a Saturday, he's making overtime—just following orders, I'm sure. The bucket drags the tent through a laundry line, spilling clothes as it scrapes the site into a heap. There's so much waste, and I'm the only one here who gives a shit.

I could retreat along the seawall and hightail it down to

Thompson's Point. I could sneak back onto my sailboat, pull up the gangplank and hide below decks and hope they stop at the water's edge. There's no reason for me to hang around, but no way I can let this go.

The excavator's deck spins sideways to tidy a gnarled pile of tree trunks. Its driver doesn't notice me until I'm cresting a mound of debris, safely inside the bucket's arc. It's a short jump from there to the deck and through the cab's open door. I knock him clear off his chair and out of the little cabin, right smack onto the ground. I leap from the deck and land on him, driving my elbow into his ribs.

Then the damn *beep* starts again—my pelts must have caught something on my way through the cab—as the excavator rolls backward toward us. I scramble off the driver, pulling him safely between the treads. The machine passes harmlessly overhead. At least his crew can't see us in this clanking, beeping, treacherous little space. The driver gasps and coughs. There's life in him, but no fight.

Good. Let it be a lesson.

Then I see it: the little black box on the undercarriage, passing slowly by with its ear-splitting *beep!* I rip the backup alarm off and toss it into the daylight, right in the path of the treads. The machine grinds it into the dirt and clanks harmlessly away.

I drag the driver behind the gnarl of tree trunks and leave him there, coughing and shaking and out of the fight. From around the pile I watch the other machines blithely wreck the camp, their drivers oblivious to my little commotion.

Good.

The nearest occupied machine is a bulldozer. Its driver bops his head to the music in his headset.

The unoccupied excavator clanks slowly away. I dash across the open ground, swing up its ladder and climb inside the cabin. The last time I operated one was for a landscaping company, digging a goldfish pond—not exactly combat conditions. But the controls are the same. So I bring it to a stop and spin the driving platform around to face the enemy. I give the bucket a test swipe, side to side, and consider for a moment taking the path of less resistance—I could cost someone a lot of money by just rolling this machine into the sea.

But what would that accomplish?

Nothing near a proper lesson about kicking people when they're down.

I reverse the starboard treads and advance the portside treads and pivot the machine until I'm lined up for a run at the bulldozer. There are more machines beyond it, and by the ghost of A.S. Gispert, I'll get them too—a front end loader, another excavator…an army of progress watched over by a bored-looking cop near a squad car out by the road.

The two fresh rounds in my derringer are no match for the sixteen in his pistol. My excavator's bucket hangs between us with the promise of righteous violence, swinging a little side to side—concealing the cop, revealing the cop. I can use it as a shield as I ram the bulldozer.

He startles, reaching instinctively for his gun. Then he turns away and sprints across the street like I don't even exist.

I'll take whatever breaks I can get.

The bulldozer backs directly into my path. I rotate the platform and aim my bucket right at it, then jam both throttles forward.

Chapter 17

Saturday, April 25th
Outer Commercial Street

Jamie Schmidt

We're the last three to the beer check, but that's alright, because we didn't leave Giggles behind. Everyone is drinking and talking, and Thor is clearly agitated. He pulls Kate aside.

"You know anything about those machines across the street?" he asks.

"It was bound to happen eventually," she says. "I just didn't think—"

"Hey guys," Giggles interrupts, wandering over. "What's up with those guys bulldozing Hash Henge?"

Thor is aghast at the sight of his blood.

"What the hell happened to you?"

"I beat up the ground with my face," Giggles says. "The ground won."

Thor and Kate exchange this look, like *what could possibly happen next?*

"Man, we've got a song for that," Thor says, seemingly glad for the distraction. "Hash hush!"

Everyone's so busy talking and filling cups from a skinny Hampshire Street Brewing Keg that they ignore him. He blows his whistle to shut them up. Soon, everyone is blowing their whistles. When it's finally quiet, he yells.

"Can I get a note for blood on trail?"

147

* * * * *

Saturday, April 25th
Yard 8

Officer Buffone

Well that was fun for a minute. But now I'm leaning against my cruiser, wondering if I'm going to get a sunburn before they're done today.

Snore...

But what the hell is that, across the street? A whistle? A bunch more whistles!

Rape whistles!

Finally, something worth my time.

The sound comes from those trees at the base of a bluff. There's another hobo jungle back there, but they keep to themselves. They'd never make a racket like that...

I'm across the street in a flash, sprinting toward the trees. Whatever's going on in there, someone needs me. Screw calling for backup. I've got this.

* * * * *

Saturday, April 25th
Sherwood Forest

Seasquatch

Excavators have no get up and go, but once they're in motion...*uuuunnngh!* I feel the power, surging through this thing! So much promise! So righteous!

That bulldozer just sits there while the guy screws around on his phone. I aim to hit him on either side of the cab so

I don't hurt the dumb sonofabitch, and because then I can drop the bucket right in line with his center of gravity. Here goes.

Smash!

"What the hell!" he yells.

My treads scrape against his machine, trying to climb over the dozer, but the angle's wrong. I drop the bucket on the far side of him and hit reverse. He has a moment to pull ahead, screw up my angle and maybe work free, but he just sits there screaming at me.

Perfect.

I pull his bulldozer over about forty five degrees and pause, giving him a little shake. He crawls from the cab and falls out gracelessly, just *thump* onto the dirt, and now he's up and coming after me. Like he's gonna climb aboard and fight me. I point my derringer at him, and that does the trick. Suddenly he has the grace of a deer hightailing it to safety in the forest he was just knocking down.

I pull his bulldozer the rest of the way onto its side. Its engine groans. They're not meant to run on their sides, and in a few minutes the lack of oil will do a number on it.

I raise the bucket and back away, swinging wide around the disabled bulldozer. Now the other drivers know something's up, and are pulling away from their jobs to see what's the matter. If they're stupid enough to charge me, maybe I can scare 'em off with a shot; they'll probably hear that over the engine noises. I just need a little space for a straight run at a different target.

Hot damn this is fun.

Uuuunnnggghh!

* * * * *

Saturday, April 25th
Outer Commercial Street

Jamie Schmidt

We've got small, medium, large,
We've got—
"Stop!" some guy screams behind us.
"Wait your damn turn!" Thor yells over his shoulder. We turn around and come face to face with a cop pointing a gun.
"Shut up," the cop says. "And quit resisting."
"Easy, buddy." Thor raises his hands.
I watch the cop's eyes glance from Thor to me, to Kate, to the picture of Marcel Marceau around her neck, to the bloodied face of Mr. Giggles kneeling in the dirt surrounded by a gaggle of sweaty, ragged mimes—frozen in a moment with his arm outstretched, ready to pour a beer into his crooked smile. I can't imagine what this looks like to an outsider.
"What in the name of—"
A gunshot cuts him off. It comes from through the trees, over toward the construction site by Hash Henge. Then there's a shriek of twisting metal and a burst of breaking glass.
His pistol wavers and lowers, pointing at the ground by Thor's feet.
"You want a beer?" Thor asks. "It's not peer pressure, sir—it's just your turn."
Wordlessly the officer withdraws along the trail, turning and sprinting toward the sound of calamity.
We wait exactly half a heartbeat before following him, carrying our beer to watch whatever is so exciting. I hide with Kate behind a tangle of brush near the trailhead, where we have a pretty good view across the street.
There's an excavator rocking back and forth on top of a

crushed cop car. It's either stuck, or grinding the car into the dirt on purpose. Maybe both.

The cop just stands there at the edge of Commercial Street, pistol pointed uselessly at the giant machine like he can't make up his mind where to shoot it, or whether it's even worth the trouble. His cruiser is totaled, and growing flatter beneath the rocking excavator.

I take Kate's hand and squeeze. She squeezes back. We're watching the same thing, but now, I'm sure we're watching it together.

The other machines idle in a kind of semi-circle—probably not cheering the madman on. Probably thankful the officer is back, so they can punt responsibility to the man with the badge. There's a bulldozer on its side farther on, and who would want to be next?

But the excavator really seems stuck now. A front end loader takes the initiative, coming around for a broadside charge. Its wide bucket rises to protect the driver from gunfire—it's probably the excavator driver who fired the earlier shot. It would be useless against the machines, so it was probably just a warning. I wonder why he didn't fire again and again for dramatic effect. Maybe he only has...

The machines collide, and now I see him: Seasquatch, leaping from the excavator, pelts billowing in the air. He hits the ground and stumbles to his feet, drawing his derringer, pointing it at the driver of the front end loader. The cop must not be able to see them from his angle. What luck for Seasquatch!

The driver drops to the ground and backs away slowly, his hands in the air. The other machines keep their distance as Seasquatch swings up the ladder. He backs the front end loader away from the tangle of excavator treads and cop car parts and speeds backward down Commercial Street—toward the heart of the Old Port, and right past the cop, who opens fire.

The bullets have no effect on the enormous rubber tires. They ping harmlessly off the bucket. Even the *pop pop pop* of the cop's pistol seems puny as the diesel engine rumbles along the street toward us.

Kate lets go of my hand and dashes into the open. I rush to stand beside her, my arm around her waist as she raises her fist in solidarity. Seasquatch sees us and the white-painted faces peeking from the shadows and opens a little window in the cab.

He speeds past, a final *ping!* echoing off the bucket as he yells.

On-on!

Chapter 18

Saturday, April 25th
Portland Police Department

Chief Boyer

"Still no word, Chief Boyer," my lead dispatcher told me.

I figure it took a while for Buffone to call this one in. He sounded like a child who knew he fucked up, scared to tell daddy that he let a nut job loose on the waterfront in a stolen bulldozer and oh by the way, the guy trashed a squad car too. It might have been a good couple minutes before he screwed up the courage to radio that in. Now the guy could be anywhere.

"How come no one's called in a rogue bulldozer?" I asked.

"It's construction season, sir. Heavy equipment isn't out of place downtown."

"But there's a madman driving it!"

"That's also not unheard of, sir."

"Well, dammit, this isn't Boston!"

And so we wait in my communications room, as on the eve of battle, surrounded by maps and computer screens. Fifty calls an hour come through here on a slow day. But today, there's not even one about the Mad Bulldozer.

I leap when a line rings. My lead dispatcher takes the call.

"Nine one one, where is your emergency?"

I motion for him to put it on speakerphone.

"This is Gladys Farnsworth," an old lady croaks through the speaker. "I'm sorry to bother you, but my Press-Herald hasn't been delivered in—"

I pound the disconnect button. We have to keep the lines open.

"Sir," my dispatcher says cautiously. "We have five more phone lines…"

"I know that! Keep 'em all open."

I pace the room, coming to stand once again in front of the map of the Old Port. Foot patrols are investigating half a dozen construction sites around there, checking bulldozers and front end loaders and excavators for signs of Buffone's bullets—if he even hit the damn thing.

Nine one one, where is your emergency?

"He shot me," a woman says from the speaker. "That no good son of a bitch shot me, and he's—"

"Ma'am," the dispatcher interrupts, "where have you been shot?"

"He got me in the boob! That fucker!"

"I'll dispatch an ambulance, ma'am, just give me your—"

"This is Chief Boyer," I yell into the dispatcher's headset while it's still on his head. "Describe the suspect!"

"Who, Kevin?"

"Apparently!"

"He's kinda tall, shaggy hair, big guy, kinda overweight, the lazy piece of shit…"

"Beard?"

"Yeah, why? He's hiding up in his apartment on Hampshire Street right now, ain't like you gotta go find him," she says.

"Was he just involved in a rampage at a construction site?"

"God, I don't know," she says. "But he's sure pissed about something. I'll give you the address."

"He has a gun?"

"Yeah! Shot me with it, ain't you listenin'?"

Then she says something through the speaker that sounds like *It was only a...* but I'm out the door already, her voice fading behind me.

We've got that sonofabitch now.

* * * * *

Saturday, April 25th
Portland's Oldest Pub, Free Street

Jamie Schmidt

"May the hash go in peace!" Thor yells.

"May the hash get a piece!" we respond, and that's it for the Mime Hash. The spell is broken. I'm just Jamie again, and now we're just people in sweaty clothes and smeared makeup standing around the roof deck of a dive bar, feeling a little self-conscious as the regulars gawk. That's how I feel, anyway. Kate doesn't seem to care.

"The thing about 'dick checks,'" she says, holding court with Thor and Cummy Bear, "isn't the dicks."

I've learned how "dick checks" are the checks on trail where the women get to take a rest while the guys either search for the next section of trail, or take a little rest after giving an anatomical display.

"It's the reactions to the dick check that I love," she says. "It's looking at your faces."

"Our faces?" I ask.

"Everyone has their own reaction. Thor, you're our religious advisor—the center of attention during circle! But you don't want *that* kind of attention. I've never seen you whip it out, you just look for trail. Least Weasel, she sneaks a peek, and Cummy Bear, you just don't give a damn."

"Gee, I wonder why," she says.

155

"Mr. Giggles…" Kate continues, looking around. He's disappeared, probably to get another drink. "…is more reserved. He plays along, sure, but if you look him in the eye instead of—down there—you'll see it."

"See what?" Hans Yolo asks, wandering over to join us, his pants pulled down so that he's casually exposing himself.

"Then there's you," Kate says. "Your dick happens to be out, but it's so casual. There's nothing provocative about it, no embarrassment. It's the range of response that I enjoy."

"Hey!" one of the regulars yells from the corner of the deck. He's sitting safely behind a high wooden table, flanked by large, strong-looking friends. "You put that filthy thing back in your pants!"

Hans Yolo gives the man a jaunty wiggle of his hips.

"I can't hear you over the sound of my cock being awesome."

"See what I mean?" Kate says. Her eyes are electric. "It's not about the penis—it's about the *reaction* to the penis."

"You dirty faggots!" the man yells.

Cummy Bear's posture changes. Kate's jaw sets. It's suddenly really quiet. The man's friends puff out their chests. My friends—the guys, anyway—lower their pants in solidarity. This bar claims to be the oldest in Portland. I wonder if it's ever seen a standoff like this.

"The nineteen nineties called," Cummy Bear yells. "It wants its hate speech back!"

The guy's voice rises uncertainly.

"Fuckin' queers better put them dicks away right now," he says. "And get the hell outta here."

I step between the groups, my waistband still modestly raised. No need setting them off further.

"Why don't you join us?" I say. "All are welcome at the hash, if you drop the attitude."

"Why? I've got a bigger dick than any of you."

"Prove it," Kate says. "I'll judge."

I don't like the way the guy holds his beer can—like he's getting ready to throw it. His friends are agitated, waiting to prove something. Diplomacy isn't working. Kate isn't exactly helping. And now, they're looking at the doorway leading inside.

So I look at the doorway.

There stands Mr. Giggles with his chipped tooth, crooked glasses, and shorts lowered to his knees.

"Am I too late," he says, "for the prick waving contest?"

A can hits the wall beside him and now the men are up and charging. Cummy Bear lunges at one of them, this big guy who looks like a longshoreman, throwing punches that come from some scary place deep inside her. His friend dodges around them, headed straight for Giggles, who doesn't see him coming—he's pulling his shorts up, waddling toward the fray. Kate kicks the guy hard in the shin, tripping him, sending him sprawling at Giggles' feet.

"Get in line," Giggles says, leering at the guy. He ducks a barrage of beer cans and takes Kate by the arm as I grasp her as well. We're both trying to hustle her away to safety.

"Let's go!" we say.

"Screw that," Kate says, shrugging us off. "Let's fight!"

She raises her fists to guard her face like a boxer and dashes away to help Cummy Bear fight the longshoreman. I'm about to follow when Least Weasel steps from the doorway and freezes, some bright colored drink in her hand. She's a regular here, she said earlier; she must know these guys. But she's one of us, too. The look on her face breaks my heart.

Then Giggles is upon her, shielding her from the melee. A bottle skips off his shoulder. He flinches, hustling her through the doorway to safety. I don't think there's any kind of moral high ground here. Everyone sucks in this fight. But my duty is clear.

The guy Kate sent sprawling to the deck is up now. He

shoves me aside and limps past, raising a fist to punch her in the back of her head. I jump on his back, slipping my arm around his neck. We stumble together past a table, the guy bucking wildly. When he softens a little I grab a bottle with my free hand, gripping it like a club. He reaches blindly for me, clawing my face. I raise the bottle to bash him, really teach him a lesson in manners, when his knees give out.

I struggle to support his weight and let go, the man falling half-conscious and gasping to the deck.

Thor brushes past and plants his knee between the man's shoulder blades.

"Stay down," he tells the guy. "This'll all blow over if you just stay down."

Thor looks up at me and says, "I've got it from here."

I lower the bottle, glad to not actually have used it, and turn around to go find Kate.

* * * * *

Saturday, April 25th
Catfish Club, Free Street

Devon Cumberland

"That's a serious camera," the waitress says.

"It's for serious work," I say. "I shoot for the paper, and some fine art stuff. I sell prints in the Old Port..."

"So you're an artist too?"

"Something like that."

She sets my beer on a coaster. I chose this table, on a little balcony overlooking Free Street, because it's quiet and out of the way and I didn't want to be bothered.

"I dated a painter once," she rambles. "That was his thing—being an artist. He moved away last year. You know how it goes."

I nod.

"That's why I also shoot for the paper," I say.

She leaves me to my thoughts, which for the moment aren't pleasant. Brigitte stormed through Bell Buoy Park this morning, and even Kate wasn't enough to stop her. Brigitte was filming on her phone, demanding names, addresses, making accusations and threats. Kate tried to intervene. She even tried to get Brigitte to focus solely on her, but in the end, it just made the scene worse. The tourists cleared out, and even the locals gave us the stink eye like we'd done something wrong. So, we all just packed up and left. Now I'm here, lying low, wondering about some commotion up the street.

It's coming from the roof deck of a bar a block away. There's some kind of brawl. It looks like a bunch of…

No. That can't be. A couple longshoremen fighting a pack of clowns? Come on, even in Portland…

My telephoto lens zooms right in, and there they are, sure as hell: a pack of *mimes*, throwing punches, getting slammed to the deck. There's no choreography to it, just a lot of stumbling and kicking and elbows and knees. I take a few pictures, but nothing stands out.

Then a shot comes together: a mime with a longshoreman in a headlock, spinning the guy to face me. The mime's makeup is smeared like it's been clawed, his shirt is torn, and his eyes are lit with mania. He raises a bottle like a club to bash the longshoreman, who ducks, revealing a third figure—watching. Then the moment is over and the art in the violence is lost.

I sip my beer and check the image on my camera, ignoring the rest of the fight. The mime has the perfect face for a front page photo: indignation mixed with glee, framed with the crook of his arm and a bottle held with the promise of violence. The paper will buy this photo in a heartbeat.

My phone chirps with a message from my editor to drop

whatever I'm doing and go photograph some kind of police activity. He says they're pouring out of the station.

For a bar fight?

No.

His next message is only two words: Hampshire Street.

I look at the image on my camera again, and zoom in on the third face—the one watching over the mime's shoulder. Smiling. Approving.

Kate.

* * * * *

Saturday, April 25th
Hampshire Street

Chief Boyer

"Chief Boyer!" this guy with a camera yells at me. "Devon Cumberland, Press-Herald. Can you tell me what's going on?"

"What the hell does it look like?"

"A military siege on the streets of America."

My officers have surrounded a three story walkup and barricaded the street with squad cars and our MRAP tactical vehicle. We've evacuated the rest of the building and those around it and taken positions that offer sightlines on every window and fire escape. The man inside has fired a gun already, destroyed a squad car and wrecked a construction site, and I'll be damned if he hurts one of my men.

I stare the photographer down across the thin blue line between us. He's not the one who has to apprehend the barricaded Mad Bulldozer.

Then again, neither are we. This afternoon has completely gone to hell, and for as long as I can hold it together, I'm the only one who knows how bad it is.

"We have movement behind the Gadsden flag, chief," my captain tells me. He's fully equipped for battle, and spoiling for it. So are the other men, the reporter, and the TV news crew setting up. It's too late now to stand down.

I turn my back on this ugly tarpaper house behind me, and follow the captain's gaze to the top floor of the tenement across the street where the windows are covered by a Marine Corps, Gadsden, and other flags. That's where the caller said a man fitting the Mad Bulldozer's description shot her, and where he's currently barricaded. My men are ready to pop those windows with gas grenades and drive him out. That's what the media came to film.

I'll give 'em one helluva show.

"Standby," I tell my captain.

My voice blasts through the public address system on the MRAP as I tell that poor son of a bitch one more time to give up. My men are hunkered behind their squad cars with their rifles and grenade launchers. I can tell when they're posing for the cameras. They're ready to make an example out of this guy, even though he humiliated Buffone and that makes him just a little bit alright.

The woman who called dispatch brazenly walks over from the ambulance.

"I'm tellin' you, he's a veteran. His hearing's shit," she says, rubbing her breast where she's been shot. The paramedics just gave her some aspirin, and sent her away.

"He probably doesn't even know you're out here."

"We'll get his attention, ma'am."

"Gimme a phone, I'll just call him. He's got one of them deaf people phones that blinks."

Buffone told me the Mad Bulldozer has a derringer—the unmistakable kind with one big barrel on top of the other. He'd heard it from across the street. He'd seen it.

This woman was shot with a pellet pistol that didn't even break the skin.

Over her shoulder I see Councilman Grant standing at the edge of our perimeter—just standing there, staring at me, phone up to his ear. I know exactly what he's here to see: a shining example of *cleaning up the streets*. Of driving the bad element out. A display of law and order that looks good on TV.

Whether it's the right perp or not doesn't matter.

"He's had his chance," I tell her. "Now we gas him."

* * * * *

Saturday, April 25th
The Titanic

Seasquatch

I resisted the urge to use that front end loader to wipe out this yuppy little oyster bar. Around the corner from the Titanic, it's a beachhead for the gentrifying assholes who've already ruined so much of Portland, but I didn't have time to remove it and also get away. Maybe that makes me a chicken, but at least I'm still a free one.

So I ditched the machine at a construction site and ran here through these little shortcuts and alleyways I learned about from hashing. It's hard to disappear in public when you're a big guy, wearing pelts, hopping off a stolen front end loader, but that's just how some days go. I broke in through Sherman's brewery, snuck past someone in the bathroom upstairs, came up here to hide in the attic.

Then restlessness got to me, so I barricaded the window onto the fire escape and covered a couple other windows, fortifying this place in case I have to make a stand. I blocked one window with the National Pie Day costume. The fabric meant to be the blueberry filling turned the sunlight purple, and in that purple light I sat pondering the offensive capability of a broken coat stand.

That's when I heard the diesel engine outside, and the squeal of brakes. I crept to the window and watched a half dozen warrior cops jump from the back of an armored personnel carrier. My barricades didn't seem very impressive anymore.

"The wages of sin are death!" the Street Preacher likes to scream.

So this is what divine retribution looks like, from three stories above. Lord knows I've tried to find my place in this city. I've tried to fit in, I've tried to leave. I've shut up, I've spoken out. In the end, the only thing that ever felt right was being myself. At some point you've gotta turn your face into the wind, bare your teeth, and just give it the old *uuunnnggghh!*

But they come for the weird ones. In a thousand little ways, they shut you up, they tear you down. They reward you for fitting in, and serving them—for trading your freedom for their approval and protection. Lord help you if you call bullshit on their plans. So where's it get you, daring to be truly free?

Barricaded in an attic, apparently, with one round left for yourself.

"We have you surrounded!" I heard through speakers. "Exit the building with your hands up!"

I peeked through the window again, around the corner of the pie costume. I saw their guns. I saw their teargas grenade launchers.

And I saw their backs.

I couldn't believe my luck.

* * * * *

Saturday, April 25th
Hampshire Street

Dan Grant

"I'm watching the strangest thing on live television, Councilman."

Max is on the phone.

The sound of sirens brought me out of my living room and down Munjoy Hill to this spot near the tacky mural on that decrepit house, at the edge of a police cordon. Chief Boyer is all puffed up, talking to a reporter. It looks very serious with the lights and the guns and the yellow police tape.

"Can you tell me why the police are laying siege to a building in my Cathedral District?" Max asks.

"I have no idea."

"Well find out! I see you just standing there, in the corner of the picture."

I wave self-consciously at a television camera across the cordon.

Max continues.

"Could it have something to do with the trouble at Yard 8?"

"Yard 8?"

"Never mind. I'm sure justice will be swift."

The police fire a volley of tear gas at the tenement. The windows shatter, the flags behind them twisting and falling. I suddenly feel very exposed.

"Are you familiar with tear gas, Councilman?"

"Not since college."

"Look for the gas coming out of the windows, any moment now. Ah, there. It's gray. Those are hot-burning grenades—the old kind. They have a tendency to catch things on fire."

"That's no good."

"Well, it wouldn't be a tragedy if that tinderbox were to

burn to the ground."

"What?"

"There needn't be any loss of life. But it's important you prevail upon the chief that when the building catches fire, it be allowed to…"

"Make way for progress?"

"Precisely. It's coming down soon anyway. Why not let the owners get two big checks instead of one—insurance, and what we'll pay for the cleared lot?"

"People live there, Max."

"And they'll be better off with a fresh start anywhere else they like, with enough insurance money to get out of our way."

"Max, you make burning people out of their homes sound like a goddamn public service."

"There is opportunity in every tragedy, Councilman."

"So how am I supposed to tell Chief Boyer to let an apartment building burn down on live television?"

"From my vantage," Max continues, "the scene doesn't look secure enough for the fire department. So long as the police keep looking tough on camera, it looks far too dangerous for the firefighters to intervene. Let them be heroes eventually, just too late to save the structure. No one needs to know why they were delayed, when the answer looks perfectly clear on screen."

There's black smoke mixed with the tear gas now, pouring out from the broken windows.

"I'll do what I can," I say.

For the greater good, I tell myself.

Chapter 19

Saturday, April 25th
Free Street

Jamie Schmidt

There's really nothing else to do in the aftermath of a bar-clearing mime fight, except run away as fast as you can.

"You, were, awesome, back there," I pant, running up Free Street alongside Kate. "You pretty much saved Giggles' ass."

"Is that what I did?" she says

In our tattered black and white striped shirts, our pancake makeup smeared and streaked with blood, there's no denying that we're part of whatever disturbance got phoned into the cops. The first siren, somewhere off toward Hampshire Street, sent everyone running for the door—hashers and locals alike. We'll each claim victory when we tell our stories, and if none of us are right, at least none of us are wrong.

A squad car turns the corner by a trendy wine bar. Kate spins me against a brick wall, stands on her toes, and kisses me.

This might be the greatest moment of my life.

Her lips move across mine, sweetly, but also in service of keeping the back of her head in the officers' line of sight. For all that we look like the people they're after, we're not running away, and they can't see our makeup, so they just keep driving. Kate pulls back, lowers herself on her heels...

...then looks up at me—tenderly. With a hopeful smile.

The smile of someone who wants to be kissed, for real.

And so I kiss her again—for real.

Coming up for a breath, I'm aware we need to get out of here before more cops show up.

"I should sneak back to the Titanic and burn these clothes," I say.

She shakes her head.

"Just follow me."

She leads me past the art museum, past a group of crust punks busking with a tambourine, through traffic waiting at a red light, and along a stretch of the main street I remember from my first morning here—when I'd wandered in the opposite direction. The buildings seemed like the walls of a canyon: high, sheer, and impenetrable. What goes on behind the windows high up there? And where do people even find the hidden passages that take them inside?

"In here," Kate says, leading me into a small coffee shop full of calm, cleanly dressed people. They stare at us in horror. Kate smiles at the barista, who smiles back, like everything is okay.

Then she pushes through the service door in the back, and we're in an alley with milk crates and dumpsters and puddles of grease.

"That's my little shortcut," Kate says. "I didn't feel like running with my keys today, so we're going in the backway."

She leads me up a fire escape to a small, flat roof. The ladder retracts noisily behind us, leaving us on a little rooftop island above the alley, with a panoramic view of brick walls.

"We've ended hashes here," she says. "We got a projector once and played a movie on that wall. Speedwanker was named in that alley."

"By the dumpster?"

"Isn't hashing glamorous?"

She jimmies a window open and crawls through.

"You coming in?"

167

* * * * *

Saturday, April 25th
Hampshire Street

Chief Boyer

"We've gone through all the old stuff, sir," Buffone reports. "All fourteen canisters. It's gotta be *toxic* up there!"

There's plenty of teargas billowing out the windows, but I'm concerned about the black smoke mixing in. Driving out a suspect doesn't take as much as we used, but I really hate domestic abusers, and anyway, my men still think that guy is the madman who crushed Buffone's cruiser and made us all look bad. So, fuck that guy.

"Good. I can use our Homeland Security grant to buy more, now that we've turned over the old inventory."

Every disaster has its opportunities.

"Sir?"

"What, Buffone?"

He nods over my shoulder. His eyes are set like a German Shepherd's. I can tell he wants to go chase something. I turn around, and see two mimes gawking from the edge of our cordon. One of them has crooked glasses and someone's blood all over his shirt. The other is a woman with rainbow colored hair, the kind that really ought to be probable cause by itself. They look like they just survived a riot.

"This neighborhood has really gone to hell," I mutter.

"There was radio traffic about a bar fight with mimes," Buffone says.

"Well, you've got the Mad Bulldozer holed up behind you," I lie. "And those twits sneaking into Gispert's. Pick one."

Frantic screaming behind us makes up his mind. We

turn to watch a naked guy burst from the front door of the tenement, clutching his eyes, wailing, coughing—it's a terrible, beautiful sight. My men keep their distance, allowing Buffone the honor of taking him down. He lowers his shoulder and charges, taking the dumb sonofabitch to the pavement. The guy perfectly matches the caller's description of our shooter.

But not quite Buffone's description of the Mad Bulldozer.

If my men don't realize it on their own, I'll have to tell 'em later, after the media leaves and the fire department saves the building and we're all done here. Grant is on his way through the cordon now, probably coming over to congratulate us. I'll let him think whatever he wants to.

I wonder where the real madman is, though I suspect he's not far away. And I wonder what he'd think of this dress rehearsal for taking him down.

* * * * *

Saturday, April 25th
The Titanic's Attic

Seasquatch

Uuuunnnggghhh!

* * * * *

Saturday, April 25th
Kate's Apartment

Jamie Schmidt

While Kate showers, I poke around her apartment. Her kitchen is so tidy it looks unused. Elegantly mismatched pillows in her living room guard her thrift store couch in arrangements so precise there's no place to sit. Even the books on the shelves and the shoes lined by the door. Are any of these things meant to be used, or are they window dressing for friends who crawl in through the fire escape?

Her bedroom door is open. I expect to find hospital-white sheets on her bed, tucked in with forty five degree corners. I'm not far off. This room, too, looks staged, ready for someone from a design magazine to come and photograph it, freeing it finally to relax.

I listen at the other bedroom door—a closed door—for signs of her roommate. It's quiet. I ease it open. Inside is an art studio—no bed. No dresser.

The wooden floor is studded with hardened drops of solder and flecked with paint. Coils of copper and silver wire line the edges of a drafting table, amid rows of jar lids full of stones and beads and sea glass. She left a mug of tea, half finished, on the windowsill. Rolled banners lean in a corner, boxes overflow with costumes, easels compete like flowers for the sunlight streaming through the single window… This room is the splendid refuge for all the disorder missing elsewhere in her home and I wonder if she lives—truly lives—in any other room.

"Find anything interesting?"

She's standing behind me, towel wrapped severely. The sound of the shower still running covered her footsteps.

"You said you have a roommate."

"Does it bother you that I lied?"

"A little, yeah."

"Then I'm sorry about that."

Her eyes soften with genuine apology.

"It's just a safety thing," she explains. "I *had* a roommate. I like people to think I *have* a roommate. Especially Evan. You know?"

"Not really."

"I guess you wouldn't."

"Isn't that expensive? Not having someone to split the rent?"

"Ridiculously expensive," she says. "But I take it as a challenge. I don't need anyone else—I don't want to need anyone, anyway. I figured, if I can make enough more money from my art that I don't have to get a roommate again, well... That's 'making it,' isn't it?"

"So, you're making it?"

"By that measure. But then I start second-guessing myself, whether I've *really* made it, or just *technically* made it, and what else it might mean to make it, and how long I've got before the rent goes up or something falls apart and I can't hang on anymore. I'm holding out against time."

"Isn't everyone?"

"I guess. For the moment, I have food and this place, but I don't have retirement savings, and I get my healthcare from the community clinic. So even now, I haven't made it like some woman with an office job. At least I'm doing what I love and have time for what matters to me, so I've made it more than someone who hasn't, I guess. It's just..."

"It's hard to know where you stand," I say.

"It's hard to feel safe without, like, being rich. Then I wouldn't have these problems."

"You'd have totally different ones..."

"And the luxury of time to worry about 'em."

"Would that kind of security," I say, "satisfy you? Or would you just rot in tranquility?"

"I'd spend every day creating, and I'd put myself, a hundred percent, into each piece, instead of guessing what other people might like enough to pay for. In my daydream world, I'd create every time I'm inspired, make enough to be comfortable, have time for a life...and time to help my friends keep the scene strong for all of us."

"You'd need a thirty hour workday."

"I'd need a miracle," she says.

"Yeah, well… I'm sorry for snooping."

"I'll forgive you," she says, "if you tell me which of those paintings you like the best…and why."

They hang from a wire strung by the window—a line of watercolor paintings, awaiting new homes. The shapes are indistinct and alluring, with hard ink lines and dashes of oil paint in a mash of styles that wouldn't work with any single detail fewer.

"The one with the gray blotches and all the blue and green."

"What about it grabs you?"

"I have no idea."

She guides me to it and stands behind me.

"Close your eyes," she says, "and breathe. Let this moment fall away. Slowly now, open your eyes, but don't focus. Let your vision be blurry, and relax until you *experience* it. See it with some other sense, and let it take you somewhere."

"Hash Henge!"

It's raining in the painting. But it's a springtime rain, the happy kind that washes things and brings new life. It's so… optimistic."

"Try another one."

I work my way through the line, finding portraits of Bell Buoy Park, of the Titanic, places I hardly know but somehow feel and connect with through the work. I'm surprised at what I see, and how it overwhelms me, so I play it cool.

"Those aren't bad."

"I knew it. You're an artist."

"Kate, I can't paint for the life of me."

"You dare to feel, and to open up to the unknown to *learn* from it. That takes courage. And that's the soul of being an artist."

"I'm flattered, I guess."

"And you're filthy. Go get cleaned up already."

I walk to the bathroom in a daze, close the door, and stare at the mirror. It's frosted with steam, making shapes and colors indistinct. I relax my eyes, try to see with my mind or heart or whatever, but it's still just a steamed-up mirror.

Then I wipe the steam away and in the reflection I see, for the first time, the face of a man I want to be.

* * * * *

She stood outside the shower curtain, holding a towel. I turned the water off and took it blindly, drying my face, opening my eyes. There she stood, stark naked and silent. She rushed me, pinning the towel between us. Our lips collided. I tried drawing her into the shower, but she pulled away, swaying her hips, leading me to the living room.

I followed, dripping. She led me to her couch, turned, and pulled me onto it.

"I want to ruin these pillows," she whispered.

And so we did. She disengaged in a nick of time, making me chase her from one surface to another. I pulled away in fiendishly timed moments as well, carrying her somewhere else—a chair, a counter, the footstool by the window with the shade rolled up and the afternoon light streaming in…

We wrecked the order imposed so thoroughly on her home, liberating the couch from its occupation of cushions and teaching the coffee table how to have a good time. In the end we collapsed on the floor, Kate in my arms, her hand on my chest.

"I need another shower," I say as our sweat pools beneath us.

"I love a good fight," she says.

"Is that what just happened?"

"Well, earlier, yeah. Just now was a celebration—of getting away with it."

She is as lovely now that we've slept together as in

173

the moments before, when lust could have blinded me to anything. Even her blemishes, and the rise of bruises from the bar fight, are at home amid her perfections. I kiss my fingertips and lightly touch them to a scar near her belly button.

"What's this from?"

"I donated a kidney," she says. "I was the only match in our family."

"To a sibling?"

"To my grandmother."

"I didn't think they let you do that for old people."

"After a fight, yeah, but not with the doctors—with my mom. I wasn't sure I was brave enough to go through with it, you know, until she said I couldn't."

"You really are a fighter."

"You're just now getting that?"

I kiss her and stroke her breasts, my hand gliding along her side, her hip, her thigh.

"I can't believe," I whisper, "you picked a bar fight."

"It was building all day." She pulls slightly away. "We got chased out of Bell Buoy Park this morning—all the artists, even the painters with their big canvases and that old guy who sells books. All of us. That's what got my Irish up."

"Got your 'Irish up'? You know, you fight like a redhead."

I take an appraising look down the length of her body, my gaze coming to rest again on her eyes. "But you're definitely *not* a red head."

She laughs, rolling back on the floor, a hand across her forehead.

"No...and can you imagine if I was?"

"I like you just the way you are."

"Really?"

Vulnerability flashes across her face.

"Really. But why were you chased out of the park?"

"There's this woman, Brigitte Kennedy... She has a

shop near the park, and she's the landlady for a few other businesses. She thinks we're competing for the same tourists, and we are, but with very different things—we sell art. She sells kitsch. If she'd sell our art, we wouldn't have to hit the sidewalks. And get this. She called us a 'craft fair!' She said, real artists don't have to sell their own work!"

"She really said you're not an artist?"

"I don't value her judgment. But yeah. Bitch…"

"Well, I know you're a real artist."

She looks at me coolly.

"I appreciate that. But I don't need you to tell me."

"Then I'll tell you this. I get what you're saying, *and* I agree. She's totally out of line. The more I see of this town, the more people I meet through the hash, the more I love the vibe, and the people who make it, and… I've just discovered all this. I don't want it to already be too late. So if there's a chance of helping, well…this is me offering. Let's figure out how."

She rolls toward me.

"Not right now."

She kisses my neck, and this time when we make love, it's tender and minimally damages her décor.

Chapter 20

Saturday, April 25ᵗʰ
Gispert's

Sherman

"Alright, Sherman dear, that'll be…"
Jude takes a long moment tallying my bar tab.
"…eh, call it twenty bucks."
The bar is all mine. The regulars, other than us, are crowded near the door, watching the drama up the street: the apartment building right across from my home is under some kind of police siege, and now it's on fire. I want to watch, but the militarized police make me nervous. That, and in this neighborhood we say things like *I've got your back*, but right now, I have no idea how to help anyone. So, I'm glad to hide from my neighbors as well as the cops.

Before I ducked in here, I saw fire trucks staged down the street, like they're waiting for an all-clear that hasn't come. I keep glancing out the door to see if they've rolled up yet.

They haven't.

I found Evan and Carrie here already, and Cummy Bear sneaked in a minute after me. They were trying to get to the Titanic, but there were too many cops all around. They look like they're fleeing a mime riot, which apparently they are—that much I gathered before I came to get our drinks.

I pay Jude and slide a little extra on top.

"Say," she says, "you're the kinda fella who knows people.

Know a good lawyer?"

"Are there any good lawyers?"

"Only when you need one, and I need one."

"Somebody might come to mind. What happened?"

"I got rolled by Buffone."

"You and me both, Jude. What'd he get you for?"

"Well that's the thing. Nothing, then all kinds of crazy stuff, and in the end...nothin' after all. He shot my car with a Tazer!"

"I respectfully doubt that."

"He did though! Then he arrested me and the whole deal, even roughed me up a little. He cuffed me to a table! And then the chief came in, and they said they'd let me walk if I promised not to say anything."

"Then maybe you shouldn't say anything."

"I wasn't going to, but today I got this."

She fishes a letter from beneath the bar. I don't bother looking at it as she explains the details.

"So basically, the city is 'reviewing' my liquor license, whatever that means, while letting me stay open on some technicality. There's something up, mark my words. They're after me."

"Do you have any paperwork from being arrested? Any citations, any proof?"

"That's what I mean when I say, they let me walk— nothin'. No charges, no paperwork."

"Then I'm sorry to say, you'll have a hard time proving to a judge, or a lawyer even, that anything happened."

"But it did! It's some kind of conspiracy!"

I smile politely. She's obviously having a rough go this week.

"I'm astonished, Jude. Astonished and furious. Any threat to Gispert's, is a threat to this whole neighborhood."

She nods.

"And if any lawyer comes to mind, I'll be sure to let you

know."

I carry the drinks to our little table, where Evan regales Cummy Bear with the story of breaking his tooth. I'm curious, but not enough to ask him to start over.

"Here's the crazy part..." Evan says.

"The part about the mime fight?" I guess.

"Crazier. It's about Seasquatch."

"Say no more..."

"Oh, but I must."

He unfurls this incredible story about Seasquatch stealing a front end loader or something and obliterating a construction site, even grinding a cop car into the dirt. It's easy to imagine Seasquatch stealing a bulldozer and going nuts at a construction site, but hard to believe he actually did it. There's so much myth surrounding the guy.

"I hope it was Buffone's car," I say.

"Whose car?"

"Nevermind. Where'd you say this happened?"

"Hash Henge."

"Wait. No!"

"Yup. We got out of there before any more cops showed up, but it didn't look good. There were a lot of trees down, a lot of machines... I'm really worried about the place."

"I don't get why they'd bulldoze Hash Henge," Cummy Bear says. "Urban campers live back there! It's their home!"

"Construction is out of control," I say. "And so is Seasquatch. What happened to him?"

Evan shrugs.

"No clue. Last we saw, he was hauling ass down Commercial Street in some big machine, with that cop shooting at him. He could be anywhere by now."

"All that got us a little worked up," Carrie says. "So when we got to Mathew's Bar, it was a matter of time before something happened. You know?"

"There were these guys..." Evan says, explaining how an

ordinary afternoon drinking with a pack of mimes on a roof deck devolved into a bar fight for the ages. I wish I'd been there—I have a little righteous indignation to work through, too.

"Homophobes have it coming," Cummy Bear says.

"I'm sure you're the bad guys in their story. A bunch of degenerate weirdos, invading their space, waving your pricks around—literally."

"Guilty," Evan says cheerfully.

"And that's why I love our friends. Maybe we should push back more, against all the fancy, politically correct bullshit. But with a little better focus, if we wanna do any good."

"What are you all of a sudden, the fun police?"

"I'm just a little rattled, too. They came again today—the cops. I'm still not over it."

Evan shoots a devilish glance at Carrie.

"Were they looking for us?"

"No," I say emphatically. "It was about the siege. Cop said they were going after this guy—kinda tall guy, strong build, shaggy hair, acting nervous like he's running from something. Wanted to know if we'd seen him today."

"That's half the shifty-eyed dudes in this town," Cummy Bear says.

"They evacuated me, 'cause he had a gun, and he shot someone already, so he's 'armed and dangerous.'"

Evan pales.

"What'd they say he's wearing?"

"Pelts, like some kind of mountain man. Why?"

"Oh, shit," Evan says.

"Oh, no," Carrie says.

"Oh, Seasquatch…"

I dash for the door and push my way through the crowd to see Chief Boyer and a couple guys in tactical gear posing for some cameramen. They're standing so the cameras can't get an angle on the burning building, whose roof is about to collapse. The fire trucks are staged up and down Hampshire Street, but they're still not in position. Are they really waiting for a press conference to end?

I can just make out the police chief's words.

"...captured our number one suspect in the disturbance along outer Congress Street. I'm proud to announce there is no ongoing threat to public safety."

The roof collapses with a *whoompf!*

"Now," he continues, "you people need to get out of the fire department's way."

The cops turn abruptly and hustle toward their tank. I catch a glimpse of officers in riot gear stuffing a writhing, coughing, naked dude into the back of an ambulance. It's a neighbor from across the street.

I hurry back inside.

"Seasquatch escaped."

* * * * *

Saturday, April 25th
Hampshire Street

Chief Boyer

"We could have saved that building," the fire marshal seethes. He'd punch me, I know it. But he's smarter than that.

"I was protecting your men."

"From some naked guy? Now we're up to our asses saving the buildings *around* that one! It's a miracle the whole neighborhood hasn't gone up yet!"

"That's a testament to your men. Don't you believe in them?"

"I'll tell you what I believe—that you're a grandstanding asshole."

"One with a job to do, for the greater good. As do you.

Now, let's go evacuate that rat's nest in case the fire spreads."

He follows me, fuming, to Gispert's. The crowd outside retreats from us, packing into that dank little bar. I pull open the door for the fire marshal.

"This establishment is over capacity," he announces, "and dangerously close to a working fire. The Portland Fire Department hereby shuts it down, for the public good. Everybody out!"

"Fuck you!" screams some hipster in pants the color of sushi.

Buffone barrels in and grabs the guy, hauling him out. The rest get the idea and flee. They're a rogue's gallery, and I hope they don't stop 'til they across the state line, but there's only one I'm really after…and there's no way he'll come out the front door.

If he's in here, we'll find him.

Buffone returns from eighty sixing the hipster. We go in together.

"Can I get you boys a drink?" Jude says.

"We believe you're harboring a fugitive," I say.

"Where's your warrant?"

"Probable cause, Jude. Come on out from behind that bar."

"Nope."

She puts up one helluva fight, the liquor display sustaining significant damage in the process. A few taps get bumped open.

"You shut those off right now!" she yells from beneath my knee.

"Go find your man, Buffone."

He's eager to oblige. I'd like more backup, but the other men still think we caught the Mad Bulldozer already and now's not the time to tell 'em otherwise.

I hear Buffone rattling around the storage area, the bathroom, even knocking out ceiling tiles. He is innocent of any suspicion that he's serving a higher purpose than finding the man who humiliated him.

And that's just fine.

Beer flows on the barroom floor. It'll be moldy before Jude can get back in this building. I'll make sure the health department gets to it first.

Maybe then this little roach hotel will stop attracting the likes of that crowd, and the Mad Bulldozer, and we can finally bring this neighborhood in line. Maybe then, Grant and Naylor will get off my ass.

* * * * *

Saturday, April 25th
The Titanic

Sherman

"Alright Sherman," Carrie says, "just about everyone is accounted for."

I can't stop watching the smoldering wreck of the apartments across the street while my housemates, and Evan, sit at the kitchen table. Carrie wrote a list of hash names on the backside of a concert flyer. She and Evan called everyone, made sure they're not arrested or hiding somewhere in need of rescue.

"I can't get hold of Kate," Evan says. "And no one's seen Just Jamie."

"According to Speedwanker, they were the last ones out of Mathew's. And there he is," she says, pointing to the man fast asleep on the couch in our living room.

"So everything's fine?" I ask.

"No it's not!" Evan snaps. Then, more calmly, he adds, "Well, it seems like we got away with it, if *that's* what you mean…"

"But I'd still like to find them."

"Oh, I'm sure they're *fine*," Evan says.

A board creaking in the attic punctuates his words.

"Jamie!"

Carrie bolts to the hatch and flings the trapdoor open. We follow her up the narrow stairs.

There stands, in ill-fitting clothes from the discard pile, Seasquatch.

"Hello there," he says, mania sparkling. He stands at grizzly bear height in his underwear with half an erection, his head and one arm caught in a too-tight t-shirt that says *'Cause 3 69s are Better Than 1.* He flexes his arms and puffs his chest and rips out the seams.

"What the hell are you doing?" Carrie asks.

"I'm trying to get out of this damn shirt," he says, peeling the shreds from his body. "Aren't any of you people normal sized?"

"It fits us just fine," I say. "Almost like they're...*ours*."

"We didn't even know you were up here," Carrie adds.

"What the hell kind of ragtag hippie cult," Seasquatch bellows, "doesn't have disguises for everyone, like, at all times? I feel discriminated against! Don't you have to be ready to escape The Man at the drop of a hat? Blend in with the civilians? Shit, you don't even have any weapons up here!"

"We're an autonomous collective," I remind him. "Not radicals. You're thinking of the Weather Underground."

"Or the Orange Volunteers," Cummy Bear adds. "Or MOVE, or the Allied Democratic Forces, or..."

"Well, try harder!" Seasquatch struggles into a pair of pants, the waist stretching to a perilous stop just above his knees. "This is an embarrassment to us all."

"The pie costume might fit," Carrie suggests.

"I'd rather fight the cops naked than run for my life in that thing."

"Which poses an interesting question," Sherman says.

"Which way would you stick out more in this town—naked, or dressed like dessert?"

"Pretty fifty-fifty on that one," Carrie says.

"Inconspicuous," Seasquatch says, eyeing his pelts in their heap on the floor. "I'm going for *inconspicuous* now. At the moment," he holds up a pink tulle tutu, "this is all I've found that fits. And I can't go *anywhere* until I can walk at least a *block* without drawing attention, you know?"

"I kept an ex's sweatshirt," Carrie says. "I could practically camp in it. That might fit you...and, some old yoga pants maybe?"

"A two hundred fifty pound man," Seasquatch's voice shakes with frustration, "with a beard like mine, in *yoga pants!* In this weather?"

"I can give you a ride out of town," Carrie adds. "No one'll even *see* the pants. That's it, though—that's all I can do. A sweatshirt, yoga pants, and a one way ride, alright?"

Seasquatch grumbles.

"...but only," Carrie continues, "if you tell us just what the hell you were doing stealing a bulldozer."

"First off, it was a front end loader. Second, they were destroying Hash Henge!"

"Yeah," I say, "and that really sucks and all, but..."

"There are some things you just don't do. They destroyed people's camps—their homes. They rolled in like they own the place, 'cause they probably do, but with flagrant disregard for others. They destroyed a community, and sacred ground of ours. I can't abide that. Progress that doesn't respect who's already here, doesn't deserve my respect either."

"It's okay, big guy," Carrie says. "At least no one died. *Right?*"

"Not to my knowledge."

"Good. But you need to get out of our house, and outta Portland entirely."

"Oh, I'd *love* to. I've been trying for years to leave this town, leave this state! But something…" he stares pointedly at Carrie, at Cummy Bear, at Evan, at me, "keeps bringing me back."

"Don't blame us," I say.

"I could borrow Captain Skankaroo's van and drive you out of town," Carrie offers.

I can practically hear Seasquatch's mind racing. His eyes dart around the attic, and then he's off, scrambling toward a pile of bolts of fabric.

"These yours, Least Weasel?" he asks over his shoulder.

"Yeah. Kate and I were gonna make some backdrops for street theater, but haven't gotten around to it."

"This is canvas! You got needles strong enough to sew it?"

"Yeah…"

He carries the bolts back to us. I can't fathom the costume he has in mind.

"I'll make you a deal," Seasquatch says. "You give me this canvas, the needles, the thread, whatever you've got, and drop me off near what's left of Hash Henge. I'll use it for…a suitably high calling. You'll be saving a life—probably mine, maybe someone else's. And I'll give you all the credit."

"I don't want the credit," Carrie says. "Just you out of our house. Peacefully."

"Fine. But I'm not going anywhere without some damn yoga pants."

Chapter 21

Sunday, April 26th
Federal Bureau of Investigation, Portland Field Office

Special Agent Nathanson

"Working on a Sunday, Nathanson?"

"It's the free coffee," I tell my boss, the Assistant Special Agent in Charge. "I can't help myself."

"Me neither."

We wait for the coffee maker to work its magic on a little disposable pod. I can't walk away without my coffee. He can't walk away without his. So we're stuck together on a Sunday morning at the coffee-dispensing altar of a little shrine to the wanted and the missing. Over the machine he hangs posters of killers and terrorists, dotty old people and kidnapped children. That way we're made to stare at the people we're hunting while held captive by the single serve brewing process.

"You see the new guy?" He points to a missing person poster above a stack of napkins. "Sticks out a bit, doesn't he?"

I nod. The terrorists have a certain look in their eyes, of mischief and riled-up hatred. You can tell they're copping a look. The murderers, usually it's a kind of madness at the edge of the eyes—like it's overtaking them. You see that in some of the missing persons, too, like there's a bad kind of madness in some people, and it's a coin toss which poster they wind up on.

186

The new guy looks like some bored junior manager. He's got the sadness of a couple others, a kind of world-weary, spiritual fatigue, although he looks healthy enough. Clean enough. Wearing a suit, for chrissakes. Who disappears in a suit?

He probably didn't disappear in a suit.

"What's he doing on our wall?"

"Forwarded from Boston. We had the space, so I hung him up."

"Charitable of you, sir."

"What do you think his story is, agent?"

I read the description below the picture. His name sticks in my mind. I look down at the coffee table. Beside the creamers are little packets of mayonnaise. They say, "Schmidt & Sons," with an address in White River Junction, Vermont. There's a little banner on the label that reads, "Three Generations of Excellence."

The missing man's name is James Schmidt the Third. Of White River Junction.

"Bored rich kid running away from daddy." I hand him one of the little packets. "A story as plain as his old man's mayonnaise."

I rescue my coffee, grab a newspaper from the table, and walk toward my office. The cover story leads with a full color photograph of an apartment building on fire, collapsing in on itself, beneath the headline, "Hampshire Street Horror." There's a smaller headline near it, "Mad Bulldozer Wrecks Yard 8." The man was apparently last seen wearing pelts, driving heavy machinery backward into the Old Port.

And I thought Portland was going to be a quiet little assignment.

I turn the paper over. There beneath the headline, "Mime Fight Embroils Pub," in a moment of gleeful violence the opposite in every way from the picture on his poster, is the maniacal face of James Schmidt the Third.

* * * * *

Sunday, April 26th
Kate's Apartment

James Schmidt

"That's really sweet," Kate says as she snaps a clasp on her paint-splattered overalls, "but I've gotta get going."

"Hey, I understand. How about dinner instead? Tonight maybe?"

"Isn't that a little forward? I hardly know you!"

I playfully throw a pillow at her. She throws it back.

"Maybe you can make me breakfast some other time," she says.

"Maybe?"

"Okay, *almost* definitely. But not now."

I spin my legs over the side of her bed to stand up.

"I thought you had to be in place around dawn?"

"We do, but I don't regret how I spent my morning."

I fish my underwear from her floor and get dressed.

"I'm going to try Tommy's Park today," she says. "It's less crowded there, and I can set up off the sidewalk. See how it goes."

"Brigitte doesn't have you on the run, does she?"

"Of course not!"

She snaps the other clasp on her overalls and sighs.

"Maybe just a little. But let's call it market research. If things are gonna change, I have to know how to adapt."

"She hasn't won yet. Why don't you attack her head on?"

"I do!" she protests. "We keep occupying public spaces. We continue showing our work, making our sales… giving tourists directions when they ask where to go, and representing our city with a smile. We stay in the public eye.

That's our head-on attack."

"Which is wonderful," I say, "but she's working against you behind the scenes, right? Through the city council and mayor? Have you tried working with them against her?"

"Kind of."

"What's that mean?"

"She represents businesses. She has people. She has power. We don't have any kind of leadership. A few of us have made a few phone calls. But no one speaks for us collectively, and if they did, we'd probably tear 'em down, because we didn't say they could."

"You're a leader."

"I speak for myself."

"Oh come on, Kate! Don't be humble *now*. You know everybody! I've seen the way they look up to you, at the Sacred and Profane, in Bell Buoy Park. If not you, then who?"

There's a look of doubt in her eyes that wasn't there yesterday at the bar fight.

"We're doing the best we can," she says softly.

"Look," I said. "Power only respects power, right? Individually you have passion, but not much power. If you can show the mayor, show the council, that the arts community is united, they'll listen to you. Then you can fight Brigitte toe to toe."

"What should we do? Go occupy City Hall?"

"You need a rally, a protest...something fitting a groundswell! Get them to notice you, then show them what you *all* can do."

"While we're going, why not a riot? That'd send a louder message."

"Seriously, Kate, you're a leader. You can get people together and make a statement so the mayor and the city council *have* to take you seriously!"

"Yeah, and what's your role going to be in all this?"

"My role?"

I didn't expect to have a role beyond encouraging her.

"I like your ideas," she says, "but put a little skin in the game. Prove to me you give a damn. Then we'll see about breakfast."

"But I'm not an artist! I'm not even from around here. It's really not my place to get too involved."

"What's not your place? To give a damn?"

"Well, to speak for something I'm not really part of. That's where a lot of people try to do right, but get it wrong."

"Do you live in Portland?"

"Technically…"

"Do you know even one, single, artist?"

"Well, you, and—"

"Then I'd think," she says, "you qualify. Really, all you have to do is care. That, and stick around for the consequences."

"It's been awhile," I admit, "since I've given a damn about anything serious. That's why I came here—I was tired of just feeling numb, just going through motions that didn't mean anything to me. So I kinda…snapped. Now I'm here."

"Everyone has a fighting spirit," Kate says. "It's just a question of how you use it, or if you spend your life afraid of it—afraid of yourself. The hardest thing, and the best thing, I've ever done, is learning to stand up for myself. That's what you're doing, coming here. That's part of what I like about you. I need more people in my life with that kind of courage—people who give a damn, and actually do something about it."

"Then I'm your man. And you're their leader. Let's march on City Hall or something!"

"First I've gotta move some pieces so I can pay rent."

"Yeah, and I've gotta move some boxes, so I can pay mine. Let's figure it out though."

"Of course," she says, eyes glistening. "Then let's fight."

* * * * *

Sunday, April 26th
Old Port

Special Agent Nathanson

As a federal law enforcement agent, I have an uneasy relationship with luck. I appreciate it, even though it isn't real—luck is just a misunderstanding of cause and effect, like whatever improbable events led to the missing man from White River Junction running in front of my car to climb in a moving van. I waited in Old Port traffic to let the van pull out, glancing at the newspaper on my dashboard.

No doubt about it—that's the guy.

I'm not specifically assigned to find him, but when a missing person runs in front of your car, it's unprofessional not to at least investigate.

Now there he goes again, hopping out of the van in front of a shabby little house on a shabby little street. There's an oyster bar around the corner, where the neighborhood abruptly changes for the better, and some place that fries their potatoes in duck fat. I'll wrap this up and have a nice, leisurely Sunday lunch.

"James!" I say, hitting the sidewalk. He stops in his tracks, turning away from the house to face me. "Hey, just a quick question."

He shakes my hand. I clasp his forearm as well, vigorously shaking his hand like a long lost friend, gently turning him around so I'm between him and the refuge he sought.

"I'm sorry," he says. "I can't recall your name."

"Don't worry about it. I'm just trying to find a guy you might know, I think he lives around here—bit of an eccentric fellow. Had himself a big weekend."

"I don't know what you're talking about, sir."

I look down at his work shirt, and back up to his eyes.

191

"You work for a moving company now, huh?"

"I do."

"Well, the guy I'm looking for—he's a big fella. Perfect for that sort of work. Say, does he work with you? Did he come with you from Vermont?"

"I wish I could help you…"

"No, I don't think you want to help me, James Schmidt."

"Excuse me?"

"What are you doing in Maine? Working for a moving company, getting dropped off on Hampshire Street for God's sake… Don't tell me this is better than what you left behind."

He tries to pull away. I don't let him go.

"It's mine, at least. And it's getting better."

"That wouldn't be hard."

"Am I under arrest?"

"Of course not. You just worried the right people, is all, and I'm gonna send you back home."

He locks eyes with me, and shows what I wanted to see: the anger, and whether he controls it, or if it controls him. Show me who you really are, James.

"Then let go of me."

I do, confident he won't run or fight. He's coming with me, and he'll do it voluntarily. I've set the hook. Now I just have to reel him in.

"I'm not going back," he says, retreating toward a parked car—mine.

"Fine. You're over eighteen. You can take a long trip home, or a short trip to my office to sign a few things. I honestly don't care. But you're getting in my car."

"No."

"Are you familiar, James, with protective custody? That's the hard way—for you, at least."

"Excuse me!"

How dare some asshole interrupt? I hear his flip-flops smacking the pavement, getting closer, and risk a glance. The guy has wild, blue hair, and stained overalls rolled up at the ankle.

"I'm this man's legal counsel. Who the hell are *you*?"

"Nathanson," I say casually. "Federal Bureau of Investigation. You know this guy?"

"I do, as a matter of fact. And I'll represent him in any further business you have."

"Then you know he's a missing person, right? And if you're involved in his disappearance, then I'll need to know a *lot* more about you…otherwise, you might wanna fuck right off."

"Is he under arrest?"

"Not if he comes willingly."

"Which," the guy says, "he won't be doing."

"You know what? It's Sunday, and I have better things to do. So I'll just have Portland PD pick him up for protective custody at their leisure, and process his ass all the way back to White River Junction. *After* they ask him about that bar fight, which incidentally, *I* don't give a shit about."

The guy can hide behind his loudmouthed friend until the police show up, or come with me and let his family know where he's hiding. Who does he fear more—the cops, or his daddy?

"Now if you'll excuse me," I say, "I'm going to lunch. Either get in now or don't. The choice is yours—Mister Schmidt. The Third."

I drive away without him, having already done the fun part. From here, it's not worth the paperwork. This smacks of some domestic dispute rather than violent crime or mental illness. Hardly worth federal attention, and least of all on a Sunday. I'll send a message to the Portland PD, give 'em the address and let them worry about wrapping this one up. As I drive past, the wannabe lawyer doesn't even look at me. His eyes are locked on James.

Looks like he's got some explaining to do.

* * * * *

Sunday, April 26th
The Titanic

Jamie Schmidt

"Here," Sherman says, handing me a homebrew. "It's not an interrogation if we're both drinking."

"How thoughtful."

"You wanna tell me why the fuck the FBI is after you?"

"Parking tickets. They take those things seriously."

"Bullshit."

"Look, I've made some bad decisions."

"So did Ted Bundy. What were yours?"

"Apparently I'm a missing person," I say. "Which is news to me. I don't think I'm missing anything. Not anymore."

"Depends on who you left behind."

"Just my family."

"Wife? Kids?"

"No, my parents. I'm the... Look, I'm kind of embarrassed about where I came from, alright? It's nobody else's business."

"You made it my business when you brought the FBI to my door."

Carrie wanders through the kitchen, pokes her head in the refrigerator.

"Hey Least Weasel," Sherman says, "you wanna know why the FBI just followed Jamie to our doorstep?"

"Am I involved?" Her eyes plead for context.

"Maybe," Sherman says. "He won't tell us."

"You're not involved, no one is, I'll fix it... Sherman, can we talk about this in my attic? It's embarrassing."

* * * * *

"If I'm not back in five minutes," Sherman says, closing the hatch behind him, "you're going to have a pacifist vegetarian go crazy on your ass. So no funny business, alright?"

"Wouldn't dream of it." I close my eyes and pinch the bridge of my nose to relieve a headache. "So...my family owns the fourth largest mayonnaise factory in America. They expect me to run it, fulfill this ideal set by my grandfather before I was born. I told them to give it all to my younger brother, who actually wants it, but they wouldn't, so he ran away and joined the Marines to spite them. Then I ran away too."

I open my eyes. Sherman stares at me cynically.

"My dreams, my hopes, have nothing to do with the role I'm supposed to embody—with the company, in our town, everything. So, I ran away to make something of myself on my own, just like my grandfather did—a fact that seems lost on them. It shoots my whole escape in the ass if I'm judged by where I came from, so can we just drop it?"

"So...you're rich?"

"My father is, I guess. I'm broke, but I'm happy."

"And living in my attic."

"You know what it's like to recognize a trap and run like hell from it," I remind him. "This is your refuge too."

"I didn't forsake my family. I'm not a missing person. I'm not being tracked by the FBI! And I don't have a fortune to fall back on if I fail."

"Neither do I."

"Oh come off it! If Carrie can't make it, she's screwed. Cummy Bear, Kate, me—any of us, what do we have to fall back on? The risks we take to be here, to make something of ourselves, are *real*, Jamie. We're not on your vacation."

"I can't go back. I won't go back. Not with the cops, and not on my own."

"What are you gonna do, threaten to kill yourself? Carry

195

a gun like Seasquatch? Spare us the drama, and spare us the cops."

"You know what I've found here? My reasons for staying?"

"Enlighten me…"

"Friends, Sherman. Community. This house, the hash, the people who've welcomed me. I woke up under a *canoe* my first morning here. You know what I found beside it? A bottle of water with a note from the hashers. A bottle of water! It meant everything to me. And since then? A place to live, a job to afford it, people who care about each other and about me, even when you're kind of being a dick about it. And Kate."

"Ah, Kate…The truth comes out at last."

"I mean every word of it. And she's helped me find a purpose—for now, at least."

"A purpose! Jamie, we're scrappin' to pay bills around here, and you've found your purpose? Well congratulations!"

"So have you."

"My 'purpose' is to not lose this house. My 'purpose' is figuring out how to turn home brewing into a business that sustains us. My 'purpose' is to pay our bills."

"Exactly. You have a community of people who need you, and who you need, too. That's what I want—a place in the world of my own making. I have a little of it right now, and I'm working to earn the rest—by helping you, and helping Kate."

"So you've dropped in from Planet Rich Kid to save us all. How charitable."

"Can you look past who you *think* I was, and let me become who I need to be? Or are you just my father all over again?"

"So who are you, oh benevolent mayonnaise king?"

"The guy you knew an hour ago. I'm just Jamie. And I'm here to help."

Carrie pounds on the attic hatch.

"Least Weasel to the rescue," Sherman says. "Your five minutes are up."

"Good, I have a question for her."

He opens the hatch. Her neon hair precedes a worried face as she climbs the narrow stairs.

"Everything okay up here?"

"Smooth and creamy."

"Sherman and I were just talking about the art scene."

"We were?"

"Well, we were about to. Least Weasel, do you know a woman in the Old Port named Brigitte?"

"Oh, yeah I do…"

"I'm trying to help Kate stop her from running the artists off the sidewalk."

"That's noble," Carrie says.

"That's neurotic," Sherman adds.

"Well, that's me."

"If you wanna help her, or us, or anyone, you've gotta look at the broader context," Sherman says. "Not to steal their spotlight, but things are changing pretty fast all over. There are a *lot* of people fighting to hang on. The affordable housing crisis, the overcrowded homeless shelters, hell, there are well-off people being pushed out by better-off people. It's not just the artists, it's anyone making under twenty bucks an hour, and those are the people who actually make this city run. Look around the hash. We're all about a paycheck away from disaster. We all have our own Brigittes."

"But they're usually not one person," I say. "Brigitte may be emblematic, but she's also a specific person we can work against. I'm open to ideas."

"Seasquatch could kidnap her," Sherman says. "But Kate will still be broke if nothing else changes. It's a hard life."

"You sound like you've given up."

"No, I'm building a business in our basement. I'm going to build my security from those gentrifying yuppies' money before they price me out of town. Karl was a dead broke hasher before he started that moving company, and now he employs a lot of us. Forget what you think victory looks like, often success is just adaptation."

"Then how can I help Kate adapt?"

"Defeat Brigitte," Sherman says. "That'll give Kate some breathing room as she figures out how to hold on. Meanwhile, look at what you built to defeat Brigitte. That'll be your base. Those will be your people. Then it's a matter of hanging on, until someone takes a shot at you."

"Is that the Hampshire Street Brewing business plan?"

"I wish it was as easy as one guy trying to run us off! Our Brigittes are dumb luck and economics. And rich assholes flocking here to buy into the lifestyle without contributing. That's not you…is it?"

"Not in the least."

"Then you've got a role in our fight. If you want it."

"Will you judge me by what I do, instead of who I was?"

"I promise."

"On-on!"

Chapter 22

Wednesday, April 29ᵗʰ
White River Junction

Carol Schmidt

"Dammit Carol, what's it say?"

I love knowing things my husband doesn't. I draw the moment out, taking my morning medications with a mug of white wine. This little vigil I keep, in front of the east-facing windows, is interesting again. Jamie's letter has hardly left my hands.

"Nothing you'd like to hear, darling."

"I'll be the judge of that!"

"Just that he's living with bohemians in some kind of 'autonomous collective.' Being young, being foolish, having a great time. You'd positively *hate* to know what all he's been up to."

The liberties I take with the details are for punishing my husband. He put too much pressure on the boy, and in all the wrong ways. This is his fault.

"A Schmidt, cavorting with bums? Living in some flop house? I can't believe it. I *won't* believe it."

"And he's met this artist girl. James, he says he's in love."

"I'll show him love!"

"Yes, dear, with an empty mayonnaise jar. Shall I continue?"

"When I find him, I'll put an end to this disgrace."

"Why not just send the police? Have them bring him home?"

"You're joking…"

"He's still a missing person," I continue. "It would be a lot rougher on the boy. I mean, it would send a *message*, darling. Isn't that what you're doing to each other?"

"It'll send a message, alright. To the front page of the Valley News! I want to keep our family name out of the paper, Carol."

"You think too highly of yourself. No one cares about our 'family name' as much as you do."

"Give me an address," he hisses.

"There isn't one, and the cancellation mark is washed out. The state is M-something. The city has an O, a T, and an N, I think."

"Boston! I've got the papers all drawn up. I'm ready to leave at once."

This is the most engaged he's been as a father in years.

"I'm sure he'll write more. Until then, dear, try not to be jealous—it's a bad look on you."

"Jealous!?"

Or perhaps that's me.

James storms from the room, leaving me to reread my favorite part—the paragraphs at the end, where he talks about his friends, about Kate, and about beginning to find a purpose. Good for him.

"I'm sorry, mom," it concludes. "But I hope you understand."

I'm certain I will, in time.

The Boston Metropolitan Police Department picks up on the third ring.

* * * * *

Wednesday, April 29th
Congress Street

Jamie Schmidt

Benzo waves me through an unmarked doorway tucked between storefronts, something I'd probably never notice on my own. Down a short hallway, Karl holds the doors open to an elevator. We're moving a couple out of their apartment within what still seems a sheer, impenetrable row of buildings. After following Kate up a fire escape and in through a kitchen window, walking through a front door of this secret urban space has me feeling like royalty despite being the hired help.

The apartment overlooks the glass-walled canyon of Congress Street, with a decent view of the Maine College of Art building and its street-facing galleries. I watch the people down there who seem shut out from this world of locked and unmarked doors. It feels so safe in here.

"Give me a hand with the bedroom set?" Benzo says. He leads me past a brightly colored child's bed and weaves around orderly stacks of boxes, many of them labelled "Books." The child is nowhere in sight, and the clients just left to spare themselves from this part of the move.

"I wonder what this place rents for," I ask as we disassemble a bedframe.

"Two bedrooms, no parking, right downtown? Twenty five hundred, easy."

"That's mortgage money. I can't imagine paying that much in *rent*."

"Hell, that's cheap compared to any bigger city…"

We finish with the bedframe and arrange boxes for Karl's hand truck.

"I heard you're helping Kate. With some issue with the city?"

"From one person, anyway," I say. "Someone wants to run the artists off the sidewalks. It's worse than it seems."

"Seems bad enough. Them losing that freedom, would be like losing a job. And jobs hold everything together for people. You know, everyone's about two or three bad breaks away from the street, whether they think so or not. For people like Kate, people like us, hell, they don't even have to be *big* things. Just dumb luck."

"It just seems so out of proportion that something so little, a stupid ordinance, could so thoroughly screw so many people and their communities. It doesn't seem right."

"My man, if you only knew how many stupid little things completely screw entire groups of people... Security is an illusion. I mean, take this move. Squared away, professional people, with a kid and two jobs, and here we are, moving 'em away 'cause a grant ran out."

"Is that what's up?"

"Yeah. She's an adjunct at the art college, right across the street! The business card he gave me says he's the director of something or other for Home Right Here—that's a city program that helps homeless people find housing, and get jobs so they can keep it. She whispered to me that HRH ran out of grant money, and that was it. Poof. His job's just gone, and now on one income, so are they. You just never know."

"She whispered that?"

"Like she was embarrassed about it! Hell, that's nothing to be embarrassed about. That's just shit luck and irony. So now, *whoosh*, off they go to Westbrook—the Siberia of Portland. You wouldn't think a six mile drive could change your whole life, but it can. They'll find that out."

I can't let that happen to Kate. I can't let that happen to any of my friends.

"You know," Benzo says casually, "You can do everything right and still lose."

* * * * *

Wednesday, April 29th
Congress Street

Dan Grant

"Welcome to Six Sixty Six, Councilman," the maître d' said. "He's waiting upstairs."

I followed him through the cocktail lounge to a grand staircase watched over by oil paintings of God-knows-who, up past rows of photographs of dining celebrities, to the mezzanine. Immaculate tables hug the wall around an opening in the floor that looks down into the gleaming kitchen and onto the dining room beyond. It's obvious when someone cranes their neck to look up. Watching those below is much more casual. It's difficult to get a reservation for the mezzanine; to succeed, is to dine eye-to-eye with power.

The maître d' led me through the mezzanine to a door in the corner. Before this moment, I had no idea there was yet a third story above.

"After you, Councilman," he says. The stairs are padded with red velvet. The banister is carved mahogany. Whereas the stairwell below is lined with portraits, these walls are elegantly bare, directing one's focus toward whoever awaits them above.

Of course, I know already: Maxwell A. Naylor. But ascending these stairs, I feel as if I'm meeting him anew. The effect is humbling.

"Your hat, sir," the maître d' says. Only after I remove it does he deign to open the heavy wooden door that meets us. The room beyond is as opulent and pretentious of the entire restaurant below, condensed into a single immaculate room. Max sits alone at the only table. He does not stand to greet me.

"Good evening," he says austerely, before addressing the silent busboy in the corner. "You may *now* clear the glass."

The lad scurries to the table and removes a single wine glass with a lipstick print on the rim. His station is filled by a stone-faced waiter.

"Sit down, Councilman. Will you have a drink?"

"If you'll join me."

Max gestures subtly to the staff.

"But just one," I say. "I have a busy evening ahead."

"As do I."

Not that long ago, Max was solicitous. On that parking garage he spoke like an artist—with passion, with vision, eager that I share his enthusiasm. Eager that I work with him. Riding along to Yard 8, surveying Hampshire Street, he seemed still to be selling me on an idea, and if anything, proving himself—to me.

But this feels like a shakedown. For all that I want to call bullshit and cut through his pretense to remind him whose city this is, and whose it won't be without me, I'm struck dumb in this damn chair.

The waiter returns with a bottle of Chateaux Unobtainableaux bearing a date from last century. He pours first for Max, and then, with the subtlest air of utter contempt, for me. The effect is complete. I stare at Max in silent fascination, waiting to listen.

"The fire in your district was a pity. I'm glad no one was hurt."

"The worst of it was avoidable," I remind him.

"No, Councilman. It was inevitable. We just helped things along. It worked to our benefit, wouldn't you agree?"

"Hardly. It displaced three families, and the buildings on either side are barely inhabitable. Their siding melted off! The whole block reeks of smoke and teargas. Those aren't things I'm happy about."

"Relax, and share in the owners' joy. Nice insurance checks will arrive today. I met the claims adjusters on Monday— miraculous, don't you think, how quickly these things can happen?"

"That's not the word I'd use."

"And what do you think they'll do, Councilman, before spending a dime on repairs, when the deal of a lifetime comes their way? To walk away with *another* check, move someplace warm, and never look back?"

"They'd be tempted, but don't underestimate my neighbors. They're proud, they're stubborn, they have roots here. And they're not foolish!"

He laughs at me, long and low.

"Foolish, would have been turning down our offers. Which they did not do. They agreed to formally close on Friday—the day after their insurance checks clear—on deals they've already signed. It's wrapped up quite nicely."

"Well good for you…"

"Good for us," Max corrects. "Need I remind you, with the Cathedral District you'll be a made man. Your campaign to clean up the streets—"

"That's *your* campaign!"

"Yes, which you so skillfully whipped into a platform, has caught on. Your presence at the fire, your quotes in the paper about community, perseverance, and hope—perfect. Merritt Capital is pleased. Your campaign finances, from different sources in name, wait only for you to announce your candidacy."

I've never had a rope around my neck, but this is what it must feel like—though to be led, or hanged, I don't know which. I have never been more certain that I hate Max, or that, alone, I'm powerless to stop him. I want to tell the smirking bastard to go to hell, but I don't know what'll come out if I try. He looks at me pityingly.

"History is written by the victors, Dan. They decide the future too. Isn't it better to be at that table—at the *head* of that table—than to be swept along, powerlessly, by the tides of change?"

"That all takes time…and building permits. Which you don't have."

"You mean these?"

He draws a manila envelope from a briefcase at his feet. "Dropped off just before you arrived."

The dirty glass—the lipstick.

Lillian.

"Then why am I here? Aren't there more important people to show off for? Isn't there someone in this town who doesn't already work for you?"

"Two reasons. The first, is to co-sign these." He slides the permits past my glass of wine. "They're for demolition and reconstruction in your district. Whether it's the permits or the wrecking balls—or other circumstances—that motivate the holdouts along Hampshire Street will be known in time."

"And the other reason?"

"Ah, that's the fun one, Dan! You're holding a press conference this Saturday to formally unveil the Cathedral District."

"First I've heard of a press conference…"

"You'll notice that it's the day *after* we close on those properties, so mum's the word before you get on that stage."

I wish he could feel my glare.

"Mayor Tennerly will announce the permits," he continues. "And you'll welcome Merritt Capital and our partners with open arms, encouraging your constituents to embrace the change. Do suggest a certain—urgency—to selling property ahead of development. Maybe hint about eminent domain. We'll pull Chief Boyer from his war room to herald the development as a boon for law and order and public safety, and to reassure our investors that there is nothing to fear anymore on the streets."

"And where," I ask, "is this supposed to take place? Just so I don't miss my own press conference…"

"On the rubble of 368 Hampshire Street. I'm told the

last coals will be out by then, so our stage won't burst into flames. It's fitting, don't you think? The Cathedral District, a phoenix from the ashes—in Portland's proud tradition of resurgence!"

"That's sick."

"One might call it poignant. And here's another secret: we've convinced the governor to appear. He doesn't poll too well in Portland, but with the Cathedral District shifting demographics in his favor, his numbers may change."

The governor won with the support of rural voters, and the cash from business owners drawn from out of state by favorable tax laws—Max's target demographic.

"Those permits," I say, "aren't for *that* many new dwellings. A couple hundred votes? What's he care?"

"Some pockets run deeper than others. Besides, Dan, all politics is local."

I stare at my untouched glass, its wine the color of blood—my blood, all over this mess.

"How'd you poll last time," he asks. "Fifty two percent?"

"Fifty three." My voice is softer than I'd like.

"Surely you'll poll better with the new demographics, especially in a citywide election. If we can get some units open by November, you'll have first crack at a new bloc of… shall we say, *our* kind of people? You'll walk through the election, right into your new office. Easy. As. That."

He snaps his fingers.

In the dead-silent room it sounds like a steel trap.

* * * * *

Wednesday, April 29th
Federal Street

Jamie Schmidt

This next move felt more auspicious, albeit kind of weird. Our client was a guy about my age, moving to Portland for a new job. We were just unloading a container dropped on the sidewalk, moving him into a brand new condo that smells like paint and fresh carpeting. We haul a wicker loveseat through the kitchen, onto a tiny deck. Less than a foot from the railing is the particleboard side of a new building under construction, completely blocking the breeze and what was probably a nice view a few weeks ago. Someone tied stubby little boards to the deck railing here, and to the decks above and below. The boards come within inches of the new construction, probably defending a property line. If they finish the wall with bricks, they'll have to cut them in half to stay fair.

We headed back to the container, then whisked stacks of boxes around our client: paunchy, gray at the temples and balding up top, yammering into the cellphone that had yet to leave his ear.

"Over there," he mouths, silently pointing to a little room that could be a huge closet or a tiny office—depending on marketing. I set down a surprisingly light box.

"Open it up," he mouthed, then yammers into the phone in jargon that may as well be another language. With his hands he directs me to slit the box open and root around, I guess to show him what's in here.

The box is jammed with clothes that pad a cut-glass trophy. He made a gesture like *well hurry up!* I removed the trophy. Etched on the glass is "Q4 Goal Leader," and the year. Neither his name, nor anyone else's, is anywhere on it. He gestures for me to set it on the narrow mantle running over a gas fireplace. I'm relieved when he turns his back to continue his call.

"What are you doing tonight?" I whispered to Benzo as he unpacks a box of office supplies.

"Drinking, cleaning kegs, howling at the moon… The

usual."

"If you have a minute, I'm trying to figure out how to help Kate, and you know this town better than me."

Karl wheeled a hand truck laden with boxes into the living room. We retreated to the container to keep talking.

"Why do you care?" Benzo asked.

"Well, it seems the art community—"

"Dude, really: *why do you give a shit?*"

"Honestly? I'm trying to impress Kate…"

"Good. Honesty is a fine place to start."

We wrestled a narrow mattress into the stairwell.

"So here it is," he said "Call it 'Benzo's Paradox.' You can't set out to impress the girl, if you want to impress the girl. Oh no. You've gotta attract that high opinion with something worthy. Find some common values, stick up for them, and let that impress her. If it doesn't work, well, self-improvement's rarely wasted."

Our Q4 Goal Leader is now screaming into his cellphone like the future of humanity is at stake. We glide the mattress past him and into the bedroom.

"What do you really want out of Portland?" Benzo asked.

"To not wind up like that guy."

"Good. What else?"

"Adventures, I guess—trying new things. I ditched this really focused life, all goals and milestones and expectations. There wasn't any room for choice, so, no room for surprises either; no room for creativity. Now I'm here, and…wow. I never thought I'd be a mover."

"Livin' the dream," he said.

"Hey, it's fun. I get to see inside some interesting lives I'm glad I don't have to live."

"Ain't that the truth!"

"But what I mean is, once I let go and drifted here, things I never would have expected started happening. The novelty is cool, but more than that, if you *don't* know what's going to happen, then it feels like *anything* can happen. Then there's reason to hope the future won't be as bad as I feared."

"So you want freedom, and opportunities—to not be told what you can't do."

"Yeah! A chance to try things, I guess. To fail and grow until something clicks, and meet weirdos until I've found my people—to see what I can make from the chaos of the hash and this strange city."

"So do a lot of people who probably couldn't put it into words. It seems like one person, one ordinance—a minor inconvenience to someone who doesn't truly get it. But *that's* what's at stake!"

"So where do I start? Do I write a petition? Knock on some doors? Burn down Brigitte's store?"

"Oh, you've started already. Let's grab dinner with Sherman. He's got a feel for these things."

We finished the job. I look one last time at our client's shiny new life: orderly boxes, plastic plants, a gleaming kitchen with a single box of unused gadgets. There's disorder here, sure, but there's no chaos—no grit, no uncertainty, no evidence of failed experiments or risks beyond the pursuit of anonymous trophies. Above it all is the weary sound of his restless voice.

As I leave he looks at me, and I at him, across more than the space between us. His eyes burn with unfocused anger, set in a mask of spiritual fatigue—a look I recall from Grace's mirror.

Chapter 23

Wednesday, April 29th
Rosie's Bar

Jamie Schmidt

"So here's the latest gossip," Sherman told Benzo and me between bites of his burger.

I miss the intimacy of Gispert's, but at least here at Rosie's Bar it's so loud we could talk privately at regular volume, thanks to some guys in polo shirts reliving their not-too-distant college drinking days. We talked in between their yelling.

"That property across the street," Sherman continued, "that's now just smoldering rubble? Some holding company's buying it. They're probably gonna put in some godforsaken condos."

"Damn," Benzo said. "I liked the people who lived there. They'd day-drink on their stoop, and always wave to me. Where'd you hear that?"

"Word on the street today. There were guys in suits hitting the buildings on either side. Betcha they weren't looking for rooms to rent."

"Anyone knock on our door?" I asked.

He avoided my question.

"Man, the world has discovered Hampshire Street," he said, "and we're not ready to capitalize on the marketing. This sucks."

"We're on the frontlines of change," Benzo added.

"Nowhere's safe. Some places go first, some places get a little more time. We've been lucky, but nothing lasts forever. Jamie, here's the thing: you've gotta figure out what's coming, and make it happen on your terms. That's where your fight is. And ours too."

"So how do I help Kate?"

"You've gotta speak truth to power," Benzo said. "And so they know not to mess with you."

"But that's not enough," Sherman added. "Just defending a status quo? That's a losing strategy. It puts you up against more than just Brigitte; more, even, than City Hall. Fighting for the status quo means fighting against evolution and against change itself. You're not gonna win that fight. You've gotta understand the process, and guide that change in your favor."

"I'd rather burn her store down," I said.

"That *would* be more efficient," Benzo said.

"She'd just rebuild," Sherman said. "If not her, then someone just as tone deaf and self-interested. No, this is an opportunity. And all this guff about the artists getting pushed around, about sidewalk ordinances, even about developers tearing buildings down for condos—it's like this at different times in every city. We're not the only ones watching the places we love get turned into Yuppie Asshole Heaven."

The Fraternity of Latter Day Bros erupted in cheering. Sherman waited for them to settle down.

"Right now is a boom time," he continued. "Developers are knocking down old buildings and putting up new ones for all the people who want to move here. We're a destination! Why? The artists have a lot to do with it—they created a vibe that was easy to sell, and they helped take the edge off the dirty and dangerous parts of the city. But it's all just part of a cycle."

"Look way back," Benzo said. "It started with the settlers.

They pushed the Wabanaki out so they could settle here. They built this fort over where our house sits—Fort Loyal—but the Wabanaki didn't like that, so they slaughtered everyone in it and burned it to the ground."

"That's your classic head on solution," Sherman said. "It didn't work out longterm, though, did it? The settlers just kept coming. They built a new fort, then a town, then a city. The British burned all that to the ground in the Revolutionary War, and those who somehow still had money and power, gobbled up property and rebuilt. The cycle started over, but with wealth and power consolidated a little bit more."

"They still needed workers," Benzo said. "So they took whoever they could hire for shit wages—immigrants, usually."

"They lived down by the docks," Sherman explained, "not far from us, with everyone else whose labor made the port city function. A lot of them were freemen from the Bahamas, unloading molasses that made its way to stills for rum."

"Like our little basement brewery," Benzo added. "It's a proud local tradition!"

"But you know what? Those workers got pushed out by other workers—immigrants from elsewhere. There's not much room to move up, so the fighting got intense to hang on...which kept wages down. There were boom times with shipping, back when shipping meant *ships*. Then, the city needed lots of workers. There were bust times, when the enormous workforce suffered. Then boom times again, with the railroad changing everything and making the port a viable exchange again. Then the mills inland went overseas, so the port went bust again...just on, and on."

"You've lost me," I admit.

We weather another storm of nearby cheering.

"The point is the cycles," Benzo says. "Boom, bust, with the people farthest down at heel—the working class—feeling it the most. We have the least savings, the least power, the fewest options."

"But then something weird happened," Sherman says. "Just before I showed up: the arts revolution. Every major city had one, and in a lot of places, they're still going, reshaping whole neighborhoods. Artists can't afford much, usually. They found Portland—it was in a bust cycle then, and there were cheap apartments and cheap studios and you could squat in buildings if you were dead broke."

"When I was a kid in this town," Benzo says, "it was pretty rough. An outsider couldn't walk around Munjoy Hill, even in broad daylight. You just didn't take the chance—people would roll you for whatever you had. Or they'd jump you just to keep you away from their block. It's a lot better now."

"A lot of things pull cities out of bust cycles," Sherman says, "but a good arts revolution is hard to beat. Word spread and more artists came, and Portland developed its own arts community—its own vibe, its own groove. Musicians, actors, painters, writers…people who can't afford much because creative professions don't pay for shit unless you're at the top.

"They took the edge off the seedier parts of town. People started coming for the vibe. People started *staying*. A bunch of other things happened, I'm no professor, but we're on the backside of that cycle now. Now, the city sells that aesthetic, that vibe. It's made a name for itself, and the people flocking here for the good life are pricing out those who helped make it good in the ways that attracted them. There are more consumers than creators, which is great for the creators who've already made it…"

"And really hard," Benzo says, "for people like Kate."

"'Artist' is shorthand for…what?" Sherman asks. "People who work for passion and purpose more than money, right? So, to be brutally honest: poor dreamers."

"Poor dreamers don't have money to fight the man," Benzo says. "They get priced out, pushed out, or forced out, when someone wants to coopt their vibe."

"Think of the condo-buying, brunch-eating, up-for-the-weekend crowd as a new class of immigrants," Sherman says. "Then it all makes sense. They're not coming here for our jobs, per se. The jobs they're bringing are esoteric, white collar jobs they do by telecommuting. They turn working buildings into office pods, and bulldoze apartments so they can live in new condos. They're vying for the same space, now that it's really nice, without accommodating those they displace…because they don't have to."

"That's a fine way of saying thanks," I say.

"They wouldn't know what you're talking about. By the time the hotels open, or the condos hit the market, hell, people like us are long gone—off to Westbrook if we're stubborn, back home if we give up. Our city doesn't have any sprawling industry, so it doesn't need such a vast blue collar workforce…so it doesn't have blue collar places to live, which incidentally, are priced right for broke-ass artists and the rest of us. I came here at the last possible moment that I could afford to settle down. Now, like a lot of our hasher friends, and the artists, and the actual immigrants, I'm too broke to stay much longer but I *really* don't want to leave."

"You could go back into law," I say. "To keep up with the white collar cost of living."

"Yeah, and *you* could go back to White River Junction."

"Ain't happening."

"Nope. So here we are. And so is Kate."

"It seems hopeless," Benzo says. "But it might not be."

"What we need to do," Sherman says, "is create a little breathing room, so we can work another angle."

"That's our plan for holding out," Benzo explains. "Once we get the brewery viable, we'll be able to employ some hashers, keep the Titanic, and stay right where we are. Let the neighborhood come up around us. It can only be good for business."

"You need a similar plan for Kate," Sherman says. "Stop

215

Brigitte now, and figure out a strategy—how she can adapt—so this city's evolution is good for her, and her scene, instead of clearing the working artists out."

"So we're back to my question," I say, "of where the hell to start."

"Well, what *do* poor dreamers have?" Sherman asks.

"Passion. Time. Unique abilities to express themselves?"

"All that," Sherman says, "plus inherent romance—which is *very* useful. Now, Brigitte's working through City Hall, because that's how business relates to power. That power is nominally based on the mandate of the people...so you've gotta show the mayor, and the right councilmen, that the people love the artists enough to get *really* pissy if bad things happen to them."

"Speak truth to power," Benzo says. "And also show 'em that you *have* power, too. Like, organize a protest or something!"

"Kate already loves that idea," I say.

"Just get their ear first," Sherman counsels, "so they know that what's coming, can be used either for, or against, them. You may win them over in private. I doubt it...but who can turn down a poor dreamer?"

"Certainly not someone with a public image on the line."

"Bingo. Work on their hearts and minds in private. Then in public, hit 'em where they live—right in their public image."

"So, should I just barge into the mayor's office with an army?"

"Well," Sherman says, considering his words carefully. "I'd knock first."

* * * * *

Wednesday, April 29th
Commercial Street

216

Evan

"You know, I've had fun tonight," I lied.

"Me too, Evan."

Of course she doesn't look at me as she says it—she's lying too.

"I'm sorry the drinks took forever to arrive."

"It's fine," she says. "Thanks for walking me home. Only until your street, I mean—don't go out of your way. Please."

She moved to Portland a month ago. We met through a dating app, because I've been shot down by everyone I already know, and everyone else I've messaged. My last hope is to play tour guide for newcomers, but she didn't want to go anywhere after drinks—not to dinner, not a concert, not a gallery. Not to a book store, not a tea shop, not a comedy show. Not even for a walk, though she deigned to let me follow her partway home, maybe so I won't suspect she's going to double back without me.

I didn't think our date had gone *that* badly.

"You know, this is a really progressive city!" I say. I want to make her feel good about Portland, and therefore, about me. "It's the perfect place for that software I told you about."

"The human resources thing?" she idly wondered.

"Yeah! Did I tell you it's race-blind, and gender-neutral? I designed it that way! Oh, they wanted gender in there, and race, because of the life insurance angle—those are big variables—but I said, 'No sir, no-can-do, it's either completely impartial or I won't do it!'"

"What'd it say about you?" she asked.

"Well, I'd have to run it on myself."

She stops walking and stares at me, shaking her head slightly.

"As if there's a question whether you ran it on yourself. Come on!"

217

We start walking again, past oyster bars and Mediterranean cafes and pizza places and taverns and just about everything you could ask for on a date night.

"It says I'm right where I need to be." I said it with a smile to hide the implication.

"So, you've peaked."

"I could run you through it," I offered. "See if it finds you a good job with our company."

"No thanks."

We walk past Bell Buoy Park, where couples share benches as they listen to a man with a guitar abuse old Beatles songs. He's not very good, but they listen politely, more interested in each other. Past them is the ferry terminal, on the Maine State Pier that juts way out into the Fore River. I'm resigned to walking her that partway home, out of a sense of duty and desperate hope, but would rather wander down the pier, past the resting ferries, the fishermen catching smelts, and right off into space. Just give myself to the sea, and be done with it. But the water is so cold.

"Hey, I don't really want to walk anymore," I said. "I'm going to head down the pier. There's a great view. I know you don't wanna come, and I'm not gonna try to kiss you or anything, but if you'd like to see the city lights, I'd be glad to show you."

"Well…" she said, taking a moment. "Alright.

I pointed out the name on the bow of a ferry—Abanaki— and tell her it's one spelling for the people who lived here before us.

"People have been drawn to this water way longer than Portland's been around," I said. "I feel drawn, too."

We steered clear of a group of teenagers smoking in the shadows, and pressed on down the pier, parting a flock of seagulls as they eat trash on the ground. The fishermen ahead watched us warily.

"We can see the city hall rotunda from the end," I

promised. "They light it in purple for some reason."

I heard a faint hiss and laughter, and turned to look over my shoulder as a firecracker popped nearby. The birds exploded into the air, a maelstrom of flapping wings and flying feathers around us and now overhead. In their terror they evacuate themselves midair, shrieking and choking and flapping and puking as the fishermen and teenagers roar with laughter. My date takes off running, back the way we came and maybe all the way to where she's from, leaving me behind in a literal shit storm.

* * * * *

Wednesday, April 29th
Maine State Pier

Jamie Schmidt

"Hey buddy," I say to Mr. Giggles, who looks like he lost a food fight. "You're looking kinda rough tonight."

"Save it, Jamie." His words have a weary edge. He's sitting on a bollard along the pier, staring at the city's twinkling skyline.

I'd left Rosie's to walk home alone with my thoughts when I heard a loud pop down Franklin Street and saw this eruption of seagulls from near the ferry terminal. Then came laughter that filled the Old Port, so I headed over. That's when I found him sitting here, like he's all alone in the world.

"I'd offer you a napkin or something," I say, "but you're kinda past that. What happened?"

"I tried to find love," he says. "Like everyone else."

"Don't be maudlin, dude. Why's it look like every bird in the world just dumped on you?"

"Because they have? Look, I just want to be alone right now."

"That's cool, but you wanna drop past the Titanic? Have a shower on your way home. I'll pour you a beer, looks like a rough night."

"Go away," he says. "There's absolutely nothing you can do to help me."

"Well I'm glad to try if you change your mind."

"I've rather made my mind up, actually."

I don't like the ominous tone, but…what am I supposed to do? He's covered in bird droppings, and doesn't want my help.

"Jamie, you know that park on Munjoy Hill? By my place?"

"The one with the awesome view?"

"Sometimes I ride my bike up there, at night. I ride as fast as I can, straight toward the edge. As I get closer, the trees recede and the city opens up and it feels like if I pull back on the handlebars and just keep going, I can sail away and merge with the skyline. That would be it. One minute I'm there, trapped in my own head, and the next, I'm not—free of everything."

That hill, with its steep drop off, is on the other side of the skyline from here. I follow his stare, past the neon signs and lights of the Old Port, past the strangely purple-lit rotunda, out into the darkness where that overlook sits. I imagine him rising up, up, up over the lights, and vanishing—part of everything, forevermore. Trapped by nothing.

What I say is more mundane.

"You'd just fall off the cliff, bro. It'd hurt like hell."

"All the same," he says, "I can't help but dream."

Chapter 24

Thursday, April 30th
Portland Police Department

Chief Boyer

"Message for you, chief. Just found it in the stack."

My lieutenant handed me a form with all the boxes filled in and a little paragraph describing what it's all about. I didn't need anything more to worry about.

"You said, sir, to bring you anything about three sixty nine Hampshire Street. This came over from the FBI."

That got my attention. Not because it was about some missing person, or that it came from the feds, but simply for the address. On my desk there's a form in an envelope that says "Disorderly House Designation." The form arrived by private delivery from City Hall, with the address filled in already: 369 Hampshire Street. I wrote the nuisance smell complaint in there, and I'll write whatever comes of this missing person, too. It's a small but growing list. Once I complete it with something truly worth bothering about, I'll send back. Then the city can serve the address with a lien and pressure them to shape up, or ship out, so we clear another nuisance property from the neighborhood. It's that councilman's idea, and it's not without merit.

"Get Buffone in here," I say. "He knows the place."

Maybe while he's playing hero to the missing person, who probably just doesn't want to be found, he'll find something

221

for the rest of my form. One can hope.

* * * * *

Thursday, April 30th
The Titanic

Jamie Schmidt

"Just like that, Jamie," Sherman says. "Roll the keg back and forth on its side."

It crunches across the basement floor, the beer inside sloshing and making it hard to stop and roll back. A clear plastic gas line connects to a little turret on the top, and at the other end, to a bright aluminum tank.

"How does this help?"

"The motion helps the CO_2 dissolve into the beer," Benzo explains. "Some kind of chemistry, I don't know. But if the beer's flat, we're gonna have an angry hash to deal with."

I keep rolling the keg, one of several we're filling for the 207th running of our kennel, tomorrow night. Sherman told me it's an auspicious number, being the entire state's area code as well.

"Your job tomorrow," Sherman explains, "is to see which kegs get hit the hardest. It's market research. We've gotta see which beers people come back for if we're going to sell this stuff for real."

Benzo moves a crate of his hand-carved tap handles out of the way, and plunks a stool down near a row of kegs. He peels labels from a sheet, and smooths them to the metal. Each beer has a name—True Trail Ale, Barley Legal Lager, Surprise Finish Saison—and a label with artwork drawn by either Least Weasel or Sherman. To the opposite side of each keg, for the sake of panache, Benzo applies identical Hampshire Street Brewing stickers. The design is a cartoon drawing of our house with the kennel gathered out front. The faces are indistinct, but I know their shapes, and there's even a pair of glasses on a featureless silhouette for Mr. Giggles. The hand-drawn original poster hangs in my attic.

"These are partial fills," Benzo says, "and they'll probably all get drained. We need to see which ones go first."

"If they leave an unfinished glass behind," Sherman says, "that's evidence, too."

From up the stairs we hear a faint knock on the front door. Neither Sherman nor Benzo moves from their stations.

"Should I get that?" I ask.

"Na," Sherman says, without looking up from the gauges on the CO_2 tank. "Our friends come right in. That's someone canvassing for a room. More and more of 'em try every day. You snapped your place up just in time."

"They coming for the summer?"

"No, just looking for a cheap room so they don't get priced out of town. Last week it was honest-to-God refugees, from Somalia I think, trying to get out of public housing 'cause they're sleeping six, eight to a room. The ones with a little money to move out, they want a decent night's sleep so they can keep their jobs. Can't blame 'em. This week, it's people from those places on Grant Street that are getting torn down. There's not enough room for everybody who wants to be here. Classic supply and demand."

"That door is a helluva border," Benzo says, smoothing a sticker. "I'm glad to be on this side of it."

"Speedwanker heard the Grant Street people are going to protest here, on Hampshire this Saturday," Sherman says.

"What on earth for?" I ask. "Isn't their street way across town?"

"Yeah, but get this. He said our councilman's holding some kind of speech, with the mayor and God knows what all, right across the street!"

"Where that building burned down?"

"Yup. I bet he's in cahoots with that holding company that bought the lot. I'm telling you—it's starting, man. It's the beginning of the end for this neighborhood, and the damn brewery's not even ready."

"But we're holding out…right?"

"As best we can," Benzo says, looking at Sherman uncertainly.

"As *long* as we can," Sherman says. "Change is inevitable. The trick is adapting, and not losing your soul. That's something I worry about, with…well I mean, that building wasn't much to look at, but clearing places and people out is a little heavy-handed. And it's happening all over town."

"I thought that fire was an accident?" I say.

"A suspiciously fortunate one, especially after they closed Gispert's. They're probably going to spin this up as some great opportunity to renew the neighborhood. And when they say it, you bet your ass they'll be looking *right* at this place."

"We should join the protestors, then," I say. "They're protesting to save their homes? That's catchy enough. 'Save Our Homes.' It resonates."

"Sure does," Benzo grumbles.

"This is bigger than one building, if it's drawing people from across town," I say. "This is a *moment*. Benzo, you keep saying Kate and I need to speak truth to power—that's it! We *will*, and we're going to hit 'em right where they live. First in private…then in public."

"Good!" Benzo says. "Go kick in some doors! Haul 'em into the street!"

"Not like that," I say, standing the last keg upright and disconnecting the gas line. "But maybe not too far off. I've gotta go find Kate."

"Let's get these loaded into Skankaroo's van," Sherman says. "Then Benzo, let's grab a burger, and Jamie—you can go foment your revolution. Just let me know if you're planning a standoff with the police, so I can buy a fire extinguisher."

* * * * *

Thursday, April 30ᵗʰ
Hampshire Street

Officer Buffone

Chief issued me the oldest, shittiest unmarked car in our fleet. It blends in perfectly to this neighborhood, but still I know he's punishing me for that madman destroying my cruiser. He assigned me this stakeout alone, and there's not even a radio in this piece of shit. Nothing to do but watch the door on 369 Hampshire and see who goes in. I knocked earlier, and there wasn't an answer.

Now let's see if these guys have better luck—there's a pair of Somali men in bright shirts and macawis, those wraps they wear instead of pants. They're knocking on the door, and of course there's no answer. They wander across the street, past that burned down place, and try another building.

There has to be something better to do with my time than stake a place out over a missing person who's my age and in no obvious distress. But this is my penance. And there he is, emerging from the side door where the beer-steam came from before. He's carrying a keg and sure as hell, matches the description perfectly. There's another one, with blue hair, and a taller one, and they're all carrying skinny silver kegs.

This pedo van rolls up near them. Any other time, I'd pull it over on principal—it's covered in this airbrushed mural with arrows and symbols and other drugged-out shit. I write down the license plate—ONONH3—and count the kegs. The driver pulls out his wallet and passes some cash to the guy with the blue hair. This just got a little more interesting.

I check out the labels through binoculars, and can't tell

what most of them are…but at least a couple kegs have labels with a pretty clear picture of that *exact* house. Stenciled across each one is "Hampshire Street Brewing." No such place exists…officially.

While they're busy loading the kegs, I step out of my car and hurry across the street. I catch their eyes, being in uniform, and James—my missing person—drops his keg and takes off.

I chase him down a side street, over a guardrail, to the edge of the Franklin Arterial. He sprints through traffic, I don't know how, and scampers up the far embankment, slipping around a fence. By the time I get across, he's gone—right past the police station I wanted to take him to, disappearing into the Old Port.

Once I catch my breath, I call the chief. We'll get the guy eventually, but there's something much more interesting afoot. Maybe it'll get me off this shit detail.

"What, Buffone?"

"Sir, you said to report anything suspicious about three sixty nine Hampshire."

"Did you catch that Schmidt guy?"

"No sir—better."

I tell him about the kegs, the labels, the money, the van. By the time I get back the van is gone, along with the kegs and men.

"Go back in civilian clothes, Buffone. Try to buy something. If they're stupid enough to sell beer without a license, in kegs labelled with a picture of their friggin' place, they're probably too stupid to remember what you look like."

"Of course, sir. And James?"

"Forget James. I'll call his family, they can wrap this up. Just make a buy, and we can put a lot of things behind us."

Chapter 25

Thursday, April 30ᵗʰ
Hampshire Street

Officer Buffone

The door opens a few inches, the woman on the other side staring suspiciously at me. She has red hair with streaks of all kinds of colors; wears a shirt that looks handmade; stands a good bit shorter than me. She looks angry, but like one of those dogs that fits in a purse looks angry and can't really hurt you.

"We don't have any rooms," she says, trying hard to sound firm.

"I don't want a room."

"Really?" She looks confused, her phony anger melting. "Everyone wants a room."

"I just want a beer! I heard you got some good…IPAs?"

"I'm sorry," she says. "Do we know you?"

"I'm just a fan of the, uh, brewery on Hampshire Street, you know?"

"It's Hampshire Street Brewery," she corrects. "And we *don't* sell any beer."

I jam my foot in the door as she tries to close it on me.

"Just a bottle or two, and I'll go away."

"You'll get your foot out of my door."

"For two bottles I will, and I'll even pay ten bucks."

She stares me down, but I can tell she's given in. When I

pull my foot back, she says "Wait here." A few minutes later the door creaks open just wide enough for two small, dusty bottles to come through. I have my money ready.

"No, really," she says. "We *don't* sell beer. Just go away."

The bottles have a smaller version of the labels I saw on the kegs. I throw my ten dollar bill through the closing door and head down the stoop before she can throw it back.

I only need one bottle to hang 'em with. I've earned the other one.

It doesn't taste half bad.

* * * * *

Thursday, April 30th
City Hall

Kate Dorsett

"I can't believe you talked me into this," I tell Jamie. "It's so…impetuous."

"That's a pretty big word, Kate, for 'just a little bit crazy'."

"A little bit! That's the *mayor's* office! We don't have an appointment. It's the end of the day. And we don't have a plan."

"We don't always *need* a plan, do we? We just need to give a shit. You taught me that."

He knocks on the door. A flustered voice calls us in. I'm thankful the secretaries went home for the day, or we might not have gotten even this far. He holds the door as I step into a large office with a stone walls that seem to pull the warmth from the air. They're lined with bookshelves. Paintings hang on thin wires from the ceiling, but the room still feels like a tomb. There's a man in slacks and a collared shirt on a seat near the mayor's desk. He doesn't stand as she walks over to greet us.

"Madame mayor," I say, shaking her hand, introducing Jamie and myself. "We'd like a minute to talk about Brigitte's ordinance."

She looks shocked. The man on the seat stands to leave, but she motions for him to stay.

"What have you heard about that?" she asks cautiously. "My office hasn't released any comment."

"Word travels fast," I say. "And she's not exactly subtle."

"No, she's not. Have a seat."

"We won't be that long," Jamie says. "We just want to know what, exactly, the arts community is up against. I think that's only fair."

"And who do you represent?" she asks.

"Ourselves," he says. "But if anyone can speak for the community, it's Kate."

I'm not comfortable with the honor, but here we are.

"We've been harassed for weeks by Brigitte," I say. "And threatened. And had our sales interrupted, our customers chased away. She's going after our livelihood, which is bad enough, but she's also a threat to the creative soul of this city."

The mayor balks, shaking her head.

"That's a pretty big claim," she says. "The ordinance— which she merely proposed, we haven't acted in any way— simply wants to structure things a little bit. It's kind of chaotic down there, don't you think?"

"Art is messy," I say. "It needs to be shown, it needs to be lived, out in public, where it can do some good."

"Good art doesn't come from cleanliness and order," Jamie says.

"But does it wind up on card tables?" she asks.

"Sometimes," Jamie says. "And other times on blankets in the park. Or with instruments, or with dancing. I only came here recently, but I'm staying, because of the amazing people I've met who give this place its character. A lot of them do it through their art."

"There are galleries," she says. "And coffee shops. These paintings are all local. I bought them off the wall in an ice cream shop."

"That's great," I say. "For those who can get their work shown. And can live on thirty percent commissions. And don't need to reach people personally to build an audience. One great thing about our community, is that you don't have to already be somebody, to show your work on the street. Come as you are. It's a lowly starting point, but it's a way to gain experience and pay some rent before going pro—in the eyes of people like Brigitte. On the streets, we test the market…and ourselves. That's not tidy, but it's part of the spirit of our city."

"Which attracts tourists," Jamie adds. "Tourists who fill your hotels and restaurants and spend a lot of taxable money."

"Undeniably," she says.

"So we'd like to know," I say, "what we're up against."

"At this stage it's just an idea," she says. "An idea put on paper by someone not officially connected to the City Council. It needs careful handling."

Her tone betrays dwindling enthusiasm for defending Brigitte.

"A lot of people would like to hear more about that idea," I say. "Maybe she'd like to present it herself."

"We don't have any public forums scheduled."

"I'm thinking of your press conference on Saturday," Jamie says. "Maybe you'd like to gauge the public's reaction?"

The man in the seat leans forward.

"You're going to talk about bringing the neighborhood up, aren't you?" I guess. "What better time for her to present her plan—to clear us out of the Old Port, and out of the whole city while she's at it. To 'clean up the sidewalks.' We'd like to know just how she wants to do that, and maybe you'd both like to see what you're up against if you try."

"You don't have to fail in public," Jamie says. "Let her."

She may not admit to claiming a side, but I recognize the smile catching hold of her lips.

* * * * *

Thursday, April 30th
The Titanic

Sherman

"I'm so, so, *so*, sorry, Sherman," Least Weasel says to me. I'm in some cold, unreachable place beyond anger. The universe is against me. There's no way out.

"I didn't know he was a cop!" she protests. I stop listening and just stare at the court summons in my hands: made out to me, as the registered property owner, for the unlicensed sale of intoxicating beverages. There's no fine attached—the really nasty charges fine you later, after wearing you down until you're desperate to pay anything to be left the hell alone.

There's a handwritten note that came with the summons. It simply lists the date and time of the nuisance smell complaint; of our sidewalk encounter with the man from the FBI, coming for Jamie; and two incidents today: the officer lighting out after Jamie, and now, the bottles of beer Least Weasel sold him.

"I didn't even take his money!" she pleads. "He just threw it through the door and ran off!"

The officer delivered the unsigned note with the summons, but it's clear it came from the powers behind him—the police, the city, the developers, seemingly the full weight of the future itself, saying that we're not welcome any longer. Any more entries on that list, especially a serious one, and we'll get hit with the city's Disorderly House designation— they put a lien on the property, forcing me to comply with a host of rules and oversight and pay some fines to fund it all. It's meant for slumlords and crack houses, but it can be used against anyone. The easy way out is negotiating a sale—through the city—and clearing out. If it comes to that, I'm sure an easy solution will present itself as if that wasn't the point all along.

I walk through the living room, past Speedwanker asleep in the bosom of the Initiative Sapping Apparatus, and stand before the windows overlooking Hampshire Street and the ruined building. Least Weasel cautiously stands beside me.

"That's where they'll do it," I say. "That's where they'll announce the future of our neighborhood. A future, I know, that won't include us."

"They're putting up a stage and everything," she says, pointing out the stacks of scaffolding off to the side.

"And whoever gets on it, intends to run us out of this neighborhood."

"We're gonna fight it though, right?" she asks. "Speak truth to power? Stick it to the man? Save our homes?"

"I'm not sure how. But we have nothing left to lose."

Chapter 26

Friday, May 1ˢᵗ
Fore River

Seasquatch

"Fill you bastard! Fill with freedom and take me home, aye sir!"

It was a beautiful sight above me—the sail filling with the wind and rocking my boat. The sea calls! Adventure calls! I listen!

It's a glorious mess of paisley and cream and plaid and green and all the colors and patterns on that canvas I liberated from the Titanic. The stitches held as the wind rocked my boat to starboard, pushing the keel against the broken pylons deep below. I ran to the bow and jumped up and down, threw myself against the rails, ran to the stern and cried and screamed and then I felt her slipping free. She scraped the barnacles off and slipped into the river, leaving behind the wasteland that once was Hash Henge.

I can raid the islands for provisions. The summer homes are insured, should they miss anything. A Casco Bay pirate can live off the fat of the weekenders if he believes in himself and the quality of his stitching. I set a course past the working waterfront, bow pointed at the bay and the freedom of the islands beyond.

I tacked into the wind, past the wharves that are slowly being overtaken by condos. They pushed the low metal buildings closer to the water, sailboats and yachts pulling past lobster boats to tie up beside parking lots. When I worked those lobster boats it was nothing but traps along the wharves, working boat after working boat tied up, changing crews and selling bugs. It was good work when I could get it, but I couldn't always get it, and in the end, I didn't always want it.

There were a couple bars that weren't completely overrun with tourists yet, and that's where we'd go—the crews coming off the boats in threes and fours and me. They always knew where they were going. I'd always have to follow. Labor forges brotherhood, or maybe it's the suffering. I worked and suffered too, but I was never one of them and it showed in the coldest ways.

The hash brought me to those same bars later, with similar results. I remained an outcast, even among outcasts—tolerated. But tolerated isn't good enough for a life worth living.

I tacked away from the wharves, toward the oil tanks in South Portland, and back again, aiming nominally for the Maine State Pier. They used to pick me up there for my job hauling docks for the coastal homes. The winter storms batter them severely, so clients paid us to haul their docks into the coves, and bring them back in the spring. Hook them up to their stairs again, so they can walk to their boats without spilling their coffee. I looked up at their houses, past landscaping that could pay good rent for a year, and wondered what twist of fate put them up there and me down here.

It's a shallow thought, and a shallow hate. I was glad to leave them both behind. And to leave Portland behind, too, with all the memories of trying to find a place here, giving up, and trying unsuccessfully to stay gone. If I'd found anything, anyone, any cause worth staying for, maybe it wouldn't feel so good to leave.

I sailed beyond Bug Light, carving around Fort Gorges.

The smell of the sea washed over the chop, filling my lungs and my heart. I'm high on the radical freedom of a life unbeholden—master of my destiny! *Unnnnnggghhhh!*

My boat roared back at me with a sound like the heavens tearing asunder. I look up to see a run ripping down my sail, heading straight for the boom. I see daylight through the gash, the wind's energy lost. I lose headway. The sail falls slack as I point dead into the wind, then puffs uselessly as the breeze pushes it sideways, spinning me slowly in place. The falling tide has slacked. In a few minutes it will rise again. Along with the wind it'll push me back the way I came.

There's a trolling motor below deck; I liberated it from a fishing boat in dry dock. It'll help me not collide with things as I make my way back to land. Against the tide, it's useless.

For the moment the wind has me, spinning me slowly with gusts and sheers. Across the bow I'm taunted with visions of the open ocean; of freedom hiding among the islands; of the mainland coming back into view, and then of Portland—it's not done tormenting me.

I drew my derringer and pointed it right at the godawful apartments on the Eastern Prom, and at City Hall beyond.

"Let! Me! Go! Goddamn you!"

But the tides and fates don't listen to man. So if I'm going back, I'm going back on my own terms. I tried to leave this city peacefully. Now it's time to fight my way out—to avenge the memory of Hash Henge, and pillage the city that won't let me in, and won't let me leave.

* * * * *

Friday, May 1ˢᵗ
Congress Street

Dan Grant

He followed me for several blocks, ever since he came up

Hampshire Street at the Immaculate Conception Church. I knew he was following me because I stopped to check my phone, and he stopped too. I rushed across the Franklin Arterial, and he waited—like he *wasn't* following me—and then, once the traffic cleared, rushed to catch back up. With all the people around, on such a clear and beautiful day, it felt like nothing truly awful could happen, even though there was someone clearly, unmistakably, following me.

At the edge of City Hall, within sight of my office window, I confronted him.

"What do you want!?"

"A word with you, councilman."

He wasn't an imposing man, but his blue hair made him memorable. I've seen him somewhere before.

"I was going to wait until we reached your office."

"Who are you? What do you want?"

"I'm a lawyer, a businessman. A community leader, councilman, and the one man you will not remove from Hampshire Street without a fight."

"Are you threatening me?"

"Maybe. Depends on what you plan to say about my neighborhood—about *me*, directly or not. I want a little preview, is all."

So he was one of *them*—one of the holdouts.

"Then I'm happy to report, son, that the future is bright. We're cleaning up from that unfortunate fire. We're giving the neighborhood a facelift, and removing the grit and rabble. It will become a shining example of Portland's future—one that belongs to those with vision, and who work with the visionaries."

"And the rest of us, who think bullying and burning your way through the neighborhood is bullshit?"

"Well…that's the beautiful thing about that future. It doesn't include the cumbersome likes of you."

"So you're a social engineer," he said. "Deciding who gets

236

to live in my neighborhood, and who isn't good enough."

"That's just the market. It's simple economics."

"Simple economics didn't close our neighborhood bar to attack our morale. Simple economics aren't setting me up for a Disorderly House lien and a forced buyout. And they sure didn't burn down the apartments across the street."

"That was an accident, simply the wrong type of—"

"Oh, can it. They let that place burn and now you're going to stand on the ashes like General Sherman."

"It's rather poignant, don't you think?"

"Do you know any of the people who lost their homes? Do you know anyone who lives in *my* house? These are hardworking people. They staff our restaurants, they move your shit when you have too much shit, and they make the art you show off to your friends. You won't have a city without them. Do you know how scared, and pissed off, they are?"

"I know I didn't poll well on your street."

"And I bet that's going to change, too, when you fill condos with people who mainly care about their taxes. You know where else they engineered whole neighborhoods and called it progress? Soviet Russia."

"I'm no Socialist," I protested. "I'm quite the opposite."

"Then you're an elitist. And a bully. And you do *not* represent anyone I know."

The hell of it was, mixed in with his wild accusations he had some valid points. Just…it's not *me* who's guilty—it's Max, his investors, his money, fate, even change itself. There are forces beyond that man's control that are conspiring against him. They're using me, too. They may work through my hands, but I'm blameless.

I tell myself again, because he would never agree, that I'm innocent of anything but riding out front, and guiding change so it does the most good it possibly can. To hold me accountable for more than that, is naïve—childish. *He* is childish. Accosting me on the street…

"Young man, I hope you're at my speech, so you can learn a thing or two and embrace the future alongside the people I *do* represent."

"I will be. And I'll bring my neighbors, my friends, and the Hash House Harriers—the people *I* represent."

* * * * *

Friday, May 1ˢᵗ
The Titanic

Jamie Schmidt

Our house slowly fills with hashers as they wake up and wander over, or clock out early from their day jobs, to help paint signs and banners for the protest. Benzo cashed in a favor to skip work, and Carrie took unpaid leave to get an early start. She spent the morning rummaging through the attic, finding old shirts to turn inside out so she can stencil slogans across them.

"I made this one for you, Jamie," she says, standing from her workstation near the living room window. She holds a bright red shirt that says, "We Belong Here." On the back is a true trail arrow, like those that led to these friends.

"I don't know if I can wear that," I say.

"Get over yourself." Sherman claps me on the back as he wanders past. Over his shoulder he adds, "You're one of us, like it or not."

I thank her profusely and slip it on.

"How's it look?"

"Revolutionary."

"I'll try to earn it tomorrow."

She distributes the other shirts to Sherman and Cummy Bear, to Thor and Sea Ration and all the rest as they arrive. Their sizes and colors vary, but the message written across each is the same: Save Our Homes.

Benzo hit the streets to recruit our neighbors, especially those renters living on borrowed time in buildings that may already have been sold out from under them. He's still gone, which I take as a good sign, and Sherman is back from having a word with our councilman. He went straight to the basement awhile, and just came upstairs carrying some empty boxes to cut apart for more signs.

"How'd it go with Grant?" I ask.

"About as well as you'd think," he says, plunging a kitchen knife into an empty box. "He's *definitely* messing with things around here, and doesn't think he's done anything wrong. But what'd you expect?"

"Certainly not humility," I say. "I was hoping for a little diplomacy though."

"You only need diplomacy with peers and superiors. But with people less powerful than you? Fuck 'em, force is more expedient. That's what he's doing. And that, tomorrow, is what we're gonna give him right back."

We dumped the cardboard near the Initiative Sapping Apparatus.

"Hash hush!" Sherman yells. The room falls as silent as Speedwanker, who sleeps innocently amidst the bustle. "We only have until six o'clock, and then I want *every one of you* to report to Standpipe Park for Hash 207. It's the eve of battle! We need to get in the right frame of mind! They're trying to run us out of this neighborhood. They're trying to run us out of this city! They don't like the way we live, the way we dress, our tattoos or our hair or the way we refuse to sell our souls to buy their fucking condos. Tonight…we celebrate how that makes us great!"

The room cheers as he leads me to the stairs and down to the basement, to a cluster of skinny kegs around a CO_2 tank. Hoses connect the kegs to a central distributor, like suckling piglets.

"Behold, the nuclear option," he says. "Each one is half full of skunked beer and foaming dish soap, pressurized to ninety PSI." He attaches a beverage line to one of the kegs with an ominous *pssst*, holding the metal faucet at the other end like a pistol.

"Watch," he says, pulling back on the faucet's tap to release a jet of foamy beer. It hits chest-high on a distant wall and splashes back before draining along the slope of the floor.

"Strong enough to go right over the good guys," he says. "And catch the baddies square in the face. Let's see 'em broadcast *that* to their investors."

"The cops burned down the place across the street," I say. "Over what, a naked guy with a pellet gun? What do you think they'll do if we hose Grant and the mayor with rancid beer?"

"Probably burn this place down, too."

The bare bulbs in the brewery shine in his eyes like madness, helping me believe he means it.

"Power respects power," he says. "It always will."

"Power is a street full of people chanting, 'Save our homes,' and meaning it."

"Backed by people willing to attack their oppressors."

"Rancid beer isn't power, Sherman."

"You're right. The will to use the force you have, *that's* power. The rancid beer is just proof."

"And when the crowd runs away and the cops fire tear gas in here, then what? What happens to our home? What happens to *us*?"

"They might spare the rest of the neighborhood awhile, after doing *us* a big favor. Look, this gear is replaceable, and we've outgrown it anyway. What the brewery needs now is money...and this place is very well insured."

It feels like things are missing around the brewery—little personal things, like the wooden tap handles Benzo carved.

Keepsakes, like the old rolls of unused labels. They'd never survive a fire, and aren't worth listing on a claim.

"You want this place to burn!"

"'Want' isn't the right word. 'Need,' maybe. If the protest gets 'em to back down, I'll back down, and we'll all sing Kumbaya. If not... Look, I tried diplomacy, but Grant's right—you can't fight the future, and the future here doesn't include us. If I hold out, they're going to put a lien on this place and force me to sell at a loss. We'll all be homeless anyway and I'll be damn near broke."

"If the cops burn this place down, we'll *definitely* be homeless!"

"Yes, but then we have funds to start the brewery...in a different neighborhood."

"And where'll we live? I mean, the day after we chant 'Save our homes,' while goading them into burning it down?"

"You have Kate. The rest of us will manage."

The rafters hummed with muffled singing voices, as if the house is trying to lift itself up with song. Everyone jumped between stanzas, and right on cue, came crashing down. Something snaps. Dust rains from the joints. I wonder how much longer our home might last on its own.

"You've really talked yourself into losing," I say.

"Sometimes the only control you have, is over your own destruction. Besides, everyone got out of the other fire just fine. No one's getting hurt. They might even have fun."

"No, Sherman. They don't know you're willing to get them gassed and burned out of our home for your business."

"Our business," he says. "We're losing the house either way, and we can't afford to live in Portland without the brewery. I'm not leaving anyone behind. I'm bringing us all a big step forward."

"Not like this. Not with my help."

"You have until Grant takes the stage tomorrow, Jamie, to figure out something better. Until then, my mind is made up.

Tonight, I'm going to Hash 207 with a clear conscience that, come what may, the future is bright for all of us—whether you like it or not."

* * * * *

Friday, May 1ˢᵗ
Kate's Apartment

Jamie Schmidt

"You're early, Jamie," she said as she welcomed me with a kiss. The living room was covered in neatly lettered signs arranged edge-to-edge to dry, each one bearing a slogan. My favorite read "We Run This City," with running shoes and hash arrows. She said she made it for me.

I recognized the other people in her living room from Bell Buoy Park, but I didn't know their names and I was embarrassed to ask. There's the photographer, and the woman who glues seashells into little fish shapes, and others. They hardly looked up from their work.

"I couldn't stay there any longer. Sherman plans to—" I catch myself. "I gotta tell you something, maybe somewhere a little quieter?"

"I'm really busy," she said, sitting on the couch in front of a partially finished sign. "Just tell me here."

The sign didn't look like her heart's really in it. The motif is a globe, with the word *Earth*, where the letters *art* are a different color, but it's overwrought.

"That's the bumper sticker design," I said. "I've seen it all over town."

"Yeah, it's been done to death, but…I'm having a hard time coming up with something better. It's the pressure, you know?"

"I don't think a sign has ever won an argument," I said.

"So it's not like getting it perfect is so important." The look she shoots me suggests there's something I fundamentally misunderstand about signs, or art, maybe about her. "I mean, maybe you should just sharpen the edges so you can swing it like an ax."

"This isn't the best time for violence."

"And that's exactly my problem! Could we step outside?"

She sighed and led me through the kitchen, past the guy who sells his books in the park, as he filled in a sign with shoe polish. The window was open. We climb outside, onto the flat roof overlooking the alley.

"Sherman plans to burn down the Titanic tomorrow and I don't know how to stop him."

"What!?"

She listened patiently as I explained his plan and his crazy rationale.

"Does anyone else know about this?"

"I have no idea. He said we could leave at any time—he doesn't want anyone to sacrifice themselves, just the house, if it comes to that. And he's pretty set on it coming to that."

She wandered to the edge of the roof, where if you crane your head you can get a look at the flashing sign on the Time and Temperature Building. The view is through some scaffolding, though, where a new story is going in on top of an old building. Soon that little glimpse of the skyline will be gone.

"I see his point," she said finally. "I *hate* his point, but he's found a way to win by losing. At least for himself. The rest of the neighborhood might be spared awhile, until the bad press dies down, but…they're going to lose in the end, too. I just hate this! Isn't there some other way?"

"I haven't figure it out yet," I said. "But I'm open to one."

"Well *my* people, the artists, we're not going to get violent. If the hash makes a stand…alright. It would send a message that none of us are going down without a fight. If it comes to that, I hope he soaks Brigitte too."

"You can't be serious."

"I don't know if I am," she said.

I folded my arms around her, as much because I need to feel like everything is going to be alright, too.

"Where would you go," she asked, "if the Titanic burns down?"

"Not back to Vermont. I'd rather move back under the canoe."

She looked at me with cautious hope, and pulled away.

"I don't want this to come out wrong," she said. "But if it comes to that—we could split my rent. It'd take some pressure off me, and you wouldn't be homeless."

Suddenly the future looked bright, indeed—but I didn't trust it. It felt like throwing the game to get paid under the table.

"Still," Kate said, "they *have* to know—anyone who's going to be in that house when he opens the taps."

"I'll make sure of it," I promised. "Even if he doesn't."

"And if you can stop him?"

"You know I will."

She kissed me and led me back to the window to climb into the kitchen.

"I need to finish my signs," she says. "I haven't given up on peace."

"Me either."

I followed her inside and stared over her shoulder at the unfinished sign. She pecked at it with a paintbrush.

"I know we're for peace and all," I said, "but 'art' is right there in 'wartime,' too. Just 'cause you don't have beer canons, doesn't mean you're not fighting."

"I'd have to start over," she said, setting the paintbrush down. "There are so many signs I still have to make."

"You've got enough people here. C'mon, make that one really quick, and let's go to the hash. It's the eve of battle, we should bond with our friends."

"They're still hashing tonight? The rally's in the morning!"

"I know!" I said. "It's perfect. The energy around the Titanic, it's gotta go somewhere. We can't keep it bottled up overnight. The walls aren't strong enough."

"This is the biggest fight of my life," she said. "And I'm going to be caught between the mayor and Brigitte in front of me, and whatever happens at the Titanic behind me, and I have to get these signs *just right,* or…"

"Or what?"

"Just let me work, Jamie! I don't have time to hash tonight, I'm sorry!"

We're drawing stares from the other artists. They keep respectful distance, but their eyes are focused on me, the object of their leader's torment.

"They just don't take anything seriously enough," she says.

"That's the point of hashing!"

"I'll see you in the morning, Jamie. Goodbye."

* * * * *

Friday, May 1ˢᵗ
White River Junction

Carol Schmidt

I imagine finding him wandering the streets alone, my boy in a big scary world just needing his mother. I rush to him and he collapses in my arms. I'm strong enough to hold him as he apologizes.

And I imagine finding him sneaking away and catching him by the wrist. He looks at me petulantly. I slap the devil out of the boy because I love him more than anything, and more than anything else he alone can wound me.

And I imagine him in some godforsaken flophouse,

abandoned on a filthy mattress in a living room, too weak to escape. I swoop in and save him, gathering him in my arms and carrying him into the light. He looks up at me and says he loves me.

I'm not sure which of these I'll find, but I've made up my mind to see. That was Chief of Police something-or-other on the phone. He gave me an address.

They've found my son.

"Where are you going?" James says as I rise from the couch and gather my purse. I grab my little amber bottle of pills, the ones he picks up at the pharmacy so I don't have to leave the house. The last one is wearing off. The rest are calling to me, but so is an address far away.

"I'm leaving to save my son," I tell him, dumping the pills down the kitchen sink and flipping the switch on the garbage disposal. The grinding and rumbling drowns James out, so he repeats himself.

"I said, the hell you are!"

"Just try and stop me."

I leave through the front door, for the first time in ages, like a bird sprung from a cage.

Chapter 27

Friday, May 1ˢᵗ
Gispert's Parking Lot

Jamie Schmidt

"Welcome to the two hundred seventh running of the original Portland's Hash House Harriers, come over here if you wanna make something of it...can I get an on-on!"

On-on!

"Here you go, Just Jamie," Least Weasel says, handing me a blaze orange hunting vest. She's wearing a plaid shirt and orange hat, while others dress in their interpretations of the theme: the Mainer Hash, gleefully lampooning the state. Sea Ration is dressed like a tourist, in khaki shorts and sandals with socks; Cummy Bear stands quietly in a head-to-toe bear costume, wearing a homemade sash that says "Good bears eat their honey."

There's no sign of impending doom, and even the shadow cast by the darkened Gispert's can't chill the warmth of our opening circle.

"Tonight, God willing," Thor says, "will be Just Jamie's naming!"

Hooray!

He explained the marks once again, for the sake of the traveling hashers, the long-ago hashers, the hashers who moved away but were roused by the battle cry to return to their comrades. They're here early for tomorrow's protest, in the largest circle I've seen. Thor recognizes an emotional Sherman, ushering him into the circle.

"Whatever happens tomorrow," Sherman says, "whether we repel the powers that be or lose our house in the end, we know that the hash is bigger than one building. Or one person. The hash is an expression of freedom that abides wherever we gather to drink our down-downs and sing the old songs and forget the words all over again. Tomorrow, we fight. Tonight…let's celebrate! On-on!"

On-on!

We dispersed along Hampshire Street, hollering when we found our marks, calling true trail, following the arrows through a bank parking lot and then in one side and out the other of a trendy hotel's lobby. We climbed a fancy retaining wall and stormed a parking garage, finding a case of beer at the top with a view back over our neighborhood.

"It's real pretty from up here," I say to Cummy Bear.

"We're too high up to see the grime," she says.

Evan haunts the periphery, abstaining from the beer and keeping away from the scrum. I call to him. He joins us by the railing.

"I like it just the way it is," I say, sweeping my hand across the panorama. "But just think of all it could be, with our little brewery right in the middle. Holding it all together."

"I think of all it could have been," he says.

"What are you fighting for tomorrow?" I ask.

"Peace," he says.

"Me too."

* * * * *

Friday, May 1st
Kate's Apartment

Kate Dorsett

I sort of like it, anyway: "Wartime," with *art* emphasized. It speaks to something deep inside that's powerful, but doesn't feel healthy—like there's enough anger and fear down there that I could go too far.

"What do you think, Devon?" I asked my photographer friend.

"Feisty!" he says. "I like it. Makes me think we should get the fire dancers to bring some Molotov cocktails. Really spice things up!"

I rolled my eyes.

"There's greater strength in resolve, than violence," I tell him.

"Yeah, I don't know about that…"

I showed my other friends and they nodded and smile and looked down at their own signs wondering if they're *feisty* enough, too, as I wondered if there might be a better way to say that we won't quietly go away.

That we…well, as Jamie's shirt said: that we belong here.

"Guys, new concept," I announce. "Let's keep what we've got, we can hand 'em out, but how about this for the next signs: 'We Belong Here.' We belong out in public. This whole city is our home—not just the private spaces."

There's a great shuffling of cardboard and swishing of brushes and they're off, and so am I, to my running shoes by the door and then down to the street. Jamie was there for me, in the mime fight. He jumped right in at the Sacred and Profane. He seems to finally get what I'm fighting for, or at least, he genuinely cares—and so do I, about him.

Now the Titanic's defense is his crusade, even against Sherman, and I don't know how I can help, but I need him to know that I care. Maybe we can figure something out; maybe we can just hold each other, and feel safe a while longer—lovers, in a dangerous time. I don't owe him anything, I remind myself; tonight, I'm going after him for me.

* * * * *

Friday, May 1ˢᵗ
Fore River

Seasquatch

I got the trolling motor clamped to the rail off the starboard bow, while I'm in the stern paddling on one side and then the other, because I'm not making enough headway for the tiller to do much good. At least there's music, from the sunset tour boat cruising the bay. A live band on their top deck plays Nordic heavy metal. Pure Viking shit. Stirs the blood! The music charges across the water. It shakes my skull. I love it. But there's also this damned cheering and the tourists' voices because they don't know how to shut up and appreciate the moment.

If they did it right, they'd throw the casuals overboard and set that boat on fire as the band plays on. They'd ram it aground full-speed and the survivors would charge the land swinging chains and leg bones and they'd lay *waste* to the Old Port. They'd sack that place in the finest tradition and leave it a smoldering wreck. March the tourists into the sea. Punish the goddamn short-ropers from the Fore River Parkway to the Eastern Prom.

This city was once a place of hard men who smelled of cigarettes and the sea and honest work, and now it's all wine bars and tourists turning red in the sun.

Give me the sea.

But the sea is pushing me back to Portland. I'm done

with it, but I can't be free until it's done with me. Perhaps we can come to an understanding in the ruins. The party boat glides past, effortlessly as I paddle like a fiend. It gives me an idea.

The drunks at the railing salute me with their cocktails. I shake my fist at them. We're headed for the same pier. They'll be gone by the time I tie up to their stern and climb aboard.

With Sherwood Forest scraped off the Earth and Hash Henge pushed into the sea, with buildings coming down and people turned out on the streets, there's a lot of unrest in the city. It needs the right kind of accelerant, then a spark, then maybe I'll finally earn my freedom.

Chapter 28

Friday, May 1ˢᵗ
The Titanic

Kate Dorsett

I let myself in through the front door, which they never lock. I didn't figure I'd find Jamie here, but it's a good place to start, and maybe someone would have seen him. But there's no one here, just signs laid out drying in the kitchen and living room. I've been here so many times it should feel like home, which it usually does, but the absence of my friends makes it feel like a place I'm not supposed to be.

"Hello?" I yell. No answer.

No one picks up their phone on trail, either, to let me know where they are and where they think they're heading. They're not supposed to answer phones, of course. It's proper etiquette to *be here now*, and shut out the world beyond the hash. What good is the escape if you let the real world intrude?

But that's damned inconvenient right now.

"Anybody home?" I yell up the hatch into Jamie's apartment. Again, no response.

Walking to the living room window I see the shape of a person beneath a banner that says "Save Our Homes." I pull it back.

Speedwanker.

He doesn't wake up, even when I call his name and kick

the ISA. His lips part, though, and he smiles, from some unreachable place on the far side of consciousness.

I'd give anything to sleep that well.

So I head down to the street and over to Gispert's, past the deadbolted door that was always open to us. I find the chalk marks from their opening circle on the parking lot, and an arrow a block away. I follow it. There are false trails meant to confound us, and one true trail that leads to Jamie. I hope I've chosen the right way.

* * * * *

Friday, May 1ˢᵗ
East End Community Garden

Dan Grant

I've come here for peace and quiet and to stare at the city lights from the edge of the bluff. This is an out of the way spot, behind the community gardens where the skyline stretches in a great, shimmering arc. I slip away here often to be alone with my thoughts.

Tomorrow morning I'll give the most contentious speech of my career, and I've been promised great resistance. I don't want to serve Max Naylor, but it's still the best bet going. Nothing can stop him, shy of an army, and even then, change is inevitable. The market's hot. Progress marches on, with or despite us.

I've lost all enthusiasm to participate, but the gears are in motion.

I sit at a large stone table, near the edge of the bluff, trying to come up with the opening words of my speech, when my thoughts are shattered by frantic yelling behind me. From the darkness appears a thundering horde of unwashed young people in tattered flannel, reeking of warm beer and marijuana. What's this neighborhood coming to?

Their shapes pass near me, and in the moonlight it looks like one of them is dressed like a bear! God knows why. Then one of them blows a vuvuzela.

It's them! The hooligans from last weekend!

They disappear into the tree line, along a walking path, where I hear them laughing.

These people, and their…

They have no right to…

Why, I oughta…

I'd like to march them into the sea! At least they'll never afford a place in my Cathedral District. And if I, as mayor, can renew the city like we're bringing up Hampshire Street, there won't be a place for their kind *anywhere!* Finally, it'll be peaceful around here. Respectable. Orderly, and calm.

I'm up and stomping toward them. My heart is sick about tomorrow, and now, about this disgrace to my solitude. Anger is good medicine. I'll follow them into the darkness and give them a piece of my mind, before I run them out of town.

* * * * *

Friday, May 1st
East End Trail

Jamie Schmidt

"Make a hole!" Hans Yolo yells.

Clutching our drinks we fade to the edges of the walking path so the guy coming toward us can get through. He stops in our midst and squares his shoulders, breathing like a bull. Poly-Glamorous, wearing a camo-print running skirt and fishnet leggings, offers him a plastic cup of Moxie and coffee brandy. The man bats it away.

"Have a drink," Hans Yolo says. "Don't cost nothin'."

"I'm Dan Grant," the man says arrogantly.

So he's the one Sherman confronted! The devil himself.

"City councilman for this district," he carries on. "Lifelong resident of this neighborhood! And just who the hell are you?"

"We're the Hash House Harriers," Cummy Bear yells from her bear costume. "Portland's original drinking club with a running problem."

"And this, sir," Thor says, stepping forward with a bottle of our homebrew, label proudly facing up, "is your down-down. Drink with us!"

*Down, down, down, down...*we chant.

"This," he says, taking the bottle and pointing with its neck, "is hooliganism! Disorder! You unwashed punks act like animals! You disrespect my community...and yourselves! You break the law!"

Down, down, down, down...

"I saw you on the sidewalk, scaring the tourists. Brawling in a bar! Don't you people have homes? Don't you people have jobs?" He points the bottle at me, looking me dead in the eye. "Just what the hell are you doing out here?"

"It's called having fun," I say, stepping forward. "In the shadows, where you think we belong. Shut down our bar, we'll drink in your parks. Tear down our homes, we'll take to the streets. We even get run off the sidewalks, trying to make ends meet. Where are we supposed to go?"

"Away," he says. "Back to whatever shithole you crawled out of."

"We have a right to exist. To do as we please, where we're not causing harm. The harder you make that, the more we'll push back."

"Oh, grow up. You're making an ass of yourself—carrying on like a frat party."

"We spend the workday masquerading in your world. At

night we have ours. It's not a crime to be free, or to want more than your condo-building, urban-renewing bullshit."

"That 'bullshit' made this place *livable*. We didn't clean it up for *you* to drag us back down! People *want* to live here now—the *right* kind of people."

"When will things be safe enough, councilman? Nice enough? There's no end to it, but a livable balance that you're overshooting. They'll push you out, too, when you're not good enough for them."

His confidence falters. I watch his grip change on the bottle, from using it as a pointer, to holding it like a weapon—like my father, testing his grip on a jar. I circle him to complicate his aim.

"But I need you to know," I say, "that there's still time to make it right. Quit forcing development on our neighborhood. Quit chasing us into the shadows. We have nowhere else to go, and a hard enough time as it is. And we come in peace. All are welcome at the hash, as in our neighborhood. Even you."

"Yeah," Hans Yolo says, nodding at the bottle in Grant's hand. "It's not peer pressure, it's just your turn."

The chanting resumes, *down, down, down, down...*

To our horror he pours his beer on the ground. Then he drops the bottle.

"You should recycle that," Cummy Bear says. "We brought a bag..."

He glowers at her but picks it up, dropping it in a bag held by Sherman. We leave without a further word. I'm last to turn and follow the group, silently along the trail.

* * * * *

Friday, May 1ˢᵗ
East End Trail

Dan Grant

"You should recycle that," the damn bear said to me. "We brought a bag…"

It was a moment below my dignity, too absurd to be real. I picked the bottle up and dropped it in a bag held by the man who accosted me on the sidewalk. Do these people *actually* have it in for me, the way they think I have it in for them?

They left silently, the young man who argued with me being last to leave. Once he was gone I turned away, pride intact, and stomped back to the garden. But each step felt like retreat, not victory. Like instead of chasing them off, they'd left me behind. I was worked up and pissed off, but standing alone in the darkness felt too much like sulking.

So I turned around to chase them and make one last point or two, maybe—shamefully—plead for their understanding. They remind me of my old friends, when our street was as seedy as theirs. I'm the only one of us left on Munjoy Hill.

As fond as I am of the memories, I'd be embarrassed to live like that again, and daunted by the work it took to come this far. Every neighborhood is a stack of memories—slices of time. I belonged to one as a young man, and a different one now, which I feel receding as a new era dawns. It's my privilege to shape that era with the powers of my office, and with Max's money. But it doesn't feel like that future belongs to me.

It belongs to those who will be around to experience much more of it, and deal with whatever blessings—or mess—they inherit. I can rule that future tyrannically, for myself and those just like me, or I can acknowledge it's just another memory we're all passing through.

Heaven help me if I'm still around when it's their turn

in power.

If all goes well, I'll be mayor in a year. I'll have a whole city to manage, rather than just a district. The worst of me wants to drive those people into the sea with bricks on their heads. The best of me wants to apologize and make room for them.

I have to put the brakes on the Cathedral District. I have to stop Max. I need to direct the next wave of development more cautiously. No more wholesale renewal; no more hotels for awhile. The people already here don't need these things.

It's hard to bring a place up organically, like we did when I was younger…but people like that group tonight, for all their insolence, have that kind of energy. They have that kind of passion. And they're already here. I should get out of their way, instead of clearing them out of mine.

Through a break in the trees I see them silhouetted against the twinkling skyline. They belong to this place, but to no time in particular, their shapes merging with the buildings and filling the spaces between.

* * * * *

Friday, May 1st
Munjoy Hill

Jamie Schmidt

"That was really great, Just Jamie," Least Weasel says as we run between ugly condos on a hillside. The views were probably pretty good here before they went in.

"Which part?" I ask. "I thought it ended kinda poorly."

"What you said to that guy. It's like you rehearsed it or something."

"It's been brewing since Kate got me thinking about it." At the mention of Kate's name, Least Weasel looks away.

258

"You watch yourself with that one," she says, running ahead of me along the trail marked in chalk arrows. "She's a firebrand."

We find a song check beneath a streetlight, and decide to sing until the rest of the pack catches up.

"Can I get a note?" Thor yells.

Note!

I used to work in Chicago, at the old department store. I used to work in Chicago, I don't work there anymore!

Diddle Acquittal steps forward.

"Someone came in looking for a hammer."

A hammer from the store!

A hammer they wanted, nailed they got!

I don't work there anymore!

And on it goes, everyone contributing verses, as Mr. Giggles brings up the rear. He arrives, unexpectedly, on a bicycle.

"I found it in the woods!" he says. "Isn't it great?"

"So it's stolen?" Cummy Bear says.

"Well not by me."

"Yes, by you! If it's not yours, it's not yours."

"I'll put it back when I'm done," he says bitterly. "So the thief doesn't lose it!"

We follow arrows on the pavement to a pale blue apartment building. On the sidewalk our hares wrote, "On-In! On-Up!" so in we go, up a staircase, to fill the living room of an otherwise empty apartment—no furniture, no art, no signs of habitation. Pabst Smirnoff and Diddle Acquittal pour beer from kegs in the bathroom, where the tub is full of ice.

"Whose place is this?" I whisper to Sea Ration.

"No clue," she says. "But with Hash Henge gone, it's lucky for us!"

I look around as we take our places for the closing circle. Several of us are movers. Perhaps they had a job here; perhaps they knew just when it would be vacant. Fortune favors the brave.

The room is thick with musk, and our group feels united for more than just a party. The thrill of this stolen space, on the eve of battle, at the end of a long run, has our nerves in a fine state. Maybe that councilman would like it here too, if he could drop his pretense and remember what it's like to be young and free.

Thor calls us to attention. We sing our opening song, then as always, excoriate the trail and the hares who laid it.

S-H-I, T-T-Y, T-R-A-I-L! Shitty trail, it sucked! Shitty trail, it blew!

…and carry on through the standards I've learned unite us with hashers around the world. We stomp to the rhythm and dance as the spirit moves us. Hans Yolo restrains his booming voice on several songs, and simply hums along.

"I learned some of these while hashing around Asia," he whispers. "It's an oral tradition. The lyrics change over time and distance."

"Hash providence provided us this space," Thor says. "We should pay it due respect. Can I have the most recently named hasher in the circle?"

Least Weasel! we cheer. In she goes.

"And the hasher we're naming tonight?"

Hans Yolo shoves me in. There's no fire, no sacred boulders to write on, no scent of the sea, either, just a roomful of sweaty, drunk people in the harsh light from the overhead fixture. But in the warmth of their embrace, I feel invulnerable.

"As a sign of respect for this space, and our elders," Thor continues, "we need a pants off, dance off!"

Least Weasel locks eyes with me and sways to their chanting—*Pants, off! Dance, off!*—moving faster and faster, daring me to keep up as she peels her costume and throws it piece by piece at me. They're joined in flight by many shirts and shorts and hats and socks and underthings of all variety in a maelstrom of solidarity. We're chanting, dancing, cheering, drinking, the naked frenzy of a community with fewer and fewer secrets between us.

* * * * *

Friday, May 1ˢᵗ
Old Port

James Schmidt, Jr.

I followed them for four hours, through probably thirty bucks worth of tolls, all the way to this new-looking hotel at the edge of the bar district in Portland, Maine. My wife got out of Grace's car beneath the portico. Grace parked behind the hotel, then followed her into the lobby.

I let ten minutes pass before parking in the rear of the lot. I have no bags, just a folder with forms for Jamie to sign—to cut him out of the estate entirely, or scare him into coming back home. I'm honestly not sure which I'd prefer. I've spent my life protecting something grand for my sons, and if they don't appreciate that—appreciate their grandfather's sacrifices, our family's history, and my charity—then they can lie down with the animals of their own kind.

"My wife just checked in," I told the night manager, giving Carol's name and a description to boost my credibility. "I presume she has my room key?"

"She does, sir."

"Very good. Did she get the room across the hall for our son? She was supposed to."

"No sir."

I rent that room for myself, the ruse working beautifully, and take the elevator up. Her door is closed. Through it I can hear them murmuring. I duck into my room and pull a heavy chair up near the door, propping it ever so slightly open so I can hear if they slip out. My son is somewhere in this town, and if Carol won't tell me where, she can damn well show me.

Chapter 29

Friday, May 1st
Munjoy Hill

Jamie Schmidt

"Before we get to your questions," Thor announces, "I have a little background on this wanker." He wraps a sweaty arm on my shoulders. For all the clothing in this room, not a stich is on anyone.

"When I first met Just Jamie," Thor continues, "I thought he was another of Diddle Acquittal's internet dates." The circle laughs good-naturedly. "But he stuck around, God knows why, and wound up fighting shoulder to shoulder at the Mime Hash bar brawl. He's the instigator, if not the organizer, of our protest tomorrow, and he's bringing Seventh Heaven and her army of artists along for the fight! But most of all…he helped brew tonight's beer!"

One of us!, they cheer, *Just Jamie!*, sending my spirits through the roof. It was a strange road that brought me from sleeping beneath a canoe to standing in the center of these sweaty, naked people chanting my name.

"He's true blue," Thor says, "and the man's got a set of balls on him!"

"True Blue Balls!" Poly-Glamorous yells, which Hans Yolo writes on the wall in chalk. Through the same wall comes a terrible thumping noise, slow and steady and drawing near. Has Seasquatch found us?

"What in the hell's going on?" bellows a voice I don't recognize. Even through the heavy front door the fury is terrifying.

"Everybody out!" Thor yells. We scoop great handfuls of clothing, legs piercing whatever underwear is handy. Mr. Giggles slips into the bathroom, probably to top off his beer for the road. Amid a stream of profanity the front door bursts open. The guy on the other side, in dirty jeans and a work shirt, is in no frame of mind to appreciate the moment's delicious absurdity.

"Who let you people in here?" he screams, stomping. It's no moment for stupid heroics, which doesn't stop Benzo from handing the guy a beer. He throws it in Benzo's face, and takes a half-hearted swing at him.

"Out!" Benzo yells, slipping a second punch and leading our retreat.

"We're really sorry," I say, getting the guy's attention so more of us can escape. From the corner of my eye I see Cummy Bear, wearing the bottom half of her bear costume, frantically throwing empty cups into a trash bag. "Just give us a minute, and you'll never see us again."

"Who the hell are you?" the guy yells.

I haplessly point to True Blue Balls written on the wall, and as he's distracted, run past him.

Poly-Glamorous stops on the stairs. We nearly collide.

"The beer!" she says.

"Screw the beer!" Benzo yells, pulling her down the stairs toward safety. "We'll make more!"

I follow them to the parking lot where we trade whatever spare clothing we grabbed, and count our members.

"Six of us went uphill," Benzo says.

There are twelve of us here now, talking about meeting up at Sea Ration's apartment, and more on the stairs coming down—the rear brought up by Cummy Bear, who wriggles into the rest of her bear costume near Giggles' stolen bike.

"I think I picked it all up," she says.

From behind her come the enraged sounds of the guy stomping into the hallway, probably looking for anyone hiding away.

"But where's Giggles?"

"He's not with you?" Benzo says.

I dart past them, back to the stairs, in time to see Mr. Giggles march to the landing with an arm twisted behind his back. The guy trips my friend and pushes him down the stairs. I catch him halfway down, and glower up at his attacker, who screams at me as I drag Giggles outside.

"What were you doing?" I ask him.

"Making sure everyone was out. Why are you still here?"

"Same," I say. "Let's get you on your bike."

I give him the last pair of running shorts between us, hot pink ones a little too small, and set him up on his bike.

"They're all going to Sea Ration's," I say.

"Not me," he says. "I'm going back along trail, in case of stragglers."

"They'll miss you," I say.

"No they won't." His look allows no argument as he pedals alone into the darkness.

Far down the street Thor yells the hash's closing words, "May the hash go in peace!"

I yell the response, "May the hash get a piece!" and flee downhill toward Kate's apartment.

* * * * *

Friday, May 1st
Eastern Promenade

Kate Dorsett

Someone left true trail arrows at each of the checks, so I

know which way to go. I want to believe it was Jamie, because I want to believe he's thinking about me and hoping I'll come for him. There are places I'm needed more, but nowhere I'd rather be tonight than with him in the communion of the hash.

I just have to catch up to them first.

The trail leads me around the east end of our peninsula, right along the water on a moon-lit jogging path, up a steep, grassy hillside with the velvet-black panorama of Casco Bay behind me, through the trees, and along a series of quiet streets. In all I pass three drink checks, each with a clear plastic bag filled with empty cups and bottles with their familiar labels, ready to be picked up later. Most hash trails have only one drink check, but on the eve of battle, this isn't most trails.

Distant sirens draw nearer. Blue flashing lights play off houses around me. Then they roar down this sleepy street, all out of place—this is not a three-squad-car, four-squad-car, five-squad-car kind of neighborhood.

In my hometown, sirens are so rare you'd ask your neighbors if they'd heard what happened. Even if they didn't know, they at least remembered the siren.

In the city they're too common to bother over. Still, I begin to worry when the sixth squad car speeds past and turns right where the others turned, because they seem to be following the trail I'm on.

I pick up my pace, running, sprinting, to see if we're headed for the same destination. My trail veers off the sidewalk, through a community garden, safely into a stand of trees. The sirens go cold somewhere ahead of me. The trail spits out in the courtyard of some tacky condos, where once there was probably a pretty good view.

I follow trail through the hillside neighborhood, then there they are: the blue lights, flashing across the homes up ahead. The trail arrows at my feet point right at their cordon, their spotlights trained on a pale blue building swarming with cops.

I stare into the shadows at the edges of their light, looking for a huddle of my friends in handcuffs—looking for Jamie—but I don't see anyone. I want to march right up to the cordon and ask what's going on. I'm just an innocent jogger, after all, wondering if there's anything I should worry about going bump in the night.

The police stand around idly, puffed up with body armor beneath their uniforms, struggling to show interest in whatever they hurried up to wait for.

Maybe this has nothing to do with the hash.

Maybe my friends got away.

The last true trail arrow is definitely Jamie's work.

* * * * *

Friday, May 1ˢᵗ
Sheridan Street

Evan

I stashed the bicycle in the shadows of a tiny side yard and crouched in the hollow between two bushes, backing all the way up against a house until the bushes swallowed me and I felt safe—from the cops and from the world. If I could stretch the moment, I'd curl up inside of it and sleep forever.

Then Seventh Heaven appeared, staring down the street. Blue lights flashed across her face. She stood right on the last check, right where Jamie drew a true trail arrow for anyone following behind the pack.

Of course…

"Kate!"

She jumped.

"It's me!"

"Mr. Giggles?"

"Quick, crawl in here before they see you!"

"No way," she said, backing off.

So I crawled out of the bushes, fetched my bike, and hurried her back along the trail and farther from the cops.

"Why are you bloody? And why are you wearing Carrie's shorts?"

"It's the mystery of the hash."

"Giggles! Is Carrie okay?"

"Yeah, she got out," I said. "Everyone got out."

Even in the blue light, her face looked pale.

"Out of what!?"

"Let's get out of *here*," I said. "I'll explain on the way..."

We withdrew along the street, past the condos, into the trees. She stood right where our councilman did when he accosted us, and demanded to know what happened to Jamie—did he "get out," and if so, of what?

"Jamie is fine," I told her. He didn't get roughed up or thrown down a flight of stairs."

I wish she'd been as concerned about me. I dodged her questions a moment and rubbed my swollen face. She daubed at the blood on my lip—pityingly. Not lovingly. Still, it was tender, so I closed my eyes and tried to kiss her.

She slapped me, opening the cut again. She let it bleed.

"Where's Jamie?"

"I really don't know, but I'm sure he's fine."

She didn't look convinced.

"Let's get out of here," I said. "Standpipe Park has a better view."

"Of what?"

"Of the city." So I push my bicycle along the path, leading her to the park.

"I feel pretty woozy. I might have a concussion. I don't want the cops finding me at all, but especially, like this."

I look back at her, and she at me, like she's trying to

decide between duty and love. Maybe she just doesn't want to be alone with me.

"Are you going to be okay?" she asks.

"I don't know."

"Fine," she says. "I'm not the kind of person to leave someone battered and alone, but you're *not* going to make any more passes at me, got it? And you're going to tell me *everything*."

What happens at the hash, stays at the hash, but of course, there are exceptions. It's not gossip if it's news, so I tell her all the lurid details about Jamie. Maybe I gloss over a few of the heroic ones. Maybe I make a few things up. But the way I feel is its own kind of truth.

* * * * *

Night
Old Port

James Schmidt, Jr.

I stood on the bridge again, staring at the statue of my father, his eyes staring back at me as cold in bronze as ever in life. I tried to ask him these questions I carry, but the words didn't come. I'm afraid of his answers. I'm afraid, too, that its lifeless silence might prove my father is truly gone and I will never know if I'm honoring him right.

Then some drunken hollering woke me up, and the dream dissolved into vapors. I'm sitting in a lumpy, scratchy chair by a heavy door propped slightly open to a hallway. The voice is indistinct, but sounds like my son's—the women's voices joining it, like harlots stealing him away. If my boy knocks someone up in this town, so help me...

They pass my door and I see them, the man wearing a shirt with an orange flame design, walking with two women who don't know what size shirts to wear. They stop a few doors down so one of them can dry-heave before fumbling loudly through a door and letting it slam.

What the hell kind of town is this? What kind of people are these? They're my son's age, but this shameful public image, this stunning lack of self-control…

Don't tell me Jamie left to keep this kind of company.

Grace would never stay out all hours of the night, tramping around with God-knows-who. Our bars aren't even open past ten, anyway! This city has too many distractions from honest, noble work.

Maybe I'll let him get a look at her first. See if she can lead him home, and end this whole debacle. She's employed, stable, financially independent…she has no aspirations beyond our hometown that would lead him astray. What more does the boy need to settle down with?

Clearly there's something wrong with him. Maybe I gave him too much freedom. What if he got his fill before she could set the hook? Is this the thanks I get for being lenient?

Tomorrow we'll see what he chooses—fulfillment, or self-destruction—and whether I let him come groveling back at all.

Chapter 30

Friday, May 1ˢᵗ
Standpipe Park

Kate Dorsett

"So it was a textbook clusterfuck," Evan concludes as I rest on a bench overlooking the blue flashing lights at the foot of the skyline. "But you know how Hashers are. We don't just flirt with danger, we propose to it on the first date."

From his first words, I knew what was coming. The energy's been building, and of course it couldn't wait for the morning for my friends to get carried away—not with a night like this. I should have been with Jamie, in that circle with him singing our songs and sharing the feeling of unstoppable momentum.

"...I mean, out of all the people I've ever met," Evan says, "there should have been at least *one* so far, right?"

"I'm sorry?"

He sighs and shakes his head at me.

"You haven't heard a word I've said."

I shrug apologetically.

"As I was saying, if there's one person for everyone out there, one soul mate or whatever, what about all the other people you could be attracted to? There's gotta be a second tier, right? People you could live happily ever after with anyway? And a third tier that's not too bad a match, each tier with more and more people in it, all the way down—like a pyramid—to a base of millions of people you'd never even get along with. I get it, finding that one person in seven billion is a moonshot, but can't I find *someone?* It's not like I have standards anymore."

"Are we still talking about the hash?"

"Yes, Kate," he says, "and how everyone ran off with someone, except me."

"Who'd Jamie run off with?"

"Well, no one, I guess. He's probably out looking for you."

"Then I really should be—"

"Please?"

I don't want to leave him alone with this kind of naked, dangerous hurt, but I also wish I had a can of mace. I've suffered his self-indulgent diatribes before, but something about tonight is different. I want to help; I want to shrug and run away; I want to get out of here without it getting even more awkward.

"You have two minutes," I say. "Then I'm out of here."

I glance at my phone to check the time, and see if anyone from the hash has gotten back to me. No word yet.

"You've known me over a decade," he says. "Do you think I've peaked?"

"That's absurd."

"It's what my software tells me, and I believe it. It says it's all downhill from here, and I'm nowhere near where I wanted to start that slide."

"Things change too much for there to be just one peak," I say, the words coming as quickly as the ideas. "Maybe, the peak of a job, or a peak to your twenties, your thirties, but how can they be related? We change too much. There's not just one peak, Evan. It's a whole mountain range."

He turns his back on me to stare at the city lights.

"I've loved you since college," he says over his shoulder.

"I know."

When he turns around his eyes are utterly lifeless.

"You've never been what I needed you to be."

"That's not on me, Evan."

"You're right. But no one else has, either. I've been on one date with every woman in this town. Rarely a second. Never a third. I just want to be loved!"

"Some people can be alright without a partner. There's more to life than love, I guess."

"Like what?"

"Like…friends? Meaningful work?"

"I've become the creepy guy who's been hanging around too long, Kate. I know that's how they see me. And at work, I can't get promoted, because my biggest success was showing them how to keep me right where I am. Did you know, I don't even dream anymore? What's left to hope for?"

"Maybe you've outgrown Portland? What's that saying, 'Change your latitude, change your attitude?'"

"I know what the problem is," he says. "It's me."

"No shit, Evan. We're the root of all our own problems."

"But now I understand just *how* I'm my own problem. That's what I brought you here to say—that now I understand the central tragedy of my life. And I've made peace with it."

I'd like to see the peace of Buddha in his eyes. I'd like to see the detachment of Zen. Instead, I see nothing.

"That's really good," I say. "Everyone should be able to accept themselves as they are, right?"

"That's not what I said."

"You're creeping me out right now. Stop."

He looms over me, dominating the skyline.

"I have so much love to give, but no one wants it. Because this isn't the face you dream about. It isn't the face you want to see when you close your eyes. Not you, not anyone."

I stand up in the narrow space between us.

"You're freaking me out, so I'm leaving now."

"Fine."

He backs away, turning his hands over to show his empty palms.

"I'm not keeping you. I just wanted you to know that I finally get it."

"It's not your face, Giggles. You're desperate, you're angry, you're creepy—*that's* what drives people away."

"I know," he says flatly. "And it's killing me."

* * * * *

Midnight
The Titanic

I left Evan alone at the bluff's edge. Once I was safely away, I doubled back on a side street and crept through the shadows to see if he was following me. He wasn't.

He was riding that bicycle around the park in a great, swerving loop, aiming for the long sidewalk that leads straight to the bluff's edge. He straightened out and aimed for the space between the benches and pedaled for it, so fast I thought he might shoot over the edge and take flight—up, up, into the night sky until he merged with the panorama, a part of Portland forever.

At the last moment he leaned hard to the left and rode away, along the edge. I lost sight of him, but confident he wasn't coming after me, I ran downhill to the Titanic to find Jamie.

"Haven't seen him," Sherman said. He was moving a giant, profane banner from the kitchen floor to the Initiative Sapping Apparatus. I helped him drape it over Speedwanker, who was fast asleep and motionless. "Most of them went to Sea Ration's place. God knows what all they're up to."

"I'll just wait for him upstairs," I said.

Sherman's eyebrows raised. Carrie left the room.

"Is that a problem?"

"No, no," he said. "Go for it."

Climbing into the attic was thrilling. What a surprise for Jamie that I'm here after all! I'll get my signs in the morning. Tonight, though, can still be for us.

So I wait in the silence, in the light of a single lamp, alone.

Chapter 31

Vacant Apartment
Midnight

Dan Grant

"We've got 'em now, Councilman," the chief growled. His officers stared at me in the harsh light of the single fixture in the completely empty room.

"Got who?"

"Buffone! Bring 'em out!"

From the bathroom came the clanging sound of hollow metal knocking into walls, porcelain, a door, like a raccoon floundering in a recycling bin. Then out came Officer Buffone, dragging two skinny kegs and a lumpy trash bag. He propped up the kegs for my inspection and poured a sample brew into a clean-looking cup for me. I drank it, and was surprised to like it. Then he dumped the bag out on the floor for inspection.

"Dammit, Buffone!" the chief snapped. The floor was clean, but for the new pile of beer-soaked cups and bottles. He held the bag over it, dripping, while the guy who owns the place lost his mind. The other officers escorted the guy out.

"This is it for three sixty nine Hampshire Street," the chief continued, pointing to the labels on the kegs and bottles alike: Hampshire Street Brewing Company, with a dead-on drawing of that house by Gispert's. "Unlicensed commercial
276

brewing and distribution, and if any of 'em were here tonight, they're in for criminal mischief and felony breaking and entering."

"Who exactly was here?" I asked. My voice was softer than I'd like it to be.

"We have our theories. There were over twenty of 'em."

"Dressed like lumberjacks and hunters? One of them in a bear costume?"

"That's what the owner said."

I walked silently around the room. The officers stood at attention, waiting for their boss, or me, to speak. The room was immaculate, aside from Buffone's pile of trash and some fresh graffiti on the walls.

It read, *True Blue Balls.*

I stared at it, muttered the words, and couldn't make sense of it. Then I ran my fingers over it, and wiped one of the letters easily away.

Chalk—harmless, easily cleaned chalk.

"Did they steal all the furniture too?"

"No, Councilman. It's an unoccupied unit."

I walked to the front door and tested the handle. It worked fine, and the frame was undamaged.

"This doesn't look broken."

"That's not a requirement for breaking and entering."

I walked through the rest of the apartment, and there were no further signs of the supposed wild debauch at all. I can't fathom how they had the time or presence of mind to even bag their trash, unless they wanted that badly to remove the evidence.

Or were just cleaning up.

"Is this just young people being stupid, or some kind of cult?"

"We think it's a running group."

"What kind of running group throws keg parties?"

"They call themselves the Hash House Harriers. They're

loud, obnoxious, and there's a lot of 'em. Previously, we thought they were harmless."

So this is the future of America—brash young people who enter without breaking. Chaotic enemies of peace and order who pick up after themselves. Crude, drunk, and pugnacious, but not without ethos. They've made some damned fine points about getting along together in a city they love as much as I do.

Any other time, I'd find that admirable. Maybe even useful.

"I don't see anything vandalized," I said. "I don't see anything broken. Your man made a bigger mess than they left. What damage has been done here?"

Chief Boyer stared at me before dismissing his men to the hallway.

"The law was broken here, Councilman. That's good enough for me. And they're running an unlicensed brewery. Don't tell me you're alright with bootleggers."

"Nothing of the sort."

"You told me to come down hard on Hampshire Street. You sent me that disorderly house form. You stood my men down while a building burned! We've got these hooligans by the balls. That neighborhood is gonna clear out once they're gone. Isn't that you want? Isn't that why you've been on my ass? Don't lose your courage now, councilman! It's almost over."

"Courage is not the issue."

"Their brewery is right across from your stage tomorrow. As the culmination of your rally, it would be a privilege to raid it and perp-walk them right past the media. I believe that's what the mayor, and Naylor, and all of City Hall wants, is it not?"

"Something like that."

"I can have a bench warrant by breakfast. We'll shut that place down on live television. Maybe then you'd do me the honor of getting off my ass."

"Get your warrant," I said. "Gather your men. And wait for my word."

* * * * *

Kate's Apartment
12:30am

Jamie Schmidt

I ran all the way to the alley behind her apartment, pulled myself up onto the fire escape, and climbed to the roof by her kitchen. The lights of Congress Street spread through her bedroom window at the far end, pooling on the posters drying on the living room floor, but there was no sign she was home. I knocked on the glass—no response—jimmied the window open, and stepped inside.

"Kate?" I whispered. The darkness felt too peaceful to yell. I flipped the lights on and winced at the brightness. Signs and banners were drying everywhere, ready to be deployed in the morning.

I made my way to her bedroom, calling a few more times just in case she was asleep. No answer. On the edge of her coffee table, surrounded by banners, sat a cold mug of tea, half empty, and an uneaten slice of fruit. When her friends locked the door behind themselves, they must have expected her back soon.

I wonder if she's with someone else tonight. Of course not. She barely has time for me!

It's been a strange week. It's been a stranger night. Our relationship is peculiar, but it brings out some of the better parts of me. She's driven, confident, serious, in ways I admire. There's a time in life to be peaceful, but I'm not there yet. Growth doesn't happen when you're comfortable.

I'm glad she makes me uncomfortable—mostly.

Still, I wish she'd ease up a little, and make more space for me in her life.

I put my shoes by the door so she'll know I'm here if I fall asleep, and leave a lamp on—I'm here unexpectedly. I don't want to scare her.

Her pillow smells like her hair as I lie down on top of the sheets, fully clothed, to stare at the ceiling and wait.

* * * * *

Jamie's Apartment
12:35 am

Kate Dorsett

My mind wanders as I wait for Jamie, lying on top of his sheets fully clothed in the lamp light. I don't want to send the wrong message; I don't want to scare him, either, when he finds someone unexpectedly in his room. What am I even doing here? I should be home, organizing the signs, planning for tomorrow—what if Brigitte *doesn't* make an ass of herself? What if she gets applause? What if that emboldens her and she expands her campaign and…

But worry without action is useless, and it's the middle of the night. Brilliant thoughts and strategies aren't coming; just the fears. So I lie here, staring at the true trail arrow painted on the ceiling, smelling Jamie on his pillow, my mind wandering back time and again to him.

If only he was a little more settled, a little more serious; a little more invested, maybe. It's like he fell from the sky, fully formed, with no past and no certain future. He lives so haphazardly. I live so intentionally. Tomorrow, I'll see two of my communities come together in the streets. I have a plan. I have people. What'll keep Jamie here, if things get rough?

I don't want to trust someone who might leave as easily as he showed up.

Somehow, though, he makes things work. A job, an apartment, a place among our friends… How strange, that the same world that rewards the planners and organizers doesn't punish that reckless fool.

My reckless fool.

I want to curl beside him, shut out the world, and lose myself in the feeling that everything is alright. I don't feel that way alone, not even in his bed. I remind myself that I'm a strong, independent woman, but wonder if I'm confident enough to make a place for someone else in my life. To trust someone with their own needs, to help me with mine.

When he swings that hatch open, if he's alone, I might cry. It would be easier if he isn't.

So I toss, I turn, and I wait.

* * * * *

Kate's Apartment
12:45am

Jamie Schmidt

I wish she'd get home soon, so I can kiss her and whisper these things and hope she doesn't hear the words, just feels the meaning and melts into my arms…but it's later by the minute and I'm growing self-conscious about breaking into her apartment. She showed me how, I've spent the night here before, but still—I'm waiting in her bed, unannounced. This is certainly over some uncertain line and won't look as sweet as it seemed, back when it was just a silly idea. Maybe there's time for everything in a relationship, but we're not yet at the breaking-and-entering stage.

I pull the covers tight behind me, refolding the corners as

281

she'd had them, taking one last, indulgent smell of her pillow. I slip on my shoes, turn off the lights, and lock up.

I'm just as lonely in the stairwell, but feel better about being on this side of the door. She'd never break into my place; she's not romantic that way.

So I'll find another time to whisper these silly thoughts, tell her these crazy things about how she drives me nuts while she turns me on. I imagine catching her eye at the protest. She smiles. I nod. I lead my housemates and all the hashers in a chant. She leads her artists in one, too. Our voices unite, drowning out the councilman, driving him from the podium. We march on the stage, seizing him by his wrists and ankles and carrying him past Gispert's, past the oyster bar, past the construction sites to the end of the Maine State Pier where we throw him into the water. The police can't stop us all, so they stand by, watching, surrendering the street to those who belong here—those chanting *Save our homes!*

Maybe we'll win tomorrow; maybe, I'll be homeless again. So long as I have my friends, I'll be alright. So long as I have Kate, I'll even be happy.

* * * * *

Jamie's Apartment
12:47am

Kate Dorsett

But what'll I say before we get to the sweet romantic part? Like, the moment he comes through that hatch—preferably alone—and sees me here, in his bed without an invitation? He's not crazy enough to break into my place, yet...here I am.

Clearly crazy.

I breathe one last time the smell of his pillow, and make

his bed so he won't notice anything wrong. I'm folding the sheet corners down when I catch myself—this is his bed, after all. I rip the sheets off and throw them back on, crowning the mess with his pillow.

"Yeah, he'll never know," I mutter, picking my way through the attic to the fire escape. I hope his housemates are asleep when he comes back; I hope they don't notice me sneaking out, so when they say I was here they can't say for how long.

I'll see him in the morning. I'll bring the "Wartime" sign and hand it out, and save for Jamie the matching ones I made for us. I imagine handing one to him on the Titanic's stoop, my artist army behind me, chanting; a house full of hashers behind him, waving banners. I imagine kissing him, feeling his hand on my hips. Pushing him gently away, a little *not right now* in my smile. We lead a chant, *We belong here!* that blows Brigitte's hair back. It drives her and that councilman from the stage. We pursue them, chanting, through the streets, our voices united, until we've driven them through the Old Port and into the sea.

Then I catch Jamie's eye again, and this time, when he wraps his arm around me, I lean into him instead of pulling away.

Chapter 32

Old Port
12:58am

Jamie Schmidt

The farther down her stairs I went, the guiltier I felt, wondering how I'd explain being in her apartment, or even in the stairwell. So I took the stairs faster and faster, two at a time, until I burst onto the sidewalk and took off at a dead run under the streetlights. I turned down the next block, settling into a jog past darkened doorways that brought back the feeling of being shut out. Should we lose our home, where would we go, and what might be lost forever? I ran as much to outrun my anxiety, as to get home.

There was a group of men in tight shirts and nautical-print shorts outside a gay bar in the Old Port, smoking and talking. A car slowed near them. A window rolled down. Then someone inside shouted, *Fags!*

I shook my head. The car had out of state plates—just strangers, being jerks and leaving again. Lack of accountability can bring out the worst in people.

Then the window rolled down farther, and the voice yelled again, *Hey, faggots!* A cigarette butt flew from it, the cherry glowing as it arced toward the group of men.

Aw, hell no. I quickened my pace. Suddenly that car was everything wrong with the world—cruelty, malice, unprovoked shots at people who can't fight back in time...

The car drove off, trailing the sound of laughter. With the other traffic and the drunks lurching through the streets, though, it couldn't get away very fast.

I caught up. Something came over me.

"Get the fuck outta my city!" I screamed.

They were stunned into silence, then rolled up the windows and mocked me from relative safety. I ran alongside, beating on the glass until it broke, screaming at them about having no respect for the locals, no respect for the ways of life here, and embodying everything wrong with the world... as if I had been wronged personally. From the depths of my being I hated them, and everyone who smears the worst of themselves through someone else's home.

So I was stressed. And it got the better of me. And window glass isn't as strong as I thought.

I stared at them through their broken window with satisfaction. But the sound attracted three policeman on foot patrol. They lit out after me.

"Get him!" the riders yelled, spilling onto the sidewalk once they saw the cops giving chase. I glanced over my shoulder, watching them fall farther and farther behind, winded, stumbling, weak, while the police kept up.

I made it to a parking garage. At the back was a low wall separating the deck from an alley.

Looking back again I saw them, three officers yelling *Stop!* and fanning out to block my escape, one of them coming straight for me. Without slowing I planted my hands on the low wall and vaulted over.

And fell for a very long time.

* * * * *

Munjoy Hill
1:00 am

Dan Grant

I ask for my check in the wannabe Irish pub this place became in the last few months. Finnegan's? Flannigan's? Hannagan's? What's it matter? It used to be a cash-only, beer-only dive the young people liked. I shook a lot of hands here before elections, but never cared for it much. The rent went up, the young people went away, and now we've got this place, trying to look like it's been here forever. Tonight, I just need a place to think awhile, safe from hooligans storming the trails, safe from the drunks wandering the streets, somewhere among the people—*my* people.

But none of my neighbors are in here, and the couple at the bar have accents from far away, as if they're just passing through. Without the locals, this place will turn over again. I can learn the newest name then.

Behind the bar they built a bookshelf around the bottles, I guess to give it some kind of old-world feel. It tries too hard, and the lighting is wrong.

"Could you pass me that collection of Longfellow," I ask as I give the bartender my credit card. "I need his words to steady my nerves."

"That?" He rudely jerks his thumb. "Can't help you, buddy."

"Why not? It's just right there!"

"That's not a real book. Dad wanted a fancy bookshelf without blowing out the bar space, so he got all these old books and cut 'em down on his table saw. We glued the spines together." He grabs a spine at random and shakes it, the whole row quivering.

"That's an insult to Longfellow! He was born in this town! He grew up on Congress Street!"

"You an English professor, old man?"

"I'm your city councilman! Don't you know anything?"

"I just moved here. Here's your check though, mayor."

"Councilman!"

"Whatever."

I leave a lousy tip and hurry outside to be more comfortably alone with my uncomfortable thoughts. So this is the future of too-rapid growth—erasure, rather than evolution, with no respect for the past. All façade, and airs of desperate aspiration. This is Naylor's legacy.

Mine too, if I keep working with him.

Wandering the streets, I look at the darkened windows of the homes around me. Behind them are people who give a damn, or would, anyway, if they knew the stakes—pay up, or get out, the question is only a matter of time. Any future worth having should be for the people who live it, not the whims of those who write the checks. Character is built, not bought, and history is earned.

I'd need an army to stop him now. I'd need boots on the ground, and fists in the air. Lawyers. Community organizers. A campaign to stir their blood, with charismatic figures to spread the message—save your community! Save your homes!

But where in Portland could I raise an army at one in the morning?

* * * * *

Old Port
1:01 am

Jamie Schmidt

The pavement broke my fall, but thankfully, not my legs. I roll onto my back and stare up at a bright light I know isn't death, but rather, an officer's flashlight. He's high above, leaning over the edge of the parking garage. The other officers join him, but they're up there, and I'm down here, and in a moment I'm up on my feet again and making a painful escape. They disappear from the railing, their shouts receding down the garage's ramp.

I limp through a group of smokers outside a bar and lurch across Commercial Street, putting as many twists and turns between myself and my pursuers as possible. I can't outrun them now, so I need a place to get lost awhile. This wharf is inviting, with all its places to hide. There are stacks of yellow and green lobster traps, blue plastic barrels, piles of rope and towers of chum buckets. It smells awful. Maybe they won't look for me very long.

I come to a cyclone fence near the end of the wharf, and climb sideways around it, hanging for a moment over the water and then stepping onto the narrow walkway beyond. Through the fence I see their flashlights—shining through the lobster traps, looking behind the barrels, washing over the chum buckets. They'll climb around the fence as easily as I did, and suddenly, I realize how foolish it is to hide somewhere surrounded on three sides by cold, dark water.

The opposite shore is too far to swim like this. Could I fight them? That would end poorly for me.

I take the plunge.

* * * * *

Evan's Apartment
1:05am

Evan

Everything is laid out on my kitchen table: a list of my accounts and passwords, bank statements with the account numbers highlighted, the title for my car with a spare key weighing it down, checks made out for each month of rent left on my lease...all my affairs, in order. I don't know the details, but I know the general shape that tomorrow will take. Wrapping this up will be my family's job. I've made it easy for them, because in my heart, I bear them no malice. My problems are mine. They've done what they could.

I've taken down my diplomas, too, and made a little stack of them off to the side. All together, these are the accomplishments I've spent my life chasing. They amount to so much ink on paper—paper on a tabletop. How can years of struggle, hope, fear, and ambition, come only to this? The empty second bedroom, the absence of a woman's things in mine, these things ache more deeply than words can soothe, or reason can reach.

The difference between my dreams and this reality is absurd and haunting. I set down my front door key, right on the copy of my lease, and back away, as if from everything on the table. That's me, in papers. Here I am, in flesh. A few things to leave, and one person, going.

I'm free. Those things on the table don't hold me anymore. There's nothing left to work for, and no future left to fear. No reason for anything but a final night's sleep.

I wonder if tonight, I'll dream.

* * * * *

Old Port
1:06am

Jamie Schmidt

The shouts draw nearer behind me. Ahead, I see only water and a sailboat with no running lights, its sail furled, yet underway slowly. There's a man at the rail with a paddle. He stands, silhouetted against the moon-shimmer.

"Seasquatch!"

"Never heard of him!"

The water is freezing but soon I'm astern, pulling myself up the boat's boarding ladder. Seasquatch looms over me, holding the paddle like a club.

"Jamie? What the hell are you doing here?"

"Hiding from the cops." I roll over the gunwale and drop out of sight. "I figured you'd understand."

"All too well."

Flashlights make him wince, and set the fringe of his hair aglow.

"You see a guy in the water?" a cop yells from the wharf.

Seasquatch grabs his crotch and thrusts.

"Unnnggghh!"

The light follows him away from me. He settles into a rhythm, paddling first on one side of the cabin and then the other to keep us more or less going straight. Before sweeping elsewhere, the light shows a hopeful little trolling motor clamped to the rail. I wonder how far he's come tonight.

"The question remains," he says later, keeping his voice low so it won't carry across the water, "what are you doing out here?"

"I was teaching some assholes some manners, when their car window broke…right under my fist."

He looks down at me, soaking wet and shivering.

"You sure showed them, huh?"

"Yeah, it could have gone better…"

I wring out my shirt and pants and hang them to dry. He gives me his pelts to ward off the chill. The derringer feels heavy inside them.

"I thought you were leaving Portland," I say. "But you're paddling us back toward it."

He squares his shoulders and cocks his head like an actor.

"Because my work here isn't done!"

Then he slumps over the rail to paddle some more.

"Let me do that awhile." He reluctantly hands me the paddle and slips below deck, returning with a bottle of whisky. I decline a taste. He shrugs and tips it back.

"You know, I've only wanted to live in peace," he says. "To be left alone. Truly free."

"Radically free," I add.

"Hell yeah! But this place won't let me go. Case in point—here we are. I was supposed to be hiding in the islands by now. Living off the fat of the weekenders! Not sneaking back in the middle of the night."

"There's still hope," I say. "I came here in the middle of the night, too, and that's worked out okay."

"I don't know why I can't get away, though—*actually* away. It makes me fightin' mad."

"I know how I got away—it was an escape from a life I didn't want. I didn't know what I could make somewhere else, so I ran away to find out."

"Sounds reasonable," he says.

"I think you have the opposite problem. Trying to be completely free of everyone, and everything, you haven't made anything meaningful enough to leave. Or much to stay for, either. So you're stuck in some kind of limbo."

"Yeah, well tomorrow's going to be different," he says, taking the paddle back. "Look below deck."

In the moonlight I see cardboard boxes packed tightly together.

"I raided the party barge," he brags. "We need their liquor more than they do."

"'We?' I just got here."

"For saving you from the cops, you're gonna help me haul that hooch to the new Sherwood Forest. There's an army of hobos to liquor up. We attack at dawn!"

"I thought you were trying to lay low…"

"I was *trying* to get out of here, but my sail ripped and

the tides pushed me back. I was *trying* to live in peace, but they destroyed Sherwood Forest beside me. I've *tried* to make a life here. Even the hash is cold to me, and they accept *everybody*. I'm done trying. This town is full of greedy assholes and malicious self-interest. It won't leave me alone, but it won't let me go, so I'll fight my way out with an army of liquored up hobos and teach this place some goddamned respect."

"Well, your army sounds more interesting than mine."

"Than yours?"

I tell him about our plans to protest Grant's rally, and about Kate's battalion of artists. He listens keenly, especially about the cops pressuring the Titanic, and laughs at Sherman's plan to goad them into burning it down.

"Move your stuff out tonight," he says, "and let him do it!"

"No! I've finally found a place where I belong. Why does everyone want to burn it down?"

"Well…"

"Look, if our house goes, the whole neighborhood goes, and there'll be no getting it back. The assholes running us out will get more powerful, and the people just trying to get by will get fucked again. We've got something cool at the Titanic—a real community. In one of the last places it can exist in this city. That's worth protecting."

"Look at you giving a shit, after what, a month?"

"I'd just rather build things up, than tear them down. It's in my blood."

"Still, let Sherman do it. The last power we have left, is over our own destruction."

I laugh. He stares.

"That's exactly what Sherman said. Man, you two would get along great."

"He hates me."

"Why?"

"Everyone does."

"So, give 'em a reason to respect you."

"Oh, I will. By sunset tomorrow Portland will be in flames, with my hobo army looting the gift shops and frog-marching rich people into the sea. We'll make new homes in their condos. We'll burn their hotels, take the waterfront back for the working man, and make the streets safe again for freaks and weirdos. The last cop in Portland will look to the clock tower over what once was City Hall, where he'll see me with my gun in one hand and a beer in the other, and with his dying breath he'll curse the name Seasquatch."

"That's certainly ambitious."

"Got any better ideas?"

"No, that's fine," I say. "It's just what we expect, actually. Might as well live up to your image, right?"

"Right..."

"Of course the guy who avenged Hash Henge with a bulldozer would muster a hobo army to sack the Old Port. That's the guy who lives out our revenge fantasies...but that's not the kind of guy we really want to hang out with. But by all means, burn City Hall to the ground, it'd buy us some time. And you've got precedent—Portland's been burned by plenty of people who've since been lost to history."

"You are a thief of joy."

"I just wonder if you're brave enough *without* a liquored-up hobo army. Just you, *making* a place for yourself, by standing up for something you believe in—peacefully. That's all."

He glowers at me.

"Dude, I respect you," I say. "You're honest in a way that's frankly terrifying, and instead of just complaining, you *act* on your values."

"Damn straight."

"We're both scared of not belonging, or having a place in the world, or having people who respect us...yet you keep

293

trying. You showed up at the Sacred and Profane, you're a hasher, you want to prove something tomorrow instead of just hitchhiking out of here. People would respect the hell out of that..."

I lift a tail from one of the creatures sewn into the pelt.

"...if they could just see past your image."

The tail falls with a thump.

"You don't need to hide the fact you care. And you don't need a hobo army, either, if you're brave enough to stand up for what you believe is right for everyone—peacefully."

"But I really want to sack the Old Port," he says. "I need to send a message, about pushing reasonable people unreasonably far."

"I can dig that. We're sending a similar message, but without using violence straightaway. I'm trying good old fashioned protest first...and I'd love your help."

"My hobos can lay waste to that guy's rally!"

"That's your choice, man. Keep being the old Seasquatch, with all the old problems...or not."

"Dude...I'm the Seasquatch."

"But who do you want to become?"

Chapter 33

Saturday, May 2nd
Hampshire Street
Morning

Sherman

The stage is dressed and ready across the street from my house. Flags neatly line each edge, leading with the Portland City Flag—*Resurgum* they say beneath the seal. Resurgence. Resurrection. Twice this city has burned to the ground, and twice it's rebuilt itself into something it could never have been without a brand new start. Those enemies of my people who will take that stage have the harder job of working with what's already here, fighting for every building, every street, as they replace our community with their vision of the future.

For my small part, I plan to have it easier—Portland's latest phoenix, rising from the ashes with a brewer's paddle in one hand and a six figure insurance check in the other.

"They've closed the streets, Sherman," Benzo tells me. "Looks like only about a half dozen cops, total."

"It's still early. Did you bring the last keg up?"

"The one labeled 'Rinse'? Yeah, it's in the kitchen. Jamie and Carrie are about done with the cider vinegar towels, and Cummy Bear is handing signs out by the front door."

"This may be the first time in hash history that a kennel is ready on time. Under other circumstances, this would be an embarrassment."

"Cut us some slack, we're not as hungover as we should be. The after party at Sea Ration's took a very different turn."

"Yeah? How's that?"

He smiles wolfishly.

"We shouldn't talk about Hash 207," he says, hustling away.

The living room bustles with hashers organizing signs and banners, eating junk food breakfasts and sneaking peeks outside. I want to get a better look at the police presence, and the spectators gathering on the street. So far, there's no sign of Kate. Walking through the kitchen I pull Jamie from his job mixing cider vinegar with paper towels in plastic bags that Carrie seals and stacks.

"Let's get a look at what we're up against," I say, leading him up the hatch into his attic apartment.

"What's the keg labeled 'Rinse' for?" he asks.

"That's pressurized water with campden tablets. We use them to sterilize kegs. It also washes off teargas pretty well. Similar to the cider vinegar wipes you're working on with Least Weasel."

"I saw the other kegs by the windows. You're really going to do it, aren't you?"

"I reserve the option, unless someone pulls off a miracle in the next few minutes."

We make our way through the maze of furniture and costumes and castoff brewing equipment to the fire escape, and climb outside. Over the low, flat roof of Gispert's I see a set of barricades manned by a single officer. Other cops stand idly along Hampshire Street, but nowhere near the number I'd hoped for. We can see the police station in the distance, across the Franklin Arterial, but there's no sign of a riot brigade mustering there, either. I hope they plan to bring an army, because mine is ready for them.

"Where's Kate?"

"I have no idea," Jamie says. "I haven't seen her since

yesterday afternoon."

"You mean last night…"

"No, I didn't get home until four. Alone."

"But she went up to your… You know what? I don't understand your relationship."

"I don't either, Sherman."

"She is coming today, right?"

He just smiles and points over to Congress Street a few blocks away. I see them a moment before I hear them: a battalion of artists in flamboyant clothing, waving signs, marching behind an enormous banner and chanting *Save our city!* They swarm through an intersection, shutting down traffic, cars honking in anger and support. It's all the same to me—rile them up! Get the police to notice, the Councilman to notice…send a message! We won't go down without a fight, and even when we lose, the anger will remain.

"Oh, shit," Jamie says, drawing my attention down the Franklin Arterial to the Old Port. There's a marching, shouting, angry mob down that way, too. The man out front is unmistakable.

"I didn't think he was going to do it," Jamie says. "I thought I talked him out of it!"

"What the hell is Seasquatch doing with a hobo army?"

"Coming to join us," Jamie says. "And he's marching them right past the police station."

"Perfect!"

"No!" Jamie runs down the fire escape, yelling *No, no, no!* He scrambles down the ladder, drops to the street and takes off running with a painful looking limp. I watch the shabbily-dressed hobos draw near, following Seasquatch, and wonder what's his problem. It's not like they're carrying Molotov cocktails or sacking the Old Port, though I wish they were. They're just carrying cardboard signs, following Seasquatch in a collared shirt and Carrie's yoga pants.

Hampshire Street Parking Garage
8:30am

Dan Grant

I don't spook easily, but I don't like the looks of this. From the top deck of this parking garage where I met Naylor and set this whole development in motion, I see my people gathering: retirees, investors, people in khakis and sandals—the kind of people who turn up on a Saturday morning for public speeches. They listen quietly and applaud politely at my rallies. They come to hear what they want to hear, and reward me with donations and votes. They don't realize yet that their donations will soon be replaced by Naylor's endless checks, and their interests, with ours.

This morning they're outnumbered, three to one at least, by the unwashed denizens of Hampshire Street. The unkempt masses loiter on sidewalks, sit on stoops, wander back and forth in groups of five and six, like there's nowhere else to be on a Saturday than here, menacing me with their existence. It's like they know they're screwed, and I haven't even said the first word about the Cathedral District yet.

Sometimes change smells like burning buildings and teargas. Was that what tipped them off?

Most unsettling is the stream of people in and out the front door of 369 Hampshire Street—young, vaguely athletic-looking people, who judging by their clothes and tattoos and haircuts, have never voted for my party in their lives. All up and down the street my constituents give them noticeable space.

A young man scampers down the fire escape of that rat trap, drops to the ground, and runs off in the direction of some commotion. There's a group approaching through the

Old Port, whom I can vaguely see in the distance. They're swarming, carrying signs, and heading right this way.

Great.

Between the tenements we plan to replace along Hampshire Street, I see *another* group marching, swarming, carrying signs and heading right for me. They don't move like my aging demographic. They outnumber those who've come to see my recent speeches. And even from here, I can cock my head to listen and tell that they're royally pissed off.

Imagine, if they were on my side. Imagine if just a small percentage of them were aligned with my goals, carrying petitions and organizing events. Imagine if a fraction of that energy were put to *good* use, instead of complaining—complaining, surely, about the inevitability of the future Naylor and I have planned.

As they draw closer I imagine them converging on this parking garage rather than in the cramped street before that stage. I imagine them chanting for me instead of against me. What would it cost? Giving them what they want—what that guy on the trail last night wanted, what that self-proclaimed lawyer on the sidewalk the other day wanted. To be left alone. To have a fair shot at making it by themselves, rather than being hurried out of the way.

That's impossible, of course. They stand against progress. They stand against change. Two groups of them converging with a third, stand in the way of…Maxwell A. Naylor. The face of the future.

At least, the face of *one* future.

But you need a few things to shape the future. One of them, certainly, is money—lots, and lots of money. The other…

…a popular mandate.

* * * * *

Franklin Arterial
8:35am

Jamie Schmidt

"You're not sacking the Old Port," I tell Seasquatch as I walk beside him toward the Titanic.

"Brought my hobo army though," he says. "And they're as sober as you'll ever find 'em."

"Glad to hear it."

"They've got a right to be pissed off, and the freedom to choose how they show it. They'll rip this place apart if you provoke 'em, but personally, I'm here in a spirit of peaceful indignation. Not to fight."

They've turned the signs they hold at intersections, where they beg for change, into protest signs that read *What about us?* and *More beds now!* and *Proud to work!* On the backsides, their signs still say, *Anything helps, God bless.*

"What do they want?"

"To not lose any more camps. A new shelter to ease the crowds. The guys who followed me don't want to fly their signs anymore, they want a way to work for real and get back on their feet. They got the same problems as me: where the hell do you start, when no one wants you?"

"You must have really struck a chord with them."

"Break of dawn, I'm in the new Sherwood Forest, pounding gas station coffee and just talking to people, and the damndest thing happened. They *listened* to me."

"Did you give them a choice?"

"Hell no. But they felt the message! I said 'Guys, there's no place for me in this town. I already feel like an outlaw, just trying to survive. Then they scraped Sherwood Forest into the sea. They set the police on me!'"

"You kinda baited the cops by squashing their car..."

"Don't interrupt. 'You know,' I said to them, 'all I want is to live in peace. To make it or not, on my own. Now there's some greedy assholes trying to tell me I'm not good enough to be here, and taking away my chance to live and let live. They're gonna hassle more of my friends this morning, and I'm not gonna take it!'"

"You really called us your friends?"

"Yeah."

"And the liquor?"

"Still on my boat. I mean, if I don't have to share…"

"I'm proud of you, Seasquatch."

"Who?"

"Seasquatch…"

"No, man. I'm tired of hiding. I'm making a stand today, and seeing where it takes me. You're lookin' at Newsquatch."

"Well, Newsquatch…I'm damned glad to meet you."

* * * * *

Hampshire Street
8:40am

Jamie Schmidt

I run back, ahead of Newsquatch's march to the Titanic. My legs hurt and I'm limping, but this is no time to falter. I want to get a better vantage to find Kate in the crowd, and get a feel for the groups massing in the street, so I run up the ramp into the parking garage, where from the top deck I can look down at our neighborhood.

I stop cold when I see the Portland PD's armored troop carrier and a brigade of riot police staged deep inside the garage. I turn around and walk casually to the stairwell, climbing up, peeking onto each of the higher decks to see if there are any more. There aren't.

Across the top deck is a lone figure leaning at the rail. I

walk over…

…and can't believe my luck.

"You…" he says.

"Councilman…" I say. "Rehearsing your speech?"

"Just wondering what the hell you people were doing last night—breaking into an apartment! You almost had me convinced that you're harmless. That there's just some generational thing between us, instead of you actually being miscreants."

"We're not without faults…or ethos. Look at us today, in the light. We're united down there for something we believe in."

"The destruction of my beloved city?"

"The preservation of it. Against you."

He shakes his head and looks over the horizon at something I may never see.

"It's a beautiful sight, isn't it?" I say. "The whole neighborhood turned out, and people from all across the city too. Sherman hit social media with the call to save our homes, and it really caught on. Over there's a group of artists, coming to give Brigitte a piece of their mind. You met their leader. You know their needs."

I'm thrilled at the sight of Kate, mustering her pack in front of the stage. I can't wait to stand beside her.

"And that's a group of hobos the city ran out of Sherwood Forest," I continue. "They want a few more beds and jobs so they can make their way, rather than begging until they get run out. And right there in the middle of it all, councilman, is the home of Portland's Hash House Harriers. My home. Which we know you're trying to force us from. We won't give it up without a fight."

"You've brought a lot of people together for that fight."

"You brought an army, too. I saw them below, by their tank."

"I promise you, that wasn't my idea."

"Can you stop them if you need to?"

"Yes."

"Then they're your responsibility, regardless."

"Son," he says, shuffling uncomfortably, "just who in the hell are you? I've never seen you around town before the last few weeks, and suddenly, you and your people are everywhere."

"I'm Just Jamie."

"Oh. Here I thought you might be the mysterious True Blue Balls, or whatever puerile dreck they wrote on that wall."

"I suppose I am."

"Then say it with conviction! Be proud of who you are."

"Sir, I'm True Blue Balls," I say, "of the Portland Hash House Harriers!"

"Good. And I'm Daniel Grant of the Portland City Council. Do you know what I actually do around here?"

"You spend money and sign things."

"Practically, yes. Idealistically, my job is to represent the will of the people. When that will changes—no matter my opinion—it's my duty to change with it. That's is not an admission of error. It's simply my job to keep up."

"Then I'd say that's a reality check down there."

"Do you lead those people?" he asks me.

"Nope."

"Then take me to the person who does."

* * * * *

The Titanic
8:50am

Sherman

"Sherman, there's someone knocking on the front door," Cummy Bear said.

303

"Why bother?" I said, confused. "It's a madhouse around here!"

"I have no idea."

I handed my end of a *Save Our Homes* banner to Benzo to finish tacking up by the window, and went down to check it out. I opened the door, and my blood ran cold.

"My God, it's you," our councilman said.

"We're inevitable," I replied. "What do you want?"

"This is Hampshire Street Brewing, right?"

I looked over his shoulder at Jamie, who just stood there grinning like an idiot.

"Yeah, what about it?"

"You're fucked, and so am I. But I have a proposition for you. Can I come in?"

"Right this way to the living room," I said.

"In the brewery, if you don't mind. It would be more fitting."

Chapter 34

Saturday, May 2ⁿᵈ
Hampshire Street
9:15am

Carol Schmidt

I wonder which of my daydreams is about to play out. Will I march into that firetrap and rescue my boy from previously unknown depravity? Will he sneak away with a petulant look, or see me and come running for salvation?

"This is the one, right, Grace dear?"

"Yeah…"

"Dreadful, isn't it?"

"Yup."

A side door opens in the mural across one side of the building, and a man dressed far too nicely for the place steps out. What business he had in there, maybe even with my boy, I shudder to think.

"I hope we're not too late."

"Yeah…" she says.

The poor dear is overwhelmed by the crowd around us, or maybe, at the prospect of getting her Jamie back. I can't tell. I've bigger things to worry about. They're chanting again around me, "Save our homes!" and it's doing terrible things to my nerves. What if a riot breaks out? Where will I find him then?

The front door opens, and a man with blue hair steps

onto the stoop. He's followed by Jamie!

"Honey!"

"Mom?"

I rush to him. He catches someone's eye in the crowd behind me. I hug him, burying my face in his shirt and breathing nothing but the smell of my child.

"You're alive, you're alive, you're alive…"

"Yeah mom," he says, catching me as my knees give out. This moment could last forever. "And doing better than ever."

"I knew I'd find you!"

"And just in time."

"Why, are you sick? What did these people do to you?"

"These are my people, mom. We're standing up for something we believe in. These are—Grace? What are you doing here?"

"It's more interesting than staying home," she says, "and your mom paid the tolls. Is that your house?"

"I live in the attic…"

"Classy."

"We're trying to save it from developers."

She wrinkles her nose.

"Why?"

"Because it's our home!"

"My, my, James Schmidt, living in a—"

"That's not my name," he interrupts her. "I'm True Blue Balls now. Of the Portland Hash House Harriers."

This strange woman appears next to him, holding signs. She has visible tattoos, and fading bruises. A pretty face, but nothing outstanding. She could take a step backward and disappear into this crowd, so perfectly is she camouflaged among the bohemians and rabble around us.

"And I'm Seventh Heaven," she says, sliding her arm around my boy. "His girlfriend."

His face lights up like he's never heard the word before, and they kiss, certainly to Grace's horror. This is not the woman I imagined for him. But the way he touches her cheek, the way she leans into him…what's a mother to do, but smile?

"You could have called," Grace says. At least she waited until they were done.

"This is Grace," Jamie says. "She's one of my oldest friends."

"And sometimes more," she adds.

"Which is some other guy's job now, apparently."

"It's like I haven't known you for years, Jamie. What happened to you?"

"I changed. It's the greatest freedom I have."

"And if you'll excuse us," his girlfriend says, "we have a rally to lead. Lovely meeting you."

"Meet me back here later," Jamie says, pointing at the house as they slip into the crowd.

My last glimpse of him, for the moment, is arm in arm with the girl, taking a sign she hands him. They take one last look my way, and raise their matching signs overhead.

We belong here!

* * * * *

Hampshire Street
9:21am

Evan

"No moving jobs this morning?" I ask Karl.

"Several, Giggles. I just wanted to see what this is all about first."

We're standing at the vehicle barricades across Hampshire Street. There's one helluva crowd on the other side, chanting, waving signs that match the banners hanging from the Titanic.

"I'm surprised you're not in there," I tell him.

"Why would I be?"

"Well, you're a hasher…"

"So are you. Why aren't *you* in there?"

There are so many reasons I could give him, but he doesn't deserve the whole truth. He wasn't there for me before; I don't owe him the closure he might want later.

"Because no one invited me," is what I say.

"It's not worth it, anyway," Karl insists. "They're not going to stop the developers, and what's their argument— that gentrification is unfair? Fairness has nothing to do with a free market. And there's no way to build a fair system, if you start riddling it with exceptions for people or things you like. They're my friends, but they're wrong, and I don't feel like standing beside them for this."

"You're a coldhearted son of a bitch, you know that?"

"I'd rather be fair, than loved."

"Is it worth it? Being right in your mind, when people just want to know that you're listening, that you understand and care?"

"Oh, they know I care."

"But they won't remember who was right," I say, leaping over the barricade. "They'll remember who seemed to care, and who sacrificed everything for their stupid, hopeless dream."

* * * *

The Crowd
9:23am

Jamie Schmidt

We're watching the councilman shake hands on stage with an exceptionally pale guy in a three piece suit, then with our mayor, then with the police chief. The chief whispers something to the councilman that makes him cringe.

"Where were you last night?" Kate asks.

"You wouldn't believe me if I told you."

"Does it involve a bunch of hashers on Sea Ration's bed?"

I stare at her in awe.

"What the hell kind of after-party did I miss?"

"I only heard rumors," she says. "I was out looking for you."

"And I was looking for you! But instead I found Seasquatch."

"I'll try not to be jealous…"

Through the crowd I see Mr. Giggles, his distant stare fixed right through me. Kate starts a cheer of *Save our art!* as I step into Giggles' way.

"I'm glad to see you here, man," I say as earnestly as I can.

"Why? I'm not here to help you."

"Then what'd you come here for? To fight, or surrender?"

"Look, the developers own the politicians, and the business owners run the Old Port. This is futile, Jamie. You can't fight city hall, especially when you're really fighting against change. Progress is inevitable. It doesn't care what you say against it, so fuck off with your banners, okay?"

"I don't believe that in the least."

"Yeah? You should have been here seven years ago, when there was still room to grow. And reason for hope. But Portland has peaked! It's all over! The best years are behind us. The future is bleak, and certain."

"I'm glad I'm not that fatalistic."

"Why?"

"Stick around, you'll see."

"I've stuck around as long as I care to."

"This morning isn't about stopping progress, Evan. It's about sticking up for what's worth holding onto, and finding new ways forward. Change is inevitable. But we demand a real say in it."

"Give up, Jamie. It's gentler to embrace destruction. That's the last dignity you have."

"Why are you even here, Giggles, if not to stand with your friends?"

"I'm here," he says, backing slowly away as he smiles a wolfish smile, "to take the humane way out."

I follow, asking what the hell he means by that, as he shoulders his way backward through the tightly packed, fervently chanting crowd.

"You are so fucking naïve, Jamie. Listen to the crowd! Feel the anger! This place is gonna explode! They wanna burn that stage down, and the developers and the cops, they wanna burn the neighborhood. Let's see who wins. All it'll take to set that off is one shot, one cop forced to shoot one person—me. In death, everyone loves you. I'll die the martyr you wish you could be, and no one will ever know or believe I wanted it this way. Except you. I want you to have to live with that."

He turns and barrels through the crowd.

* * * * *

The Stage
9:26am

Dan Grant

It's an intimidating view from my podium: hundreds of angry people waving signs at me, the building behind them draped in angry banners with slogans like *Save our homes!* and *Stick it to the man!* and my favorite, *We kill fascists*. That's the kind of energy you want working for you, not against you, and where there's great tension, there's also great promise.

The crowd falls silent for my opening remarks. Even the

chanting subsides.

"I'm joined today," I say after introducing myself, "by our outgoing mayor—Lillian Tennerly."

She winces at the reminder but smiles and waves politely.

"And from Merritt Capital, Mr. Maxwell A. Naylor, the face of the future of Hampshire Street!"

I pause to let the chorus of profanity wash over us. I'm off-script already, and Max looks furious at my adlibbed introduction. Good.

"And by Chief Boyer of the Portland…" fresh booing drowns me out. Boyer faces the invective with a straight back, sharp eyes, and a subtle sneer. He's posed in dress uniform behind me to lend a certain air. The effect is not lost on the crowd, who don't know that half of his force are standing by, out of sight, to execute their warrant across the street. They brought, he whispered to me, the rest of their hot-burning teargas.

"Last week's fire, right where I stand now, was a tragedy," I say. "The owners came out ahead, but five families and a military veteran were displaced. There's no room for them to return here. Not at the moment, anyway. The fire reminds me that nothing lasts forever—neither plans, nor thankfully, mistakes. We built this stage over the ashes so that, in our city's finest tradition, we may rise like the phoenix to embrace a bright new future for this neighborhood…and all of our city!"

"We don't want it!" someone yells, and the chanting starts again: *Save our homes!*

"Mayor Tennerly has a few words," I continue, "to mark the occasion."

Withdrawing from the microphone, I see Jamie shoving his way through the crowd, pursuing a man as he flees for the perimeter. They're leaving the bohemian section, heading for a group of hobos led by a towering man in an ill-fitting shirt and, inexplicably, women's yoga pants. He stands at the head of his unwashed horde like Genghis Khan. Jamie carries a sign, which he holds high so it won't get ripped to shreds, the paper cutting like a shark fin through the crowd. The Khan tracks it with his eyes, easily stepping in their way near a pair of officers. The fleeing man shoves his way through the last of the protestors, and right into the Khan's arms.

He only struggles a moment before Jamie catches up.

* * * * *

The Crowd
9:31am

Jamie Schmidt

"Let me go," Giggles mumbles as Newsquatch bear-hugs the air from him.

"Calm down, little buddy," Newsquatch says.

The officers behind them keep their distance, watching cautiously. Newsquatch eases his grip to give Giggles a gulp of air.

"You really mean it, don't you?" I say. Giggles, his face turning dark red again, nods. "What is it with all my friends wanting to start a riot today?"

"I'm not your friend," he croaks.

"But fuck the chance, right? You're done with all your friends? And every plan, every dollar you haven't spent, all the beer in your fridge? Just ready to leave it?"

He nods.

"Then brother...you've done it. You're free."

"Dude?" Newsquatch says, looking at me seriously.

"But you've done the heavy lifting," I continue. "The spiritual work, the mental work. The rest is redundant. Giggles, you've put an end to your life, in your heart. But your body's still going. And wherever it goes next, that's a clean start. You can kill yourself tomorrow, or whenever, if it doesn't work out. But why not see what happens first?"

Newsquatch relaxes his bear hug, holding Giggles just firmly enough to hold him upright as he gasps. The novelty of our altercation has worn off, so no one is watching us anymore, just staring at the stage as the mayor drones on.

"Because I'm absolutely done with my life," Giggles says between coughs. "I know *I'm* the cause of my problems. It's *me*. I can't run away from myself."

"You're right. But you're free to grow again now, to start completely over and rebuild. It's a radical kind of freedom to completely leave your life, even yourself, and begin fresh. Something like that saved me, too."

"How? You're here on a lark."

"I came here with nothing to lose. I hated my job, my future, my life, and it was exhausting even thinking about how to fix it. So I didn't. I left, in the night, and now here I am, taking to the streets with people I care about. We have a lot to lose. I've found people, a place, and a future, worth fighting for, that I couldn't even imagine before."

I see hope for the first time in his eyes.

"Death is always an option," I say. "But you have a much more exciting one now: get the hell away from everyone who knows the old you, and let life show you what else you might become. See where you wind up! You can always end it all, but you can only do that once. Starting fresh, though, you can choose many, many times."

"So I should just walk off into the sunset?"

"No, it's still morning."

"Then what am I supposed to do? I'm not going back, and I'm not staying here."

"Get the hell outta town. Maybe..."

I look at Newsquatch, whose smile suggests he's having the same thought.

"...trade your old place for a boat."

The Crowd
9:37am

I find Kate easily enough: right in front of the stage, leading a chant of *Save our art!* as our councilman walks Brigitte timidly to the microphone. He introduces her as a last minute guest, come to talk about reshaping the Old Port for the benefit of commerce. His words are carefully chosen to incite, and should karmic justice compel her from the stage at this moment I have no doubt she'd be torn limb from limb.

"We need to keep public spaces open," she says, "for the public to pass through. There's too much congestion on our sidewalks that calls itself art. It hurts local businesses, and is nothing more than an unlicensed, unregulated craft fair."

Save our art!

"We're not unreasonable! The artists can stay! We just need to separate the *real* artists!"

Boo!

"And we need some kind of schedule, so our public spaces aren't mobbed!"

I'm surprised the artists haven't stormed the stage and carried her to the sea. They follow the rise and fall of Kate's sign, chanting and booing when it's up, letting Brigitte box herself deeper into a corner when it's down.

Save free speech! they chant.

"But this isn't free speech! It's madness!"

She stares in white-hot fury at the crowd. Behind her, the mayor looks at Grant with a conspirator's grin. Slyly the mayor unplugs the microphone cable from some kind of box, and the podium, Brigitte's once-imagined pulpit for preaching to the masses, becomes a hangman's scaffold. She's trapped there, clutching the edges of it with white-turning

314

knuckles, blathering impotently into the dead microphone.

Kate's sign goes down. The artists clam up, and soon, the rest of the protest falls silent as well. Kate pushes her way to the stage, where the councilman is quick to help her climb up.

I feel a hand on my arm. It's my mother.

"What's your girlfriend up to, dear?"

"Her full potential," I say.

The mayor gives Kate a quick nod, and seems to say *microphone*. Kate takes it from the podium, and stares Brigitte down.

"What makes my city great—" she says, her voice booming through the speakers and joined by uproarious cheering, "—is the room in our hearts, and on our streets, for so many different communities."

From civic pride she celebrates the value of art in public, and the need for disparate voices to maintain rich and inspiring communities. Her voice thunders, channeling the pride, the grit, and the hope of her artists. When at last she switches the mic off and drops it to the stage, she turns her back to Brigitte and raises her fist in the air.

"Resist!"

Resist! they chant.

"I like her style," my mother says.

* * * * *

The Stage
9:43am

Dan Grant

"You'd damn well better fix this," Naylor hisses.

"I assure you, I'm in complete control."

I make Brigitte pick the microphone up and hand it to

me before she scuttles off the side of the stage, disappearing behind a line of policemen. The chanting continues, driving her farther away, leaving me at the front of the stage with Kate.

"Jamie told me you'd probably storm the stage," I say.

"He did?"

"I'm glad he was right. Thank you for reminding me of so many things I love about our city."

"Those things need people, Councilman. People you're driving away."

"Stick around a minute…" I raise my arms for quiet, to no avail. I look over at Kate, who gives a little gesture. A few signs drop into the crowd, and then it's quiet.

"So what do you think," I say to the crowd, "should we drive the artists away?"

Hell no, we won't go!

Again she silences the chanting.

"That about settles it, I think. I will not sign any ordnance that restricts the arts community, or freedom of speech, or freedom of assembly."

I can feel Naylor's stare burning into my soul. Kate shakes my hand and climbs down from the front of the stage, to join Jamie in the crowd. Behind them, I see the enemy of my enemy—my new friend, Sherman—standing proudly on his stoop beneath a *Save our homes!* banner.

"Now, with gratitude for your patience…our main event!" On cue, Naylor carries a cloth-draped easel to the front of the stage. I pull the cover away with a flourish, revealing a pastel-colored rendering of Hampshire Street's potential future.

"It is my honor to reveal the Cathedral District Redevelopment Plan."

I pause in the face of the boos and jeers and profane threats from the house across the street. It's Sherman's turn, now, to manage his people, which he accomplishes by yelling through a bullhorn.

"Hash, hush!"

"Last week, a building stood where I stand now. It was home to five families, and a military veteran. They have nowhere to live now, and the burning of their building is mere growing pains on the way to Merritt Capital's vision of a new, more exclusive Hampshire Street. Through the police department, they've put pressure on your community, even closed down Gispert's. Through private deals, they've already bought this lot and several buildings. And through the City Council, they've pushed the permits to accelerate their developments all around our city."

Naylor, reading the crowd's hostility and the depth of my betrayal, sneaks toward the steps at the rear of the stage. Boyer stands in his way, shaking his head *no*.

"To create offset housing to get those permits, they scraped an urban camper settlement into the sea. The proposed development won't help a single displaced person, nor will any of the projects planned for this neighborhood. Merritt, and other developers, are heavily involved in shaping our future for their investors, and the clients they market us to in New York and beyond. Their vision of our home is a playground for people who buy into lifestyles without coming to contribute. But our city is our home, and our home is not a product!"

The residual booing and jeering cease, dead calm taking the place where I'd certainly like applause.

"Neighbors, I was wrong. I'm guilty of helping the developers, because I believed the future belonged to money. I let my cynicism and fear alienate me from you and bind me instead in the service of capital. Many of you are not as old as me, don't look like me, don't live as I have lived, and I let that come between us...even as I appreciated the better parts of this community we share. I've taken more, lately, than I've put in. And we're here, staring at plans for a future you don't want, that does not even include you, because there are those who believe it's inevitable. But is it?"

"Hell, no!" Sherman yells through the bullhorn, setting off a chant.

"Tearing down our neighborhoods, replacing our housing with unaffordable new units…this is a waste of the communities we love. Of the Portland we've built, much more slowly, over years and whole lifetimes. Change is inevitable, but it doesn't have to be artificially accelerated.

"Individual circumstances," I continue, "not urban renewal or backroom deals, should determine who lives where, and who may stay in their homes. The market is cruel enough without outside meddling…and a city loses its soul when it ignores the human cost of outrageous progress."

Through the thundering applause I hear the Genghis Khan-looking guy yell *Uuuunnngggh!* He waves a sign saying "Remember Hash Henge." I'm glad he's with me, and not against me.

"There's someone here," I conclude, "who can say it better than me." I tip my microphone to Sherman. With the crowd turned to face him, Naylor stalks up to me.

"What the fuck are you doing, Grant?"

"Representing the people—my job."

"You're ruined! I'll bankroll everyone who runs against you until the end of time. I'm gonna take your house, too, and turn it into a public bathroom. Your legacy is fucked. *You* are fucked."

"They're driving one of us out today, Naylor. And it's not me."

Sherman raises the bullhorn and quiets the audience.

"The city has no legal means," he says, "nor enforcement mechanism, to decide who is an artist or not; what is art, or not, or who is allowed to stay, and who gets cleared out of their homes. When they overstep their authority, it's our job to push them back! In the courts, and in the streets. Today, tomorrow, and as long as we have a city worth protecting."

He basks in the cheering. When it settles, he raises the bullhorn again.

"But instead of threats, let's celebrate what makes us great!" Then he points into the crowd, and tosses the bullhorn. Kate catches it, and hands it to Jamie. Surrounded by close-packed protestors, his voice seems to rise from the crowd itself.

"I came here not knowing what future I'd have," Jamie says. "I stayed, because of the community I found. A thriving, creative, energetic community, that didn't really care where I'm from. They made room for me, asking only that I contribute, give a damn, and stick around for the consequences. Those who are willing contribute, can make whole new lives."

The crowd cheers, none so loudly as those from the windows and stoop of Sherman's house.

"The people I've met are diverse in character and philosophy. I'm glad that people can change, because in their company I've become a person I like a whole lot more. Places change, too, but that change should come from the people—not from outside. We protect our homes, and communities, while keeping them open, when we invite others to join. We can't do that when we're too busy fighting among ourselves to hang on. And we must hang on. Communities like ours help you find out who you can become. That's worth fighting for!"

"Which is why," I say, commanding the stage once again, "I stand in direct opposition to the Cathedral District, and to our current trend of irresponsible and unsustainable growth. And I will stand with you—*all* of you—in our mutual defense against unchecked greed. We can stop it, and we will."

It'll take a moment for the applause to die down again, even with Sherman yelling "Hash, hush!" I knew this morning what needed to be done, but it was after talking again to Jamie and seeing Sherman answer the door that I felt it might actually be possible. It's crazy, but these people have the gall, the courage, and the manpower, to pull this off…and they're going to have history on their side. I've been wrong. But luckily, I have this chance to turn an apology into a crusade.

"That's not realistic for just a councilman, though." I look back at Naylor.

Boyer holds him firmly by the arm, keeping him right here to witness the undoing of so many things Boyer as well is glad to be rid of. Naylor knows what's coming. His eyes could melt steel beams.

"Which is why today, I'm proud to announce my campaign for mayor. This is my platform. Let's save the soul of Portland!"

Grant! Grant! Grant!

"In the interim," I say, "there is one crucial change to this neighborhood that I feel I *must* make." They quiet to a nervous whisper, reminding me what fun I used to have at stump speeches. "Any cohesive neighborhood needs its gathering place. I called Jude this morning, and she's unwilling to reopen Gispert's…but Hampshire Street needs its bar! A local establishment—founded by locals, employing locals, serving as a gathering place for your community."

Sherman, across the street, smiles like a man overwhelmed with good fortune he can't possibly hope to maintain. He confided in me that, chief among other factors, what's holding them back right now is the money. I'm betting he comes up with it.

"There's an up-and-coming brewery already on this street that needs a home. They've got the brewers, they've got the beer, and they've got a little trouble with the law. What they need, is to be legitimized."

Chief Boyer is flabbergasted. While holding Naylor, who may spontaneously combust with rage, he mouths, *We're ready to raid that place!*

I shake my head.

No you won't.

"Rather than punish those who are a little over-excited in their entrepreneurship, I intend to use the powers of my *current* office to fast-track their licenses and get Hampshire Street Brewing out of their basement and into a lawful space. You're getting your bar back, folks, and better than ever..."

Grant! Grant! Grant!

"...because it's important that our communities support the better ambitions of our friends and neighbors, and that we let the people sort these things out themselves. Also, my campaign needs a headquarters, and they make a damn fine brew."

* * * *

The Crowd
9:57am

Jamie Schmidt

I push my way through the crowd, holding Kate's hand so we don't get separated, until we're at the Titanic and up the stoop with Sherman, Benzo, and Cummy Bear. Our stoop is an island right now on a vast and tumultuous sea, but for the moment we're safe, and so, apparently, is our home.

"Have we really done it?" Kate asks.

We look across at the stage as the police chief lets go of the man in the three piece suit. The suit disappears down the ramp, banished like Brigitte, stealing away behind the protective line of officers. The chief has a word with Grant, shakes his head, and slips away, leaving upon the stage the mayor and the councilman. He smiles at us. Sherman waves.

"For the moment, at least," Sherman says. "But we're gonna need a lot more people, really quickly. And we're going to need to brew a lot more beer."

"I'll brew with you," I say, shaking his hand.

"And, we're going to need artists for the labels and the marketing."

"That's me," Kate says, "and my friends."

"And a fixer—someone we can absolutely trust, who makes problems go away."

"Like that dude?" I say, pointing at Newsquatch, who has commandeered a "wartime" sign he spins like he once spun his flaming staff.

"Not that dude!" Sherman says.

"Exactly that dude. Newsquatch. We can trust him. I give you my word."

"He lives on a freakin' boat!"

"I'm pretty sure he's gonna live at Giggles' place now," I say. "And we're not gonna see Giggles for awhile."

"Why?"

"Just a little idea I gave them. I hope it works out."

Sherman chuckles, shaking his head.

"Okay, buddy. But we still need pennies from heaven—lots of pennies from heaven."

I look for my mother and find her standing in a little open space near the stage. Grace appears beside her carrying two cups of coffee, and hands one to my mother. I slip my arm around Kate and smile at them. They wave. Their lives are in White River Junction. Mine now is here, and I know it, breaking the fearful spell my hometown held over me. I can contact my family again, even go back some time to visit my hometown, without fear of my old life dragging me back.

"Pennies from heaven? I know just the guy." Sherman looks at me strangely, afraid to hope too much. "And by God, here he comes!"

My father bulls his way out of the crowd, yelling over their final cheers, "James Schmidt the Third! I knew I'd find you among the rabble!"

He storms up the steps, a folder in his hand, anger and vicious disappointment in his eyes.

"This rabble," I say, "is my girlfriend, Kate. *That* rabble, is Newsquatch, and *this* rabble," I sweep my arms to encompass the Titanic and the crowds, "is the company I'm *proud* to keep."

"Then you're no son of mine!" he yells, thrusting his folder and a pen at me. "If you've truly chosen these people over your legacy, then you won't mind making it legal. Sign these, and never speak to me again."

"I have a better idea," I say, pushing the papers away. "What did grandpa, for all his success, never get to do?"

"He wanted to be a brewer again," my father says, "and keep the old traditions alive. Why?"

"And he was crazy to flee, wasn't he?"

"He fled the Soviet Union, Jamie. You fled Vermont."

"He chased a dream of freedom. What he built wasn't what he imagined, but it was what he, and the community, needed. That's what I have here—community. Opportunity. A brewery, apparently, to build with my friends, so we can save our neighborhood. So instead of shutting me out, I'd like to invite you in—as the financier of Hampshire Street Brewing...dad."

* * * * *

Sunday, May 3rd
Casco Bay
7:24pm

Evan

A stiff sea breeze fills the sail over my new home, bowing the canvas so it glows in the sunset. Least Weasel and I repaired the rent sail with a bolt of canvas, shaping the patch

DAVE NORMAN

into a giant true trail arrow. I adjust the tiller and trim the sail the way my father taught me a lifetime ago.

I'm out past where I know the islands by name, in territory altogether new to me. I have no destination in mind, but I'm provisioned for awhile and have time to figure things out. I could slip overboard at will to merge with the ocean's infinity. Every moment I don't, I freely choose to live.

I wonder how Seasquatch likes my old place. I wonder if my cat accepts him as his new benefactor. I wonder how long until Seasquatch drinks through all of my beer...but it's not my beer anymore, or my cat, or my place. My future lies somewhere out past the bow, each moment washing slowly into my glistening wake.

The breeze is chilly, so I pull on Seasquatch's abandoned vest of pelts. It's enormous on me. I adjust it, his derringer falling at my feet. I hold it overhead, in the sunlight's last gleaming rays, drawn to the abyss within its cavernous barrels.

Then I flick it overboard and prop my feet on a case of good liquor. Here beneath the true trail arrow, things are truly looking up.

Epilogue

One Year Later
Kate's Apartment

Jamie Schmidt

Kate runs her finger down my chest, parting the sweat we've worked up, and with a sigh climbs down out of bed.

"Any more, and I'll be late," she teases, backing away toward the door.

"I think Mayor Grant can spare you," I say. "At least for a few minutes."

"They're pitching a new street arts fair today, and I should probably be there...since they're pitching it in my office and all."

"Your work as Commissioner of Arts and Culture is never done."

"Thankfully."

She slips away to the shower as I spend a moment savoring the breeze across my body. It gently flutters the art on the wall, the original drawings and paintings for our labels. The newest is tacked near the door—clusters of ripe blueberries dangling from a true trail arrow, advertising our new blueberry ale: True Blue Balls.

Later this morning Sherman and I have a teleconference about that name. Our Chief Operating Officer doesn't like it. He thinks the hashing connection will be lost on the average consumer, and finds the insinuations puerile. But that's just my dad, and I've come to accept him as an otherwise brilliant voice of reason.

I dress in my brew-day overalls and pack a lunch. When she's dressed, Kate and I carry our bicycles down the apartment stairs to the sidewalk.

"See you at the release party tonight?" I ask.

"Wouldn't miss it."

We kiss, and pedal off in our different directions.

* * * * *

Portland City Hall
Midday

Dan Grant

"I'm glad most of our city is on a peninsula," I tell Kate in the privacy of my mayoral office, "and that the towns around us are built right up against our borders. I've been to cities that just sprawl and sprawl, gobbling up forests and farms every time developers get some bright new idea. Here? We can't sprawl. It means we have to improve what we already have."

"I hope you're not planning any new hotels," she says.

I laugh.

"Well, I'm not, anyway. You know those derelict warehouses at the far end of the waterfront, downhill from the new public housing?"

"We've staged some guerrilla theater in there," she says.

"How'd you like to make that a little more legitimate? I'm thinking a performing arts space, some studios, and the like—whatever the incoming tenants want, within reason. An arts space by the people, for the people, so long as they keep it regularly occupied."

"Does some developer have his eye on the land?"

"Of course. But done right, I'm sure you can hold 'em off

a good long time."

*****

Hampshire Street Brewing Co.
Evening

Jamie Schmidt

I tape a sign across our taproom's door, "Closed For Private Event," though we don't plan to turn anyone away. Newsquatch guards the door, as usual, to lend a sense of security. Behind him, we converted Gispert's into the taproom, served by lines directly from the tanks in the brew house we built in the old parking lot. Artists pack the taproom this evening, alongside our neighbors, while the hashers circle up in the brew house to sing the old songs. Tonight we celebrate the first anniversary of saving our homes...

...and keeping the *art* in "wartime."

My cellphone rings. It's my father.

"Jamie! Dammit, you've worn me down."

"How's that?"

"Go ahead and name it True Blue Balls. We'll just see how it does."

"It'll be fine," I say, threading a tap handle onto a faucet of tonight's special release. True Blue Balls is already flowing freely. "Wish you were here, dad."

"Yeah, well... How's your mother?"

She's sitting down the bar, drinking club soda and laughing at the tawdry hash songs floating in from the brew house.

"Doing just fine," I say. "I'm always glad when she visits."

Kate breezes into the taproom, so I hurry to get off the phone and greet her.

"What did I miss?" she says in my arms.

"Dirty drinking songs, casual nudity, and Mount 'n Dew Me hitting on my mom—the usual."

Time stands still as we kiss.

"Get you a drink?" I ask.

"What're you pouring?"

"The special release," I say, ducking around the bar to prop a glass beneath the newest tap handle: Sailboat Saison, the label on the handle featuring a pastel painting of a boat with a true trail arrow on the sail. At the stern is the silhouette of Mr. Giggles.

"I love that label."

"It's one of my best," she says. "I wonder how he's getting on."

"I'm sure he's in a better place, having the time of his life."

Newsquatch stirs uncomfortably at the entrance. Through the glass I see a man in uniform whose face I instantly recognize. I excuse myself to get the door.

"It's been about a year, huh?" Officer Buffone says.

"It has."

"Can I get a drink?"

"I've got just the thing." I lead him to the end of the bar, where I brazenly pour a pint of Mad Bulldozer Diesel Stout into a Viking drinking horn. "You ever catch that guy?"

Over his shoulder I see, through the window into the brew house, that Newsquatch has abandoned his post to carry Least Weasel on his back around the circle of hashers.

"Of course we did!" Buffone brags. "We pulled him out of that apartment fire up the street, where they built the new community clinic! We stopped his rampage, saved his life from the fire, and booked his ass, all in the same day!"

I shake my head, smiling.

"Is that how the story goes?"

"Yeah," he says. "That's how the story goes."

"Then far be it me to correct you."

The hashers are winding down their circle in the brew

house. Surrounded by our dearest, sweatiest, drunkest friends, Thor yells his closing cheer.

"May the hash go in peace!"

The End

Acknowledgements

I began writing *Hash 207* with a Pilot V7 pen and a yellow legal pad, beside a pond in St. Louis, Missouri. At the time I was living in self-imposed exile from Portland, Maine, and missing it dearly. Three years and seven drafts later I was back in Portland, in a little writing studio one block over from Hampshire Street. I thought I was just about ready to send the manuscript off to publishers, but wanted a professional to help get it into shipshape.

That's when I reached out to Alan Rinzler, a developmental editor who sharpened his pen working with some of my author heroes, including Hunter S. Thompson, Clive Cussler, Toni Morrison, and Tom Robbins. Alan sent me a two page manifest of every problem in my manuscript that I hoped no one would catch. He took me on as a protégé, and we spent the next year *rewriting the whole thing from scratch*.

So to Alan I owe enduring gratitude—for believing in my story, in me, and in the power of the written word to affect reader and writer alike.

The encouragement of Kim Millick, author of *Rookie Warden*, kept me going through the eighth draft. Thanks to Dr. David Collins, author of *Accidental Activists*, for editorial assistance and years of support through critical times in my career.

After years of rejection by editors and agents from sea to

shining sea, Dave Swillum of the band Broadwing convinced me to lean into the DIY ethos I admire in punk bands like his, and publish this work through the independent publishing house f/64 Publishing.

I owe a kind of gratitude to mainstream publishing for unambiguously rejecting this manuscript, without which brutal discouragement I would never have met contributors like cover designer Jessie Darnell-Boynton, peer reviewer Kim Millick, and the amazing community of supporters and new friends who have rallied around this project. Making *Hash 207* created paid work for four professionals, involved scores of volunteers, and utilized absolutely no generative artificial intelligence.

For helping me believe in myself, and in this work, I appreciate the encouragement (and editorial guidance) of Walt Moore, Heather Auman, Micah Edwards, Randy Salisbury, and my friend-family in the PorME Hash House Harriers of Portland, Maine. Cheers to Jessie Porcaro, for permission to use her original artwork as part of Jessi Darnell-Boynton's subsequent design.

Cheers to Bill and Wendy Norman for their unending support, and to my children for their understanding when daddy had to work late...for ten years. I believe this to be the book that turned my grandmother's hair white. On-up to those we lost since undertaking this work: Herb and Leola Schueler, Stacie Thoma, James and Anne von Brecht, and Tim Durbin—shades of you all persist in this work, and in my heart.

Thanks more than words convey to my wife Anastasia for her support, compassion, and years of understanding through long nights and existential crises. I wish I could promise I won't do this book writing thing again...but you know me better than that.

Please Help This Book!

The creative team behind *Hash 207* needs your help reaching a broader audience.

Now, while your thoughts are fresh, may be the best time to leave a review on Amazon, GoodReads.com, and elsewhere—no matter where you bought your copy. Take a picture of the book beside your favorite beverage, or take a selfie with it, and post on social media. That really helps!

So does adding *Hash 207* to reading lists and recommending it to book clubs!

I measure the success of my books by the extent of my readership—through new and used copies, e-books and Little Free Libraries, even tattered copies passed between friends…so please, pass this copy along to someone you think will love it. Maybe write your name on the inside cover first, and post a pic of all the names there already, to celebrate how books connect us as we pass them around!

If you'd like me, the author, to visit your book club, book store, or library, in person or anywhere via Zoom, please reach out—I give book talks frequently across New England and online. Encouragement and well-wishes are also welcome any time. Thanks for reading, and for supporting *Hash 207*!

hash207novel@gmail.com

Also by Dave Norman

Following Josh

White River Junctions

A Small Town Celebration

501 Paintball Tips, Tricks, and Tactics

www.hash207.com

www.f64publishing.com

www.ingramcontent.com/pod-product-compliance
Lightning Source LLC
Chambersburg PA
CBHW071201020726
47502CB00002B/499